Live Free *or* Undead

PLAIDSWEDE PUBLISHING
Concord, New Hampshire

Live Free
or Undead

by Diverse Hands

Edited by Rick Broussard

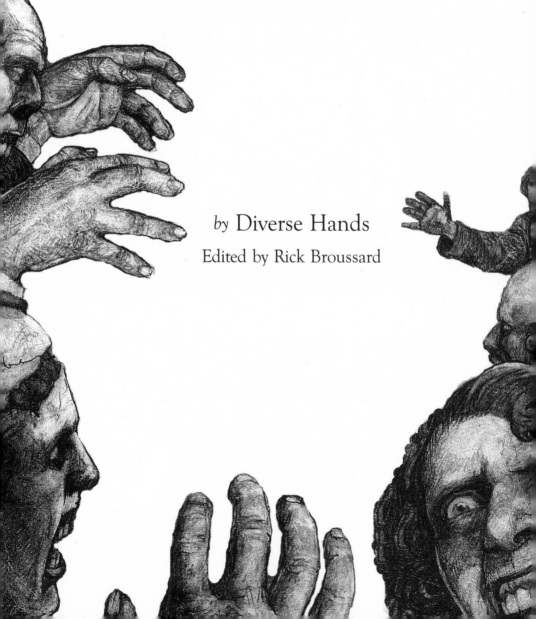

Designed and composed at Hobblebush Books, Brookline, New Hampshire (www.hobblebush.com)

Printed in the United States of America

ISBN 978-0-9840650-9-7
Library of Congress Control Number: 2010936384

Volume #1 of the New Hampshire Pulp Fiction Series

Cover art and illustrations by Marc Sutherland

Published by:

PLAIDSWEDE PUBLISHING
P.O. Box 269 · Concord, New Hampshire 03302-0269
www.plaidswede.com

Contents

Introduction

My first love was monsters. Well, there was also Kay Chestnut, the vixen of my 4th grade class, but she was really my buddy Dick Porter's girl and therefore more of an imaginary entity to me than, say, the Creature from the Black Lagoon.

Like girls, monsters offered a tantalizing blend of fear and familiarity when I was growing up. You got to know them from afar, but you could could choose one and establish a kind of voyeuristic intimacy. Monster-wise, most of my friends dug Dracula. I identified with the Wolfman, the lonely peasant with the Gypsy curse, more than with the evil blue bloods: the bloodsucking counts, embalmed pharaohs and mad scientists.

Of course, it seemed like there were fewer monsters to choose from back then, hanging out at Jimmy's Newsstand thumbing through the latest issue of *Fantastic Monsters of the Films*. You essentially had your vampires, your werewolves, your Frankenstein monsters, your mummies, your creatures from outer space and your giant radioactive animals and bugs.

Nowadays those archetypes have metastasized into all sorts of monsters from the Id. These are mostly fabricated in Hollywood by other former boys—geeky guys who lucked out and make a living turning their childhood fears and fantasies into scripts and films.

As much as I enjoyed the creature features, I never really aspired to make movies. Hollywood seemed too technical and glamorous for a pimply kid like me. But writing—now *that* was within my grasp. All that took was paper and ink. And a little inspiration.

So I set out to be a writer, and for my inspiration I immersed myself in the words of some of the greatest writers of all time.

No, not Dostoevsky, Nabokov and Hemingway. I refer, of course, to Edgar Rice Burroughs, H. P Lovecraft and Robert E. Howard. The fantastic stories these men and their peers crafted were more vivid to my young mind than the best modern 3D cinema. The writing was engorged with blood, illuminated by pagan fire and rich with the smells of black oceans and perfumed palaces. It was so alive it came as a shock to me to discover that most of the writers I admired had died years before I was born.

Much later I learned that many of their stories might never have been printed were it not for a group of shady publishers churning out cheap, often salacious magazines with titles like *Argosy*, *Weird Tales* and *Spicy Detective*. Unlike the glossy upscale magazines, printed on slick paper for the professional set, you could still feel the wood grain in the pages of these books, thus the moniker: pulp fiction.

For the first half of the 20th century, these American pulps defined what would later become known as pop culture—horror, mystery, adventure, lust, stars and schmucks, heroes and heels, all larger than life and available for the price of some pocket change. The pulps were created to make a profit, not to cultivate talent, but the fast new printing presses and the growing demands for escapist entertainment kept well-known authors busy and gave opportunities to unknown writers who might never have a shot at being picked up by a mainstream publisher.

Here in the first half of the 21st century pop culture increasingly defines America and the printing presses are no longer fast enough to keep up with the flow of new ideas, new artists and new monsters and heros. So the presses were genetically spliced with computers, resulting in a viral explosion. Soon, like some irradiated sea creature, the mutant publishing/entertainment industry grew to Godzilla-size proportions and began belching radioactive fire at its own foundations. And now the Internet crests overhead like a digital tsunami with the power to sweep away everything solid in its path.

With this online Armageddon shambling ever closer, does the primitive, sacramental act of writing and reading stories using elemental paper and ink have a future? Or is the world of literature doomed to march lockstep into a disintegration chamber where fragrant magazine folios and creaking book bindings are scanned and discarded, only to be replaced by coded impulses of light on thin plastic screens?

So it would seem.

But in a move that could have been scripted on a clacking Underwood typewriter, a counterinsurgency is already under way. As the infinite appetite of the Internet consumes information at the speed of light and converts it to sizzling white noise, small presses and local booksellers are reasserting themselves. They secure their territories by offering readers something familiar and meaningful—a feeling of belonging. Writers are likewise rising up to defend their towns and states, instilling a sense of place into their stories and making true human contact in underground readings at independent bookshops.

Just as punk rock ignored the czars and potentates of the music industry and delivered its message from garages and abandoned warehouses, the new writers and publishers are not intimidated by the Gog and Magog of the Google age. They can take advantage of the virtual global networks and still remain as grounded as lightning rods in their own communities. They can have their blogs and work their social media, and still produce books that are as real and organic as the people who will read them.

That's the idea behind the New Hampshire Pulp Fiction Series, the first volume of which is the physical object that you hold in your hands. This book contains stories by well-known, award-winning writers, seasoned amateurs and unknown first-timers. No matter how many accolades or publishing credits they have, each one is thrilled to appear in actual print and eager to have you read their words on real pages.

Future editions in this series will delve into other great pulp fiction genres: Mystery, Science Fiction, Adventure, even Romance. But we start with Horror, because in an uncertain world on the brink of apocalypse, a little fear is a healthy tonic.

And because my first love was monsters.

—Rick Broussard, Editor
Concord, New Hampshire

Note: Many of the writers of the 160 stories originally submitted to *Live Free or Undead* have given permission for their works to appear online. Visit www.NHPulpFiction.com for a catalog of links to them all and for information about future editions in the series.

Acknowledgments

First of all I want to thank my daughter Eleanor for her help with this book. She assisted me at every turn, read every story, helped narrow a list of 160 submissions down to my 20 final choices and even assisted with the cover design. Her enthusiasm for the project is a clue to a deeper debt. Practically from the day she could select her own books from a shelf, she embraced fantasy and myth-making in all their most vivid forms. Recently, both as a diehard fangirl and as a creator of visual and literary art, her influence has resulted in my re-examination of popular storytelling — both classic genre literature and newer manifestations such as fan fiction, role playing and online gaming.

Without this rejuvenation of my own sense of wonder, the New Hampshire Pulp Fiction series might never have come to life.

Special thanks go out to the many dozens of writers, both professional and wanna-be, who submitted stories, endured rejection or simply contacted me and affirmed this project.

Early in the process my brother-in-law, Greg Nicoll, a talented writer of fiction and a well-known music critic, provided practical guidance and encouragement.

George Geers of Plaidswede Publishing believed in the Live Free or Undead concept when it was merely ink scrawls on a coffee-stained breakfast napkin at the Corner View Restaurant in Concord.

Finally my dad, Bruce Broussard, a psychologist, puppeteer, poet and raconteur who turns 90 this year, bought me my very first Edgar Rice Burroughs book, "A Princess of Mars," in a beautiful hard-bound edition when I was 11 years old. It's one of those rare memories that has not faded — a paternal gift that launched my imagination on a fantastic journey that continues to this day.

Live Free *or* Undead

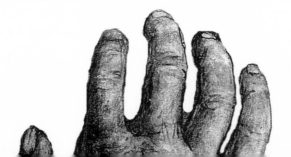

Memento Mori

Elaine Isaak

James tried once more to stride across the Keene State campus. He struggled to lift his right foot, and finally grabbed about his knee with both hands, lifted the recalcitrant limb and set it down again. The left followed more easily, but still tended to drag at the toe. He growled and grabbed his pant leg to coax it along. He hadn't been striding for, well, a long time, but he remembered what it used to feel like—the bouncing roll of his steps, the swing of the rhythm, the sheer, ground-eating beauty of it. He remembered kicking leaves and vaulting the backless benches in front of the library, one arm supporting him, both feet briefly in the air, like maybe he could fly. He couldn't fly any more.

Groaning in defeat, James shambled. He lurched, he shuffled, he even let himself stagger as he got close to his destination, hoping the ordeal would be over sooner.

At last, he fetched up against the brick corner of the new science building, a scrape of flesh peeling off his cheek. Growling, he pushed himself upright, and frowned furiously. Standing up should be easy. Squaring his shoulders, planting his feet, lifting his chest into something like military bearing. Shouldn't be that difficult. He pulled himself erect, forcing his shoulders down and his chin back.

"James!"

Startled, he released his concentration and slumped again, his fingers dangling.

"You shouldn't be here." Lydia glanced both ways around the door.

"I told you I'd call, didn't I? Wait for me to call!" She swallowed hard and stared at him. "Please."

"S-sh-s-sorry." James tried swallowing as well, to see if that would help. She must have been watching for his approach from the lab window. "My phone . . . " He groped in his pocket, his fingers feeling chubby and unresponsive. "Got." He grinned at this success, but Lydia recoiled, looking as pale as her lab coat, as he held out the phone.

James lost his grin and something rattled inside his chest. He opened his palm, the phone lying there, framed by his graying flesh. At least that hand was mostly intact. "It's dead. The phone."

Lydia bit her lips and her eyes shimmered, but she shook her head, a few blonde hairs escaping from her cap, and took the phone. "Have you been remembering to charge it?"

Something about her shimmering eyes made James's chest feel more hollow, and he shook his head. "I . . . no, I don't think so."

Jabbing her fingers—her nimble, delicate fingers—at the device in her hand, Lydia said, "Do you remember where to go?"

James pushed his hands into the pockets of his overcoat and tried. He pictured meeting her outside this door a few days ago, and he could even picture her lips moving—her lush, pink lips in her expressive face. "Homeless shelter?"

"Yes! That's right, James. Yes, the homeless shelter. They'll let you in, and you can plug in the phone by your bed." She held it out toward him and dropped it into his hand, her own hand hesitating. "You do have the cord?"

James nodded. He had no idea. If he had been to this homeless shelter before, it might still be there. Or he could search his pockets after she'd gone back inside. For now, he just nodded.

"Oh, James," she sighed, almost too low for his ears.

"Do you have . . . ?" He looked up at her, forcing his eyes to focus.

"I don't have anything." She stood there, still stopping the door with one foot, not quite coming out to him, and her hands pleaded. "That's why we were supposed to call."

"Nothing," he echoed. His body started to sway and he stopped it, jamming his hands deeper into his pockets, his ragged nails gouging little bits of skin. "When?"

"I don't know. I'm sorry. Maybe the weekend—" she broke off, then said more carefully, "In two days, James. That's two." She held up her fingers to show him.

She didn't have anything for him. Two days. In one day, he'd have forgotten to plug in the phone again, a thing that used to be as natural as, well, breathing. He huffed an imitation of laughter at his own joke. In two days, he'd forget to come here. He would forget her. "No!"

Lydia jumped back, her hands up, her body edging behind the door.

James tried to make a placating gesture. "S-sorry. Didn't mean to speak out loud."

She gripped the rim of the door, and he caught the twinkle of a diamond on her finger. She still wore the ring. A terrible piercing feeling throbbed in his chest, as if he tried again to breathe and forgot how. His eyes itched as if they, too, had forgotten.

"I'll bring you something," she said suddenly, urgently. "Wait here." Lydia moved inside with the grace of the living, swinging the door shut and trotting off down the hall with magnificent speed and coordination. He gazed after her, just watching her body move, until he couldn't see her anymore.

James waited. A light buzzed overhead, and he glimpsed a few students hunched up and laughing. Their moist breath blew out in misty clouds that dissipated as they moved through and disappeared again into the twilight.

The door clanked open again, and Lydia stood there, propping the door a bit wider with her foot, her skirt swaying. She held out a metal tray with a few shriveled, gray slices, crumpled at their edges like over-cooked bacon. "This is all I can get. It's not fresh, I'm sorry. I hope . . ." but she didn't speak any more, just held out the tray with both hands.

The smell of it awakened organs he'd forgotten he still had, and James shot out his hand to grab the slices all at once. He stuffed them into his mouth, his cheeks bulging as he chewed, his teeth grinding into the rubbery texture, barely aware of the formaldehyde clinging to the bits. He swallowed a little, and kept chewing.

Lydia hunched in the doorway, the tray held close to her now, her shoulders up, her face downcast, wincing slightly at any little sound he made.

James swallowed hard and gasped in a breath. A rush flowed through him from his lips to his toes, just reaching his fingers as he stretched them out before him. "Thanks, Lydia. I'm so sorry I forgot the cell phone. I'm such an idiot." He ruffled his fingers through his hair.

A smile crept onto her face and she peeked at him, slipping back her loosening hair with one rubber-gloved finger. "You better go, James. That wasn't enough to last you long, and I want you to get back to the shelter before—"

"Before I start to forget. I know." The overhead floods should have bleached her to nothing, but to him, she glowed like a snow princess, a porcelain figure, delicately painted. "I started reading that book you gave me. I loved the part about the car, how it always seems to backfire when he's got something important to say. I mean, it's a little obvious, but it works for the story, you know?"

"Yes, exactly. My friend—ah, this other lab rat read it, but he thought it was lame, especially about the car." She chuckled.

"Danny Duke." The name aroused a fury in him, but James fought it down. He remembered what it was to be angry, and he didn't like it.

Lydia stiffened. "You guys used to be friends."

"Yeah, well, that was then." James released his clenched fists. He only had a little while before the effects wore off; he didn't want to spend his lucid moments on a jerk like Danny. "I listened to your recording again." He patted the pocket containing the fancy, multi-function phone he barely remembered how to use. "I really love what you did with the glissando."

"Did you?" Her eyebrows pinched together, then smoothed out. "The director wasn't sure about that, but it just—"

"It felt right. It flowed straight from your heart to your hands."

She smiled, in that radiant way that transformed his state from confusion to certainty, and he remembered love. "Yes," she breathed. She gazed back at him, then quickened. "I made a new one, that Bach piece I was working on. I'll email it, okay? Will you be able to . . . ?"

"I'll make sure. There's one of the volunteers at the shelter who keeps track of things for me. Here—" he fumbled through his pockets again and found a ragged notebook "Write me a note, okay?" He found a pen as well, but had trouble keeping a grip on it.

Lydia slipped out her own pencil and wrote "Look for email from Lydiasongs and download. Big headphones, if poss." She handed it back to him. "I'd better go back. I still have a lot to do. I'll call you when I have more." She twiddled the pencil back and forth. "Will you be okay? For two days?"

"I'll be okay," he promised her. If he remembered to wait that long. If the vitality he knew now did not ebb away to nothing even as he found his way back to the shelter. "Thanks."

Her lips parted to say more, but she just gave him a quick smile and slipped away again. She liked to leave him like this, as if she'd see him back at the dorm, or at the coffee shop in the morning. As if he still lived.

Walking back across campus, almost like the rest of the late evening denizens, James inspected the damage to his hands. He'd cut little divots in, but the skin was still attached. He had some superglue in his stash back at the shelter, so he could fix that up. He felt around the scrape on his cheek. Superglue might not be enough, but he would have to face a mirror in order to be sure. He walked faster, his joints temporarily buoyed. With this newfound energy, James turned toward the library.

The librarian's eyes flared when she saw him and she jumped up, trotting around the desk. "Here, why don't you wait in the staff lounge? I assume you're looking for the usual items." She put out a hand as if to guide his elbow, then hesitated.

"It's not contagious," James murmured, pretending he remembered this, but he walked before her into the little room with its huge oval table and let her shut the door after him. Zombies aren't good for business, even quiet, library business. He caught a glimpse of movement from the corner of his eye and started. A gaunt, gray face stared back at him, a peeling swath of skin dangling from one cheek exposing the edge of the jawbone and even a back tooth. James groaned. He tried to pick up the flap and pat it back in place, but it wouldn't stay. A quick survey of the smooth cabinets and squeaky drawers provided him with a first aid kit. Two band-aids later, his face looked, well, normal would be putting it too politely. His brown eyes sank deeper in their sockets daily, and his fine motor muscles, like those responsible for his expressions, weakened.

The door opened and the librarian scowled in at him. "You might have asked." She set a handful of journals on the table. "Just because you're—dead—doesn't mean you should go rooting about where you don't belong."

"Sorry." He put a hand to his cheek self-consciously. "I thought this would be better."

"Yes, well—" but she cut herself off, with a curt nod of agreement, then held out a clipboard. "Sign for the topic file."

James wrapped his fist around the pen and started laboriously to inscribe his name. The list was long, mostly his own signature, slowly deteriorating over the last four months, with Lydia's on occasion, and even Danny Duke's. Probably trying to figure how long James would last before he could put the moves on Lydia. That anger stirred, but James finished the name and dropped the pen back onto the board. He tried to use the Internet sometimes, but his fingers could no longer pick out the keys.

As the librarian departed, he settled at the table and scanned the articles from the topic file. AMA had a cover story about pinpointing the genetic markers for potential zombiism. Psych Today had some schmoe claiming it was all about unfinished business keeping the dead from their rest. James snorted. Brainwaves mentioned promising research into ongoing treatments that might allow for longer revivals. "Revival," James thought. Just like those old-time religious meetings where people suddenly felt moved by the spirit. He skimmed the article, but it didn't sound too promising to him. The last title was a kid's magazine featuring tasty ways to present brains for your young zombie. The lead photograph showed a happy mother holding out a plate of stir-fry—tofu for the family, and brains for the zombie. James's eyes throbbed and he squeezed them shut.

Only one in a hundred thousand dead would still be walking, and most zombies didn't last long after—how many kids could that be? Then he recalled the statistics from his criminal psych class last year. Most of those kids would have been killed by their parents. Not so many perky child-killers eager to serve up brains, then. His own parents held a funeral and moved away, though his brother still urged him to go in for an exam, a sort of walking autopsy, to answer all his questions about James's "death." What with wandering the woods around Mount Monadnock for a few days before he found his way home, James couldn't see the point. His best bet was on exposure from hiking after sundown, just not getting in on time. He didn't think he had enough injuries to have fallen to his death. He couldn't remember what happened before, though he got close a few times when Lydia procured a whole brain.

James shoved the magazines away. If his stomach had been alive, he might have felt revolted. Instead, he could only remember the sensation of revulsion, almost on a par with the craving that came over him at the sight or smell of the brains. He didn't want them, but he needed them. Without a regular supply—without Lydia—he would forget his humanity and crumble into nothing. Sometimes, he thought of that, of not returning and just going back into the forest he used to love until he forgot everything and let himself decay. Then he thought of her face, and patched himself up for another day.

A rap on the door told him his time was up. James shambled back to the shelter, to the special room where three or four like him might bunk on any given night. Once in a while, a zombie forgot too quickly—or maybe didn't have that much humanity to begin with—and James rose from his bed to find the next one filled with a mess of skin and bones as one of the walking dead let himself go. Maybe he finished that unfinished business. James chuckled as best he could.

"Lydia called," said Raymond, the towering volunteer, then he patted the air. "Don't get excited, James, she just wanted to be sure you plugged that phone in. Got some tunes coming your way." The guy even smiled as he took the phone. "She plays real pretty, that lady of yours."

"She sure does." James felt for the superglue in his little box of supplies and got to work on his palms. Raymond pushed some buttons on the phone and gave him a thumbs up. After a minute, the slightly tinny tones of an electronic recording flowed through the cramped room. James fumbled the glue into the divots one by one, pressing them shut carefully so he didn't stick to himself. Careful, careful with his sausage-y fingers. He pictured Lydia's fingers flying over the neck of her cello, the dance of the bow as it leapt and swooped, that amazing night she played down at the Redfern. Did she treasure the agility of her body? Maybe after what happened to him, she did.

James passed the next day close to the shelter. Raymond let him push a mop around the floor, and he helped to carry out the ruined blankets and remains of a stranger who mouldered in the night. A lot of the zombies were nocturnal, either because they got restless not needing to sleep, or because they were just too embarrassed to be seen. Others chose that time to die at last. Raymond hosed him down and found him some fresher clothes from the donations bin. Halfway through getting dressed, James couldn't figure out why he'd want to do that, and Raymond helped him. "You got a hole here, dude. Might want to take care of that," Raymond told him, patting his chest gently.

James nodded, returning to his bunk. He reached for his box, and stared at it in his hands, wondering why he had wanted it. He rifled through the contents: glues, patches, band-aids, pictures of a woman with a man. No good. He tried to read a book, but the letters swam and lost meaning, and he found that he was randomly crumpling pages in his hands. He sat on the bed and swayed, his muscles twitching here and there, like they wanted something. Unfinished business. That should be funny. Why?

A telephone rang somewhere. It might have been his. Lydia. When she called, he should go to her. He remembered something, a bright, winged something. Hope—that was it. Maybe it wasn't his phone. What did his phone sound like? James looked around, but the ringing had stopped. His twitching legs pushed him up and he lurched from his bed. He could go anyway. Maybe it was her.

James kept the image of Lydia in mind as he shuffled toward campus, but he did not find her by the door where they usually met. He swayed there a long time. A student brushed past him, tapping fiercely at a little device in her hands. She shoved her keycard into the door slot and popped the door open, gliding inside as it began to close. James caught the door and followed her in. He wanted something, something tender and tasty. His own shuffling steps echoed in the hall, or maybe just in his head. Formaldehyde lingered in these halls in spite of the daily cleanings. James snuffled, discerning individual scents below. He moved forward. At the end of the hall, the student trotted upstairs and was gone. James followed more slowly, sniffing out the labs, the mixture of scents he remembered on her: Lydia, the one thing he could keep clear in his muddy, decaying mind.

Voices rose into the hall as he drew near. "Look, Danny, it's just too soon," said Lydia's voice, still ahead of him.

"You've been saying that for weeks, Lydia. James is dead—he's not coming back." A nasty laugh followed, then, "Except when he wants braaaaaaaaiins."

"Don't, Danny." She sounded—hurt? Angry?

James tried to hurry, but he stumbled, his weak left foot twisting the wrong way.

"Relax, you gotta take care of him, I understand that. But you've got to take care of yourself, too. Or let me take care of you," Danny's voice grew husky. "You know I've been in love with you for years."

"Please stop. I have work to do."

"You work too hard."

James rounded the door and swayed against it. In the gleaming fluorescent lights Lydia froze, her hips pressed against the lab table, Danny pressed up behind her, his hands stroking her hair as he kissed her neck.

Roaring, James pushed through the door.

Danny shouted, leaping back, and Lydia spun, her hand at her throat, her shoulders instantly relaxing as a smile flashed across her face.

"You," Danny spat, overcoming his surprise. "Get out of here, you shambling thing. Go die in the forest."

Fury swept through James as if he had never forgotten it, but Danny was his friend, or had been. He just had to take no for an answer. "Leave Lydia 'lone," James managed, his mouth working extra for each syllable.

"Oh, Christ." Danny shook his head. He moved up closer to Lydia. "The living don't need you, James, don't you get it? She's still got a soft spot for you, but you're the one who's gotta do the right thing and get lost."

James clenched his trembling fists. "You—you—" he tried to form a sentence, but it didn't come.

"Please, don't fight. You were friends, remember?" Lydia edged away from Danny again.

"It doesn't. It doesn't remember anything before the minute it died, right, James?"

Rage stiffened James's weak ankle and seemed to burn inside him as he glared back. He felt that rattling sensation in his chest again, something shaking loose, and he bared his teeth.

"See?" Danny now looked more relaxed, his grin growing expansive. "And you have to forget us, too." He slipped his arm over Lydia's shoulders. "Just go."

Lydia's glance darted toward the wall, to the alarm box. She twisted under Danny's arm, but he hugged her a little closer. "Stay calm, sweetheart. James knows what he's got to do, don't you?"

He did, oh, he did. The urgency grew in him, much as he tried to restrain it. His arms jerked with the effort. They started to reach toward the metal stool Lydia had been sitting on, but he pulled them back. He pictured the crack across Danny's skull, the glistening brain laid bare before him. It had to be done. He had to do it. No! He had to go while he still cared enough not to kill. His teeth ground together and his body swayed.

"You," James said again, carefully. "I hate you."

Lydia's eyes widened, and Danny's throat bobbed with a quickened breath. "No," she said, "you don't. We're your friends, both of us." Danny tried to smile again, but it looked twisted and wrong, like James's smile.

"James," Lydia cried. "There's a few slices left, in the big bottle. They'll help you calm down." She gestured toward something behind him.

"No!" Danny cried.

"Hush," she murmured. "They'll help him remember. He'll be human again."

He heard their voices, saw their faces, but all from a distance. He wanted something. He could take it from the big one, oh, yes, but the little one didn't want him to. A ring flashed on her hand as she pointed. Lydia! He caught hold of the name again, and swung away to seize down the big bottle where a few ribbons of dissected brain still floated. Something smashed into his side from behind.

James staggered and the bottle broke on the table. Lydia screamed. James's shirt snagged on a screw, tearing over his chest as he tried to right himself. Liquid spilled over and he slipped, catching himself on the stool. A piece of glass carved into his hand. His fingers groped on the seat of the stool, where one of the shriveled brain sections lay.

"Get out! Get out of here!" Danny shouted, thrusting out a gun in both hands. "Don't make me shoot you again!"

Again?

James glanced down. That rattling sensation. The hole in his chest. "You want me to forget." He grabbed the slice of brain and stuffed it in his mouth. The gun fired again, slamming him back against the table, but James pushed himself up, gripping the stool with both hands. "You want me to forget," he repeated, "but I remember." The chewed brain struck his innards like a shot of speed. Memories flashed before his eyes. The hike from the base of the mountain. A new trail Danny had discovered. A secluded place. A single shot and a makeshift grave.

James roared.

Danny shrieked in response. He seized Lydia's shoulders and swung her against him, shoving the gun against her temple. "You want her, right? You still want her? I'll give her to you. Zombie girlfriend, zombie love. She's what you want."

They could be together again. The memories kept flashing: the two of them together, walking the woods, studying in the library, making music. The incredible skill of her agile hands.

He swept up the stool and slammed it into Danny's off-side. The gun leapt and fired, but Lydia dove away, scrambling for the alarm. James swung again, cracking the stool down on Danny's skull. Blood spurted over the slick, polished surfaces. Danny fell, his head hitting hard, lips groaning. Brains. James could smell them. Danny wasn't dead, not yet. But he deserved to be.

The shrill alarm dashed red light in a swirl around the room.

"James," Lydia sighed. She held her arm against her, blood trickling between her fingers, staining the ring she still wore.

Brains. He could remember. He could be almost himself again, for her. He stared at her beautiful, agile hands. "The glissando," he said. "It was perfect." He took an awkward step toward the door and the wilderness not that far away.

She bit her lip, tears blossoming. "Don't go," she whispered.

But he knew that he was already gone.

One day, he would forget his name. Two days, he would forget her. In a little while longer, she would forget him, too. James turned away and he strode out the door, strong enough for now to remember how to love.

Elaine Isaak dropped out of art school to found Curious Characters, designing original stuffed animals and small-scale sculptures, and to follow her bliss: writing. She is the author of *The Singer's Crown* (Eos, 2005), and sequels The *Eunuch's Heir* (Eos, 2006), and *The Bastard Queen* (Swimming Kangaroo, 2010). A mother of two, Elaine also enjoys rock climbing, taiko drumming, weaving and exotic cooking—when she can scrape the time together. Visit www.ElaineIsaak.com to read sample chapters and find out why you do not want to be her hero.

Wonders in the Woods

David O'Keefe

I don't care if you don't believe me. If I cared I wouldn't be talking to you. Just put the drink down for a second.

You want to know why I'm here?

Because the music's too loud, the smell of fried rice is overpowering and the drinks are poured strong. I come here when I just can't stop thinking about it. I don't have any other escape. I don't *want* another escape. I can stay here until they close, and if they kick me out there's a Mexican place right next door that would love me to buy their drinks. And when they close? Well there's a Denny's on the other side. They've got a seat and a stack of pancakes waiting for me. Twenty four hours for 15,000 calories. It's just what I need.

You're still here so I'll give you some credit. Folks who know me move on when I start getting chatty. They don't want to hear it again. You'll feel the same when you get home. You'll tell your wife about the head case you met tonight. Before you do that, look up Charlene Massey sometime. It'll make you think.

We didn't get out much, Charlie—Charlene—and I. I guess they'd call us yuppies. We were young and professional, but Merrimack's more of a suburb. Charlie grew up here and I moved in from Vermont. I was a middle manager at an electronics store. They shut it down recently; I can't get you discounts. Charlie telecommuted to a software company in Boston. She was making the money. I was bringing home some nice tech, though. She had a thing for new stuff, you see. Plasma screens,

surround sound, anything that was new and different. I didn't complain, though. I mean look at me. Here's a photo of her I keep in my wallet. You see that long red hair and those eyes? Do I look like a guy who deserves to be with someone like her?

Right.

But I wasn't complaining and, wonder of wonders, neither was she.

Trouble was, neither of us made all that much in the long run. We shared a tiny apartment. Vacations came cheap and infrequently. We made it work, though. Twice a year we took a trip up north. That's what everyone comes to New England for, isn't it? Head far enough north and you get beautiful scenery on a budget. We'd go twice a year. Once in the winter for ski season and once in the summer for hiking.

She packed our minivan with a cooler of beer, water and sandwiches. I grabbed our sleeping bags and yanked the seats out of the minivan. No hotels for us. We parked in a rest area and slept in the car's midsection. If we were sore we might go right to sleep. If we had some energy left? Well, we usually found some energy. I won't say we smelled great when we got back. We were away from everything that mattered besides each other. And you know what that meant? It meant we had all we needed. We'd come back dying for a shower and a soft bed. That was our recipe for happiness. I dare you to get more out of Foxwoods.

We were on our trip. We'd already had one night and were thinking to stretch it out an extra day. This was in summer. Just pleasant mountain climbs and the scent of mosquito repellent. Ever been on Kancamagus? It's beautiful. Make sure you have gas to spare because you're going to be a while. A long while. That, my friend, is what Charlie liked about it.

"Wow, will you look at that?" she said. I looked out the window. "You know, the human eye can see for miles if unobstructed." She looked at me, then back to the valley.

I was always a good driver. Keeping tabs on the road wasn't a problem. "It's just that we spend all our lives looking at walls," I said.

"Yeah." She was humoring me, I think. "So much green." Her hair was matted. It did that after a night in a sleeping bag. Yeah, this grin is because it was my bag that night. Hey, shut up. Let a man reminisce will you?

We didn't get another night. That was when we found the rest area. You know the drill. Anywhere north of Tilton you leave popular culture behind. Instead you get mountains and valleys and every town along the way built to sell it to you in the form of key chains. If you can't find what you're looking for at Wal-mart you're in for at least an hour drive. That's where the rest areas came in. Some have all the amenities: working toilets, pamphlets for Six Gun City or Story Land, and a couple of vending machines. Others are just a clearing with a parking lot and an outhouse. I wasn't a fan of the outhouses unless there was no other choice for miles. Charlie was the brave one in those situations.

This was one of those last types. We parked and Charlie was the first one out. She didn't bother to throw her socks back on, just pulled boots over her feet. I pulled all my gear on. The only reason I didn't spray myself was because we'd be back in the van shortly. We hadn't even had breakfast.

"See? This is why we come up here every year," she said, gazing at the view.

I slid up next to her and took her around the waist. The valley looked like someone had draped a giant green blanket over it. Shadows of clouds added depth. We stood there, quiet, just enjoying the breeze and each other. I go up there sometimes. Thinking maybe I'll get up the courage to go into those woods again. I always spend some time look-ing at the valley. It taunts me. I'd love if it was one of those things that disappears and no one can find it. But it's still there. Even the stinking outhouse is still there.

That was when we heard her: "Not bad, huh?"

We both turned, startled. There weren't any other cars in the lot.

The newcomer wasn't much to look at, but after sleeping in the van, neither were we. She was about 50, dressed like a life-long woodsman. I don't mean like Native Americans. She just had that look like she'd never set foot in anything more civilized than an L.L. Bean. She wore a red plaid flannel shirt and a pair of blue jeans. Her feet were bare, odd thing. Hair was a washed-out brown tied in a braid. Being the deductive sort I assumed she lived nearby and came out to enjoy the view, same as we did.

"Not bad?" Charlie answered. "It's beautiful."

"I come out here a couple times a week. Helps me get my spirit back, you know?" She took a spot next to Charlie and me. I didn't really like the way she smelled, either. "I'm Francesca. Friends call me Frannie."

"Good to meet you, Frannie," said Charlie. She was always eager to make a friend.

"Hi," I said.

We stood there for a few. Charlie was lost in it. Me, I meant for this to be a romantic moment. The stranger horning in had turned it awkward.

"Hey, you wanna see something else?" Francesca asked.

"Huh?" Charlie said, coming out of her reverie.

"Well this is nice, don't get me wrong." She pointed back towards the woods. "I live in these woods, not far from here. I can show you some real sights."

"Like what?" Charlie asked.

"You'd be amazed," she answered with a smile. "Most people just drive by and stop to look around. But if you live here you really get to know the land."

We both listened.

"Think about it for a second. You only see this narrow strip of land as you drive along. That's all you see for the whole ride until you get to Conway or Ossipee or wherever you're headed. So all you're getting is the place you started, the place you finish, and a long road with yellow lines on it. But if you take a look around you'd see stuff no one even remembers is here."

"How long would it take?" I said. I'm suspicious of people. Yes, yourself included.

"You in a hurry?" she asked. "That's fine. One's only a ten-minute walk from here."

"Then let's go see," Charlie agreed, impulsively. She does that. Did that.

"I don't know," I started, but Charlie was already on her way, red curls bouncing.

"Right up here," Francesca beckoned. I made them wait for me. Fact is, with Triple E and West Nile I wasn't going anywhere without being hosed in bug spray.

We climbed a couple of rocks and then we were in the woods. There were no paths, but Francesca knew the way. She walked on, bare feet on sticks and nettles, without a pause. I relaxed a little. I thought maybe she was a thief luring tourists and—I don't know. Not many bandits up north, are there? But it was clear she knew the place like someone who lived there. She had a habit of touching the trees like they were pets.

The first thing she showed us was pretty damn impressive. I'll admit it. It was a mushroom.

"What do you think of that?" she asked.

The mushroom was glowing in the shade. Not the pale firefly glow but a full, bright orange light. I held my hand over it and could swear I felt heat.

"Glad you came, now?" Francesca asked me.

"Very impressive," I said. "What makes it do that?"

"Damned if I know," she said. "Might be some chemical like those deep sea fish have. A lot brighter than you'd think though, right?"

Charlie and I both nodded.

"So why does it do that?" Charlie asked. "I mean what's it for?"

"Don't know that either. Sorry girl, I'm no botanist. I'll tell you this, though, it glows even brighter at night. Sometimes I don't know why passing cars don't see it."

"It's beautiful," Charlie said. Light from the mushroom danced in her eyes. I was glad we came.

"Well, if that's all you've got time for, I'll wish you well on your way," our guide said.

"Wait!" Charlie exclaimed. "We weren't really going anywhere today. If there's more like this I'd love to see."

Francesca laughed, and so did I. That was so like her, getting excited over something new and shiny. "Well of course there are, you didn't think I was lying did you?"

"No, no, just . . ." Charlie shrugged and looked at me.

"Just that every town on the way up is selling us on everyday stuff and claiming it's unique to the area," I finished. You didn't really think the Lakes Region was the origin of maple sugar candy, did you?

"Yeah, I get it," she said. "Don't worry. I'm not charging you ten bucks to ride a ski lift in summer. My home is back this way. You can turn back whenever you want."

"Cool." Charlie started following.

Now I won't deny the mushroom was cool, but I wasn't that interested. I still sort of hoped for some Burger King that day. But where Charlie went, I was soon to follow.

"How long have you lived here?" I asked.

"Most of my life," Francesca answered, "I was born around these parts and always had a thing for the mountains. I tried city life for a while, but around 25 I simply headed up and didn't look back."

I meant to argue that you couldn't really survive totally isolated these days, but I was interrupted. We'd come across her next little curiosity.

"What's—oh my God!" That wasn't Charlie. That came from me. It took seconds to figure out what I was seeing. We'd walked into a clearing bordered by red bushes. Bushes with moving leaves. Leaves with legs and antennae. They were butterflies. The bushes were so covered with butterflies I thought they were foliage.

"What do you think they're sitting on?" Francesca asked.

"They're completely covering the plant. I can't tell."

"Are they eating it?" Charlie asked.

"They already ate it, right down to the stump," Francesca said.

"What?" I asked.

"Yell 'boo' at em, and stand back."

"OK—" I did yell "boo," and the reaction was awe-inspiring and terrifying. Amazing because the bush essentially exploded. A cloud of butterflies flew out and kept coming. By the time they'd swirled out, funneled into the sky above, there was nothing left on the ground but a root. The butterflies had been the entirety of the bush. It was terrifying because those wings were razor sharp.

I cried out in shock as two of them cut open my cheek. The two women were at my side in an instant.

"Sorry!" Francesca said. "I told you to step back!"

"Too fast!" I said.

"Oh God, you're bleeding," Charlie said. "Hang on." She took a tissue out of her pocket and pressed it against the cut.

"Ow!" I said. It hurt!

"Yeah, that's gonna sting for a bit," Francesca said. "Just tough it out."

"You could have let me know beforehand."

"I did tell you to step back, didn't I? But you yelled boo with your face over them. I couldn't have stopped you."

"Come on, Charlie, this is special and all, but I want to get out of here." God, I wish she'd just said sure, let's go. Instead she was quiet.

Then she said, "What? We might not find this place again. It's just a small cut."

"It might get infected," I protested.

"We'll wash it when we get back."

"You're serious?" I asked, but I could see she was. I looked at Francesca, whose eyes said nothing. "Fine, if you really want to keep trekking on."

"Yeah," she said. "I do. This is really amazing."

I should have argued.

"Just keep your distance from the next one," Francesca said. "You really don't want to be touching it."

"Just give me all the facts this time, OK?" I said, pulling myself back up off the ground with Charlie's help.

"Will do," she answered.

This time we walked for at least 20 minutes. When we stopped, it wasn't a clearing, just a break along the path I hadn't noticed before.

Francesca stopped and pointed. "Now you can look at them but don't touch. It's bad news if they get on you."

We came to a mound. I purposely kept my distance this time. She herself didn't go too close. The mound looked like a pile of fine mulch. Dotted on it were little green spots. Charlie took a few steps forward and looked. Reluctantly I followed. Those things—out of everything we saw that night they're the only ones that give me nightmares. They're the reason I'm checking myself every day like a leper and I freak out at the slightest tickle.

They were little emerald spheres embedded in the mulch. They shined in the light and sparkled like the stones they resembled.

"Very pretty. What are they?" Charlie asked, probably feeling as confused as I did.

"Watch—right here," she answered. "And again, don't touch."

I watched. A few moments later one green bead moved. It turned and wiggled. Beneath the bead, a set of thin legs withdrew, one by one, from the mulch, each one leaving a red spot in its place. The legs stretched, and the total creature was at least five inches across fully extended. The legs transported the small bead a few inches down the mulch, where it dug its way in again. The mound shivered.

"What the hell are they?" I asked.

"They're not exactly spiders," Francesca said, "but close. Definitely arachnids. If you could see under them you'd see the mouthpiece. It's sort of a cross between a knife and a straw." She pointed to one end, "Take a look at that side of the mound."

We did, and this time even Charlie cried out in surprise. The mound was a deer. I could see its eye and, now that I knew what I was looking at, make out the form of its body. The entire deer was covered in that weird fibrous mulch that I now saw for what it was: webbing. The things had somehow brought the deer down and were slowly eating it. A deer that was still blinking.

"It's alive," I said in shock. Charlie had her hand over her face. "Oh, God, it's alive."

"That it is," Francesca said. Her voice was like a tour guide in a museum. "They immobilize their prey. Some kind of paralytic venom. Then they start feeding and multiplying in it."

I could barely hold my stomach with that one.

"Can we help it?" Charlie asked.

"The deer?" Francesca was incredulous. "The poor thing's infested. It's not coming back from this."

"Kill it," I said.

"Try. I'm not risking having those goblins on me."

"How long will they be there?" Charlie asked. She didn't like seeing things hurt. She couldn't even watch slasher movies.

"Til it dies," she answered. "Probably a day or two. They'll all come out and go looking for more prey. Most of them get eaten by birds and the like."

Charlie shuddered, "Let's just go."

"Sure, come on." She led past the unfortunate deer. I didn't even care that we weren't heading back. I wanted to be away. I couldn't believe the woman walked around those things barefoot. As we walked away I could see they weren't just on the deer. Some of them were on the trees or in the grass. That's when I started swatting myself. I haven't stopped.

I won't tell you everything we saw on our walk. Some of it I missed, still thinking about those bugs. The day quickly went from morning to noon to late afternoon. I started to get worried.

"You know, we should head back," I said.

"Why?" both women answered. Once she'd gotten over her surprise at the bugs, Charlie got her pep back.

"I don't know about you, sweetie, but I don't want to be out here when it gets dark," I said. "Do you, Charlie?"

Charlie looked at the sky, "He's got a point, Frannie. We should head back soon."

"We're almost there," she said. "You'll be on your way back soon."

"Almost where?" I asked.

"You wanted to see what these woods had to offer, didn't you?"

"Mostly her," I said, pointing at Charlie.

"Mostly me. He just likes watching my butt on the way."

"Well," Francesca began, then stopped. She pointed into some trees. I saw nothing at all. And then it moved.

"Oh, wow," Charlie said.

Whatever it was, it was big. We could only see the general shadow of it. But there was motion so vast I couldn't estimate its true scale. Then it took a slow, plodding step. The earth shook. I could feel each step even if I never saw the whole thing. What I did see, just for an instant, was a bright orange eye. The pupil was slitted like a cat's. Then it moved upwards and rows of saber long teeth came into view.

"What's that one?" Charlie asked.

You're probably wondering why we didn't question what we saw. You know what the police thought when I told them the story? They started and ended with the mushroom. They thought I'd eaten something I shouldn't have and hallucinated the rest. You understand seeing is believing. We were seeing that stuff. Watch the Discovery channel sometime and see how many weird things are out there. We just—we figured it was normal. Francesca wasn't alarmed, right? This was apparently everyday stuff to her and, for all we knew, the people who lived around there.

"Big fellow," she said. "I've never seen it up close but I've seen its meals. It leaves a bloody mess in its path. You're lucky, Charlie. I never know where it's going to be."

"Are there a lot of them?"

"Could be," she answered.

The thing thumped again.

"I wouldn't want to get caught in its path," I said.

"Luckily you can hear it a long way off," Francesca answered.

"I would," Charlie said.

"What?" I asked, shocked.

"I'd want to see it up close. See what it really looks like. I'm amazed. Aren't you? Did it ever occur to you what could be out here?"

"Some of it's neat, yeah. But I don't want to be too close to a lot of it," I gestured to my cut cheek.

"Oh, let it go," she said. "Come on."

So I let it go and went on. Fifteen minutes later, I stopped.

"What's wrong?" Charlie asked.

"Look at the sky, Charlie. The sun's setting."

She did. "Oh crap."

"We need to go now. It's going to be hard enough finding our way back with what little light we have."

"You don't have two minutes?" Francesca asked.

"No," I said at the same time Charlie said, "Maybe, why?"

I glared at her but she just gave me an annoyed look. "What's left?"

"Well my place isn't far from here, kids. I've got something really amazing in my yard. And if it's too dark you can just crash there until dawn.

"What is it?" I asked.

"What's what?" she asked back.

"The thing in your yard; what you want to show us."

She grinned, "It's the reason I stay out here."

We followed. No, Charlie followed. Charlie, who was just so damn enamored by all this she had to see more. Me, I followed Charlie. I followed her because she was the love of my life. She still is. I still drive up there every year. I wait at that same spot where we went in and I hope and pray that this time, this time she'll come out. This time she'll find her way back to me. But you know what? She's never come out. She's never going to.

What was in her yard? I don't know. It's hard to describe. Her house looked like an old shack. It was the kind of place kids would egg and taunt the owner for being a witch. The yard wasn't a yard—it was just a place where the woods had been hacked into submission. And in that yard was—a thing. Everything else I had an allegory for. But this thing was—I don't know. Hang on, I need another drink.

There was a hillock in the middle of her "yard." Just this big mound of dirt overgrown with grass and weeds. I was already thinking back to that deer. Francesca whacked it with a stick. The hill opened. Right. The whole hill opened like a flower with thick meaty petals twirling and splitting and finally coming to rest on the ground. None of the dirt or weeds moved aside. They were rooted into it. A thick, cloying odor came from it. Something spicy and sweet, but with a tinge, like raw meat, just under it. There was writing on the petals. They were veins. But the veins were arranged like writing in a language I didn't know, with letters I didn't recognize. This was it. Charlie was as flabbergasted as I was disgusted.

I know what was up with Charlie. I know. She just loved wonder. A soul like hers was stifled in a world of sterile programming and sheet-rock walls. That's why she walked right up to it. The sun was setting now. I don't think we even had a prayer of making it back before dark.

"And this?" Charlie asked, approaching it and peering over the edge.

"Looks scary, doesn't it," Francesca answered.

I nodded, but Charlie shook her head, "I don't know. I've never seen anything like this."

"A lot of people think there's nothing undiscovered in the world," Francesca said. "They think when mankind started moving and building they trampled everything in their path. Not everything, though. Some things were here even before the natives came over from Asia. Just here waiting. Waiting for the right people, sometimes."

"People like you?" Charlie asked, staring into the maw I was too nervous to even approach.

"People like me," she said. "The ones who always press on. There's secrets in this place, Charlie. You could be here a lifetime and never see them all."

"Charlie," I said, but my voice sounded small and afraid. I didn't like how close I was to the thing. Watching Charlie stand on its rim was like seeing her dangle from a cliff and not know it. "Charlie please come down. We gotta go back."

In response, Charlie reached her hand down to me. "Come on up. You've got to see this."

I didn't want to see it. I didn't want to see anything else. I just wanted to take her and go back home. We were supposed to be eating dinner before pulling in for the night.

"Come on, Charlie," Francesca said. "It's not that far in, and you can head back whenever you're ready." With that the crazy woman simply hopped into the maw as though she were walking down a flight of stairs.

Charlie should have been afraid.

"Come on," she urged me. "Just a little bit."

"I want to go back," I said, resolute. We had to stop. There was just no way I could take that step. "I'm not going in there."

She looked at me. Then she looked at the hole. Then back at me.

The last words I heard from my Charlie were, "I'll be right back." Then she was gone.

I scrambled up after her and stopped just short of jumping in. I couldn't see into it. There was just blackness surrounded by purple-red flesh. I shouted her name but there was no answer. So I waited for her. I walked around the thing. I inspected the terrain. I even went into Francesca's house to kill time. No one's lived there in decades. It was bare walls and rotten floors. It finally hit me that the hole was Francesca's home. She lived in the thing.

The sun went down and I waited. The hole closed up and I waited. I knocked it with a stick and it opened again. I looked in, but it was even darker. I waited. It closed.

I waited until I started to feel them. I don't know what they were but I could feel them landing on my skin and crawling on me. You can guess what I thought. So I lost it. I screamed and wiped at my arms and legs. It was too dark to see them. But I could feel it when they bit. Oh yes. They drew blood. I wanted to wait for Charlie. I wanted to believe she'd be right back but you know what? There's only so much you can take. I could see myself covered in brown webbing with little green spiders crawling all over. And when I felt the thump sounding in the earth—I ran. I ran on and on. I couldn't see. I hit one tree after another. All the while, things bit me and crawled on me, under my clothes, in my hair. I never found one or caught one. Finally, I saw the light. Literally I saw light. It was the bizarre mushroom we'd seen first. The one we'd led in on. I knew where the car was from there.

I kicked the fungus. I don't know if I meant to or not, but I'm glad I did it. It broke open and scattered glowing pieces all over the ground. There were small bones inside.

When I burst out onto the road I stripped. I couldn't stand the thought of even one monster on my body. I turned on the van and stood in the light, examining my whole body. I was welted all over so I scratched at them. Nothing that got in my body was staying in.

That's how I was when the only state trooper for a hundred miles pulled up. He took me to the station, then to the hospital when I wouldn't stop scratching my wounds. When I finally calmed down they did a tox screen. They were obviously surprised when it came back negative.

There was a search party. It lasted for a week before they finally gave Charlie up for lost. I don't know if they saw the things we did. Maybe they only came out for Francesca. Without her, I couldn't lead them any better. It turned out no one really knew her. Some had heard of her and maybe seen her from afar, but that was all. Charlie's obituary was in the paper a month later.

So there you go. That's the whole story for you.

Now if you don't mind I'm going to finish my vodka and maybe forget everything I just told you.

David O'Keefe carries a notebook to record ideas and a book to pass the time. He penned scores of stories while growing up in New Hampshire, having taken to writing as soon as he could read. While completing a bachelor's degree in history, Dave was recognized for his creative work and changed focus to develop his skill. Since then he's made other academic strides, is working, and is pursuing a career as a professional writer. "Wonders in the Woods" is his first published work and, he believes, his first step toward making a career of his imagination.

The Couple Voted Most Likely to Stay Together

David Elliott

When his mother told him that the Malabrands had a "surprise" for him, Jamie balked. He disliked John and Muriel Malabrand nearly as much as he disliked his own parents—if such a thing were possible. But it was the mention of a surprise that roiled his stomach. At seventeen, he figured he'd had enough surprise to last him the rest of his life. But years of living-with his mother had taught him that she would meet his resistance with a ruthless, unrelenting assault, and the weapons in her arsenal, though silent, were lethal. Furtive glances. Quivering smiles. Sudden tears. He didn't have the energy to withstand it. Not now. Maybe not ever. Easier, much easier, to capitulate. And so on a wet afternoon in late May, he found himself standing at the door of the Malabrands' grotesque suburban McMansion, cursing under his breath and steeling himself against the boozy good cheer of its occupants. But then came the unexpected offer of the cottage on Lake Winnepocket, and he was glad he had come.

"It's nothin' fancy, Jamie Boy," John Malabrand said from his perch on the enormous couch in the great room. The walls, a sickly shade of green, highlighted the rash of exploded blood vessels that stretched over John's broad nose and down his heavy cheeks, reminding Jamie of the maps of pandemics Mr. Taylor had shown them last year in his human

geography class. "Nope. Nothin' fancy," John repeated. "Just two rooms and a loo."

Loo. The man was ridiculous, peppering his speech with British-isms like that, as if it somehow disguised what everybody already knew—he'd been born in Belchertown, M-A.

"We bought the place furnished a couple of years ago," John went on. "Built in 1922. Thought we'd fix it up, but one thing led to another. I don't think we've gone up there but twice. Probably should sell it. Muriel never liked the place."

"It's in *New Hampshire*, for God's sake," added Muriel, lighting another cigarette. "I practically had to have a transfusion the last time we were up there. The mosquitoes! Jesus Christ! The mosquitoes!"

Between the chain-smoking and the suffocating strength of her per-fume, Jamie didn't believe a mosquito would be able to get within ten feet of her.

"Don't listen to her," John said. "It's lovely up there, really."

Lovely? Had John Malabrand, with his bad skin, his thinning hair, and his waistline locked in mortal combat with his belt, actually said "lovely"?

"And I suppose it's lovely to hear those ducks at night?" Muriel asked, taking a long drag on her cigarette.

"Loons," her husband corrected.

"Honestly, it's like the criminally insane are out there paddling around in the dark. No thanks. I can understand why Jamie might want to spend a week or two up there in God Forsaken, New Hampshire after everything he's gone through, but between you and me, I've squashed my last mosquito and heard my last duck."

"Loon."

"Screw you, John."

Muriel stood up and walked into the kitchen—so much stainless steel that it might have been a factory, one that manufactured highly specialized medical equipment or something. There she mixed herself another drink, leaving her husband to explain where the key was hid-den at the cottage and give instructions about its many idiosyncrasies. "Don't try to open the back door. You'll never get it shut." And, "Oh, I almost forgot. The water in all the faucets will run brown the first day or so."

"Like blood," Muriel yelled from the kitchen.

After everything he's gone through. The words had stayed with Jamie. They were with him now, as he headed out of Boston, driving north on Interstate 93. He could hear Muriel's smoke-ravaged voice and see her flaccid mouth forming the words, her garish red lipstick contrasting so violently with the yellow of her teeth that Jamie had had to look away.

I haven't gone through anything, he'd wanted to shout. *Nothing! That's the problem!* But he hadn't uttered a word. There was no point. Muriel was clueless. Like everybody else. His parents. Barry Pryce. The friends he and Jannie used to have. There *was* no going though. There was no going anywhere. There never would be. Jannie had died. Jannie was dead. Do not pass Go. Never pass Go again.

Concord, New Hampshire. 60 miles.

As Jamie read the sign, his lips nearly curled into a smile. He was thinking of the way he had fooled Barry Pryce, Ph-fucking-D—the so-called grief counselor his parents insisted he see after the accident. The man was a dick. Him and his five stages of grief, as if what Jamie was feeling was nothing more than a recipe in one of the glossy, household magazines his mother subscribed to. *Want a surefire fix when the love of your life has kicked the bucket? Follow these five easy steps and you're sure to please both yourself and your friends and family standing at the coffin. Start with a healthy dollop of denial. Now fold in a little anger....*

No, it wasn't that simple. Hadn't he and Jannie been voted The Couple Most Likely to Stay Together? Hadn't they sworn they would never be apart? Jannie and Jamie. Jamie and Jannie. That's the way it was supposed to be. Forever. Forever and ever.

"I'm feeling better now," Jamie lied in the session with Pryce after the Malabrands' offer of the cottage. "My appetite is coming back, too."

Pryce smiled and bobbed his head, the tip of his beard stabbing at just about the spot his heart would have been. "What did I tell you?" he said to Jamie. "You've moved through the first four stages and are entering the last one: acceptance. Right on schedule."

Jamie tried to assume the demeanor of someone dumb enough to believe this prefabricated bullshit.

"I'm—I'm glad to hear that," he'd said. "It's—been rough." Pryce continued to nod and smile. Jamie had him right where he wanted him.

He knew his parents would never let him spend a week at the cottage alone unless Pryce approved it. "I—I really feel like I could use some time to myself. You know—to get my head together and everything."

"That's only natural," the good doctor said. "In fact, I think you deserve it."

And that was that.

He pulled into the left lane to get around a white, late-model Ford tootling along at 45 miles an hour. When he glanced over to check out the driver, his pulse increased so suddenly that, for one terrifying moment, he thought he was going to black out. It was an old woman. Short white hair. Glasses. Her arthritic fingers gripping the wheel like leeches. He lowered his speed so that his Volvo ran parallel to the white car.

With each click of the odometer, his anger grew. What would it feel like to run an old woman off the road? Pin her against a tree? Watch her choke on her own blood? An eye for an eye, isn't that what they say? The woman looked to be the same age as the man who had stolen Jannie from him; the old man who had run the stop sign. Who's to say the woman wouldn't murder someone just the way the old man had murdered Jannie? Who's to say Jamie wouldn't be doing someone a favor?

If she so much as glanced at him, he would do it. Swear to God! It would be easy, too. All he had to do was turn the wheel to the right, just the slightest downward pull of his right arm. That's all it would take. Easy! Easy-peasy! Easier, when he thought about it, than not doing it. He tightened his grip, getting ready. *Look at me! Look at me!* But the old woman kept her eyes straight ahead of her, oblivious, never veering an inch from her path. He jammed the accelerator to the floor until the Ford disappeared behind him.

Welcome to New Hampshire, the sign said. Bienvenue!

Bienvenue . . . Bienvenue . . .

Bon jour, mademoiselle. Je m'apelle Jamie. Je suis un garçon français.

Bon jour, Jamie. Je m'apelle Jannie. Je suis une Americaine. Je suis une étudiante.

Tu es très belle, Jannie.

Merci, Jamie.

Jannie?

Oui, Jamie.

Voulez vous couchez avec moi?

Oui, Jamie.

Je' taime, Jannie. Je' taime.

They loved rehearsing these dialogues, cobbled together from snippets from their junior year French class. Sometimes Jannie would be a secretary from the Netherlands. Other times, a teacher from Germany. Once, she was even a doctor from Morocco. But no matter how the dialogues began, they always ended the same way.

"Tell me again, Jamie," Jannie would whisper. "Say it again."

Je' taime, Jannie, Je' taime.

Jamie got an A in that class; Jannie barely passed, even with Jamie doing most of her homework.

He drove further into the state. In Vermont, it was the cleared land that predominated, the fields opening the land to the warming sun. But in New Hampshire the trees conspired, or so it seemed to Jamie, to keep it out. Even here along the interstate, battalions of hemlocks and pines grew right down to the shoulder, trunk to trunk, waiting for the right moment to send a dark root out under the surface of the road. The beginning of the end. If Vermont was a sigh, Jamie decided, New Hampshire was a startled gasp.

He tried to remember the last time he had visited the state. He was certain he had been here before, maybe at a summer camp or on a weekend with a childhood friend. But his mother insisted that he had never crossed the state line, unless he and Jannie had snuck up there. *Snuck up there.* Those had been her exact words.

He turned off 93 and circled onto 89, only three exits now from the exit John Malabrand had told him to take. When he left Framingham earlier that afternoon, the sun had been shining, but the New Hampshire sky had gradually faded to a dirty gray, the color of granite. A light drizzle began to fall. By the time he was on the two-lane road that would take him to the cottage, heavy drops were pelting the windshield, last rites for the flying things that had died there. He switched the wipers to high as lightening flashed over the trees. According to John Malabrand's directions, he was only a couple of miles from the cottage now.

He kept a lookout for landmarks. Yes, there was the farm stand sitting next to a big, white colonial house. The house sat in the eye of a large tract of cleared land. The Courser Farm, the sign read. Jamie wished he knew how big an acre was. Did the fields rolling behind the house represent five acres or fifty? A hundred? He didn't know. And at the back of the fields, the dark line of trees, always the trees.

Suddenly, as if he had summoned them out of the rain, a trio of deer burst onto the road. Jamie slammed on the brakes and swerved to the right, narrowly missing a disastrous collision with the last of the three, a huge, russet buck, exactly like the deer on the tapestries he had learned about in art history. His right hand shot out to prevent the laptop, loose in the passenger's seat, from crashing into the dash. His heart was racing. He slowed down.

The cottage was exactly where John Malabrand said it would be, at the end of an unmarked dirt road, sitting by itself on an isolated spit of sandy lawn. John had been right. It wasn't fancy, just a squat, shingled box with a porch attached like an afterthought to the front. A thick stand of evergreens encroached on its back wall, some of the branches looking as if they were reaching out to tag the shingled roof. The ground in front of the cabin, Jamie noticed, was littered with pine cones. The effect was that of a party that had been quickly abandoned.

Still sitting in the car, Jamie turned to his right where the lake stretched out for a mile or more, like an arm, bent slightly at the elbow. *Jannie would have loved it here.* Had he said it aloud? Or simply thought it? He remembered the first time he saw her in the water. Her long, thin torso buoyant and lithe, her legs softly churning behind her, and all the while the steady rhythm of her arms, slender and white, entering and leaving the surface as effortlessly as blades of a windmill, slicing through a low-lying mist. Appearing then disappearing. Appearing then disappearing. She was more herself in a lake, she'd told him, than on the dry land. Jamie had tried to convince her to join the swim team. *You could get a scholarship to a great college*, he'd said more than once. *You're that good.* But she wasn't interested. *I'm not the college type*, was all she'd said. Jamie himself was not a strong swimmer, having nearly drowned years earlier when an older cousin dunked him one too many times. It was silly, he knew, but he still didn't like to put his head under water.

Eventually, he left the car and carried his sleeping bag through the rain and onto the front porch. Walking back to the passenger's side, he grabbed his laptop, protecting it from the wet by sliding it under his shirt. But he left the box of groceries his mother had packed for him on the back seat. "Don't forget to eat," she'd begged, reminding him once again that over the last months, he'd lost more than twenty pounds. "Promise me you'll eat while you're up there."

Inside the dim, half-light of the cabin, the air was damp from the rain and chilled from its long, undisturbed interment. *Jesus*, he said. *It's like a movie set.* A faded chintz-covered sofa. A matching chair. Old paneling on the walls. A stray rocker.

He took the laptop from under his shirt and put it carefully on the painted table that sat in front of one of the two windows. Then, he unzipped his duffle bag and pulled out the yellow sweater, a birthday present from Jannie. She'd made it for him, her first effort. Two sizes too big and the wool so heavy and rough that the first time he wore it, his arms and neck broke out in a burning rash. His mother always said that the color made him look sallow. He slipped the sweater on over his tee.

Next he unrolled the sleeping bag and threw it on the couch. The minute the cottage had been offered he'd decided he would sleep anywhere rather than in a bed in which John and Muriel might have had sex. Once or twice, he thought he smelled a trace of Muriel's perfume as it mixed with the smell of dust and mouse droppings. He opened the windows. He was ready now. He pulled a rickety, spindled chair over to the table, switched on the candlestick lamp that sat in its middle, and sat down.

"There's electricity, of course," John Malabrand had told him. "But you won't get reception for your cell. And if you want the Internet, you'll have to go to the library in the village. No connection at the cottage."

Jamie had practically laughed in the man's face. Didn't he understand? Connection was why he was going.

While he waited for his desktop to appear, he stared out at the cove and the narrow expanse of water beyond, wondering what kind of fish were in the lake. Bass, maybe? Bluegills? Perch? Rain continued to beat the surface of the lake. Did the fish know it was raining? What a stupid question. Fish didn't "know" anything and didn't think in words like "rain." In fact, now that he considered it, he was certain that fish didn't think at all. They simply swam through the lake's dark water, unaware that they were swimming or even that they were fish. Not conscious that they were alive until, perhaps, a fisherman's hook yanked them out of the water or a snapping turtle got them. Did Jannie know? Did she know she was being yanked out of the lake when the old man hit her? What had she been thinking when she died? Of him? Of Jamie?

Jamie turned back to the laptop and clicked on a folder he'd named Calculus Homework. (His mother would never look there.) He selected one of the files; a picture of Jannie appeared on the screen, on her tenth birthday, a half-eaten cake topped with a now-fallen Barbie and Ken on the table in front of her. The snapshot lingered for a moment and then faded as the next took its place. His breath came in short, sharp gulps. Jannie in a cap and gown, graduating from elementary school, her uncontrollable black hair sticking out from her head like a fright wig. "I told you," she'd said to Jamie. "I'm part gypsy."

Next came a series of snapshots that Jannie had emailed from her room, taken on a weeknight and sent late. Some of these he'd deleted. He was sorry now that he had. So what if his mother found them? So what? She'd never liked Jannie anyway. *Snuck up there.* That's what she'd said.

A more recent picture appeared on the screen, Jannie standing next to him at the junior prom. He would never forget that night. "Tell me again, Jamie. Say it again." His fingertips brushed the screen just as the photo faded. *Jannie,* he whispered. *Jannie.*

Oblivious to the chill that was settling into the cabin, he pulled his chair closer and leaned in to the screen as the Vermont pictures began. *Pick me up in the morning for a surprise,* Jannie had texted just after midnight. He'd been awake, studying for an AP history exam the next day. Mrs. Connors was crazy about the New Deal. When Jannie got in the car, she was carrying a picnic basket. She shoved a piece of a paper into his hand. "Starting point: Framingham, Massachusetts," he read. "Ending Point: Putney, Vermont." They were already in Greenfield, just miles from the Vermont border, when he remembered the history test.

The cycle of pictures ended and began again. And then again. As the full moon rose behind its veil of clouds, he remembered what Jannie had said. What she wore. The way she smelled. Occasionally, he would catch himself thinking that Jannie was there with him now, in the tiny bathroom off the kitchen or maybe sitting on the deck of the porch. Sometimes, he would pull himself back from these fantasies. Other times he would stay with them as long as he dared, in his mind calling her to come in from the damp air or to come and see this or that picture. This was why he had come here. To be with Jannie. Just him and her. Without the concerned looks from his mother or the endless invitations from his dad to go to a ballgame. The empty calls and texts from the friends he and Jannie used to have. The prying questions from Barry Pryce. For the first time in months he was alone with her, with Jannie. He felt giddy, almost like a kid again. *Jannie and Jamie. Jamie and Jannie. Forever. Forever and ever.*

He lost count of how many times the pictures cycled through their progression, but by the time he stood up from the table, the rain had stopped. He stepped onto the porch, breathing the moist air deep into his lungs. Overhead, thick clouds blanketed the moon. A silver mist hovered over the lake.

"Jesus Christ!" he said, slapping his arms. "It's cold!"

The Malabrands had warned him that the nights could get chilly on Winnepocket, but he hadn't been expecting this. He was surprised, in fact, that he couldn't see his breath. Unzipping his jeans, he peed off the front steps, then went back inside, switched out the light, and crawled into his sleeping bag, fully dressed.

He and Jannie had spent more than one night together in this sleeping bag. Why wasn't she there with him now? Her hair temporarily tamed behind her ears as she lay on her side, her eyes half-closed, her lips parted. This is what he was thinking, what he was remembering, when he heard it. The series of deranged pitches floating through the dark, wet air, a horse or maybe two horses, across the lake, in some kind of trouble. Then he remembered. No, not horses. What had Muriel had said about the loons? *Like the criminally insane are out there paddling around.* He closed his eyes; then opened them again. There was no difference, and he realized that he had never experienced the kind of darkness that seemed to have descended on the cabin. It was as if the entire state had lost consciousness. Listening to the loons, he drifted into a fitful sleep.

Was it the chill that awakened him just two hours later? Or the loons? He lay on his back, eyes shut, his teeth chattering in spite of the sleeping bag. Out on the lake, the demented calling of the birds—how many were there?—echoed over the water. No wonder Muriel had complained. It was like sleeping next to an asylum. He opened his eyes, then, suddenly frightened, closed them: Somewhere in the cabin, a light was on. His heart was pounding so loudly that he was sure it could be heard across the room

Maybe he'd been dreaming. Maybe he wasn't quite as awake as he thought he had been. He opened his eyes once more, this time slowly. To his left, the computer screen cast its weird, other-worldly glow onto the surface of the table. He must have forgotten to turn it off, and now it seemed to have frozen on a blank screen. Swearing, he wrenched himself out of the tangle of the sleeping bag, and stumbled over to the machine.

He blinked, thinking perhaps that his eyes were playing tricks on him. The screen wasn't blank after all. A photograph filled its black frame. Water, a lake maybe or a pond, taken from the perspective of a swimmer so that the photo was little more than a rectangle divided into two halves, the upper half a cloudless sky, the bottom half, the surface of the calm water. It might have been taken at any time of day. The photographer had captured a ripple in the left foreground as if he (or she?) had suddenly dipped an arm below the surface. Jamie swallowed, trying to keep down the sour taste that was rising from the pit of his stomach. He had never seen this picture before. Never. And yet, somehow it had found its way to his computer.

He sat at the table, barely conscious of the cold that was working its way from the chair's plank seat through his jeans and into his skin. He studied the picture. There was nothing to distinguish it, no rough edge of shore, no boats, not even a cloud in the sky. It could have been almost any body of water anywhere in the world. But it wasn't. Somewhere, this specific lake existed. It had a name. People fished it, swam in it. And someone had captured its image from this exact perspective. Someone, yes. But who? And why? And when? He looked up, wishing he had locked the door.

He swallowed again, and put his hand on the mouse, trying not to notice that his fingers were trembling. When he clicked forward, the photo faded and was replaced by a familiar one of Jannie, that day in Vermont sitting at a picnic table at a state park. When he clicked back, the picture of the water was gone.

Don't freak out, he told himself, *you're in an unfamiliar place. It's the middle of the night and it's so frigging cold. You're not thinking straight. You'll be able to figure it out in the morning. In the morning everything will make sense.*

He looked out the window. The clouds had lifted from the moon but the mist still hung over the lake like an ill-fitting garment from another century. As he crawled back into the sleeping bag, the loons called to each other. It sounded like they were laughing.

The next morning, Jamie awoke confused, not knowing for a few seconds where he was. Then he remembered. The Malabrands' cottage. And someone was knocking on the door. He opened his eyes, noting immediately that the bad weather from the previous day had been replaced with bright sunshine. He looked at his watch, blinking to clear the sleep from his eyes. 11:33.

He squirmed out of his sleeping bag, still dressed in the yellow sweater and jeans, and stumbled in his stocking feet toward the door. Through the old bubbled glass and the filmy grain of the screen in front of it, Jamie could see a man, balding, a beard but no moustache. The man smiled. He was missing a front tooth. Jamie opened the door.

"Name's Eldred, " the man said through the screen. "Moses Eldred."

Jamie, still half-asleep, said nothing.

"I keep an eye out on the place for John Malabrand. Him and Muriel," Moses Eldred continued. "They phoned. Said you'd be comin'. I told 'em I'd come over and make sure you was settled in. I live right ovah theah." That was how he said it: they-ah. Two syllables. The man turned and pointed to a peninsula extending into the lake about a quarter mile from where the cottage stood. "Right through them trees. Deepest part of the lake."

Jamie looked in the direction the man had pointed, but still said nothing.

"Everythin' okay?" Moses Eldred asked.

Jamie nodded.

As if that were an invitation, Moses Eldred pulled back the screen, stepped into the cottage, taking in the laptop and the sleeping bag with the eye of a man used to decoding the telltale signs of trouble.

"The loons were kind of noisy last night," Jamie mumbled. It was an idiotic thing to say. "I had a hard time sleeping."

Moses Eldred used his chin to point to a small window at the back of the room. "That sill needs replacin'" he said. Then he turned and walked out of the cottage as abruptly as he had walked in. Standing on the lawn, still damp from yesterday's storm, he looked up at Jamie, who stood with one hand holding the screen door open.

"Ain't no loons on the lake this year," he said plainly.

Jamie thought he had misunderstood the man. It must have shown in his face.

"Audubon fellah just out here," Moses Eldred continued. "Couldn't find no signs of 'em." When Jamie said nothing, he went on. "You mighta heard a fox."

Jamie squinted at the man as if he were speaking Urdu.

"Screamin'," Eldred explained. "They do that sometimes."

With that, Moses Eldred walked to his truck, a beat-up Chevy with the license plate hanging at a forty-five degree angle. Jamie read the state motto printed at the bottom of the plate: Live Free or Die. The man turned to Jamie a final time. "Whatevah you heard," he said. "It weren't no loons."

Jamie stepped back into the house as Moses Eldred drove off.

"It weren't no loons," he said aloud in an exaggerated imitation of the man's Yankee dialect. "Local yokel." If only Jannie had been here to have heard him. Yes, if only Jannie had been here. "It weren't no loons," Jamie said again.

He spent the rest of the day in almost exactly the way he'd planned, listening to the playlists he and Jannie had made together, and reading through all hundreds of cards and notes she'd sent him. On every one, he traced her childish signature with the tip of his finger. *Je' taime, Jannie. Je' taime.* He tried to put the picture of the water out of his mind, but by late afternoon, he decided to search every file on his hard drive, all his documents. He didn't know if it would bring him more relief, to find the picture or not find it. By the time it was dark, he had convinced himself that he imagined the whole incident, chalking it up to the strange surroundings and his lack of food the day before. (In spite of his promise to his mother, he hadn't eaten since he'd arrived at the cottage.) That night, before he went to bed, he made sure to turn the computer off, closing its screen until he heard it click shut.

This time, in spite of what Moses Eldred had said, he was certain it was the loons that woke him, their wild ululations floating across the lake like the loud wailings of professional mourners. Lying there in the dark, his eyes closed, it came to Jamie that Moses Eldred was trying to frighten him by telling him there were no loons on the lake. He'd heard about these old-time Yankees and their weird sense of humor. And he'd also heard that they didn't much like summer people coming up with their city ways and their easy money and gawking at the locals as if they were there for their bemusement. Moses Eldred was probably lying in his bed right now, laughing his ass off as he thought about the city boy over there in Malabrand's cottage listening to the loons that he'd said did not exist.

Local yokel, Jamie thought.

Still, he wished that before he'd come to New Hampshire he'd gone to one of those bird call sites to check it out. At least then he would have something to compare the loons' call to. He thought maybe he would go into the village the next day and check it out at the library.

Suddenly, Jamie felt thirsty. He'd awakened facing the back of the sofa. Now, he rolled over to get up, finally opening his eyes.

How long did he lie there?

How long did he lie there staring at the computer with its lit screen and the photo it framed? He didn't know. It might have been five minutes. It might have been an hour.

Shivering, he forced himself out of the sleeping bag and walked to the table. The photo was exactly as it had been the night before. He leaned in closer, his eyes inches from the screen, his heart thumping so violently that he thought it would break his rib cage when he saw what he had not seen earlier. Just beneath the ripple, the faint shadow of a hand, the barest outline of fingertips. He ran onto the porch and threw up.

Faint as the image was, he would know those fingers anywhere. How many times had he kissed them? Held them? And how many times had they lain against his skin bringing him the kind of pleasure that he hadn't known existed.

"Jannie," he whispered, leaning over the wooden railing, "Jannie."

Once his stomach settled (there had been almost nothing in it), he forced himself back inside. He sat in front of the laptop, afraid to touch it.

Get a hold of yourself, Jamie, he whispered. *It's only a machine. It can't do anything you don't tell it to. There's an explanation. You just haven't figured it out, yet.*

He reached for the mouse and clicked NEXT. Just as the night before, the next image was familiar to him, and just as the night before, when he clicked back, the photograph of the water had disappeared. He was sorry now that he hadn't brought his printer.

Jamie shut down the computer, but sat at the table the rest of the night, waiting. An hour or two after the sun came up, when he was convinced that the image would not appear again, he went to the couch and pulled the sleeping bag around him. Though he told himself he would stay awake and watch, his eyelids fluttered and closed almost immediately. He dreamed of Jannie.

By the time he woke, groggy and with a fierce headache, the earlier promise of fair weather had turned to the threat of rain. He looked at the computer. Nothing. Once again, he began to wonder if he had even seen the image, if he had been experiencing some kind of lucid dreaming, the kind Mrs. Meade had talked about in his psychology class. Then, he remembered hearing about how native people would fast in order to bring on the hallucinations that would guide them during a vision quest. Maybe that's what was happening; he was hallucinating because he wasn't eating.

He got up, went to the car and brought in the box of food. The milk was already congealing in its carton, but the banana bread his mother had baked was still fresh enough. He ate the whole loaf.

That night Jamie sat at the table, the computer on, the photographs set to SLIDE SHOW. He waited. The temperature felt as if it were dropping a degree a minute, the cold settling onto every surface. After midnight he got up and wrapped the sleeping bag around him. At just before one, as the prom picture came onto the screen, he heard the loons. Their tremolo filled the cottage as if it had been built soley for that avian purpose, to hold the sound of the loons. Jamie waited. The prom photo disappeared. It was replaced by the picture of the water. He sat up straighter, staring at the screen. He swallowed and looked at the ripple. The hand was still there, but had changed position. The night before he had been able to see only the outlines of her fingers, the lower part of the hand disappearing into the depth of the water. But now, the entire hand was visible just inches beneath the surface, palm up, the delicate fingers extended and slightly curled in a kind of beckoning gesture. There was no mistaking it now. It was Jannie's hand. Jannie's, as clear as his own.

The loons called. Again and again. Louder and louder . He turned to the window. The moonlight shone brightly on the lake and Jamie could see far out into its surface. He blinked and looked back to the computer screen. How could he have been so stupid? The photograph. It wasn't of *any l*ake, but *this* one. Lake Winnepocket. It had been taken just where he was looking now, out by the peninsula where Moses Eldred said he lived. He picked up the laptop and held it next to the pane of window glass. There was no mistaking it; the image on the screen was identical to what he saw framed through the mullioned window.

He let the computer drop. For a moment he did nothing, thought nothing, felt nothing. Then he stood up. He walked out onto the porch and down the steps. He continued walking until he stood at the shore of the lake. The loons called.

He had been expecting it, waiting for it even, but when, just off the tip of Moses Eldred's peninsula, her arm rose slowly out of the water, white as marble in the moonlight, he thought he would be sick again. But then the silvery light caught her legs, her beautiful legs, barely breaking the surface of the calm lake, and his fear left him.

Why should he be afraid? He understood it now. She had come here for him just the way he had come here for her. The local yokel was right. It wasn't the loons. It was her, Jannie, calling for him, her voice distorted in the twisting corridor that leads the living to the dead.

His first step into the lake was so cold that it took his breath away, but that wasn't important. Nothing was important. Only Jannie swimming back and forth in the moonlight, waiting for him. He remembered the look on his cousin's face that day so long ago when he'd pushed Jamie's head under water for what felt like the hundredth time. He wished his cousin could be here now. To see him, to see him moving through the deep, cold lake to be with Jannie. The sandy bottom turned to a Jurassic muck sliding up and over his ankles. He was mid chest now, and the water was wicking up into the heavy wool of the sweater, pulling him down. For a moment, Jamie was confused by the fish. Hundreds of them, thousands maybe, all sizes, floating up to the surface on their sides, their soft bellies exposed, their o mouths gasping as they took in the deadly oxygen. Was it tragic? Or hilarious? It didn't matter. Her face was turned from him—why couldn't he see her face? Her hair trailed out behind her as she swam. He could hear her more clearly now too, calling his name over and over. Or was she singing as she swam? Yes, that was it. She was singing, chanting their names to the same three-note phrase. Over and over as she swam back and forth. *Jannie and Jamie. Jamie and Jannie. Forever. Forever and . . . .*

Water rushed into his mouth and down into his lungs. How silly he had been that day with his cousin. How completely silly. And how silly he had been to be so frightened earlier. After all, hadn't he and Jannie sworn they would never be apart? Hadn't they been voted The Couple Most Likely to Stay Together?

David Elliott has been undead all his life and plans to continue that way. An award-winning children's author, he has published more than fifteen books for young people including The *Transmogrification of Roscoe Wizzle*, *And Here's to You!*, *Finn Throws a Fit!* and most recently, *In the Wild*. Currently, he is working on a collection of Young Adult ghost stories. He teaches at Colby-Sawyer College and in Lesley University's Low Residency MFA Program in Creative Writing. If telepathy fails, contact David at www.davidelliottbooks.com.

Misty Rain

Michael J. DeLuca

The misty rain collected on the hemlock boughs and clung like frost or ashes to the moss that covered the stones and the trunks of the trees. In the lee of the ridge, Ann huddled in Evan's cloak, her back to a shaggy gray birch. The raindrops beaded on the hood and shoulders, then slowly seeped into the wool.

Evan stood on a stone at the crest of the ridge, squinting into the rain, frozen in the hurried act of salvaging the last dry clothes that remained to them. His pack lay open at his feet, collecting dampness.

The tolling of a bell hung in the air, the sound distorted by the thickness of the mist so that it seemed if he only leapt towards it and threw out his arms he could catch it before he fell.

"Did you hear that?" he asked his sister.

"No."

"The bell!" he shouted. "Didn't you hear it?"

She shook her head, not looking at him.

"It's the train!" He ripped at the drawstring of his pack, pulling it closed. He slung it onto his shoulders with a heave that almost sent him toppling from the ridge. Then he leapt the two steps down to his sister's side and fumbled for her hand. "Come on!" he urged. "We can catch it!"

His voice would carry through the fog, just as the sound of the bell had carried. The thing that was chasing them would hear, even from miles away. It would follow. But Evan didn't care anymore. He needed to feel hope.

45

Ann struggled to her feet, her head bowed. One long lock of dark hair spilled out below the folds of the cloak, damp and clinging to itself in the rain, the spiral bough of a mountain tree gnarled and aged beyond its time.

"There isn't any train," came the words from invisible lips. He could hear them trembling.

Her hand was cold—but so was Evan's. He spun away from her and pulled her stumbling after him along the trail.

They climbed the few steps to the top of the ridge, then descended. The mist slanted into their eyes, blurring on their lashes. Evan squinted, studying the rain-slicked trail ahead, searching for the safest path among the treachery of green-gray stones. He tried not to look up.

After all, there was nothing to see. The world was nothing but cold, gray mist, and one jagged isle of earth and stone. The mountain changed as they moved, just enough that he could go on believing they were making headway, that they would eventually escape. But the mist closed behind them, and waited ahead, and Evan had lost count of the days.

The sound of the bell came again, clear and full and real despite the mist. "There," he whispered. "Listen!"

Deep in his belly, a nervous buzzing seemed to answer it. Was it closer? Was that the roar of pistons far away, or only the hiss of the rain? "You hear it now? So close—we can catch it if we hurry!"

Ann's breathing was ragged. "I have to rest."

Evan stopped above a ten-foot fall. He took Ann's hand in both of his. "Walk down backwards. Slowly."

He dropped into a crouch, leaning back, using the pack as a counterweight. It dug into his shoulders, empty though it had become.

They had a sack of oatmeal, a jar of precious honey almost gone, some salt, and a tiny stove with a single burner. It could last them days if it had to.

She looked up at him as she descended, the hood slipping away to reveal a pale and pretty face without emotion, smudged and shining slightly from the rain. Even her eyes were gray.

"You'll have to jump the last few feet."

She didn't even wince. She let go, collapsed into a little ball of knees and elbows as she hit the ground, and stayed that way until Evan landed beside her.

Ann took a long breath, pressing her fingertips into the mud. "Remember how Father used to let me grab his thumbs and climb up on his shoulders? Mother called me Possum."

Her eyes clouded.

Evan hugged Ann to his side. He pulled the hood up over her head and tried to brush the damp from her shoulders. "Keep it on. Wool will keep you warm, even in the wet." He had told her that already, a dozen times. But he had to say something. "Come on."

She walked right out of his embrace and on down the mountain.

Evan saw her knees and ankles shaking. She grabbed at branches for support; her dirty hands showed pale and thin against the gray world. He watched her shrink and dim, fighting back the panic, the fear the mist would take her if he let her get too far away.

Evan swallowed. He wondered if she would ever be the same. He bent his head against the rain and hurried after.

He knew the tracks were this way. They had crossed them once already in the twilight, long and cold and comforting. They had walked along them while they could, followed them across a narrow gorge, and then for miles along the mountainsides in the dark. The grade was easier there, where the will of unknown men had cut a line through jaggedness. They could move much faster.

But no train ever came. It made him uneasy. The rails and the ties and the gravel on either side went on and on. It felt like they were walking in place. Then late one night the hunter thing howled in the distance and he struck back out into the wild.

Evan caught up with Ann as she crossed a swollen stream, splashing through the shallows where it pooled at the foot of a ledge. The icy water swirled around his boot seams, and Evan thought what a relief it would be to strip off all his muddy clothes and let the current wash away the sweat and dirt, let the coldness numb away his exhaustion. He thought of giving up—of laying back until the water took him, of closing his eyes and never waking.

Then Ann slipped and cried out as a stepping-stone sank beneath her feet. She caught at Evan's hand.

They made it up onto the ledge and saw the tracks empty below them. They scrambled down the last slope, slipping and sliding where the stone gave way to dirt. Evan lifted Ann to her feet and pulled her the last few steps along flat ground.

Beneath the rotted birch trees at the edge of the railway embankment, he stopped and shivered. At his feet, there were paw-prints. They were huge and deep and shapeless—as if the thing that left them wasn't made of flesh, but mist, the same leaden mist from which the whole of this warmthless world had come.

He touched the handle of the little folding knife he kept in his pocket—their only weapon. He peered up at the edges of the rain, searching the clouded mountainside for the dark shape of their enemy. He saw nothing but the shaggy trunks of trees and hulks of stone.

"Let's go," he said.

They climbed up the bank onto the gravel.

The tracks spread north and south, granting for a narrow mile the illusion of order, of direction, until the thin lines faded and the world came to its end in mist. A timber post drove up out of the ground with a thick black wire snaking around it like a strangling vine. The bell hung gleaming dully at its top, suspended in an iron frame.

Evan bent, put his ear to the rail, and waited a long time. The silence was as thick as sound. The mist began to darken.

Finally, he raised his head. "We'll get out of this," he promised feebly, for the thousandth time. "I'll protect you."

Ann sank to the ground, brushing the rain from her eyes. Insidious mist fell between them.

"There isn't any train. These tracks are old and dead."

"How can you say that? Look! Don't you see the bell? You can't say you didn't hear it." He clutched at a handful of gravel. It stung his skin. He hurled it, and a few pieces pinged off the iron. "The train is coming." He tried to grin. "Or did you think the hunter beast had learned to ring a bell?"

"Nothing is hunting us either, Evan. It's all in your head."

Evan searched her face for he didn't know what—madness, or cruelty. He saw nothing but despair.

He shook his head. The miles. The mist. A tin mug half-full of oatmeal and honey, twice a day. There was blood caked with the dirt on her shins. He understood. She was exhausted.

He got the stove out of his pack. It scraped against the gravel when he set it down: a harsh, sharp sound.

They sat on the rails with the stove between them, watching the bubbles forming at the bottom of the pot, the bits of dirt and hemlock needles swirling in the heat. The tiny blue flame roared like a demon.

He wanted her to talk about their parents again. A memory they could share—that was what they needed. Something they could hold, and know that in a mile it wouldn't fade like everything else.

But he wouldn't do that to her. He couldn't force her to remember.

"What are you thinking about?" he ventured.

"Nothing."

He brought out the oatmeal and poured some into the pot. He stirred until it started to bubble, then shut off the stove and filled her cup. He gave her half the honey that was left and ate his own with only salt.

They gulped it in silence like animals hunched over stolen food.

When they had scraped and licked everything clean, the bell began to ring again. Evan stared at it. Was it only here to mock them—a railway bell in the middle of nowhere, warning no one of the danger of crossing from empty mist to empty mist?

They only heard the howl as the third stroke died away. Evan flicked open his knife, fighting the nervous urge to laugh. Ann put her hands over her ears. Would it finally come, with its empty hunger, just when their escape seemed closest?

Of course it would. That was how the hunter worked. It wanted not their flesh, but their fear.

He shoved everything into his pack and got up. He told Ann to get behind him, but she just sat there on the rail with her head in her arms. With the woolen cloak around her, the mist and the gathering dark, she hardly looked human at all—just a shape, gray and distant as a mountain, hollow as a cloud.

Evan turned away, thinking it was just as well. He didn't know which way the thing would come.

He thought with terror of her death, of loneliness.

The ground shook. The air all around them rumbled with sudden power. The headlight of the train loomed up above the mist like the lantern of a phantom ship.

For an instant, Evan saw the beast caught in the beam, its huge shape blurred with rain and speed as it hurled itself across the tracks: a sleepless nightmare, as big as the train, its ghostly howl mingling with the roar of the machine.

He looked with despair at the little knife in his hand. He put it back into his pocket.

Then came the scream of the whistle that blasted everything else away.

Evan shouted at Ann to move, but he lost the words, and still she sat there, slumped over her knees like a dead thing. He threw himself towards her, grabbed her by the hood of the cloak and dragged her back.

The train thundered blindly past them, huge and black, its iron wheels churning: the Boston and Maine. Its path was already chosen, its speed the only thing in its control. Steam flooded from the engine, mingling with the sky.

Evan stumbled in the sudden rush of air. He fought against it, clutching Ann to his breast. The shapes of the cars blurred together, rust and bare metal and meaningless words. In a minute it would be gone—their last hope of escape.

With a low, inarticulate growl, a desperate call to the last of his strength, Evan lifted his sister in his arms and ran. She didn't cling to his neck, she didn't shriek, she didn't even whimper. Nothing. The gray beast bounded behind them, closing the distance with every step. Evan didn't dare look back.

An opening gaped in the side of a wooden boxcar. Evan heaved Ann up over the spinning wheels onto the floor of the car. He wrenched the pack from his shoulders and tossed it inside. He caught at the handle of the door as it sped past and hung there, his feet dragging in the gravel, until he found the will to pull himself up.

The thing behind them gathered its huge legs beneath it and leaped, clawing and growling—then fell back into the mist and was gone.

Ann lay in the corner, curled in a ball. Evan crawled to her side. She was crying. He leaned his head against her shoulder and listened to their breath, shifting in and out of rhythm. He thought of their parents, torn and wretched on the Pemigewasset's bank.

"We're safe," he whispered, when the thudding of his heart had quieted. "We can rest now. When we get to the next town—" Holderness, or Laconia, he couldn't remember which. "We can find a place to live. I'll look for a job, and you can go back to school. A new life, Ann."

He rolled over, sat up, looked around him. Sacks of grain or pillows surrounded them in piles. Outside, the misty mountainscapes rolled past like part of some other story, made beautiful by distance.

And in the back of the car, the giant, predatory creature sat on its haunches, brooding in the dimness.

Evan screamed and clawed at Ann's motionless form. He tried to lift her up again, to carry her back to the edge of the train and leap to safety, or even to death, so long as it was away from that horrible hungry thing that waited in the dark. But he couldn't. All his strength had left him in a moment's dreamed relief. How many days and miles had he led his sister blindly through the wild? He couldn't help her any more. He couldn't save her. He couldn't even lift his arms.

Evan swayed on his feet. He looked at the beast, seeing it clearly for the first time: a strange, amorphous mist-thing, featureless and immense, filling the whole of the car from floor to ceiling. It wasn't a mountain cat. He didn't know what it was. But there was something familiar about it: the way it crouched there waiting, its eyelessness, its single, knifelike claw.

It wasn't coming for them, he realized. It hadn't even moved.

Evan took the little knife from his pocket, pulled it open with numb fingers, and weighed it on his palm.

What would happen if he struck? Would the blade pass through the hunter's flesh like light through fog, or would it enter, be drawn in and disappear? Would the creature howl in rage and raise its deathly claw to strike him down, or would it burst asunder like a dream in daylight?

The train wheels rattled on the rails. The boxcar gently rocked beneath its riders, like a cradle lulling childhood fears. Neither Evan nor the creature stirred. Outside the fine mist went on falling. At their feet, Ann rested peacefully.

Finally, she uncurled her body and sat up. She stared at Evan, and he imagined the way he must look—his bloodless face, his body listing drunkenly, the cold sweat on his brow.

"I'm sorry," he said. "I wasn't a very good guardian."

Ann just shook her head. *You still don't see,* her gray eyes seemed to say.

But Evan was beginning to think he did.

He closed the knife and closed his hand around it. Then he took a breath and hurled himself out through the open door into the rain.

Ann and the train disappeared into mist. The creature crouched beside him in the mud.

He knew she'd be safe. The part of Evan that harbored mad hope of rest and sunlight sighed with relief and passed away.

 **Michael J. DeLuca** brews beer, bakes bread, grows tomatoes, hugs trees, and prophesies doom, all from the comfort of his rotting, sun-drenched Adirondack chair in the backyard. He writes about brewing for Small Beer Press, and his fiction has appeared, among other places, in *Interfictions*, *Clockwork Phoenix*, *Murky Depths*, *Beneath Ceaseless Skies*, and *Shroud*. Read his blog at michaeljdeluca.com.

Acalia

Joyce Wagner

My partner Claude enjoyed no interest in the marvels of this century, so it was especially ironic that it was he who discovered Acalia on the Internet.

We were living, at that time, in a beautiful old parsonage in Orange, New Hampshire that we purchased for a pittance. It was perfect—remote, woodsy, private, but a quick jaunt to Plymouth State University one way and Dartmouth College the other, so our cultural needs were met. If you didn't mind flying—which I am a touch averse to—it's an easy flap to Boston. Also, the hunting was excellent.

Since Claude was the one with an eye for color and style, I allowed him a free hand to decorate our abode in his archaic tastes. Except, of course, my own little rooms that I furnished as thoroughly modern—including a computer, a large-screen plasma TV, and a sleek, new, state-of-the-art casket that Claude sneeringly called my "Sleep Number coffin."

I am loathe to say I was disappointed in my housemate, but, about a century and a half before, I selected him specially for the afterlife because he was different from the usual gang of ghouls that frequented my parlor. He was a cowboy—a range rider—and as exotic to me as a pasha. As luck would have it, it seemed Claude desired to be more *my* type and within two decades of his conversion, he completely lost all gun-slinger affectations and changed his name from Clyde to Claude. Now he thinks he's the bloody Duke of Marlboro. I swear, it's like living with my grandfather. That's why I thought I'd bring in a bride to liven

things up. When I suggested it, Claude was surprisingly enthusiastic. He must have been as bored with me as I with him.

Against his protestations, I insisted on the Internet—a Goth-ish dating website called "É-ternité." We sought someone thoroughly modern (for me), yet with an interest in historical aesthetics (for him). We hoped for a college girl—athletic, intelligent, but not too young. We do not convert children or teenagers. There are rules.

Because of our unique requirements (and some pickiness on Claude's part) we trolled the website for weeks with little or no luck.

Finally, one evening, I awoke and found Claude intently peering into the monitor of my computer. "You're up early," says I.

"*Au contraire,*" Claude responded without raising his eyes from the screen. "You, my dear Michael, have overslept again."

"Are you on to something?"

"Mayhaps."

Mayhaps. Couldn't you just burn him? Couldn't you just toss him out into the noonday sun?

"Well, what, pray tell, M'lord, have you found?"

"Well, if you're going to be snotty . . ." Claude's amber eyes glowed even more eerily than usual in the green light reflecting off the screen. "I believe I have discovered the perfect gentlewoman for the two of us." The luminous orbs traveled across the monitor as he read off her attributes. "A senior in college—Plymouth State! Close by! She's into medieval mysticism. Dabbles in sorcery. Says she's read all of Aleister Crowley. She's tall, adventurous . . ."

"Sounds perfect—for you . . ."

"No, wait! There! She likes the Grateful Dead and has read all of *Twilight.* You see? Perfectly modern. And beautiful. Ob-*serve.*"

I leaned over Claude's shoulder for a better look. He was right. Her deep brown eyes held a fathomless darkness, seldom occurring in the living. Her hair fell in long ebony waves, a black and heaving sea. Lips stained a deep red that paled her ivory skin. She wore little makeup—a good thing since, if events worked to our advantage, she'd soon be unable to access her reflection.

Claude turned his eyes to me. "What do you think? Shall we?"

"Absolutely."

Once the meeting was set, I was scarcely able to sleep. Images of our bewitching bride capered through my dreams. Her name was Acalia. *Acalia.* So, so ancient an appellation. Could I dare believe she might be one of us already? I tasted her name, rolled it over my tongue, as I repeatedly whispered it to the satin lining of my sarcophagus. *Acalia.*

Finally, the hour of our meeting was upon us. Midnight in front of the Silver Center at Plymouth State. Our plan was to grab her up on the fly and bring her to our home. There we could interview her at our leisure and determine if she was, indeed, the lady of our daydreams. If not, then she'd simply be—well, dinner.

Our prospective bride lurked in the entrance of the gray stone building. We almost didn't see her, she was so encased in a long black coat, clutching the hood against the wind. Claude was far less clumsy in the air than was I, and she stood only a foot or so clear of the entrance. The approach would be tricky, especially with the prevailing wind conditions, so we decided, in a torrent of mid-air shouts, he would be the designated snatcher.

I held out a tiny hope that, as he made the capture, a bit of the old Clyde would appear and he would slip out a raucous "Yah-hoo!" Alas, as he swooped down gently and caught her up from behind, the only sound was a very surprised "Whoop!" coming from the girl herself.

Instantly they were airborne, his arms clutched tightly around her waist. Death had magnified Claude's strength many times over but her thrashing seemed superhuman. Although there was no danger of his dropping her, he did seem to lose altitude here and there. All cries of objection on his or her part were swallowed up by the jet stream.

About the time they reached the peak of Cardigan Mountain, our fiancé abruptly ceased her struggles. I assumed she had suddenly realized that escape would mean a substantial fall to rocky terrain. Her hands rose from Claude's encircling arms to gather her hood around her face. I scrambled next to them, ineptly trying to remain in flight while catching glimpses of her. In my awkwardness, I had to content myself with quick flashes of thick full lips and long delicate fingernails the color of a fine Bordeaux.

Our little house came into view and Claude pulled out ahead of me. In his preoccupation with the lady in his arms, he blew his approach and, as he flew into the window of his den, Acalia's toes knocked against the sill. The wind carried a shrill, nasal voice from within her cowl to my startled ears.

"Hey! Watchit' willya'?"

My heart sank, the first of a long, tedious succession of sinkings.

Acalia touched down first, lost her balance, pitched forward and disabled Claude's landing. He collapsed on top of her. I tumbled through the window, bounced off the flailing duo, and slammed into the far wall.

The two of them writhed about on Claude's ancient Kirman rug, bumping an insubstantial table bearing an eighteenth-century porcelain. I made my way back to the melee, reached in, found an arm and pulled. I set our guest on her feet and held her aright until my partner was able to reestablish his balance. Claude's breath came in fits and his face was much redder than death normally allows.

Acalia stood panting, still hidden in the masses of the black wool. She listed slightly to the left, toward the foot that had lost its three-inch platform sandal. It lay between us, framed by the lush medallion of the rug.

My eyes traveled up her body to where her face was still half hidden in the depths of the cowl. I inhaled, took a step forward, grasped the garment by the jowls of its hood and yanked it back from our prize.

It was not our bride. The lips and nails that appeared in the darkness of night to be the shade of a fine wine, now seemed to be the peculiar brown of spoiled blueberries. Her hair, however, split down the middle and flipped up over her ears, was a completely aberrant shade of burgundy. Her skin was pink and clear, but powdered an eerie white. Her standard-issue brown eyes were framed by badly applied circles of black eyeliner. A flimsy gold ring poked through her left nostril. Her height was difficult to assess, what with only one shoe on, but my guess was five foot one. White underdrawers glowed through the ill-fitting slinky black dress that was obviously commandeered from the closet of someone much older. Acalia was not a day over thirteen.

"Can I have my shoe now? Puh-leeze?"

The voice alone was punishable by death—a high pitched whine that took all the hairs on the back my neck straight out then knotted them. When we didn't reply, when we stood gaping at the child, she rolled her eyes, lunged for the shoe, and dropped to a sitting position on the floor where she proceeded to fit the sandal over too-big dark stockings.

Claude circled behind her. I could see his lips draw back and his extending canines gleamed in the artificial light of the desk lamp. He began to lean towards her. As I lurched forward with a unambiguous "No!" Acalia leapt to her feet, catching Claude squarely under the jaw with her head. The room vibrated with his howl.

I was barely able to insinuate myself between him and the girl before he could attack her again. I pulled him into a far corner and, as the girl stood grimacing and rubbing her head, Claude and I had the whispering clenched-teeth, swallowed-word, gesturing dispute of two men with secrets. I was able to remind him that we don't kill children. Period. And turning her into one of us was out of the question. His point was that she was not a child, but a deceiving little she-devil and had walked into the situation anyway. Besides he was thirsty. He'd conveyed his arguments with just a trace of Western drawl. With much effort I was able to calm him and bring him around to my way of thinking. We began to discuss our next move when Acalia once again took our attention.

"Wow! What is this? A movie set?" While we talked, Acalia had begun to wander about the room, picking up objects of art, fingering bookbindings, and was now bouncing on a leather-covered sofa. I assumed it would become necessary to restrain Claude once again. Surprisingly, it was he who responded.

"Yes! Yes it is! We're film-makers, specializing in special effects. We were testing a flying effect and we incorrectly assumed you were the guinea pig we were to meet. No harm done, though. We'll just pay you the hundred we agreed to pay her and put you right back where we found you." As he spoke, Claude unlocked the money drawer in his desk and withdrew a thick stack of bills. She sat now, stock still on the oversized couch. Her eyes narrowed and followed him like one of those unsettling portraits. He peeled off a hundred dollar bill and placed it in her diminutive palm. She stared at the bill for a moment, then peered up into Claude's glowing eyes.

"I'm not goin'." The little girl clutched the money, tucked one arm into the other and looked straight ahead.

"What?" Claude spoke first. "What do you mean you're not going?"

I snatched the wad of bills from Claude's hand and peeled off another two hundred. "You know, Claude, our little friend here did so well, I think we'll include a large, lovely tip!" I held the bills out before her. She snatched them out of my hand, added them to the original, and folded like a carnivorous flower.

"I'm not goin'."

"What?"

"What?"

"There's something goin' on here. You're no movie-makers. I'm not even sure you're real, but I know I'm not dreaming. You kidnapped me." She shook the handful of bills in her small white fist. "But you obviously have more money than my folks do, so it ain't for the bread, and if you're lookin' for somethin' kinky—well, just try it and see."

I felt Claude bristle next to me.

"Anyway, somethin' spooky's goin' on here and I'm stayin'."

"You certainly are not. You're leaving right now." Claude took a step towards her.

The girl crimped up tighter. "No."

Claude motioned me towards the door. We had another of those half-grunted conversations and decided to simply overcome the girl and fly her back to Plymouth State. She found her way there on her own, we reasoned, she could find her way back home.

Amidst much clawing and struggling on Acalia's part, we were able to snatch her back into the night air.

It was fairly simple to dump her where we had found her, and she seemed none the worse for the adventure. Not so, in our case. We hunted and dined silently and headed back to our cozy home, all thoughts of a bride banished. We retired early.

I awoke at noon to a sharp rapping on my casket. I raised the lid to the sight of Acalia. I closed my eyes and hoped against hope it was only a daymare.

"Wake up, bonehead. I want to talk to you."

That voice. This was no dream. I sat up. "Acalia, what are you doing here? How did you get in?"

"I found my way back."

"Acalia, what do you want? Do you want more money?"

"No. I want to be a vampire."

I lied back down and let the cover slam shut. It opened slightly and I could see snatches of the girl struggling with the heavy lid on the other side. It slammed shut again, and she began pounding on the bronze-coated metal over my face. I could hear her muffled whining voice right through the steel and satin. "I mean it, mister. I know what you guys are and I want to be one." Could you imagine spending eternity with that?

"No, you don't. There's no such thing as vampires. We're just eccentric." At that, I realized the stupidity of lying in a casket in the middle of the day while staunchly denying what it is I was. I pushed open the top. "You don't want to be a vampire."

"I do, too."

"It's not what you think it is." I crawled out of the casket and snatched my dressing gown from the chair. She followed me to Claude's room where we found him at rest in his carved oak coffin. I nudged his shoulder. He said "snark." I leaned over and whispered in his ear, "She's baaack."

Under lamplight in Claude's bedroom, we drained the afternoon trying to reason with the child. I perched on the edge of an overstuffed chair and she stood near the window, picking at a seam in Claude's hand-screened silk wallpaper. I could see veins standing out on my partner's forehead—rare for one of our ilk.

"Look, Acalia," I pleaded, "we need to get you home. Your parents will be very worried."

"I want to be a vampire."

"No, young lady, you do not want to be a vampire. Don't you have brothers and sisters you want to see again?"

"No. I want to be a vampire."

I listed the downsides of our afterlife. She was not convinced. I counted all the wonderful events she would miss in her life. She didn't care. Claude threatened to drop her in the center of Concord in the middle of the night. She reminded us she'd already found her way back once. I told about the rule concerning killing or converting children. She insisted she was older than she looked. All the while I kept a careful watch that she didn't get close to the draperies. The windows were covered against the sunlight, but one quick move on Acalia's part and Claude and I were toast. We hoped she didn't know that. Turns out, she did.

Around sunset, Claude and I huddled and decided one of us would have to go back to the college and see if we could find out where she belonged. Also, both of us were getting hungry. I won the toss, and, on my way out the door, I made Claude promise, no matter what occurred, he wouldn't kill her.

I hunted and dined off the mountain on the way to Plymouth State. I would pick up "carry-out" on the way back for Claude.

In the darkness of the bar at The Lucky Dog, I found a bit of success. The whole establishment was abuzz about a runaway girl. I tuned my preternatural hearing to the tables until I found the one that seemed to have the most accurate information. When I absorbed all I needed to know, I interrupted their conversation. "Excuse me, but I couldn't help but overhear. There's a little girl missing?" The gaggle of coeds was more than happy to repeat to new ears the information they'd been bouncing off each other for the past several hours. It seems one of their classmates' little sister was missing. She hadn't shown up at school that morning. She had a history of running away from home, but had never been gone this long before. I told them I had seen a very strange little girl in front of the Silver Center the night before and would one of them be so kind as to put me in touch with the sister? They would all be so kind and produced cell phones.

I got her voicemail. Either she was busy searching for the girl and didn't hear her phone, or worse, she was talking to the police. I left a message to please ring me up immediately, but included few details.

I thanked my companions and departed.

The house was trashed. Ancient volumes and first editions splayed in tatters on the floor. Brocade upholstery slashed. Rare prints skewed on the walls or knocked onto gouging shards of porcelains.

I found Acalia and Claude in his den. His skin was pallid almost to translucence, making his eyes appear as two brilliant amber marbles in sunken sockets. His usually perfect hair stuck out in spikes and the left sleeve of his silk shirt was attached to the rest only by a very short seam. A large rent traveled down one side of his trousers.

Acalia sat gagged with a silk scarf and bound by curtain tie-backs to a wing chair in the center of the room. The pitching and thrusting of her body in her efforts to escape made the chair itself appear possessed. Claude's voice was of a pitch that almost matched Acalia's. "Where the hell you been, anyway?" A hundred-plus years of civilizing himself had vanished and the erstwhile cowboy dialect infected Claude's speech patterns. This was not good. I rested my hand on his shoulder. "Claude, what happened here? Did she do this?"

"What the hell do you think?" My partner sunk into a chair and ran his hands up his face.

"Claude, you have the strength of a god. How could you not stop her?"

"Sunlamps." The word was lost in his palms and I had to ask him to repeat it. He picked up his head and glared into my eyes. "She brought sunlamps! Must've set them up while we were sleeping . . . here . . . and downstairs . . . and . . . and . . . Michael, I couldn't get to her without gettin' burnt."

He swallowed hard and continued, his words climbing into higher registers as they flew from his mouth. "Michael, she just ran around like some kind of whirlin' dervish trashin' things and yellin' that she wouldn't stop till I made her a vampire. I finally got the drop on her when she knocked the lamp over in here and the bulb busted."

"Where in hell's name did she get sunlamps?"

His eyes turned from desperation to rage. "Well, I don't know. Let's see if we can figger this out. She moves around during the day when the stores are open. She had three hundred dollars in cash that *you* gave her . . ."

I was about to remind him he gave her the first hundred then reconsidered. "How the hell did she find us?"

"Damned if I know! I didn't ask her a lot of questions, Michael. It was all I could do to not slaughter the little bitch." He swallowed again and his eyes softened back to desperation. "Can't we just kill 'er? Please?"

"No!"

I guided him toward the door with the hand on his shoulder. I told him I had hunted, dinner was in a cage in the kitchen, and that I'd handle the situation from then on. I watched him lope, bowlegged, out the door.

I closed us in softly and turned to Acalia who was glaring at me with a hatred thirteen-year-olds usually reserve for their parents. My cell phone buzzed in my pocket. I retrieved it and snapped it open before the first ring was complete. "Hello!" I'm afraid I rather shouted.

"Hello. I was told to call this number. You have information about my sister, Callie?" The voice was deep, yet somehow youthful. It made me forget the intruder only a few feet away. "Hello?"

I found my voice. "Oh, sorry. Yes, she's here. At my home. We found her last night and took her in. She wouldn't tell us who she was nor where she lived or you would have heard from us sooner. Much sooner, indeed."

"Oh, what a relief! May I pick her up?"

"Couldn't we drop her at her home?"

"Oh, no! The neighbors would be so disappoint . . . that is, you've gone through so much trouble already. Just tell me where you are and I'll be over as soon as I can."

I gave her the address, rang off, and went to inform Claude of our good fortune. His color had returned somewhat, but his hands still trembled. I had no sooner broken the news when there was a knock on the front door. Could that be Acalia's sister already? "I'll take care of this," I told Claude. "You just relax."

Upon opening the door, I beheld one of the most lovely creatures I had ever seen. It was the woman in the picture on the website and she was even more striking than her image—the eyes, the hair, all of it. She opened her mouth and I floated on the depths of her voice. It stopped, then started again. "I said, 'Are you, Michael?' Is my sister here?"

"I'm sorry. Yes. Yes, she is. Please, come in."

"Is she all right?"

"Yes. I think so. She's right up here." Just as I opened the door to the den, I realized that I hadn't had the opportunity to unleash the little she-devil. The sister spotted her, gagged and restrained, before I could intervene. She turned to me, eyes huge, red lips apart.

As I opened my own mouth to speak, I was aghast as I heard "I'm terribly sorry" in the sister's voice, not my own. "She must have given you an awful time. Help me untie her and I'll have her out of your hair immediately."

"You mean you're not angry we restrained her?"

The sister turned those remarkable eyes on me. "Michael. This has happened before. My sister is—precocious. In fact, I've often felt tempted . . ." Her eyes left mine and traveled around the room, inspecting the carnage. "Oh, dear. I'm sorry for all the damage. I'm sure we can find a way to reimburse you." She stooped and picked up a well-ravaged book of illuminated medieval music sitting at her crimson painted toenails. "Well, I'm almost sure." I moved into her field of vision, wanting to lose myself in those eyes again.

"Please, think nothing of it. None of this is real anyway," I lied. "Clever reproductions, all of it." We stood like that for a few moments, just breathing (her, not me) and gazing into each other's eyes. I finally found my voice. "You might be wondering why we didn't call the police when . . ."

"Michael." She touched me lightly on the arm. "Everyone has little secrets and Callie is quick to find them. I'm guessing she found a little stash of marijuana or something she threatened to tell the police about. As I said, she's done this before."

"Indeed."

"You know, Michael, you have an accent I haven't heard before. It's how I imagine Chaucer might have spoken. Very enchanting."

"You're familiar with Chaucer?"

"Oh, yes. I'm working on my masters in Medieval Lit. Very romantic times, those."

The thumpings of Acalia's chair brought our attention back to the juvenile intruder. The sister sighed. "I suppose we'll have to untie her."

"I suppose."

While her hands were unfettered, Acalia looked daggers at her sister then yanked down the gag. "It's about time you got here! These guys are vampires and they're tryin' to kill me!"

The sister's eyes left their task and she gazed sideways at me over her shoulder. Again, she apologized. "She has quite an imagination, I'm afraid. I really am very sorry."

"I mean it! Look at his eyes!"

That I had already dined caused my eyes to appear a bit more human. They would look, at most, unusual and, I hoped, intriguing.

An eternity passed then she turned back to Acalia. "Of course, they're vampires. And you're a devil child. Let's go home." She grasped Acalia's shoulder with a sort of Vulcan death grip and marched her out of the room and down to the front door. All the way she spent apologizing and assuring me that all damages would be covered. I assured her that it wouldn't be necessary. At the door, she turned and blasted me again with those eyes. "I would really like to make this up to you somehow. May I buy you dinner or something?"

My tongue, of its own accord, caressed my left canine. I was about to propose a date, when I felt a sharp blow to my shin. I looked down to see Acalia squirming in her sister's grip. She kicked me again. "You're a vampire and I'm telling everyone."

With a final desolate sinking of my heart I politely declined dinner.

"Too bad." The sister shrugged and flashed a line of perfect white teeth, then turned and wrestled Acalia down the flagstone path. Halfway there, the girl snaked out of the woman's grasp. She turned and the moon cast her face in half-shadow.

That sinewy, whiney, nose-infected voice made one final stab at my sensitivities. "I'll be back. I know where you live."

I dashed to where she was standing, and, squeezing her bony shoulders, demanded to know, "How? How did you find us again?"

The sister replied. "Oh! Didn't you know? My family lives just down the road."

As we tossed clothing into suitcases, Claude vocalized the disaster over and over, a therapy I encouraged, until all traces of Clyde were gone.

We would stay at our escape cabin in Maine—with its rough pine coffins and gamey food chain—for a decade or two until we could regroup and plan for another move. We agreed that it seemed an awful pity to leave all those valuables behind. Or rather, what remained of them, but once relocated in a city somewhere—I've heard Dubai is lovely—we could begin collecting all over again.

In the larger scheme of things, that seemed all right. We had, after all, each other, and our entire deaths to do it.

Joyce Wagner's fiction has appeared in several anthologies, including *Night Bites: Vampire Stories by Women*. She is the author of the collection *Random Overthoughts: The Best (Give or Take) of the Humor Column 'Overthinking.'* Her non-fiction work has appeared in many regional publications including *New Hampshire Magazine*. She is currently finishing a historical novel (World War II) and lives on Cardigan Mountain with Mr. Holland, her music teacher husband, and Traction Jackson, a retired racehound. Her favorite Stooge is Curly. She can be reached at www.toothlesscougar@live.com.

Live Free or Undead

Ernesto Burden

"I don't mean to scare you, son," The Coach said, "but I think we've got a zombie problem." I was sitting at my desk in the press room at the statehouse, down in Concord. The Coach was standing in the doorway, looking old, disheveled and threadbare, which was normal, and almost worried, which was not. The Coach was not what I'd call a happy man, but he didn't worry.

Anxiety was a weakness of the sensitive types, he'd told me more than once.

With the implication that I was one of those sensitive types.

"Zombies?" I asked in a low voice. The Coach may not be a young man anymore, and maybe he's not the most eloquent speaker, but he's not exactly Gabby Hayes, either. I was pretty sure he'd said zombie, but I wanted to mumble the word enough so that I'd have deniability if he barked at me in that distinctive, disdainful grumble, "Zombies? Clean out your ears, pup. I said lobbyists! How's somebody who listens as poor as you do claim to be a newspaper reporter?"

But The Coach didn't say anything of the sort. Instead he said, "Yep, that's what I said, Donny boy. Zombies. Damn zombies." As if there were any other kind.

I'd been the statehouse reporter for *The Denmark Record* for almost a year. Before that I was city reporter for the paper, though it was more than a stretch to call Denmark a city. It was about two and a half hours north of Concord, a tiny peninsular near-island bordered on three sides

by the rocky, foreboding shores of the mighty Lake Washabagog and almost entirely on the fourth by the roaring Pemistinoonkook River. If it was, as the town fathers claimed on the city letterhead, "the jewel of the Great North Woods," it was an undiscovered jewel. Our paper's claim to fame was that we were the smallest daily newspaper in the country to send a reporter to Concord full time. Not that anyone in the broader world of journalism had ever acknowledged this claim. But we were proud of it anyway. Our paper's owner, an ancient and reclusive former timber magnate with enough money to pursue his passions, no matter how unprofitable, was said to love newspapers, politics, and medical science. He lived in a near-castle of a home at the pinnacle of the highest point of land at the very center of Denmark. I'd never met him.

"Okay," I said. "Zombies." The press room is a sunny, shabby little office a lot like what you'd imagine. File cabinets. Beat up old industrial steel office desks buried under teetering piles of paper. Newspapers stacked on the odd straight-backed wooden chair pushed against the dingy yellow wall. Tall, wall-length windows covered with a layer of comforting grime and bound by warped wooden frames. Ironic clippings of old headlines, an odd assortment of buttons and stickers from New Hampshire presidential primaries past, a menu for the diner across the street tacked to the wall near the door. I laughed. The utterly prosaic setting demanded I be misunderstanding The Coach. Of course he didn't mean zombie zombies. Man, was I wet behind the ears. This was the New Hampshire Statehouse; The Coach was talking politics.

"I get it," I said. "Incoming class of state reps walking in lockstep with their party, arms out in front, eyes straight ahead, ooarghhhh, must vote party line, eat braaaaaiins. Who you thinking? Jensen? Markland? Wilburham?" I winked at The Coach. His face twisted into something like an imitation of a man who's just chewed up a hunk of steel wool and washed it down with a cup of lemon juice.

"Get that ax," he said, gesturing to an antique-looking implement hanging on the wall next to an equally geriatric fire extinguisher. "And come with me."

I leaped to my feet but didn't make any move to get the ax. "Coach," I said. "You feeling okay?" Coach stank like he'd just smoked a whole pack of cigarettes in the elevator on the trip from the first to the second floor. His yellowing-white hair stood out in bristly spikes around his balding liver-spotted pate and his eyes bulged behind soda-bottle-thick glasses. Nothing unusual. But it was worth asking.

"I just saw a puss-oozing zombie lose an arm climbing out of one of the bushes by the statue of old Dan Webster on the front lawn and not even slow down. Gobbled the brains right out of a cocker spaniel and ate the cerebellum of the old lady walking the poor critter like it was gelato. Would you be okay after that?" His voice was as steady as it was the afternoon he told me he'd just seen a meter maid putting a ticket on my car.

When I didn't answer he strode to the wall, flipped open the glass case and yanked the ax from its bracket. He may have been scrawny, he may have been old, but suddenly I realized how much I looked up to The Coach. He'd already been a veteran New Hampshire politics writer back in the days when *The Union Leader* made Ed Muskie weep, or Ronald Regan told *The Telegraph*'s editor John Breen, by way of explaining who was setting the rules for a debate, "I am paying for this microphone." He looked liked a barbarian warrior: If a barbarian warrior had retired, and spent the last 30 years of his life losing his muscles behind a desk working as a near-sighted tax accountant with a hardcore diet pill and Wild Turkey habit. I followed him out of the press room and down the hall toward the elevator.

"Shouldn't we call someone?" I yelled after him, trying not to appear to be scurrying.

"Phones are out," he barked. "Landlines, cell phones, the whole telecom enchilada." I pulled my cell out of my pants pocket and flipped it open. No bars.

The visages of great statesmen of the past glared down at us from portraits that hung between office doors as we tramped along the ornate but now threadbare runner. I shuddered. Their stern expressions condemned us. If The Coach was right, if he wasn't crazy, and if there really were zombies overrunning Concord, New Hampshire, these our grizzled forebears, men who'd hacked the state out of the unyielding granite hills, who'd faced bitter winters, terrible hunger, savage animals, and native populations oddly unwilling to relinquish their homes and hunting grounds to pushy newcomers, *they* would know our chances were slim—that their diluted descendants, softened into loose gelatin by generations of malls, fast food, central heat and air and prime time television, would be no match for the monsters.

The elevator was at the end of the hall—chipped gilt frame gleaming dully around brown veneer doors. The arrow on the little semicircular dial above the doors was moving, slowly, from one to two. We stopped about five feet away and watched. The little arrow settled on the two. There was a muffled ding, and the door slid open. I heard The Coach suck in his breath. "Holy mother of rivers," he muttered. "Shave my salmon and call me Donny."

"Hey," I said, embarrassed.

Out of the elevator stepped the most beautiful woman I'd ever seen. She had long, strawberry hair and shocking green eyes, as perfectly oval as a cat's. She wasn't tall, but she looked tall—possibly because of the relative shortness of her gray pinstriped skirt or the relative length of her lean, muscular legs. She was wearing a smart gray coat that matched her skirt, all business, except the way it would have made it impossible for anyone looking at her to actually think about business. The left sleeve on her coat was torn from the shoulder, as though someone had been pulling on her arm. She had a smear of blood on her left cheek.

"Are you . . ." she began, then shook her head.

"Zombies," I said. "No way."

She shook her head again. "I was going to say, 'here to help.' But I see you're media, so that's not likely."

"Today we're all in it together," The Coach said. "You work for the governor, don't you?" She nodded. "Yeah," The Coach went on, "you started last week. Marion, uh, Marion, right?"

"How'd you know we were reporters?" I asked. She just stared at me.

"There are zombies downstairs," she said after a minute of awkward silence. "They're eating the legislature." I pulled my spiral bound reporter's notebook out of my back pocket. Pure instinct. I put it back without writing anything. It wasn't likely I'd forget Marion saying, "They're eating the legislature," anytime soon. Partly because of how disturbingly sensual the words seemed coming from her. She could have turned "The Wreck of the Edmund Fitzgerald" into a torch song.

The Coach hefted his fire ax. "We're getting out of here, ma'am," he said. "If you want, you can come with us."

"Where will you go?" she said. Then her eyes widened, focused on something over The Coach's shoulder. I turned and saw the thing come around the corner from the direction of the press office. It wasn't moving particularly quickly, but it was coming on with an implacable, lurching determination that made me think of post-election repositioning on campaign promises. You don't break them all at once—you have to save something for the second term.

It used to be a Democrat I'd known fairly well. I could tell by the graying ponytail, L.L.Bean sport coat (sporty Republicans tended to wear Orvis) and wide-wale corduroy pants: Rep. Thomas Martin. Most of its chest had been torn open and I could see an empty place in the chest cavity where its heart had been.

"Aw hell, Tom," The Coach shouted at the beast, "I told you that whole grain bread and organic salad dressing wasn't going to add a day to your life."

Marion turned to bolt back toward the elevator but the door had already closed. The little arrow began to swing back across the half-moon toward the one. Marion stopped at the door. Raised her hand and laid her palm flat against the cheap veneer. "Well, that's a bitch," she said and turned back to us. She nodded at The Coach. "I hope you know how to use that thing."

"Let's just say I saw my share of combat," The Coach said. "Back in Korea, they called me The Sarge, not The Coach."

"My God," she said. "You're old."

The Coach didn't have time to respond. The zombie that used to be Rep. Thomas Martin lurched a final few steps down the hall and was upon us, arms extended, blood-blackened fingers clawing, guttural moans wrenching out of his savaged throat. I wondered how he made so much noise with his lungs mostly torn out.

The Coach swung the fire ax at its head. The blade bit deep into the zombie's skull and it staggered backwards, wrenching the ax handle from The Coach's gnarled hands. The zombie glared at us, soul-dead eyes seeming to rage with an inner fire that could have only been hell-born. It shuddered forward with a violent jerk. The Coach reached to his right and flung open the nearest office door. The door caught the ax handle and the zombie flopped over backwards, arms and legs flailing the air like an overturned beetle. The Coach strode forward, caught the ax handle, put his workbooted foot on the zombie's face and pulled the ax free. He brought it down four times on the monster's skull and the former Rep. Thomas Martin stopped moving. The Coach was wheezing

with the exertion. He tossed me the ax. I fumbled it and had to scramble
on the floor to retrieve it, conscious the whole time of Marion's assessing
gaze. "You get the next one," The Coach gasped. "I think I'm having a
heart attack."

Behind us, the elevator dinged again and the doors slid open.

"I think we'd better go this way," Marion said, dashing past us down
the hall.

"There's a back stairwell around the corner, past the press office," I
offered. "You okay to run?" I asked The Coach.

"Better than you, fat boy," he said. That hurt my feelings. It'd been
a few years, well, a dozen, to be honest, since my college baseball career
ended, and sure, maybe I'd put on a few pounds since then, but what
do you want? I type stories for a living. I could still get into my 36 waist
pants, if I didn't have to do anything afterward that required too much
breathing. I wondered if Marion had heard what he said. I gripped the
ax tightly in both hands, trying to look as tough as possible. "Let's roll,"
I said. And instantly regretted it.

We made it down the back stairwell without meeting any more of
the zombies and hunkered down behind the Dumpster in the back parking lot. There were zombies in the streets behind and alongside the
statehouse, roaming almost aimlessly, trailing body parts and bits of
gore, heads back, all groaning on and on like the one inside had been,
like each was undertaking a filibuster from hell.

"My car's down on Main Street," I whispered. "I left it there when I
came back from lunch."

"I walked today," The Coach said.

Marion held up a set of keys. "The governor's Town Car," she said
and gestured across the back parking lot. A long, black car gleamed in
the late morning sunshine.

"Hey, where is the governor, anyway?" I asked. "Should we try and
help him?"

She shook her head, which made her hair dance around her face in
a beautiful, terrible way. "He's with his family, up on the lake today," she
said. "God willing, these things haven't made it that far."

"I guess that depends on where they started out," The Coach said.
"Maybe they're Canadian, in which case they might not have made it
to Boston yet, but the Big Lake is probably overrun six hours back and

the governor's already shuffling this way with black fingernails and a hankering for brain pâté."

"My God," she said. "Do you have to talk like that?"

"It's germane," he said, "in terms of the direction we are about to pick to decamp."

"I say Boston," I said.

"You mean as in the zombies came from Boston or that we should escape toward Boston?" Marion asked. I liked when she asked me questions. Even under these circumstances.

"I think whatever happened started south of here," I said. "About two hours ago, I was reading *The Globe*'s Boston.com website and I noticed the last news update was already an hour old. It was just a paragraph or so on an odd outbreak of war protests throughout the city. The police were speculating that the protesters, who'd covered themselves in fake blood and dressed up to look like collateral damage, were using the Internet to coordinate meet-ups at a variety of locations throughout the city."

"So three hours," The Coach said. "That's bad. Means this thing is going to spread fast."

"What do you mean?" asked Marion.

"No zombie walked from Boston to Concord in three hours," The Coach said. "That means somebody got bit. And then got in a car and drove, maybe running north from the outbreak, just like we're planning to do. And by the time he got up here, he was going zombie. Maybe that's why he stopped. Car crashed. He staggered out into the street, bit a few more people, and here we are. Zombieville, New Hampshire."

"My God," Marion said. "It's going to spread like a plague."

"That's exactly what it is," The Coach said. "A plague. You get a look at Rep. Martin? I talked to him on the phone an hour ago, and he was right as rain. Five minutes ago in the hall? Refugee from a George Romero movie."

"Look, we've got to go," I said. "You okay to drive?" I asked Marion.

"Why? Because I'm a woman? I'll be less capable of driving a car during a zombie attack than a newspaper reporter?"

"What do you have against newspaper reporters?"

"What do you have against women?"

"Besides," I asked, "how do you know I work for a newspaper? Maybe I work for WMUR. I could be a TV guy. You consider that?"

She looked me up and down, took in the faded khaki pants, the rumpled button-up shirt in which I masqueraded as "dressed up," the too-short, knit tie with lumpy knot, the grubby white basketball shoes, and sniffed.

"What?" I asked The Coach. "It's not like the TV guys dress *that* much better."

The Coach stared at me. "Son, I get my clothes for free after the Salvation Army throws them out. Don't ask me for fashion advice."

I was about to ask him how that deal worked and who you had to talk to to get on the list, when I saw Marion staring at us and I clamped my lips shut.

We sprinted across the back parking lot. A couple of dozen zombies began to shuffle toward us, but we made the car with time to spare. The fire ax handle felt slick in my sweaty hands while Marion unlocked the car. The Coach took the back seat, wheezing wildly, and immediately lit up a smoke. I took the passenger side. Marion put the car in drive and mowed down four or five of the creatures that were blocking the exit. Bits of gore sprayed the windshield, and one disembodied hand landed palm down, fingers splayed on the hood. It looked like Thing's hand from the Adams Family. I half expected it to start crawling. Marion slewed the car wildly around the next corner, aiming us toward Main Street and the closest on ramp for I-93. The hand slid off the hood and vanished. Marion turned on the windshield wipers, smearing bloody lumps of tissue and bone across the glass.

"What a friggin' mess," The Coach said from the back seat.

"You can't smoke in the governor's car," Marion said.

"The world's ending," The Coach said. "If it doesn't, I'll pay for the detailing."

"You never get the smoke smell out," I said. "It gets stuck in the air systems. Stinks whenever you turn the heat or the AC on."

"You put some vinegar in a big flat pan under the hood. Leave it over night, that'll do it," The Coach said.

"Are you two serious?" Marion asked.

"Which way are you going?" The Coach asked as the car swayed onto 202. "North, south, east?"

"North," Marion said. "If we can make it to the governor's place on the lake we might be safe. The house is like a fortress. And he's got a security team there."

"Makes sense to me," I said. God help me, it almost sounded romantic. At least when she said it. A lake house. The cry of the loons, the
slap of the waves on the dock. The comforting sound of security guards
chambering fresh rounds of ammo in very large automatic weapons.
She cranked the wheel and the big car shuddered onto the ramp. I sup-
pressed a smile.

We pulled onto I-93 and the gold of the statehouse dome shrank
in the rearview mirror. There were no other vehicles moving on the
highway, though there were plenty abandoned, some in the breakdown
lanes, some right in the road, skewed across lanes, doors ajar. Zombies
wandered among them.

"I'll bet there were plenty of drivers swerved to miss these bastards
and ended up crashing," The Coach said. He had a finely honed instinct
for observation and he read the devastated road the way a backwoods
tracker reads a game trail. "Others probably stopped to help. One way
or another they all ended up the same way—ghoul chow."

"Not a mistake I intend to make," Marion said coldly, plowing
through a rotund zombie in a blue dress who'd been blocking the passing lane, still clutching an oversized white leather purse. "Did you see
those shoes?"

"I'm sure *you* wouldn't be caught dead in 'em," The Coach rasped.
She didn't answer, unless you took the small gagging sound she made at
the back of her throat to be a response.

"We're going to need more windshield wiper fluid," I said.

By the time we got to Tilton the road was impassible. Cars were piled
like timber in a logjam. We got off the highway and headed toward the
big lake, following Route 3 north toward Laconia. Each time the road
we were traveling was blocked up by a stack of cars, an overturned
truck, once a broken-open trailer that had released a flock of goats to
wander in the road, we'd take yet a smaller side road, which seemed to
present itself with odd convenience, as though we were being funneled
onto narrower lanes that would eventually peter out altogether. Which
the last did, turning from a dirt fire road to a grass track that meandered through a small forest of trees and came out at the back lot of an
austere, if somewhat dilapidated white board church. A hand-lettered
sign by the double doors at the bottom of a short flight of steps read,
"Tuesday, June 14, 5 p.m. to ?, Lakeside Congregational Ham and Bean
Supper. $5. Come on in!"

"It seems quiet," Marion said. She reached for the door handle. "Should we go in?"

"We're nearly out of gas, and we have no idea where we are," I said. "We're going to have to go in somewhere before too long."

"I don't like it," The Coach growled.

Marion paused, finger on the latch. "What?" she asked.

"It's going to be trouble in there, one way or the other," The Coach said.

"What do you mean, one way or the other?" I asked.

"Well," The Coach said, pushing past me and Marion and grasping the door handle in his gnarled, nicotine-stained fingers, "either we go through these doors and the basement's filled with rotting, flesh-eating zombies, and that's bad . . ." He tested the latch with his thumb and nodded. He pressed and the door swung open. "Or it's full of church supper wimmen," he grumbled. "And that's prob'ly worse."

It turned out The Coach was wrong about some things and right about others.

The basement wasn't filled with zombies or church supper women. There was just one church supper woman. But she did have a big, double-barreled shotgun pointed right at us as we came out of the passage and into the dinner hall. So that was pretty bad all the same.

She was tall, lean as jerky, somewhere between age 50 and age 110, as near as I could guess. She had snow white hair done up in a bun, a pink turtle necked sweater with roses embroidered around the collar, a leather bandoleer of shotgun shells slung over one shoulder, and a pair of wire-framed golden spectacles on thin golden chains.

"It's all right, Barbie, Dough Boy, step away from the zombie and I'll take care of it," she said, gesturing with the barrels of the gun for us to move away from The Coach.

"Hey," I said.

"Thanks, kid," Coach whispered.

"What's that supposed to mean, Dough Boy?" I was sort of hoping she meant dough boy as in American soldiers in World War I, not the Pillsbury sort.

"It means," she snapped, "that if you don't get back right now, you're going to make more than a meal for that creature you stumbled in here with."

"I'm not infected," The Coach snarled at her. "Now put that cannon down before you hurt yourself."

She stared at him, then very carefully drew her spectacles down so her ice-chip blue eyes could peer over the tops of them.

"I've never heard one talk," she said. "Just growl. And make those sucking, snorting noises while they eat."

"I don't doubt that The Coach does both," said Marion, stepping forward and extending her hand. "But that goes to show how important good breeding is. He's not a zombie. He's a newspaper reporter."

The church supper woman had been lowering the shotgun as Marion approached, but I swear I saw her start to lift it again before thinking twice and letting it drop to her side.

She drew in a deep, shaking breath and sighed. "Thank God you're here," she said. "I've been here alone all afternoon. Except for them." She nodded over her left shoulder. I don't know how I'd missed the pile of zombie corpses stacked in the corner next to the old upright piano and the Formica-topped table with the stainless steel coffee urn and neat stacks of Styrofoam cups on it.

"You sure they're dead?" The Coach asked with an odd, respect-tinged skepticism in his voice.

"How many zombies did you kill today?" the church supper woman asked him.

"One," The Coach said. "I mean, urr, a couple I guess."

"So you're an expert then?"

"I don't doubt that you're getting very good at killing zombies," Marion interjected. "But as strange as it feels to be saying this, I have to say, I see where The Coach is coming from. That is an awfully big pile of zombies, if it turned out a couple of them were still alive . . ."

"Okay, Bambi," the church supper woman said. She casually flipped the shotgun in her hands and pivoted toward the pile of undead flesh. The first barrel thundered and remaining bits of a zombie head exploded. The second barrel flashed and most of the zombie's neck vaporized in a spray of red. She broke the shotgun in one smooth motion, flicked away the spent shells even as she dropped two more that she'd somehow plucked from the bandoleer into the chambers and flicked the break closed again with strong snap of her wrist. "Here's how it works. You shoot them once with a 12 gauge shell and they don't have mouths left to bite you with. Shoot 'em twice and they've got so little left up top that they'd have to slap you to death with their exposed lung meat if they were to get back up and come after you. Now why don't you and the boys sit on down there while I make us some coffee. Then we can figure out what we're going to do."

"My name's not Bambi or Barbie, it's Marion," Marion said. But she sat down all the same.

"I'm Ethel," the church supper woman said. "Welcome to the end of the world, and Lakeside Congregational's last ever ham and bean supper."

It turned out Ethel had a lot more to offer our little party than ham and beans.

Once Marion explained where we were headed, Ethel was able to tell us we weren't more than 15 miles from the governor's place as the crow flies, or as she said rather mysteriously, the Jeep wrangles. We finished our dinners and she took us out to the front parking lot of the church. There, like an elephant among a herd of sheep, was a monstrously large, yellow Jeep with tires the size of a dump truck's and bulging shocks that reminded me of the arms of a steroid-abusing bodybuilder.

"My son's," Ethel said. "He had my car's exhaust system in pieces when I left the house this morning so he told me to take this. He built it himself. It's got a GenRight Legend Extreme suspension and 14-inch-travel, 2-inch diameter King coilover shocks. This leviathan will crawl right up over whatever's blocking the road, whether it's a zombie, a car or . . ." She trailed off then and lowered her head. When she looked up again, there were tears in those amazing ice-chip eyes, but her face was as rigid and implacable as a plaster saint's. "He's dead now," she said. "My son's dead. He was a good man."

"He might not be dead. You're alive; we're alive," Marion said.

"If he were alive, young lady," Ethel said briskly, "he would have been here by now to get me."

"I'm sorry for your loss, ma'am," The Coach said. He shuffled his feet, fumbled in his pocket for the pack of cigarettes, lit one. "Okay," he said. "We'd better be on our way. Do you have the keys?"

"I'll drive," Ethel said, her voice as precise and controlled as the detonator on a bomb, safe and sane but sitting right on top of a big ball of fire.

We had no trouble getting to the narrow access road that led around the lake to the governor's house. It would have been a straight shot with a few monster truck style climbs over piles of cars in the road, except Ethel kept detouring to run down zombies. "There's three in the woods back there," she'd cry, and the massive Jeep would lurch off road and crash through the brush, mowing down small trees and eventually the animated corpses in question. The truck sat so high off the ground that Ethel never even had to use the windshield wipers. The black metal tubing of the front bumper was designed specifically not to hang up on trail obstacles, and it didn't hang up on zombies, either. It flung them to the left, right, or channeled them down under the monster-tires, which ground them into chum that collected in the cavernous wheel wells. "Die, you hell-borne bastards," she hissed as they went down.

"I think she's gone crazy," I whispered to The Coach as we slammed against each other in the back seat. Marion was riding shotgun, with Ethel's shotgun in her lap.

"I dunno," said The Coach scratching the grubby-looking white and gray stubble that covered his cheeks like the last grimy snow by the side of the road in March. "I think there's something sexy about her."

I looked at the gray bun of hair on the back of the head of the elderly church supper woman in the front seat. She slammed the Jeep into reverse, backed over a pile of zombie bits and then drove forward again, grinding the gore into the leaf litter. She'd begun to cackle, very quietly. It was disconcerting.

"I can see what you mean," I said.

We found the governor's motorcade a mile up the road from his house. Judging from the direction they were pointed in, they'd been heading away from the lake. Fleeing the house. Ethel stopped the Jeep and we all climbed down to look around.

"Stay close," Marion said. "We may need to get back into the Jeep fast."

The two black SUV's were empty, and the governor's car was on its side. Bits of the driver were strewn around the front seat. The governor was nowhere to be seen.

"Does anybody else smell smoke?" I asked. We all looked up, scanned the horizon. A plume of black smoke rose from beyond the tree line in front of us. The governor's lake house.

"Aw, crap," The Coach said. "Poor little guy."

The governor was a tiny, sprightly, fair-haired man of Scandinavian descent who always looked as though he ought to be wearing a blue and white knit sweater with blocky looking reindeer on it. He was perhaps the most beloved man in New Hampshire, in part because of his consummate skill in taking tough stands on controversial and divisive issues, typically shortly after they had been decided by the legislature and the outcome had been generally accepted by public opinion. It was hard to picture him shuffling through the woods, gnawing on a dismembered arm and growling. Sort of like trying to imagine Ernie the Keebler Elf in colors and a pair of Doc Martens kicking somebody's teeth in at a motorcycle rally.

"I can't believe it," Marion said. She was shaking, holding herself tightly with both arms. "He was, he was . . . the best boss I ever had." She was on the edge of bursting into tears.

"Pull yourself together," Ethel snapped. "A lot of good people died today."

"Maybe I don't need to pull myself together," Marion said. She pulled herself up straight, drew back her shoulders and glared at Ethel. "Maybe you need to let yourself feel something. Maybe you need to let yourself grieve for your son."

"What is wrong with your generation?" Ethel asked. "What did we do to turn you into such self-absorbed twits?"

"I blame the Internet," The Coach said.

"There may be a time and a place for grief someday," Ethel said harshly. "But look around. It isn't here, and it sure as heck isn't now."

Marion looked as if she'd been slapped. Which may have been what prompted Ethel to stride forward and slap her hard across the cheek.

"What did you do that for?" Marion asked. "It's not like I was hysterical."

"Bush doctrine," Ethel said. "It was preemptive."

The Coach nudged me and winked. He mouthed the word, "sexy."

"So where to now?" Ethel addressed us all. "Shall we head back to the church basement and wait for the end, which will probably come sooner, rather than later, and will likely be a blessing, or do any of you have another bright idea?"

I stepped forward. "I do," I said.

That's how we ended up piling back into the Jeep and heading north, skirting Lake Winnipesaukee and picking our way northward along back roads, through the mountains, toward the Great North Woods, where the grim stony shores of Lake Washabagog meet the raging Pemistinoonkook River, and where we'd find the tiny, near-island town of Denmark, New Hampshire. I didn't know if there was any place in the state, the country or the world that was safe anymore from the zombie menace, but if there were such a place, it seemed likely to me that it would be the fortress-like home of the mysterious and reclusive owner of *The Denmark Record*, high on a hill in the center of town.

"I've never met him, or even seen him," I told Marion, The Coach and Ethel as we swerved around a black and white VW Bug with a Geek Squad logo on the side. The driver's side door was open and there was a smear of blood on the window that suggested the shape of a hand.

"So much for anti-virus," The Coach quipped humorlessly. "Get it? Computer viruses? Conicker worm, zombie computers?"

"His name is Langston Pierce," I went on, ignoring The Coach, who would have still been typing his stories on an Underwood if he had his way, and considered the old TRS-80 unnecessarily advanced technology. "He comes from a timber family, old money. They owned paper mills, and forests, and logging operations. He sold it all off years ago, invested in biotech and a bunch of other stuff, then settled into his castle on the hill and hasn't come out since. He owns the paper in town, *The Denmark Record*, and has been running it a loss for the last five years. His interest in politics is the only reason a paper the size of the record actually fields a statehouse reporter anymore. On top of the stories I file for the paper, he has me write him a personal weekly report as well."

"The governor knew him," Marion said, leaning around in her seat. "They spoke often by phone. And he and the chief of health and human services have visited Pierce twice in Denmark since I started working at the statehouse."

"What?" I asked. "We never heard about that."

"Not surprising," The Coach said. "Open government's something between a myth and a euphemism for 'We'll tell you what we want you to know when we want you to know it. Now put your hands on the back of your head and spread 'em.' "

Ethel sniffed loudly. "What a mouth on you," she said.

"I'm a diamond in the rough," The Coach said.

"I imagine that whatever it is that festers under that rough exterior bears little in common with a diamond," Ethel said.

"Oh yeah?" asked The Coach. "You know where the word diamond comes from?"

"I'm afraid I don't, Mister Coach," she said primly.

"Greek," The Coach said. "Means unbreakable."

"I see." I thought she was going to say something else but she didn't. Neither did The Coach. They both seemed somehow satisfied with the exchange. I nudged The Coach but he didn't look at me.

What would have been a two-hour ride from Concord ended up taking closer to eight on the back roads. Occasionally Ethel had to stop the Jeep and The Coach and I got out to move cars off the road. Many still had their keys in the ignition. A few still had the engines running. But the further north we went, the fewer abandoned vehicles we found.

"I have to say," Ethel said after driving a half hour stretch without seeing a single zombie sign, "that maybe you were right. Seems like the outbreak, or whatever it is, hasn't gotten this far north."

She may have regretted those words when we came down the hill toward the bridge over the Pemistinoonkook River that led into Denmark. It was close to ten o'clock, and beyond the darkness of the forest and the black water of the river, we saw a hellish red glow: Denmark was burning.

Half the town was ablaze. The Jeep shouldered its way past scorched cars that blocked the road and ran down the zombies that came at us, some with their hair and clothes afire, flames licking the wind of their groans as they opened their mouths and reached for the doors. Their gray fingers never caught hold of the handles. Ethel drove ferociously. She swerved the mighty Jeep from left to right, pinning a zombie against a burning building, then driving another into the bumper of a stalled truck. She seemed to have recovered from the strange mania that had possessed her earlier, and she didn't cackle this time, just pressed her lips together and gripped the wheel grimly. I could almost imagine a voice in her head speaking to the undead hordes she ground beneath the gargantuan tires of her dead son's tricked-out Jeep. "Now this hurts me just as much as it hurts you."

All the while the great hill at the center of town, with its castle perched at the summit, grew closer. I knew that at the bottom of that hill was a high iron fence tipped with spikes and a gate heavy enough to withstand a tank. If Mr. Pierce was dead, or not at home, there wasn't much chance of us getting through. Or back, I thought, looking back at the burning town that seemed to be collapsing upon itself in our wake.

In the end, it was a small thing, a cat, that finished the Jeep. It was a little black and white one, skinny and ragged looking, and it dashed across the road like its tail was on fire. Which it probably would have been before too long.

Ethel, our own church supper lady version of Conan the Barbarian, gasped like an old woman, which I suppose I finally realized she was, and jerked the wheel madly to the right. The top-heavy Jeep rolled like a die and we came up unlucky, upside down in the middle of the street. I could hear the wheels spinning above us.

"Get out," Marion screamed. "We've all got to get out!"

I felt The Coach grab my arm. "Shake it, Donny," he said. "My door's jammed and we need out. It's Custer time." He pushed me toward the door and I fumbled with the handle. The metal frame groaned but the door opened as I threw myself against it. The Coach crawled out after me into the street then went to work on Ethel's door. He dragged her out, and she dragged the shotgun out. Marion crawled out behind her and I helped her up then reached back into the Jeep for the fire ax.

Sounds strange to say, but you don't really notice exactly how many zombies there are out walking the street when the vehicle you're riding in is simply mowing them down at will. They start to blend into the overall ambiance of the drive. Like frost heaves and potholes. But now, as we stood in a tight little circle next to the overturned Jeep, I realized there were a lot. A real lot. I saw the Pierce castle rising on its hill in the distance. Four blocks maybe? Six? I pointed at it.

"Run," I screamed.

We ran, though without hope. There were too many of them. Marion and I soon realized we'd outpaced The Coach and Ethel. We stopped and turned. The Coach was also turned, reaching back for Ethel, who had also turned to raise the shotgun she still carried. A half dozen creatures shambled toward her, arms out. She fired twice and two fell, heads blown off. She reloaded. Fired again.

"Come on," The Coach screamed. "We can get to the big house."

Ethel dropped two more zombies and turned to him.

"There are too many for all of us to get through. And I'm tired," she said. "You go." He shook his head. Turned to me.

"You kids run," he said. "And don't look back. We'll be along when we come along." I started to go back to get him. He was the most critical, insulting, odoriferous and generally difficult man I'd ever known in my life, but he was also the closest thing I'd ever had to a mentor. And he may well have been the last truly veteran statehouse reporter in the whole United States of America.

Actually, given the situation with the zombies, that was probably more true than it had been even a day before. And that had to count for something.

"No way, Coach," I yelled and started toward him. Marion grabbed my arm. Her eyes, shining with tears, met mine, and she shook her head. I heard the blast of the shotgun again, and snapped my head back in time to see Ethel fall beneath a mob of clawing hands and gaping jaws. The Coach never looked back at us, just dove in after her. We turned and ran then. God help me, we turned and ran. A block later I heard the roar of the shotgun, then again half a block after that. But we didn't stop.

There were a couple of dozen zombies wandering aimlessly in the cold white lake of a floodlight on the street outside the main gate of the Pierce Mansion.

A gravelly voice boomed from a hidden speaker.

"Wait a second, kids. I'll clear you a path." Then concealed machine guns in two skinny towers on either side of the gate opened fire and grated the zombies milling about in front like soft, gory cheese.

"Nice, huh?" the voice said. "Remote control. Been fragging these douchebags all night. It's like a video game. And to think, the damn zoning board thought the machine guns and guard towers were overkill. Come up to the gate and I'll buzz you in."

We ran for the gate and waited in the glare of the floodlight. He must have taken a minute to study our faces.

"Donny?" the voice from the speaker said with a note of amused recognition.

The gate buzzed and we pushed it open a crack and leaped through, slamming it shut again behind us. "Good to see you boy! Come on up to the house."

Zombies moaned, growled and roared as they flung themselves against the stout metal gate, knocking bits of gristle off themselves in the process. After each surge against the gate there was a light pattering and plopping sound, as though it were raining tongues. Marion and I made our way up a broad brightly-lit walkway that ran next to the crushed stone driveway toward the massive steps that rose to the regal front doors of the Pierce mansion. I carried the fire ax in my left hand. At some point Marion slipped her left hand into my right hand. I glanced at her as we walked, but she was staring straight ahead. Her strawberry blond hair was tousled and tangled, her fine, pink cheek smeared with grime, her slim gray jacket torn at the shoulder. She was as beautiful as Eve must have looked to Adam. Somewhere in the back of my mind, behind the place where my conscious thoughts were dealing with the animated dead and the apocalypse, I pondered at the unfairness of it all. The world had to end for me to get a girl like this. Another more ruthless voice in my head suggested, well, if that's how it has to happen, so be it.

The front doors swung open as we approached. I saw another camera pivot just above the upper right hand corner of the door frame. Mr. Pierce was watching, making a way for us. The door slammed behind us as we entered a massive foyer. Another swung open at the far end of a walkway at the top end of a huge spiraling staircase that wound three stories toward the curved ceiling of what must have been a cavernous ten-story dome. We climbed the stairs.

Pierce was tucked into a wheelchair before a bank of video monitors. To his right and left rose more monitors, keyboards, computer towers. As we entered, we saw our own faces on the main monitors. The wheelchair rotated to face us with a dexterous hum and then rolled up a short flight of steps before coming to a stop in front of us. While the chair looked almost nothing like an ordinary wheelchair, its occupant looked much as I'd imagined a reclusive billionaire might. The chair was shaped like an executive quality office chair. It had four knobby wheels set close together on a casing of engine and gearing beneath it, and two smaller ones out in front by the footrest. As it had climbed the stairs the wheels had adjusted their levels relative to each other to keep the chair balanced. Now they shifted again bringing the chair into what I can only describe as a standing position. This maneuver brought the chair's occupant to eye level. He was a wizened creature, with cold, gray eyes and a goblin grin that revealed two rows of perfect white teeth; totally incongruous in a face with the texture of a deflated basketball. His head was completely bald, and bits of the scalp had flaked away to reveal patchy glimpses of what almost looked like bone beneath.

"Donny," Pierce said. His voice was deep and rumbled and crunched like a rock tumbler as it wrestled its way out of his emaciated frame. "And you're Marion. The governor's aid. How is the governor today?"

"He's dead," Marion said. "I hope."

"I know what you mean," Pierce said. He nodded back toward the screens.

Our images had been replaced by a shot of the front gate. Zombies thudded against the bars. "Wouldn't want to be one of those things. Of course, I'm half a kind as it is," he said, and laughed hoarsely.

"What do you mean?" I asked. Though in a way, I already knew. I felt like someone waking up from a bad dream and into a nightmare.

Pierce smiled at me with those hideous, perfect teeth. "I'm afraid some of my treatments might have gotten a bit out of hand, Donnie. You understand. "It wasn't just for me. I mean, I paid for it, but it wasn't just for me. We were doing it for the good of the state, of the country, the world even."

"Biotechnology experiments," Marion whispered in horror.

"Meh," Pierce said. "It wasn't much. A little gene splicing, some embryonic stem cells, a radioactive spider, you know the drill." He looked at us as though waiting for something. "I was kidding about the spider part."

"Oh," I said.

"A virus," Pierce said. "A good virus, we thought. Only it turned bad. And then it got out. And, well, you know the rest of the story. Three quarters of the world is eating brains and the other fourth is gettin' its brains eaten."

"What can we do?" Marion asked.

"Do?" Pierce mused. "Do? Nothing, so far as I can tell. Shoot until the machine guns in the towers run out of ammo. Watch until the screens go dark. Die, if that's even possible anymore. May be easier for you that it is me. The original version of this virus has been keeping me alive for ten years now. Not sure I can die even if I want to. But either way, I'm not going anywhere. I've got everything I want right here."

"There must be something we can do," I said.

"You could make a run for it," he allowed. "Get far enough north to be free of people, and you'd be free of zombies. Find some tight little hunting cabin up in the Canadian wilderness. Put in a winter's worth of wood and smoked fish and venison and hunker down. You two might make a life of it for yourselves. For a while. Until one of you broke a leg, or got appendicitis, or needed a root canal. Then things would go bad pretty quickly. You're not cut out for the pioneer life. But you'd buy some time, anyway."

"So that's it," I said. "We run or we die."

"Live free or die," he said and cackled.

And that's what we did. Though not before I raised the fire ax that my good friend The Coach had used to save my life back in the state-house, what seemed like an eternity before. I'd intended to put that evil old bastard Pierce out of his misery, but I couldn't bring myself to do it. Instead I shook the ax at him and then took my reporter's notebook out of my back pocket and threw it in his face.

"Here," I said. "Take this. It was a lie all along, wasn't it? I was never a reporter. I was just your mole in the statehouse." In truth, it wasn't the lie that bothered me, though. I'd just realized that an age had passed. Maybe there'd been a time on earth when the pen was mightier than the sword. But not anymore. I will never write again, I told myself. There's no reason for it anymore. I shook my ax again. "I want all the guns and ammo in the house. The keys to an SUV. Supplies."

He smiled. "You don't have to threaten me, Donny. There's a Hummer parked in fourth bay in the garage. It's already packed. Everything you need. I knew you'd come."

"How?" Marion said. "How could you know it would be us?"

"Not you two specifically," Pierce said. "Just two. To start fresh. A new experiment. There're maps in the Hummer. GPS isn't good for much anymore. The cabin I'm talking about is marked on the last one. " He smiled at her, and for a moment the rest of his face seemed to match those teeth, and he was almost charming. "I was handsome once," he whispered.

"We have to go," I said, trying not to gag. I tossed the ax in my hand. I liked the heft of it. It made me feel better.

Time's passed. I'm not fat anymore. I'm lean and strong, my skin's weatherbeaten, and I have a beard that goes all the way down my chest. I've killed deer, bear, wolves, trout, salmon, and plenty of zombies, though none of the latter in the past year or so. We're as far north as we could get. After the last logging roads ran out, we pushed the Hummer on up trails until it couldn't get between the tall pines anymore. Then we packed north until we came to the edge of a lake. There was a cabin there, and a dock. Maybe the owner used to land a pontoon plane and spend weekends there fishing. Maybe that had been Pierce, once upon a time. If so, he'd left no clues.

There are three of us now. Marion gave birth to a son a month ago.

Up until that point I'd made good on my unspoken vow; I hadn't written a word. But the day after my son was born, I dug through our supplies and brought out paper and pen. Pierce knew how to run an experiment, and he knew what we'd eventually do. He'd made sure to pack all the necessities.

But regardless of what he may have wanted, it's not for posterity or science that I begin this journal. It's for my son. Because you never know, out here, when you might break a leg, or get appendicitis, or need a root canal. Things could go bad pretty quickly. And just in case they do, I'd like for my son to know how he ended up here, and who his father was, and why we keep a fire ax by the door and machine gun next to the bed.

It's not for the trout or the bears. It's because we don't know how long those damn things will live. Or how far they might someday walk.

Ernesto Burden writes fiction, non-fiction and poetry. He's the vice president of digital media for a New Hampshire publishing company. He has been a print editor and reporter with daily and weekly newspapers. He is also a marathoner, musician and an avid student of technology, literature, religion and the Spanish language. He enjoys single malt Scotch, dry martinis and fly fishing. He lives in New Hampshire with his wife Kristen their son David and daughters Sofia and Isobel.

Little Ones

Kristopher Seavey

Chuck and Rusty roared along some back road in Chuck's beat-to-hell Chevy pickup, blasting WOKQ at top volume, although the signal was starting to fade. Tim McGraw crooned about the southern experience, which seemed appropriate even in New Hampshire, pure Yankee territory. Rusty rode shotgun, a half-empty case of Red Hook beer on his lap. Another full case was stowed in the rear along with a pair of Winchester 30-aught-sixes, a Remington twelve-gauge, a spotlight, and enough ammuntion to invade Canada. They zigzagged crazily through the woods, deeper into the domain of outdoorsman fantasy.

"What's the name of this place we're lookin' for again?" asked Rusty.

"For the bah-zillionth time, Delacroix Notch. Damn, your brain's got more holes n' a leaky radiator."

Rusty had a vacant, walleyed expression that seemed to suggest he had stuck a lot of things up his nose as a toddler. There was little doubt that at some point in the future his mug would be displayed on the Walmart bulletin board coupled with the words "sex offender."

Chuck was by no means Mensa material himself, but he kept Rusty around, mainly because it made him feel like a Nobel laureate by comparison.

"How much longer we gotta go?" Rusty asked.

"Dunno, never been there."

Truth be told, Chuck himself was not entirely sure they were going

the right way, but with five Red Hooks in his system he was beyond worrying about it.

"There sure are a lot of trees out here. Been a long time since I seen any houses. Freaks me out a little," Rusty said.

"Yuh. This is New Hampshire, there are going to be trees. Get used to it." Chuck withdrew his last Marlboro from behind one ear as if by magic, and produced a speck of flame from his trusty Zippo upon which the words BAD ASS were engraved.

"Yeah, I know, but these trees, well, they don't look right."

Chuck said nothing, but was already thinking it to himself. The trees did look different. He first noticed it about half an hour after the turned off of 101. It was only midday, yet there was an odd, gloomy murk. Something about the shadows, the way they played tricks on the eyes, was unsettling. Dark shapes danced just on the periphery.

Chuck decided he was just not drunk enough. He polished off another Red Hook, crushed the can against his skull and, with a resonant belch, held his hand out for the next.

"Hit me."

Obediently, Rusty popped a fresh one and on cue the truck hit a dip, became momentarily airborne, then came down hard sending up a geyser of warm froth. At some point, the pavement had given way to dirt mixed with ice and snow. The truck bounced around like a rubber raft in rapids.

"Christ, don't they mind their goddamned roads out here in no man's land?" Chuck spat.

"Y'know somethin', Chuck? I ain't even sure this *is* a road."

"Course it's a road, dumbass."

"But we ain't seen—" Rusty stopped, squinted at something in the distance, then hollered, "Chuck, look! A sign! Up ahead." He bounced up and down in his seat, spilling more beer. Sure enough, up ahead a sign stuck out by the road. It read: TOOKIE'S GAS & EATS.

"We need smokes," Chuck said.

He pulled in; there were no other cars in the lot, nor any tire tracks. In fact, the place seemed deserted. The pumps were antiques, with numbers that turned on a wheel rather than a digital screen, and there were no prices listed. A handwritten sign in the window, brown and almost too faded to read, said: NIGHTCRAWLERS 1$.

"Damn. This place looks all shut down. Probably for the winter," Chuck said.

"Well, what should we do now?" Rusty asked.

Chuck slurped his beer, which got his brain juices flowing.

"Okee-doke. Here's what we're gonna do. Hand me the Persuader, willya?"

Rusty dutifully reached behind his seat and pulled out a long crowbar that had definitely seen a lot of action.

"What'cha need that for?" Rusty asked.

"We're gonna bust in, you egghead. We ain't got no cigarettes. This is serious business."

As Chuck stepped out of the cab, a blast of arctic air hit him, hard as a well-wound fist to the gut, which sobered him up a little. He felt the insides of his nostrils instantly crystallize. The mercury was probably hovering somewhere in the single digits, and that was not taking into account the wind chill. He moved around to the passenger side and dragged Rusty out by the collar.

"Awright, I'm comin'. Lemme go."

There was a good seven inches of snow. It piled against the door, and there were no footprints in sight. The place had definitely been abandoned, but for how long they could not be certain. They crept up onto the porch, whereupon Rusty unzipped and emptied his bladder. Chuck peeked into the window, but could not make anything out. He gave the door a look over and discovered, much to his surprise, that it was unlocked. It swung open easily and they slipped inside.

Immediately, a voice cawed, "Pump don't work."

An old woman leaned over the counter. Her face, shriveled as a piece of cheap jerky, lacked any semblance of compassion or geniality. A beak of a nose protruded over scaly, reptilian lips.

Chuck hurriedly stashed the crowbar, and without thinking, blurted out, "Uh—pack o' Marb one hundreds."

She squinted her bird eyes.

"We ain't got no cigarettes."

"No cigarettes?" He could not wrap his head around that one. "Uh—Awright, never mind. Say, Delacroix Notch around here someplace?"

"Delacroix Notch?" There was hostility in her voice.

"Yeah. Me an' my buddy here are lookin' to do some deer huntin'. Heard Delacroix Notch was the place."

She shook her head. "You're a ways off from the Notch, but if you're lookin' for game, I know a better place. It's not far from here, and there's plenty of deer. In about four miles or so this road comes to a dead end. Just park there, and head on in." A wide toothless grin spread across her face. Chuck noticed something about the counter. It was a chopping block, the type a butcher might use. The surface was crusty with dark stains. He backed off and regarded his surroundings. There were hundreds, perhaps thousands of tiny fairy statuettes. Or at least they kind of resembled fairies. Unlike the storybook variety these were ugly little things, more like winged goblins than anything else, with leering faces and long barbed fingers. It creeped him out the way their little glass eyes stared.

Behind the counter hung a painting of a large man, only he had the legs of a bird, and a long forked tongue like a lizard. He was eating an infant, and behind him the walls of his lair were covered with pale skins, presumably from other children.

Rusty asked, "What's up with all these dolls an' stuff? They're kinda freaky."

The hag chuckled, a coarse, inhuman sound, like a bullfrog.

"You don't like my collection?"

Rusty poked at one of the figurines, which looked old and expensive. A tiny hand-painted wing snapped off and floated to the floor like an autumn leaf carried by the wind.

"I don't know. They're kinda weird. What are they supposed to be anyway? Fairies or somethin'?"

The woman croaked, "Some might call 'em that. They got many names, the old ones. Been on this earth a long time." There was an ominous color in her tone.

"What're you talkin' about? There's no such thing as fairies an' stuff," Rusty said.

"They're out there. Men just don't know how to look, an' that's just as well. They ain't the cute pixies you seen in movies. They don't grant wishes. They used to be feared. They eat people you see. They're particularly fond of . . ." she licked her lips ". . . the liver."

A mouse scurried out across the counter, and with the precision of a hawk she snatched it up quick. Chuck noticed something strange about her hands. They were more like talons, with gnarled, misshapen fingers and nails that curved to a point. She squeezed the tiny rodent until the insides came through her fingers.

"Nasty pests." She smiled.

Chuck's stomach lurched.

"Well, thanks. We'll just be going now."

He grabbed a hold of Rusty and started out the door.

"Happy hunting boys," she shouted after them.

The truck fired out of the parking lot and kicked up a spray of ice and dirt as it went.

"Dude, that lady was weird," Rusty said.

"Weird? She was outta her freakin' mind." Chuck felt a little spooked himself, although he would not let it show. He pressed down on the accelerator and cracked a fresh Red Hook to ease his nerves.

They proceeded four miles to the dead end, parked as instructed, and set off into the woods.

Chuck felt uneasy from the get go. The peculiar manner in which the trees melded with the shadows had a disorienting effect. It was difficult to judge how far away anything was. He clutched the rifle tightly.

Out of the blue, Rusty said, "Hey Chuck. You hear that? Sounds like people talkin'."

They stopped and listened, but there was only the soft creaking of trees bending in the wind.

"Ain't nobody talkin', you egghead."

"Wait. Can't you hear it?" Rusty tilted his head in a rare display of concentration.

Chuck strained to hear. There was something, a faint whispering. The noise swirled around them; there was no way to pinpoint where it was coming from.

"Hello?" Chuck shouted.

Silence.

He was about to call out again when Rusty said, "There's a naked chick over there." His voice was low and distant, like he was in a trance.

"For Christ sakes, Rusty, I really am gonna pop y—"

And he saw her. The girl was stunningly beautiful and completely nude, with ivory skin and full breasts. She stood about thirty yards away, seemingly unaffected by the cold, and stared back at them with blank eyes.

Chuck dropped his beer.

"Hey baby," Rusty hollered. He catcalled, and made wild humping motions.

"Shut up, you jackass. I'll handle this."

"You got a name, honey?" Rusty said, not shutting up. She seemed not to have heard him.

"You all right? You hurt?" Chuck asked.

Again, she said nothing.

He took a cautious step towards her. Without a word she turned and disappeared into the thick underbrush.

"Awww, Chuck. You done spooked her."

The sight of a beautiful naked girl fleeing was all too much for Rusty and he took off in hot pursuit, still carrying the full case of Red Hook.

"Rusty—"

But it was too late. In seconds he was out of sight.

"Rusty, get your fool ass back here," Chuck shouted.

No answer.

Chuck waited. A minute passed and Rusty did not return.

"Rusty, you son of a bitch. Where you at?"

Still no answer.

Another minute went by and it became clear Rusty was not coming back. Chuck picked up the trail and came to an odd discovery: there was only one set of tracks. Rusty's footprints were quite obvious—it looked like an elephant had just charged through—but there was no sign of the girl's. He ignored it for the time being and started along the path Rusty left behind, rifle at the ready. The only thought in his mind was how hard he was going to slug Rusty when he got a hold of him.

He followed the trail through the woods. Again he heard the sound of voices, louder than before but still indistinct. He could almost make out vowels, and laughter.

"That you, Rusty?"

There was no response.

The tracks led into an empty clearing and, about halfway across, they came to a dead stop. The abandoned case of Red Hook was the only evidence that Rusty had been through.

Chuck stared at the spot in disbelief. He looked back toward the woods and something caught his eye. There were thousands of tiny lights, flickering away and flitting about like a swarm of fireflies. But they were not fireflies.

"Oh my God," Chuck gasped.

His bladder let go and warmth trickled down his legs. He raised the rifle to fire, but the beer had slowed him and there were too many of them. He did not even have time to scream.

Kris Seavey is a personal trainer who lives in Northwood, New Hampshire, with four cats and a guitar. One of them is pleasant to listen to. He recently played in the pit band for *Moby Dick the Musical*. This is his first publication in an anthology.

A Lot Like Life:
An Automortography

Trevor F. Bartlett

People don't like me much. This I know and I don't blame them. I'm a very demanding person. Sometimes I'm not as articulate as I'd like to be. Sometimes I get so down that all I can do is grunt and finger. When I been fed and I'm up, I can get pretty excited, and I gibber and drool and sing really loud and try to get people to sing along but mostly they never do. I wave my arms around when I'm inclined and I get real angry when people don't understand me and then I cry. Sometimes this'll bring the waitresses close enough as I can grab 'em at and people hate that about me.

My eyesight's something kind of dreadful, so I never recognize anybody and people think I'm so rude, I'm sure, but sometimes I just don't see who they are or if I know 'em. I got to get right up on them like before I have a clue who they are and by then it's pretty much too late. Awkward, yeah, in a word, that I'll give you. And I got no peripheral vision to speak of, neither, so I'm always bashing my shoulders into people and I got bruises on me like a goddamned world atlas but welcome to my nightmare.

Pinch my lip . . . C'mon, pinch it. Does it feel numb to you?

I'm always tired, like, and didn't used to be like this. Always tired, you know, but I never sleep and when I do, I sleep in a chair. Up all night and all day most every night can wear on you. Hard to focus sometimes,

you know, and I drift away now and then even when I'm trying to pay attention or driving to the laundromat for dinner. Sometimes I'll fade out, I guess, but never on purpose and mostly I seem to just go about my business anyway. What gets to me is the dreams. You know what I dream about and it really gets to me? Get this: always I dream about being awake. Swallow that. I'm up awake, like for weeks at a shot and I finally maybe start to drift off and I get immediately the dreams about doing my taxes or driving to the laundromat. Sometimes I jerk awake and realize that I'm parked at the laundromat or the DMV so then I start screaming. Hard to tell the difference some days, if I'm really piloting this thing or not. Never felt like I was really behind the controls like I'd like, and I remember one time I woke up on the railroad tracks with a bite out of me and my coat got stolen. Never did get her name.

I got a condition, see? Like among other things, my blood's mostly thick like molasses. Don't so much pump most days as just kind of slops around by gravity. Only moves when I do, really, and I guess that's natural enough so I go to the gym whenever I remember. Mostly I get along best with the treadmill okay but even then my joints get difficult and I whine like a cracked puppy and that always gets me the looks and they hate when I borrow their towels. They peg me that I ain't no body builder, apparently, and don't seem to like it much when I sometimes jam myself into the lockers or wait in the showers. I tell you those folks at the gym can move fast when they want to.

I got a kind of sidewise staggerlurch, like a hippie sometimes since my ankle got all wrunched over and my foot it went numb and black. Skin 'tween my toes sloughs off like mashed potatoes. I got a terrible trouble with curbs, and stairs are just rotten. I fall down in the damn gravelmud sometimes if I snag a toe on the tracks when I drag myself to town, and that's no good for first impressions, either.

I suppose it'd be tough to warm up to a guy like me and you're all right not to like me. Tired and busted and grumpy and damn, you don't know what it's like when I get hungry. Man, when I get hungry, I tell you, all bets are off and I'm always hungry. All kinds of weird endorphins pumping through me and I get the twitchfits and everything speeds up and at the same time slows down and I can never explain it to anybody when it's happening and they never understand this ain't my choice and I get really mad. Man, my world'll go all kind of koyaanisqatsi on me and there ain't nothing I can do about it, and yeah, I'll bite you. We all got our crosses, I figure, but brother, don't get me hungry. You wouldn't like me when I'm hungry.

Doctor tells me the crankiness is an expectable symptom of my condition. I suppose I could blame my condition but I'm not always so sure 'cause I can't help but just hate life mostly and it don't feel at all conditional. I love parties though, and going to the mall. And the tax office never fails me or the DMV, though the other folks in line sure hate the puddles I leave and how I don't always move forward even when it's my turn so they push at me like sometimes and I stick them with my pencil.

And I'll never go to that damned hardware store again, man, I tell you that. It's just not worth it. How's the saying they say? Fastest way to a girl's heart is with a pickaxe? That's how it goes, man, and ain't it the truth, though, and I'll tell you. My memory's mostly patchy at best and I ain't the quickest study, but man, there's a lesson a body learns once and don't forget. Hardware stores, man . . . and basements and tool sheds, too, while we're on it—no good places any of 'em, all full of all damn manner of implements and some as run on fuel even though a pickaxe seems to do the job. That's the truth. Wouldn't find me dead in one of those places. That's the scary truth.

When I'm washing myself at the Dunkin' Donuts they always holler at me don't smoke in here and close the door and buy something or just get out or put that thing away so I just rock in the corner back behind the dumpster out back till they come out close enough I can show them why I got to wash so bad. I can see they don't want to know, usually, but I show 'em anyhow and they always hate when I do that but I'll smoke if I damn well please.

My car don't look like much these days and the tires are mostly flat but the trunk still works just fine. I know the gas stationary guy hates how I pull out without never paying for my fuel but seemed he hated it worse when I'd go in to bargain at him so there it is and I do us both the favor. I try sometimes to make it up by helping other folks at the pump but nobody seems all too happy with that neither as everybody's always with the shrieking at me and I tend to leave kind of a mess. And the hitchhikers are forever getting so loud how I drive with my foot like either completely off the pedal or jammed right down on the metal and traffic lights mostly don't mean so much to me. I don't know which they hate worse as when I sit at the crossroads waiting for a reason, or when I keep rolling as I'm supposed to stop, and ain't that just the story of my goddamned life. Damned if you do, damned if you don't, you know, just the story of my goddamned life.

I don't always remember where it was I parked, and you think I'm something like the shambling inescapable, well I tell you, you oughta see this town's ticket brigade. Those guys'll take you downtown every time and brother, they hate me, see, 'cause I remind them of themselves, and I'll tell you it's mutual. Seem as to move real slow like and casual but then can get all quick on you and usually when you're not looking. Those guys hate me, I know it, and that lady at the parking ticket place had me hauled out again as she don't deal so well with a citizen that has a legitimate gripe or the stains I put on her dress.

But I get rejected out of a lot of places these days and I totally understand. I recognize I don't always present so well. Skin's oily, and hair is dry. Gums are black and lips are cracked and what teeth I got left are just a foul ruin. Mouth's a goddamned breeding ground, really, and there ain't been a deodorant invented yet could put a dent in my shields. Folk never care to see how my hair comes out in clumps and not just from my head.

And people around the Square act mighty agitated sometimes when I'll put my fingers in their coffee or their dog but it's only as my hands get cold like ice. Can't feel a damn thing mostly and a body needs some warmth sometimes, 'cause I'm no good with keys or forks or needle-work. My autograph is just about hopeless which is okay by me as my checks always bounce and most days I can't remember my name so good anyhow, so I just leave the fingerprints and let it go at that. They never say thanks.

As you can imagine I got trouble working that clipperthing so my fingernails are always grown too long or cut too bloody. Always sharper than I think they're gonna be, the nails, you know, all woody thick and brown and I wonder when the damn things will just stop growing. Looking forward to the day, I tell you that, and some days I just walk the old tracks and that's what I got for hope.

Never got her name, that one, you know, on the tracks, but she was something else. Changed my whole outlook on life, didn't she, and then just left me there under the stars. On my knees and all beat up like and sticky from the tussle and looking at the heavens and all alone. I don't blame her so much as I maybe wasn't her type at the time but she was something else. She showed me, you know, what it's all about giving yourself over. You gotta learn to let go, sometimes and selflessness, man, and give yourself over. A creature don't just live off itself, you know, but it's got to be fed, like, right? A body's gotta get nourished. And you give what you got, and sometimes you get a little back and that's the way things are. Folks get this impression somehow that I'm all antisocial like but they got it all backwards 'cause I think you got to break down those barriers like and get into each other, right, or what kind of life is that?

And for one thing, I got a stink on me. A real stink, like you can see, you know, like rises off me like gas fumes. This I know, but what can you do, it just fills a room when I step in and a man can tell when he's not wanted. I call it the eight-foot perimeter, and it's quite a trick how quick it'll establish itself in a crowded bar or at the pool or in the lobby at The Music Hall and I don't blame them one damned bit. I sneeze grease and sweat syrup and got colonies of bacteria like thriving all over me. Stuff grows, eh? Life will find a way, ain't that how they say? Like, I'm a freakin' petri dish. Somebody's damned science experiment gone too far, only for real, yeah, 'cause I'm like still right here. Still right here. But, man, it can be a real fright see how shit can just spread in the real world. Always starting small, these things, little congregations in those secret places. Always from the dark corners they start and I gotta s'pose they got as much a right as you or me. Armpits, toepits, crotch and ears . . . yeah creepy enough, maybe, but who'da thought a bellybutton could ever get like this? Just goes to show, you never know what's been in the pool.

I only got two pairs of underpants left worth a damn and I ain't wearing either of 'em. Rub all you want it don't stop itching, and believe it. Skin failure's a bitch and I'm covered with the scars and nothing ever heals 'cept of course that goddamed foreskin. I'll tell you hand to god that the world just ain't the same after a foreskin heals over shut. Scratch myself all the time and on account of my jagged fingernails I get kind of scabby like and people hate it when I scratch myself and smell my fingers. They hate it worse when I have them smell my fingers. I won't lay blame as I admit they do stink pretty wretched like and the scabs never taste as good as you think they're gonna.

Like my breath? Didn't think so . . . gags me awake sometimes. Sicky sweet like old bananas and twice as many flies. Damn. You try living like this.

I saw her just one more time, a while later, you know, once, that one, at the damned hardware store and I think she didn't recognize me but by the time it was over I got my coat back. Didn't catch her name, but got my coat back except it hardly seems worth it. Got a nasty big hole punched in it now, see, and reeks like used pork. It's a lot like life. Yeah, it can be a challenge for me to get close to people but Doctor tells me good news is, I can still get hit by a train.

Raised by seagulls in the wild streets of New Hampshire's pre-gentrified Seacoast, **Trevor Bartlett** has prowled the alleys of Portsmouth for four decades. Having spent his youth watching movies from the dark balcony of the decrepit Civic Theater, he became manager of building's film series in its current incarnation as The Music Hall, in the late '90s. He co-authored a book about the theater's history in 2003, and after a long stretch writing promotional copy for nearly 100 films per year, he gleefully started actually speaking his mind in film reviews for the Seacoast-based newspaper *The Wire* in 2007.

Mairzy Doats

Lorrie Lee O'Neill

In a perfect world, problems don't compound one on top of the other until a breaking point is reached. No, idyllically, roads are cleared of snow for travel, gas tanks aren't running on fumes, and your entire night doesn't involve a pregnant nanny goat bleating mercilessly in pain (how human-like they can sound!) through a breech birthing with twins.

If life were fair, the coffee maker would have been programmed to start brewing at 6 a.m., not 6 p.m., the water tank wouldn't quit just when the one thing you needed most of all was a hot shower, and your sister wouldn't call you in the middle of another one of her nervous break-downs when you were trying to hold your own fragile world together.

"You're breaking up, Callie. I can't hear you!" Becca yells into her cell phone. It is only a partial truth: Network service this far out of town is sketchy. The whole truth is that Becca sees the ice on the road a mere heartbeat before her front wheels lose traction.

Tossing the phone on the passenger seat of her Jeep, Becca spins her steering wheel into the skid and fumbles for the four-wheel drive stick shift. Pumping her brakes, she feels the vehicle lurch to the left and lets out a strangled string of curses as her grill dips down with a hard bump straight into the roadside ditch.

"Crap! Crap! Crap! Crap!" she emphasizes each word as she pounds the dashboard with her balled fist.

The engine cuts out on impact, her foot having lost contact with the clutch mid-skid, and she sits listening to the ticking of the cooling dead

motor. A light snow hits the windshield without sound and quickly melts away, forming rivulets of water that make the pristine snow-covered hill looming before her seem out of focus. Under any other less-stressful circumstance, the moment would be serenely calming. But now, aware that her breath is beginning to come out in short cloudy bursts in the frigid early-March air, hypothermia becomes a real possibility.

She tries turning the motor over five times, realizing that she isn't going anywhere further by means of the Jeep. Unlatching her seatbelt, she begins rummaging around to take inventory of her supplies. A bundle of firewood, two empty sugar pails with their respective taps (have to get those up soon), an oversized man's wool flannel overcoat (that will prove useful), one snow shoe (who knows what happened to the other one), an empty bag of potato chips, receipts for the utility bills she paid in town last week, a second-hand book on organic farming, (she's read only one chapter so far), and a spare tire.

Brilliant! The word darts around in her head like an angry wasp. Frustration wells up inside of her and her father's words come flooding back.

"You don't know what you're getting yourself into, Rebecca. You have no idea. You're walking into this blindly. Think about it for a long, hard moment."

True, Becca had no idea what she was getting into at first, but she still felt compelled to assume the responsibility of the farm. The idea planted itself as a fertile seed when her frail Aunt Adella had taken Becca's hand and clasped it in both of hers. Becca felt her aunt's fingers—cold, mottled with spots and veined—tremble like tiny barn swallows flickering over her own palms.

"You can never, never leave it." The elderly woman's blue eyes held Becca's brown ones in an intense gaze. "You are needed, and you must take care of them."

Becca smiled and patted her aunt's hand, thinking about the small tribe of goats Adella had tended at the farm. She had supported herself off the sale of soaps and lotions made from their milk through a mail order business run out of her country kitchen.

Long before Becca even proposed the idea of buying out the interest of her family while the farm was still in probate, the concept of ownership and all the associated pros and cons had consumed her on a daily basis. By the time she introduced her intentions to her father, she had already quit her job as a lawyer's assistant and put her condo on the market.

Fortunately there were no liens or back taxes on the family property; no one associated or connected to her great-aunt's farm cared about it—other than what monetary value they could glean out of its sale. By the time she turned the key on the kitchen door and let the sunshine stream in, she was nearly broke but so much happier than she had been since—well, she didn't know how long.

For Becca, the farm represented many fond memories from her past; the smell of freshly-hewn hay cut by the oil-spewing 1962 John Deere with its chipped green and yellow paint, flapjacks cooked in a cast-iron pan on a woodstove, wearing oversized winter boots stuffed with several layers of wool socks to break ice on the watering troughs with her heels, hot summer days where her own sweat mingled with the sweet smell of roses gone to hip, and sipping lemonade that didn't come in a frozen can of concentrate.

She remembered being a young girl, fearful of the hens pecking at her as she reached for the warm eggs from underneath them, planting vegetable seeds in old cardboard egg cartons and putting them in the mud room to germinate, and washing the windows with the prior week's newspaper and a bottle of distilled white vinegar.

"Oh! Mairzy doats and dozy doats and liddle lamzy divey

Oh! A kiddley divey too, wouldn't you-oo?"

Aunt Adella would croon in an affected Scottish brogue. "Now, how does that go again, my dear little Becca?"

"Mares eat oats and does eat oats and little kids eat ivy,

Oh! A kid'll eat ivy too, wouldn't you!" Becca would sing back to her in a fit of giggles.

Becca, fifth generation of McMurphys to inhabit the farm, felt a personal inspiration to breathe fresh life into the rustic heirloom.

Yet here she is now, six months into it and stuck in a snowy ditch, up to her chin in problems.

She could give it all up before she buries herself deeper, but what would that mean? Running back to a mediocre career in the fast-paced city, looking for reasons to turn down invitations to social engagements that always managed to leave her feeling more and more introverted, or spending her free time nursing her sister through one dramatic hiccup in life after another?

The prospect brings a shiver to the marrow of her bones and she brushes the hair off her forehead in sight of her rearview mirror, pushing her glasses back up onto the bridge of her nose.

No. She isn't done yet. Becca takes in a breath laced with icy cold air, and blows it out in one long exhalation through puffed cheeks.

Coming up on her right side, from around the curve of the road, she hears the sound of a motor and a transmission grinding into gear. The round beams of headlights cut through the haze of snow and fall on the back of her Jeep, illuminating her rearview mirror like a lighthouse beacon.

"Thad, thank goodness!" Becca says, jumping out of the Jeep to greet the driver who sets his truck in park behind her. "Got a tow rope?"

"Might so round 'bout here," the old man says, turning about a quarter ways in his seat to try and see what cargo his cab might hold. Seated next to the driver is Thad's son, Ansel, who peers at Becca through thick scratched glasses.

"How's that there nanny comin' long?" Thad asks while he moves items around by his seat.

"As a matter of fact," Becca says, "I've was heading down your way cause she isn't doing so great. She started birthing last night, but I'm afraid she's not going to move either kid at this rate. Do you mind coming to look her over?"

"Ansel!" Thad suddenly barks, making Becca jump. Ansel shifts his attention slowly away from her and focuses onto his father's stern face instead.

"Get yourself out and find that tow rope in back," Thad orders.

Becca watches as Ansel rolls down the window and reaches outside the vehicle to unlatch the door lock. The door opens with a protesting squeal, and the younger man takes a tentative step out onto the ground as if the act of walking were painful. He lumbers around to the back of the truck in a plodding stride that gives him the appearance of being a couple of decades older than his 30-ought years.

"We'll get her all set," the elder man says. Becca isn't exactly sure if he means pulling her out of the ditch or assisting the birthing goat, so she just nods in reply, grateful for him in either case.

Ansel brings out an orange and frayed tow strap from the bed of the truck and hitches one end to the front bumper of their truck. The other end he fastens to the Jeep's frame. He climbs into Becca's vehicle to put it in neutral, and then gives his father a slight nod.

In minutes, Thad has the Jeep back on the main road. Ansel rolls up the tow strap, re-stows it in the truck's bed, and strides back to the passenger side door of his father's truck in that slow and awkward wide-stance gate of his.

"I can't get her started," she confesses to Thad, leaning in his driver's window.

"Well, should be we oughta just head on back your way now and take a look at that goat." says Thad, in his peculiar way of making suggestions that sound more like statements.

"We'll come on back for this later." He indicates the Jeep with a nod of his chin.

Ansel doesn't move as Becca squeezes by him to climb up into the cab of the truck. She notes the strange man's dirty and threadbare plaid jacket, his unkempt hair that is receding in a spiral from the top of his head outwards, giving him a monkish appearance, his red-tipped black rubber boots, his grimy and dingy jeans and his strange smell, a mixture of manure, body sweat and diesel oil.

The ride back to the farm is fraught with a silence that Becca feels an impulsive need to break. But no matter what words form in her head, her mouth can't seem to shape them into reality, nor does she find the breath to cut into the quiet. Squashed between father and son and jostled along the bumpy fifteen-minute ride, Becca struggles with a confusion of emotions; thankful for Thad and his no-nonsense, take-charge manner, and fearful of and revolted by his son, who sits stone still, staring straight ahead through his binocular-like glasses and pressing his unwelcome thigh against hers.

Relief floods over her as they pull up to the farm. Becca slides past Ansel, who stands holding the creaky truck door open for her with a dull and vacant look, a hint of a grin on his thin, dry lips. She mumbles a fast "thanks," and strides quickly into the barn.

The birthing doe is in bad shape. Becca finds her lying on her bloated side in the corner of the pen panting in short quick puffs, her bleats reduced to mere heartless grunts.

She knows breech births will most likely result in serious complications ... or worse. Becca turns away and finds herself walking straight into Ansel's chest, the pungent odor of him stinging deep in her nostrils. She stumbles backwards and breaks her fall on the pen's wooden railing.

"We'll be needin' clean blankets," Thad says, coming into the barn. He carries with him an Amalie Oil cardboard box that contains veterinarian implements, tools that he travels everywhere with in the cab of his truck. "And some boiled water."

Thankful for the interruption, Becca regains her footing and eases past Ansel, then half-runs towards the farmhouse.

She hand-delivers a pile of old towels and sheets to Thad at the pen and then returns to the house without so much as a glance at Ansel. Stoking up the stove with more split wood, she sets about opening and closing cabinets, looking for a pot large enough to boil a substantial amount of water. As the pot fills with water, Becca focuses on Thad's peculiar son through the kitchen window as he walks back and forth between the barn and the truck, supplying his father with requested items.

Of course, Ansel means her no harm, or does he? He is just a little strange, that's all. And Aunt Adella had always reminded her that people come in a wide variety of colors, shapes, sizes and kinds.

"People don't get to choose who they came into this world being, and life is measurably more pleasant when you practice acceptance of others," Adella had said to her once. "It's not our place to judge others. We've got enough love and caring in us to go around for everyone."

A knock on the kitchen door's pane shakes Becca back to reality. The pot of water hasn't even started to warm when Thad walks into the room, stamping snow and barn dirt onto the welcome mat. The old veterinarian takes off his cap and sets it on a hook behind the wood stove, a gesture so familiar that he must have performed it many times over the years he tended to Aunt Adella's livestock.

"Sorry to say the nanny didn't make it, Miss MacMurphy," Thad informs her. "One kid died, but the other'n is doin' just fine. Why don't you come along and take a look?"

Becca wipes her hands on the kitchen towel and grabs her aunt's dark brown and stained waterproof jacket from the hook behind the stove. She casts a meek smile at Thad and digs her hands into the oversized pockets of the jacket, fingering the random items inside: three matchsticks, a bottle cap, a rusty bolt and washer, and two quarters.

Her mind welcomes the comforting concept that no matter what she touches or does around the farm, there is always some earmark of her aunt's presence in the guise of hidden tokens. It is as if Adella had always planned on immortality, and every last thing she did or touched was left as if to say; "I'll just take care of that tomorrow morning."

"We'll go ahead and take care of the animals for you," Thad says as they walk slowly to the barn. Becca knows he means disposing of the dead doe and her kid.

"You're gonna need some goat milk, as none of your other does are nursing or with kid. I'll have Ansel run that over to you later on." Becca nods silently in response, grateful for the elder man's expertise.

"It'll be rough goin' at first," Thad warns her. "She'll be a wantin' to nurse every two hours or so."

"Thad, I don't know how to thank you enough..," Becca begins.

"Ain't much," Thad interrupts her. "Just the way 'tis, is all."

They arrive at the barn in silence. Ansel has the muck rake out, and is spreading fresh bedding into the birthing pen. Without having to look, Becca knows that the back of their truck contains the corpses of the doe and her dead kid. The vet and his son have even removed the soiled implements, shavings and linens from the barn. It is as if, by some sterile and sanitary miracle of birth (she thinks of the nativity), this one tiny kid came into the world and stands wobbling, and shivering, on knobby legs in the middle of an immaculate goat pen.

Father and son work wordlessly in conjunction while they pack up their belongings and load them back into the truck. When Becca suggests that they send her a bill for their services, Thad waves her off and says, "Up here, we take care of our own."

Becca blinks back a tear at the implied compliment. Despite losing the nanny and the kid, perhaps through her own negligence, regardless of being "from the city" and a bit green about farming and even with all the challenges she has faced so far and failed miserably, she is still accepted by the locals.

Even before she turns back to the barn, before she wraps the fragile newborn kid in a towel, before she lifts the infant gently in her arms to carry her back to the warmth of the kitchen, she watches Thad's dented and chipped blue GMC pickup nose down the long, winding driveway.

Ansel, hunched over in the passenger's seat, seems content to focus his attention on a bundle of bloody blankets that he clutches to his chest, the content of his morbid parcel shielded from Becca's view.

Back in the kitchen, Becca places the new kid in a wooden berry crate lined with blankets and removes the pot of warming water from the woodstove. She smiles, knowing that Thad really had no use for the water after all; he had sent her into the house with a purposeless mission as a means of distraction to spare her the events unfolding in the barn.

While she waits for Ansel to return with the goat's milk, Becca sits at the kitchen table with a cup of herbal tea contemplating how to word a generic response to the pile of letters stacked beside her.

"I'm sorry to inform you that your order for 5 bars of Soft-As-Silk facial soap cannot be fulfilled, and we are returning your check in the amount of $26.45. The proprietor of Adella's Goat Milk Bath Products has passed away as of . . ." she pauses.

Is "proprietor" too official and uppity sounding?

The kid bleats at Becca as if speaking very real words, "maaaaamaaa," and sniffs the air with its soft pink nose. She stoops to run her hands over its boney, warm head as an idea forms. She could just continue Adella's kitchen-table mail order business as a means of income. Why not? If she could find Adella's recipes and formulas for her goat-milk bath products, she could simply pick up where her aunt had left off.

Inspired, she begins searching through the house, starting with Adella's recipe books in the kitchen. She yanks open utensil drawers, drawers of miscellaneous junk, and rifles through the cabinets. She removes canned goods from the pantry shelving and rummages through the linen closet. She inspects the curio cabinet in the dining room, and sorts through the paperwork in her aunt's roll-top desk.

Where would her aunt have kept all her supplies? Where did she hide her records of sales and receipts, delivery shipments and bills of goods? Where are the empty bottles and canisters, or the printed black and white labels displaying a nanny goat in profile, and "**Adella's Goat Milk Bath Products**" in Bookman Old Style font? Had her aunt stashed them somewhere in the barn?

"Ansel!" Becca almost screams his name. She came around the corner into the kitchen to find the skulking figure of the vet's son standing just inside her kitchen door, unannounced. His eyes are focused on the tips of his boots and he is holding a crate of goat's milk in 12 oz bottles. Each bottle has a rubber nipple secured to its rim.

"I suppose I ought to get used to people coming and going around here without so much as a hello," she snaps in irritation.

She manages to bring herself close enough to the strange man to relieve him of the crate and then mentally scolds herself. The man is thick-headed, that's all. Just because he is mute and creepy, that doesn't mean he is evil. Adella would have accepted him exactly for who he was. She probably fed him homemade cookies right from this kitchen when he was a boy. Perhaps he had cut her lawn or brought her the newspaper, or made deliveries to and from the post office for her aging aunt. What if he were the one who kept the John Deere tractor running, or brought up wood for the fire? Who was she to come along and make such rash criticisms?

"Look, Ansel, I'm really sorry . . ." Becca begins, brushing the hair back off her forehead and shifting her weight from one leg to the other. Seemingly unimpressed with her attempt at an apology, Ansel turns away from her and points his gaze out the window. Becca follows his unaffected stare and sees her Jeep parked in the driveway.

"Oh, you managed to get it here!" she exclaims.

With his head turned to her in profile, she notices how small his eyes really are behind his distorting glasses. When he turns back to face her, she realizes that each eye strays off in different direction, never really ever focusing fully on her. To look at her, he lowers his head and sets his attention on the middle of her forehead through his dense lenses.

In the silence that creeps through the kitchen, Becca considers some things. Could she outrun this man? Could she fight him off if he made an unwelcome move towards her? And what is that awful chemical-like odor emanating from his clothing, on top of the other offensive smells?

Becca subconsciously repositions herself, putting the table between her and the lurking figure. Unsure how to end the interview, she says; "Thank you, again, for all your help. I have some chores I need to get to, and I'm sure the kid is hungry." As if on cue, the kid bleats long and hard, which makes Becca look over at it, laughing.

When she turns back to face the door, Ansel is already through it and closing it silently behind him.

By two o'clock in the morning, Becca is down to only six bottles of goat's milk. The kid finally drops off to sleep, giving her a much-needed respite. Easing silently into the outdoors to take in some fresh air, she wanders over to the barn where the bright moon lays long gray shadows across the ground, like brushstrokes of watercolor on the untouched snow. The birthing pen is empty, but there are six other nannies standing in the adjacent pen, nuzzling and chewing at the wood barrier.

She should go get some sleep, but her mind races. Could she really make a go at a life up here in the backwoods? Could she resurrect her aunt's mail-order business? Is Ansel a potential threat or a harmless simpleton?

As she stands, she hears a small, scurrying noise come from the dark far corner of the barn—most likely a rat or a mouse. She reaches out to touch the head of the nearest goat tugging at her coat sleeve when she hears a new sound; a low murmur as if a person is humming a wordless tune. Straining harder to hear, she listens for a few more moments, frozen until she makes out the particulars of the ditty and recognizes it as a nonsense song her aunt used to sing to her.

Oh! Mairzy doats and dozy doats and liddle lamzy divey

Oh! A kiddley divey too, wouldn't you-oo?

The humming continues from the area in the back corner where light from the moon can't quite reach; a place that even the spiders refuse to build their webs for lack of life. With her hand still poised in mid-air, Becca feels her heart pounding hard against her sternum.

Oh! Mairzy doats and dozy doats and liddle lamzy divey . . .

"Hello?" she manages to squeak out of her constricted throat. All at once the humming stops and the barn is consumed with a deafening silence. Even the goats have turned to face the rear of the barn from which the ditty had issued, chewing with indifference.

She backs slowly out of the barn, trying to convince herself that she is simply overtired; her mind is playing tricks on her. She is sure that, come daylight, she'll find nothing amiss in the barn after a thorough inspection.

Outside, under the light of the moon again, she turns toward the house intending to walk calmly back to it like an adult, not a frightened little girl. After two steps her legs nearly buckle. From a distance of several yards, Becca catches a quick glimpse of a two-legged hunched figure lumbering across her back lawn towards the woods behind the farmhouse. Not entirely human in appearance, but appearing to be clad in clothing, the creature stops and turns in her direction once, before undertaking a galloping lope to reach the cover of the far brush.

Becca sprints for the house, charges through the kitchen door, trips over the threshold and sends herself sprawling across the floor. Spinning around on her butt to kick the door shut behind her, Becca suddenly freezes. She feels herself quivering uncontrollably, her eyes widened in stunned disbelief.

There, stacked neatly in the corner of her kitchen away from the damaging heat of the woodstove, are half a dozen cartons of Adella's Goat Milk Bath Products, neatly packaged, sorted by item, and ready to ship.

By noon the following day, Becca jolts awake. Sunlight is filtering into the living room where she had spent the night on the couch under an old quilt. Throwing off the heavy covering, she half-runs to the kitchen to check on the all-too-quiet baby kid and finds the newborn teetering across the kitchen floor inspecting everything with its curious nose.

She opens the refrigerator to grab one of the last remaining bottles of goat's milk when her hand stops. There, on the bottom shelf, are twenty more fresh glass bottles with rubber nursing nipples. Turning around, her eyes fall on the blockade she had constructed against the kitchen door in the early morning hours; a lamp table, an overstuffed floral divan, a coat rack with wrought-iron hooks, a bar stool and the heavy oak bureau from the front hallway. None of it appeared to have been moved since she packed it up against the door.

"How in the . . . ?" Becca turns back to the stocked refrigerator to blink and confirm what she is seeing. She takes out a sealed nursing bottle with a shaky hand and sets it in a pot of water warming on the stove.

"I'm absolutely *not* losing my mind," she mutters.

Addressing the baby kid as she tests the milk's temperature against the inside of her wrist, she says; "This is going to have to stop. I may not be from here originally, but this isn't right. People around here simply feel it's okay to just walk right into other folk's homes any old time they want. And I don't like it."

That's what Callie needed to do, Becca concluded, suddenly

wrapping her thoughts around her younger sister. Callie ought to just face her problems straight on instead of letting things build up to the point were her entire life crumbles and then come running to Becca, expecting her to pick her up and set her right again.

There are minor inconveniences in life, like being fired from another dead-end, low-paying job, or realizing you gained six pounds by drinking too many fruity happy-hour specials and worrying that your boyfriend no longer finds you attractive. Or totaling your last car before you've even paid six months on it because you were driving back from a party stoned out of your mind, and now you just can't decide which replacement to buy—the cute little blue one or the yellow convertible?

How do these issues manage to melt her sister's reason into a puddle of drama and self-pity? There are limits; there are boundaries. Becca knows this. That's exactly why Aunt Adella placed her trust in her to take on this farm.

"Promise me you'll take care of them." Her aunt's dying words haunted her.

After all, there are other issues in life, like putting on a pair of baggy overalls and kneeling in a greasy puddle in the basement to fix the water heater pump; bucketing feed and water into the barn and wheeling out a barrelful of manure; hauling armloads of firewood into the kitchen; herding the animals out to the lower field; worrying about hungry coy-dogs the whole time they're out there; feeding a new-born kid every two hours in your kitchen—and never once feeling the urge to complain to your sister about it for hours on end.

That Callie and Becca are related at all makes her stop and won-der. Where Callie sticks her head in the sand like an ostrich refusing to address a problem, Becca digs her heels in and gets right down it. How different could two sisters possibly be?

So yes, that's what she is going to do. She'll head on down to Thad's farm this very evening and sit down with him to explain her position on this issue. There is no harm in that, is there? It will be just two friendly neighbors working things out over a cup of coffee.

She'd even bring some home-baked muffins as a peace offering. They could sit and chat about Adella's Goat Milk Bath Products; how the cartons mysteriously appeared in her kitchen, and about the lack of materials, supplies and recipes at the farmhouse. Perhaps she'll casually suggest that Ansel be instructed to knock before entering her home, and she may even ask Thad about the odd things she thought she heard and saw in the earlier hours of this morning.

But first there are the chores to attend to.

By four o'clock, Becca has the water heater pump running smoothly, the animals are all fed and bedded for the evening, the coffee maker is reprogrammed, the kitchen's wood pile is well stocked, and she has a dozen raspberry muffins baking in the stove. Taking a flashlight, she throws on a plaid wool jacket and a pair of galoshes and walks out to the barn.

The sun is still low in the sky, affording her some light to guide her. First she inspects the goat pen to make sure all are secure for the night. Next, aiming her beam towards the back of the barn, she follows it tentatively. In the ray of light before her she recognizes an old wooden wheel barrow stored in the upper beams, a hay rake leaning against a low dusty window, two canisters of motor oil, a stack of quart-size berry buckets, four stainless steel milking buckets, a pair of leather boots flopped over like hound dog ears and an engine block on wooden boards suspended between two saw horses—nothing out of the ordinary for a barn.

Inching her way further into the coldest and darkest area, she feels a wisp of air blow the hair off her forehead, as if an invisible hand had reached to brush it out of her eyes. She feels a chill creep up her spine, but takes two, three, four reluctant steps closer into the dark and cold, sweeping her flashlight to the left and the right.

Here the floor is slightly more giving than the main section and almost spongy underfoot. She notices that it's also clean, as if intentionally swept, and there are no items stored in this corner. Her beam arcs up to the roof where a wooden pulley and rusty chains dangle from the overhead rafters, sweeping over an abandoned swallow's nest resting between the cross beams. She traces her light down the unadorned wall and fixes it on the floor. Fishing inside her pocket, Becca removes a slip of paper, a gas station receipt, and places it on the barren floor. As soon as she releases it, the paper skims across the floor and rises up, like a leaf in autumn, and swirls past her head.

With her flashlight tucked under her arm, she uses her hands to feel along the back wall, applying pressure as she moves along the face of it. Suddenly the boards give. She presses harder and the boards push outward. The back section of the barn swings away with a groan and she stares out at her darkening farmyard through a secret barn entrance.

Becca flits her flashlight beam across the lawn and sees a series of prints in the snow leading away from the barn and her house, and then disappearing into the woods. She calculates by the tread that the impressions were made by a pair of boots.

So the figure she had seen last night had been a human after all.

She follows the path from the barn to the house and then off to the line of trees at the back of the property. She keeps the flashlight trained on the trail, hastening to find where it might end.

At the tree line, Becca kneels down and trains the light first on the prints, clearly boots, leading into snowline at the edge of the field, then on the prints heading into the labyrinth of trees. These, she notices, are the imprints of cloven hooves.

Her mind swirling, Becca heads back to the kitchen. She gathers up the muffins in a basket, secures the kid in a make-shift pen made of sofa cushions, various furnishings and duct tape and throws on a heavily padded jacket.

Surely the old veterinarian who has lived and practiced his trade in this region his entire life will have some answers for her. Climbing into the Jeep, she tries the motor. It sputters, coughs and dies. Now what is she to do? Resting her head against the steering wheel, she lets out a heavy sigh of frustration.

But, wait, the John Deere tractor still runs!

Grabbing her basket of muffins, Becca ties a scarf around her head and adds another overcoat to her first layer. She turns the tractor's motor over and pulls some leather blacksmithing gloves over her hands.

In a plume of oily smoke, she backs the antique beast out of the barn as the nannies circle and stamp in the far corner of their pen. Easing the equipment's narrowly gapped front tires down the driveway, Becca works the clutch until she finds third gear.

Sputtering along at 20 miles-per-hour, she keeps the machine aimed down the main road in the direction of Thad's farm with burps of blue cloud following behind her. She laughs, imagining what kind of impression she's making, but her heart is already feeling much lighter. What would the people in her "old life" think of her now? No matter. Thad will help her. Thad will ease her mind.

With her farm four miles behind her, Becca's thoughts settle on the poor pregnant doe and kid she recently lost. In due time she will have to search for a buck to sire more kids. As for now, with none of her six nannies producing milk, there's no way she can start to make the soaps and lotions that Adella built her cottage business on. Maybe she can pay Thad to use of one of his bucks to sire more kids for her until she can afford one of her own.

Then it occurs to her.

With no billy-goat at the farm in the last six months, how did that nanny manage to become impregnated with twins?

As she pulls into the drive at Thad's farm she spots Ansel coming out of the barn carrying a sack of feed on his shoulders. Becca manages a weak smile and cuts the John Deere's motor out.

"Hello," she calls out. "Do you know where your father is?"

Ansel turns slowly and looks back at the barn door. Taking this as her cue, Becca jumps down off the tractor and starts walking towards the barn. Before she is able to come within a few yards of the door, Ansel steps between her and the building.

"Ansel . . ." but before she can utter another word, Ansel drops the bag of feed on the ground with a thud and claps Becca's wrists in his large, rough hands.

"What do you think you're doing?" Becca struggles to get free but his hold is unbreakable.

The basket of muffins she is carrying flips over and dumps its contents on the ground. She smells his horrible acidic body scent, and turns away from his hot breath on her face.

"Let me go!" Becca yells, twisting within Ansel's deadlock hold.

"Release her," says a firm voice from the barn doorway. Becca feels Ansel's grip loosen and she yanks herself out of his hands.

Standing in the doorway is Thad, holding two fresh pails of milk in either hand. He nods at Ansel who backs away from Becca. Ansel stoops down to hoist the bag of feed back onto his shoulder, and then steps back as if he had never touched her at all.

"Thad . . ." Becca begins, but stops short. Gone is the benign countenance of the wise and fatherly farmer. Instead, Becca is met with a cold, hard glare from an unfamiliar man.

"We're not used to unannounced visitors," Thad says. He jerks his head in the direction of the barn, and Ansel steps around Becca, heading towards the barn. "What is it that I can do for you, Miss MacMurphy?"

"Thad, I . . ." she stutters, feeling ridiculous for standing there like a vulnerable child; having come seeking comfort but being met with a scolding instead.

Then the irony hits her; the real reason why she is here. She needs to discuss Ansel's invasion of her *own* privacy.

"There seem to be some strange things going on at the farm," Becca blurts out. "Perhaps you might be kind enough to fill me in on a few of them."

Thad stands still, watching Becca closely, weighing his next words carefully.

"Perhaps you oughta just come inside with me," he finally says, a sense of defeat pressing on his wrinkled brow.

Thad sets down the buckets of milk and turns back towards the barn doors.

"You don't always get to choose who you come into this world being," he says.

Becca hesitates. Those were Aunt Adella's exact words to her so many years ago!

"You see, Miss MacMurphy . . . life up here is right awful hardscrabble." Thad picks up his cap and scratches his head.

"It was worse'n your great-great granddaddy's time. Not a lot of folk was settled in this area, especially not a lot of women. Not but a handful could hack the hard life."

Then Becca hears a child laugh, from behind Thad, coming from the interior of the barn. His hand poised on the door, Thad scrutinizes Becca's confused face.

Oh! Mairzy doats and dozy doats and liddle lamzy divey . . .

Becca peers back at Thad, a question frozen on her face.

"The MacMurphy family tree goes a long way back," Thad tells her, ". . . and it includes branches that not a lot of people know about. Nobody ever sees."

Thad pulls the door back, its wheeled track squeaking for lack of oil.

In the low light of the gas-lit barn, Becca takes in the scene unveiling before her. Seated at low benches along the whole length of the barn is an assortment of people, half-human, half-goat.

A woman (or is it?) seated nearest to her is applying Adella's Goat Milk Bath Products labels to a stack of glycerin soap. Her head bears two nubs where horns may have grown, and when she smiles at Becca, her teeth are pushed forward in a narrow underbite.

A child giggles and dives under the table, chasing after a ball, his eyes positioned far apart on the sides of his head. Ansel, seated on a bench, gives Becca his customary blank stare and rubs the sore hoof he has extracted from his red-tipped black rubber boot. Nursing bottles, like those delivered to her farm, sit empty on the bench beside him. He lifts a blanketed bundle from a crate at his feet and pulls back the linen to reveal the sleeping distorted and elongated face of a newborn half-human, half-goat infant.

"Pan," Ansel says, the only word he's ever spoken to her since she's known him.

This is the other twin.

"The world just won't accept them, can't accept them," Thad says. Becca's hand strays to her mouth and flickers like a hummingbird.

"But," Thad adds, "they *are* family. Generations."

Becca braces herself up against the frame of the doorway, the latch pressing into the small of her back. The barn, she notices, has been set up like an assembly line. In full force, from raw milk to finished product, is the production of Adella's Goat Milk Bath Products. Empty boxes and cartons line the back wall, as goat-people manage the stirring, pouring, molding and mixing of Adella's various goat milk by-products.

A goat-child, teetering on hoofed feet, tentatively approaches Becca. He reaches out a malformed hand; a hand consisting of four human digits and a protrusion like a split-hoof in the place of a thumb. He grasps her hand and tugs on it.

"I want a bike," the child tells her, and holds out a picture torn from a magazine, "a real bike!"

Becca summons the presence of mind to kneel down to his level, and takes the picture of the bike from the clutches of the goat-child.

"Well . . ." Becca tries to swallow, her throat sore and dry, her voice raspy. "What a fine looking bike!"

"Do you think they have it in blue?" the goat-boy inquires.

"I'm sure I could ask," she tells him. Thad affirms her with one of his signature paternal smiles.

For Becca, reason starts falling into place. No, this isn't a perfect world. Things don't always turn out the way you expect. Life certainly isn't fair. But you deal with your lot. You handle what life hands you. You can let it buckle you under, or you can face it head on. That's what Aunt Adella had done.

That's what she will do too.

 Born in Peterborough, New Hampshire, **Lorrie Lee (Hammond) O'Neill** grew up in the Monadnock region of the state, and graduated from Dublin High School. She attended Emerson College in Boston where she received her Bachelors of Fine Arts in creative writing, literature and publishing. Lorrie's writing history includes publication of poetry, magazine articles, newspaper articles, radio and television script writing, business writing and press releases. This is her first published fiction short story. "I thoroughly enjoyed the refreshing and inspiring challenge that this project has offered me," Lorrie says.

Road Rage

Gregory L. Norris

A mechanical thunderclap blasted through the kitchen. Steff reached for the radio's volume as the last of the emergency bleats powered down.

"This is a safe travel advisory," an emotionless female voice droned. "Please be aware that this advisory may change without notice or warning, but that the federal government will do its best to update you as information becomes available. Travel to the Boston Green Zone is now recommended for the following New Hampshire counties: Rockingham, Merrimack..." It rattled off two more before finally announcing, "...Hillsborough."

Steff exhaled a bottled breath and turned toward the bags she'd readied for the drive. The power had still been on when Andrew killed the old woman. Ever the smart and organized one, Steff had boiled the few dozen eggs they found in the fridge on the gas range and then stored them in the basement freezer, which still hadn't fully thawed. The last of the eggs, peanut butter sandwiches, woody fruit from a tree on the property, and two gallons of bottled water were packed in canvas shopping bags, along with the weapons they'd accumulated, survival necessities, and Steff's personal organizer.

"...avoid back roads and Route 28. Stick to Interstate 93, where you will encounter military checkpoints and assistance. Avoid contact with contaminated individuals and any shrouded bodies you may encounter at roadsides, as these have been treated and laid as bait for the infected

and are part of the military's ongoing solution to resolve the present crisis . . ."

"Come on," Andrew said, heading to the kitchen door.

"Wait," Steff hissed.

"Why?"

She tipped her chin at the backpacks and bags while lowering the volume and picking up the radio. "We can't leave without—"

Andrew grunted and grabbed the bags. So typical of him, she thought. Like a lot of men, Andrew walked through life wearing invisible blinders, aware only of what was staring him directly in the face, never the bigger picture. Never tomorrow, or the day after that. Leave the food and their weapons behind and find your stomach aching and empty—or hanging open, entrails exposed, because you forgot to bring the foot-long carving knife you pulled out of the old woman's butcher block.

He huffed an expletive under his breath on the return march to the door.

"Keys?"

Andrew jiggled his pocket. It wouldn't surprise her if he'd left them on the table. While waiting for the update, she'd caught him playing with them, along with his old credit cards, which he'd folded into plastic footballs to punt around the kitchen with his idle fingers.

Steff hated the sight of him, especially how, since the world went to hell, he'd stopped shaving. She still put on a morning and evening face, applied deodorant, and the occasional spritz of perfume while Andrew grew steadily hairier and more odious. She was the brains of the outfit, no doubt, and always had been. But she'd also contributed mightily to the brawn. Case in point: when the old woman had tumbled down the stairs, somehow picked herself up from a mess of compound fractures, and lurched at Andrew. Knocking her block off her shoulders with three hard swings of a cast iron skillet had evened them up: fourteen kills apiece since setting out for Boston. The old woman hadn't been any easier to take down than Steff's share of the dead bikers who'd cornered them in Concord. The Brains *and* the Brawn. Steff wasn't pleased.

She only wanted to get back to the way things were, when the world ran to a schedule. When there was order and reason. Grabbing her purse—which still contained her credit cards, because you never knew if they'd need them in the Green Zone—she reached into the correct bag and withdrew the carving knife. She'd gotten good at wielding a blade. Blades, axes, shovels, golf clubs, even frying pans. Practice made perfect—and she'd gotten plenty since the outbreak turned the world upside down.

Heart galloping, Steff opened the door. They hadn't nailed over the windows because too much banging to secure the place would invite unwanted attention. The old woman was plodding around upstairs when they'd broken into the farmhouse, arguing over details that no longer mattered. They'd dumped her in a flower bed; now she was more fragrant than anything else in bloom. Steff caught a whiff of her as a billow of humid night air swept into the kitchen. Andrew swore again.

"Shut up," Steff admonished. "You want them to know we're here?"

Andrew started to argue, but Steff spun around, got up in his face, and aimed a self-manicured finger right at his lips—lips submerged beneath a week's worth of prickle. Andrew shut up. He wasn't the smartest man on the planet, but at that moment he showed excellent judgment.

A bloated full moon grinned down from the sky, bracketed by wisps of sallow-colored clouds. The moon's size shocked her. Had it swung closer to the earth in its orbit, or had cowering in a succession of cellars, strange houses, and—for two memorable weeks—garden sheds left her shell shocked and unaccustomed to being outside, in the open? She thought about asking Andrew but didn't. Andrew was useless. Why welcome unnecessary aggravation (or worse) by inviting that most-galling of Andrew phrases: *I don't know what to tell you, babe.*

The moon looked bigger, closer and, given the fundamental shift in the world since the previous spring, she could believe that it was.

The one right thing she credited Andrew with was parking their car in the farmhouse's winding driveway to face out, toward the road. Turning the car around had felt like the longest ten seconds of Steff's life, almost as terrifying as the trek around the house to reach the kitchen door. Andrew had started the car twice over the past week to insure the battery wouldn't die, leaving them stranded.

Unlocking the door, getting into the car, and then closing it seemed to take forever, the seconds passing with the weight of minutes. Steff jumped into the front passenger's seat, convinced that hands were grabbing at her, from the shadows. Filthy, diseased hands, seeking to claw at her throat and drag her back into the night.

She slammed the door, a loud and unwise action given that Andrew hadn't yet inserted the key into the ignition. Steff cursed herself, but him even more. In typical Andrew style, he took his seat, buckled his belt, adjusted the rearview mirror, and played with the lights before starting the damn car or waiting to see that it even would.

"Hurry up," she groused, corner-of-the-mouth.

"Calm down," Andrew said.

A hand pounded on the trunk. Startled, Andrew dropped the keys.

A low, throaty moan burbled in the shadows behind them.

At that moment, Steff realized the depth to which she hated him. Hated his inefficiency, his lack of focus and instinct for self-preservation. But the burning emotion was quickly smothered by cold, naked fear. It slithered over her flesh, spurred on by the jarring screech of nails dragging along the trunk, to the rear wheel well on the passenger's side. Closer, coming closer toward her.

She forced her eyes to the mirror and caught a hulking outline, silhouetted in the giant moon's silver glow. It was missing a section of shoulder, a jagged chunk bitten right out of the meat, which explained the dragging arm and scraping nails that had reached all the way to the rear passenger's side door. It was so close now she could see its dead, full moon eyes.

A scream clawed its way up Steff's throat. She choked it down as the engine turned over, blasting out more noise than she'd heard since taking down the old woman. Andrew gunned the gas and peeled out, just as the ominous shadow pulled even with Steff's seat and was creeping at the edge of her vision. The car lurched forward in a squeal of tires and fan belt. She half expected the engine to stall. It didn't, and she swallowed the scream, bottling it in her stomach, where she worried it would settle into the soft tissue and turn cancerous, like so many others she hadn't released.

The car tore down the driveway, bumping over divots and a fallen branch.

"Which way?" Andrew shouted.

"Which way *what*?" Steff fired back, unable in her panic to comprehend what he was asking her.

"Right or left?"

The country road appeared ahead of them in the car's headlights. How could he not know they needed to go left? They'd turned right into the farmhouse, hoping to find not only shelter but fresh vegetables in a garden, not suspecting the old farmer's wife had only gardened marigolds and posies for Christ-knew-how-long. Or that she was lolling about upstairs, ravenous for blood.

"*Left*," she spat, aggravated that she had to remind him.

But, she remembered, this was Andrew. Andrew who, in the old, sane world, would drive around aimlessly for hours instead of pulling into a gas station to ask for directions; who'd never met a map he liked and almost always took the long way around, rarely the shortest, most-direct cut.

"Watch it!"

"I see it," he snapped in response.

It was a pickup truck, lying on its side, directly ahead of them. Andrew drove around it and over the remains of the corpse in the road. Steff tried to ignore the sickening crunch of wheels over bones, felt the vibrations, shuddered.

"Radio?" he asked.

The car only had satellite, which was useless now. She turned through the dial on the transistor until she found a signal.

". . . a safety corridor, leading down to the Boston Green Zone. Be advised of traffic jams as you near the city and expect to pass through multiple security checkpoints. Please cooperate fully with the authorities, who are doing everything they can to help you. Remember, it is imperative to avoid any and all shrouded corpses you might encounter at roadsides and in open areas. These are part of a vital step in controlling the infected populace and should be considered extremely dangerous."

"This road leads to the highway?"

"Yeah, about ten miles ahead, remember?"

"No," Andrew snapped.

"Right after that big natural food outlet in Bedford. You know—"

"I don't know what to tell you, babe," he said.

Had they not seen the red lights up ahead, Steff might have killed him then.

"See that?"

"Yeah," he said.

"See what's chasing it?"

The vehicle numerous lengths in front of them made a turn. As Andrew matched it, their car's headlights strobed the backs of half a dozen racing bodies, each in pursuit. Andrew accelerated.

"Don't get too close," Steff said.

"Stop telling me how to drive."

"Two extra eyes, in this case, is a bonus."

"I know what I'm doing!"

Steff turned away, shaking her head. There were times, she swore, when he would have driven straight off the edge of a cliff just to spite her for pointing out the danger, taking her with him to prove some ridiculous point.

As she eschewed this ugly truth about her husband of six years, he ran over one of the infected individuals chasing their new travel buddy. Steff saw the face of the man—what had been a man, at another time—before the car collided with him going fifty-two miles per hour. The lanky bag of puss, what had once been somebody's son, brother, perhaps husband, sailed over the hood and briefly connected with the windshield before rolling over the roof and landing on the road.

"Are you crazy?" Steff shrieked.

"Fucker came at me."

"You idiot! What if you broke the windshield? How the hell would we get to Boston?"

"Looking through spider webs, I guess. But I didn't break it, did I? Huh? *Did I?*"

No, but he did dislocate one of the wipers, which they discovered when Andrew tried to wash the umber splatter of fermented blood off the windshield, on Steff's side.

"Do that intentionally again and I'll—"

"You'll what?"

Kill you, she thought. But she didn't say it out loud.

Apparitions chased the small convoy of cars responding to the emotionless beckon of the emergency alert voice that promised safety within the Boston city limits; ghosts in the shadows, the howling damned, driven mad with hunger and primitive emotion. Horns blared, proof of safety in numbers. Only Steff didn't feel safe.

A female with matted blonde hair and one eyeball threw itself at her window when a pileup on the last leg of the country road forced Andrew to slow the car. The glass barely smothered the creature's screams.

"Shit," she heard Andrew curse through the cacophony of wild, rabid barks.

"Do something, will you?" Steff pleaded.

"I am—I'm keeping us from going into a ditch, so zip it."

In order to circumnavigate the pileup, the convoy was forced onto the soft shoulder, over a patch of sedge and at a precarious angle. The she-devil matched their course. Andrew turned onto the detour. The car in front of them dug in, chewed its way through, kicking up dirt. The world then canted to the right and, for several terrible, horrifying seconds, Steff had the sensation of falling toward the dead woman's snapping mouth and the clotted seam where an eyeball should have been. Steff's face struck the window. The creature, running along her side of their car, lunged. She felt the impact, heard the scrape of its teeth on the glass, even through her screams and Andrew's swears to shut up, would she, *just shut the fuck up*!

Then the world righted to its normal plane and the road ahead widened. The organic grocery outlet appeared on their left, along with the ramp to the interstate and the first sign of the military they'd seen since Concord. Steff counted eight troop transports in the store's parking lot. Uniformed men on the roof were tossing bodies in white shrouds over the edge.

Shrouded bodies littered the roadside. The she-devil with the destroyed face ceased lusting after Steff and fell upon one of the corpses. As the distance between them widened, a powerful explosion rocked the night. A bloody, burning chunk of meat slapped the rear windshield.

"Are you kidding me?" Steff chortled, aware of the mad, disconnected sound of her own voice. "They're booby-trapping those dead bodies with explosives?"

Another blast lit the darkness, this one in the parking lot.

"Whatever works," Andrew huffed.

Struggling to breathe, Steff covered her eyes with shaking hands and tried to forget what she'd had to endure in less than ten miles of travel—and what she might yet be forced to face in the sixty-plus that separated them from Boston.

"You need to calm the fuck down," Andrew grumbled.

Steff wasn't aware that she'd started crying until her breath hitched with a sob and the rant she wanted to lace into him with log-jammed behind it, choked off and then choked down to fester with the rest of the anger and terror in her gut. Calm down? She pinched her eyes and found them soaking wet.

". . . gonna be plenty of *that* between here and—"

Boom. Another explosion tore across the roadside, several car lengths back.

"—Boston, and it don't help me to have you coming apart while I'm trying to steer the fucking car. It's stressful enough, Steff."

The next explosion created a sharp whistling sound, like a teakettle only a hundred times more powerful. Turning, she saw a fiery rocket shoot straight up into the night sky, then plummet back down. A rocket with four flame-covered limbs but no head.

Stress? Was he joking?

Highlights of their journey through one war-torn town after another flashed through Steff's memory. Weeks of traveling and ducking, hiding, fighting when they had to and, above all, surviving. She was the one who'd plotted their course before the computers went down, taking the flow of information with them. She found the vehicle, the gasoline—not an easy task, because what little the hoarders hadn't seized, the fizzling power grid put out of their reach.

If left in her husband's hands, they'd be dead by now, she was sure of it. Dead and dead again, driven insane, like the she-devil that had attempted to chew its way through her window.

Steff completely understood that creature's extreme rage. Sucking in a deep lungful of the sour, Andrew-scented air helped uncork her emotions. She turned toward the driver's seat, exhaled, and mumbled something unintelligible beneath her breath. Something that sounded even to her ears like the primitive grunts of the infected.

The interstate loomed directly ahead, the green highway sign lit by a mobile spotlight. It was perhaps the most beautiful sight she had ever seen.

". . . individuals and families free of the infection that are unable to find transportation into the Green Zone on their own may do so by reaching military checkpoints where buses have been provided. Those checkpoints include the weigh station in Windham and the bypass in Allenstown. All evacuees must pass screening checks before being allowed to board government-provided transportation. Be prepared to cooperate with military, medical, and government personnel, who are doing everything in their power to assist you during this crisis."

The military presence on the highway grew, as did the procession of civilian vehicles. Steff counted twenty cars ahead of them, three behind, based upon the lights. Counting gave her something to focus her attention upon, like a nightmarish, adult version of that license plates game kids play on long drives. Going was slow, not even thirty miles per hour, and treacherous. Traffic clogged the lanes. One set of taillights would blink, and then the one behind it followed, in succession, all the way down the line. The cars crept steadily forward uniformly, weaving from one lane to the next around mangled wreckage and the occasional body.

A fire raged through the town of Londonderry. Oily, noxious smog oozed across the highway, making it almost impossible to navigate. The putrid smell of burning plastic bit into the soft lining of Steff's nostrils and throat. She refused to roll down the window when they came out of the cloud, but felt a gust of air across her cheek and heard the dull moan of wind whisking in through Andrew's.

"Put that up!"

"Huh?"

"Are you freaking crazy?" She realized that the question, once screamed, was completely rhetorical.

"No, I'm gagging on the stink of those burning houses."

Funny, she thought humorlessly, how he hadn't gagged on his own unwashed stench. "Roll up that window."

"No."

"Andrew, I swear . . ."

His hairy mouth pursed shut, but the window remained open.

"Do you want one of those things to reach in and get you?"

"We ain't seen one of those things since we got on the highway. Didn't you see the military firebombing their asses all the way to the stratosphere?"

Steff shook her head. "So you think that's reason enough to let down your guard, invite the chance for one of those things to kill you and, in the process, me? Roll up the fucking window right now!'

Andrew rolled the window, but only two-thirds up. "When you're behind the wheel, you get to make the calls. Until then, shut the fuck up and just be glad I'm saving your ass. Okay, babe?"

In a moment of shocking clarity, Steff remembered those many occasions when Andrew had fucked up before the world went to hell. The times he bought the wrong things at the grocery store, even when she'd sent him with a list; bounced checks; bad decisions that had cost him one job after another, leaving her to work even harder at her career to keep them afloat. Steff, organized Steff, who made lists and embraced goals, who never left the bathroom light on or a window open while the air conditioning was struggling to chug out cool air or bought a bottle of regular soda when she specifically wanted diet, and who still carried a calendar with her in a world where dates and months were as useless to most people as dead religions.

This was the mother of all Andrew fuck-ups. Driver's side window open. Monsters lurking in the dark. Blinders on, unable to see the bigger picture, as usual.

But it only held that notorious distinction for a few minutes, before he trumped it with a mistake even more colossal.

Stacked like cordwood, surrounded by military trucks and spotlights, bodies were being burned en masse in a patch of open field between the Londonderry and Derry exits. The pyre sent a towering funnel of yellow smoke into the sky. Steff realized the clouds written in the sky around the moon like parentheses originated here.

More bodies, this faction on its legs, followed the flow of traffic.

"Can I get a ride, lady?" a man asked, aiming his thumb in the perceived direction of Boston. "I'll pay you."

"I'll fuck you," another plodding beside him offered.

They were people, real living people, traveling on foot.

"Poor bastards," Andrew said.

A lump of lead formed in Steff's stomach, born of the kind of precognition that couples who understand one another's faults experience.

"Wouldn't want to be out there, walking in the dark," he continued.

"They don't have far to go before the weigh station."

"That's nine miles away."

"There are buses there," she said, covering her stomach, hoping to push that rotten ingot out of her system and back into the ether. No, he wouldn't do that to her.

"Look at them, babe."

"I'm looking. Keep your eyes on the road."

"Don't tell me how to drive."

And there it was. The inevitable. There would be no avoiding it, like the window, opened willingly, inviting death and chaos into the car with them, undoing all her diligent work to save their lives. She'd packed smartly, moved wisely. Even her choices of where to hole up had been on the money—Andrew was the one who'd instigated their tango with the bikers through his bumbling around in the gas station. Steff had resorted to taking up arms in order to survive because that's what you did in this chaotic, horrific new world.

"Don't do this," she threatened, begged.

"We got two extra seats in the back. Three if they squeeze in."

"And what's to stop them from slitting our throats and stealing our car?"

"You always think the worst of people."

"And you never do, except when it's about me!"

Andrew sighed. "I don't know what to tell you, babe."

"Don't you dare."

"When you're driving your car . . ."

"I got us this car, got us as far as we've come safe and alive!"

"Yeah, that's right. You're perfect. You never fuck up or make bad decisions but you know what?" Andrew's voice rose to a shout. "You also never make good ones, babe. You're worried about saving our lives. What about our souls?"

"I'm warning you, Andrew."

Andrew glanced toward the passenger's seat—not at Steff, but the window. Stragglers took shape ahead of them in the headlights.

"I'm serious—don't pull over."

But he did, navigating their car—her car—out of the orderly flow of traffic. By the time they were even with the slow-moving bodies, she was screaming at the limit of her lungs, screaming holy terror, screaming until her voice went hoarse.

The old woman with the boy stared into the window. It didn't matter that they weren't infected, part of the last desperate living populace in

Northern New England. Andrew had willingly put her life in jeopardy again, and had crossed a line from which there would be no going back.

"There's food in the back, M'am," Andrew said. "Hardboiled eggs and fruit, some peanut butter sandwiches. Help yourself."

Steff held her tongue at the notion that he was not only bargaining away their safety to strangers but also their resources.

The old woman and the boy, a snot-nosed urchin in a dirty baseball cap Steff assumed was her grandson, thanked them in words and tears. Steff didn't even flinch when she heard them rustling around in her neatly-packed bags, touching her things, her organizer and its many important lists, shuffling their weapons aside, out of order and accessibility in their scramble to find the food. She didn't say a word, not one, merely sat in her seat, feeling the air from Andrew's open window crawl across her flesh, aware of the smug little smile on his rotten, unshaved face. Getting his way, apparently, was so much more important to him than playing it safe. Helping out complete strangers took priority over protecting his own wife.

He'd done it to spite her, not soothe his soul. This was Steff's punishment for being right.

"I only wish I could have saved more people," he blathered.

Such the hero, she thought. And he was—to complete strangers, to people who didn't know what a mean child, what a loser, what a total piece of shit he was beneath his tarnished suit of armor.

But she let him have his moment of glory and didn't say a word, not even when the old woman, her mouth full of sandwich, said, "Young lady, you are married to the finest man on the planet."

The weigh station bustled with activity, military and civilian. Armed soldiers patrolled the entrance and surrounding woods. Spotlights lit the area with a cold white glare. The images of buses, survivors huddled together a few hundred strong in columns on the pavement, even the lines in front of the portable toilets, spoke deceptively of a return to a sane earth. There was order here, organization. It empowered Steff.

They dropped off their two hitchhikers at the welcome center to be processed for boarding on one of the buses. According to a government rep, they themselves would need to be cleared at numerous checkpoints between Windham and Boston before being allowed access into the Green Zone. They could expect to have their car inspected, top to bottom, by corpse-sniffing dogs so as to insure nothing unwanted crept into the city in a trunk or under a fender. The military rationed them five gallons of gas, which gave them nearly half a tank—the American armed forces, they were told, had cleared enough abandoned vehicles from the highway as it was without people running low on fuel and adding more obstacles to the gauntlet.

They were then God-blessed, good-lucked and sent on their way south to the city.

Calmly, Steff said, "I need to pee."

Andrew slowly turned the car toward the portable toilets.

"No, I don't want to wait in line." She aimed a finger toward the far end of the parking lot and the woods brooding beyond. "Over there."

"Aren't you afraid that one of those things'll come running out of the trees and bite you on the ass while you're hunched over doing the skier's squat?"

He was mocking her again, making fun of her discomfort, her needs, her fear.

"I'll be okay. I've got you to rush in to protect me, in case an infected person somehow makes it through the soldiers. I'm married to the finest man on the planet."

Andrew pulled into a vacant spot along the pavement. Steff leaned between the seats and reached into the back.

"What are you doing?" he groused. "Thought you needed to take a leak."

Her neat, orderly bags of survival provisions were a mess. Steff fumbled through the plundered food stocks, extra batteries, the precious pharmaceuticals and cash and her organizer, her beautiful organizer, tossed aside with utter disrespect, spilling its contents onto the floor.

At long last, Steff found what she was looking for.

"I don't know what to tell you, babe," she said.

And then she drove the carving knife through Andrew's throat. The look of hatred he gave her right before he slumped over the wheel removed any and all doubt. In order to stay alive, her husband had to die.

She dumped his body at the curb and buckled into the driver's seat.

Wasting no more time, she put the car in drive and pulled back onto the highway, headed south. The only time she opened the window between Windham and Boston was at the Massachusetts border to toss out her wedding ring.

Gregory L. Norris writes for a number of national magazines and fiction anthologies. A former writer for *Sci Fi*, the official magazine of the Sci Fi Channel, and a screenwriter on two episodes of Paramount's modern classic, Star Trek: Voyager, he recently penned the handbook to all-things-Sunnydale, the *Q Guide to Buffy the Vampire Slayer*. He lives and writes at the outer limits of the Merrimack Valley in New Hampshire.

Deer Island

Catie Jarvis

I. August 11

They piled up on Broad Street. Three cars full of human life, which dimmed and then disappeared before Eliot's eyes. The whole thing was caused by a deer in the road, frozen and holding its ground. The first car swerved to the right to avoid the deer and slid into a tree along the road, while the second slammed on its brakes to avoid the first car and the deer, only to flip onto its side and skid in a slow circle. The third car lost control and spun across the left lane of traffic in between two other unsuspecting cars that tried hard but couldn't quite avoid the vehicle flying sideways. The deer stood still in the middle of the lane unharmed. A doe with narrowed eyes and a white patch in the shape of a flower on her left cheek. She was lovely there amidst the ruins.

Eliot had been walking, scoping out the new area and going over the lesson he had planned for the first week of classes at Southern New Hampshire University. Now, he ran to the first car, then the second, then the third, to find that there was no one he knew how to save. He kneeled and held the head of a child, nine or ten. A boy with dark skin and smooth features who smelled of urine and rust. Blood flowed out of his side, things were still pumping, churning. The boy coughed up blood, and Eliot instinctively pulled back to avoid being splashed in the face. Eliot took off his sweater and wrapped it around the boy's middle. He applied pressure. He screamed for a doctor. He placed his cell phone by

133

his side where a taut voice chanted *Sir, please describe for me what is going on.* *Sir, I can help you. Sir, you need to pull the bodies away from the cars in case of an explosion. Sir, the medics will be there soon.* Eliot rocked the body of the boy. There was no longer breath. There was no longer pulse. Eliot pounded at the boy's chest in a meek attempt at CPR as cars and people gathered around. "A doctor, is there a doctor?" No one moved to help him. It seemed to Eliot that nothing moved at all, except his fist, pounding, pounding, and the deer, who walked slowly away from the crowd and back into the woods, satisfied.

* * *

Mary was rearranging the bedroom furniture. The long dresser, she thought, should go against the wall instead of under the window. And the bed might face the center instead of the side. She worked up a sweat pushing the large objects around and had to sit down and breathe for a few minutes. She was feeling nauseated and thought that maybe she should eat. She toasted the bread. She took out the tuna. She cleaned the lettuce and sliced the tomato. She put the sandwiches together and arranged a pickle at the side of each, certain that Eliot would be home by the time she finished. He should have been back already.

Mary ate her sandwich and wrapped her husband's up and put it away in the fridge. She finished reading the last chapter of her novel with her feet propped up on the recliner which still sat in the center of the living room since neither the couch nor the television stand had been delivered yet. And then she began to worry. She mistook the call of sirens as a meow from her cat and she went to let her in. When she opened the door her mistake was realized. There was no cat. She sat on the stoop in the front of the house and listened to the yelling sirens as the sun retracted from her knees to her toes and then onto the grass below her.

There were a lot of pine trees here, more than anywhere she'd lived before. They were tall and slender and swayed in the wind so far from the left and the right of their bases that she feared they might crack or uproot. The front yard was covered in cones with no space to walk in between. She thought of raking them up but stopped herself. The doctor had told her she should begin to take it easy now that she was in the third trimester. He did not recommend the stresses of moving across the country, but she insisted that she'd be fine, and that the move couldn't wait. It was a good opportunity for Eliot and for herself, and she had always wanted to live in New England in the fall.

As the sun moved from the backyard onto the street, Mary caught sight of Eliot coming up the road. She stretched out her legs and sighed with relief. The sight of him moving slowly, arms held out in front of him and covered in blood didn't alarm her. It was as if she had expected him to return this way.

"You're all right," she said as he approached her.

He was crying, eyes tight and squinted.

"Yeah, I'm all right. It was a car accident, I think a young boy died, they were all hurt badly. Three cars."

Mary stood, she reached her arm out to comfort her husband in some way but she couldn't find a clean place to touch him. Her arm fell back to her side.

"You need to go in and shower," she said. "That's the best thing to do. It'll be a nice night for a walk downtown, and some dinner out, I haven't even unpacked the kitchen yet so . . ."

"That's it?"

"I'm sorry Eliot."

"Just shower off?"

"People have car accidents, Eliot. People die all the time, every minute, they always have."

Eliot covered his face with his bloody hands and crumpled up there on the granite front stoop."

"It's okay," Mary said. She stroked his hair. "It had nothing to do with us."

* * *

The Nashua River widened and narrowed like a woman; she rushed with life. The deer gathered to drink of her. The water was cool and glistened in the dusk as a doe tried to catch the diamonds of light with her tongue. Every time she tried for one the water rippled and the sun jewel disappeared. Eventually she gave up.

She had gathered the local deer near the foot bridge in town. This was not a usual spot for drinking but she wished to watch the bustle. The movement and senseless chatter of people heading out in the evening.

Most walked in small clusters, slow-paced steps. Their movement was organized by lines and lights, they did not move freely. The sight of the town weighed on her. It was all hacked up, covered in bricks and pavement, and it seemed to be expanding.

She led the deer up from the river and onto the tracks, empty for now and packed with a light soil that matched the deer's skin. The deer, twenty or so, followed her in a line across town. They walked slowly and straight along the train tracks. People from the town stopped and pointed. *Sh! Look! Get out the camera. Aren't they beautiful.* The deer paraded deliberately along in their parody.

II. September 1

"The purification of water by heterogeneous photocatalysis is one of the most rapidly growing areas of interest to both research workers and water purification plants. We have finally proved that this technology can completely destroy organic pollutants dissolved or dispersed in water into harmless substances and nearly every plant in the country has taken to using it.

"The two most important recent discoveries which allowed this new technology to finally take off, after years of preparation, are light distribution inside the reactor through the absorbing and scattering liquid to the catalyst, and providing high surface areas for catalyst per unit volume of reactor. And, ta-da, the scientist becomes rich and famous, which of course is all of our number one goals."

The students in the lecture hall let out a mumble of laughter.

"This semester we are going to work to understand the photocatalysis process and reenact the tests that scientists used to prove its capabilities. Teaching this stuff to you is how I make my living, yes, but I also firmly believe that there are some of you in this room, not all of you but some of you, who can use what you learn about the trials of scientists before you, to better the current water purification technologies, maybe even move them in a new direction, a better direction.

"As we move into the future and continue to grow and dump our waste upon this world, there is nothing, I mean nothing, more important than the technology of purification. When the water goes bad, so too do we."

* * *

Mary wheeled the garbage can out to the side of the road for pickup the next morning. Her neighbor, a man leathery and small, was bringing his out as well. A chorus of wheels against the pavement.

Mary felt swollen, she couldn't sit still. She'd spent the afternoon going through every "miscellaneous" drawer in the house, throwing out what was unnecessary, or potentially hazardous to a baby, and then labeling each drawer with what it contained so that nothing would ever be lost again. She imagined that knowing every object that was in the house and where it was would provide her with clarity. Time wasn't valuable to her just now when she had so much of it, but once the baby was born and she went back to working at the university with Eliot, it would be.

"Lovely day, isn't it," said the neighbor, looking out at the road. He had a patch over his eye, petite and round like the one that Mary had worn as a child to cure her lazy eye—a poor, treacherous, burden of childhood.

"Sure is."

She introduced herself and reached out her hand—his palm was tan and dry. Perhaps he'd lost the eye in a hunting accident or some old war. She wished she had had the fortune of living next door to a nice young couple, perhaps with a child themselves—potential companions.

"They call me One Eyed John. I've always had just the one eye."

"Oh."

"Nothing to be alarmed about. The other one's fine. Where you all from?"

"California, actually."

"That's a ways away. Me, I've always been here. Other people, they come and go, but I've been here for as long as my house behind me, as long as this street, as long as that sky hanging above us. I'm just stuck here waiting. "

The man smelt like burning leaves.

"Baby's on the way?" he asked.

"A few weeks now. I can't wait. At the start I dreaded the idea of it coming out of me but at this point I say, bring it on!"

"My daughter had one this past winter. Water birth. The poor thing didn't make it."

Mary didn't know if he meant his daughter or the child. She didn't know which would be worse. "God, I'm so sorry . . ."

"It's all right. We can't all have everything. Nope. We all have things we have to give up."

"That's right, isn't it? Not that it'd be consolation, really." Mary put her hand on her garbage can for support. Sometimes she could feel the pressure of earlier times. She could manage to erase the cars and the streets, the houses and the people in their pantsuits. She could see the forests spread out and feel their breath. She could see the long hair of men and women living with the land. The symmetry of the camps. The smell of fire. The sounds of their songs that were lessons and truths that came from the whispers under rocks and in the privacy between leaf and stalk. And she wished that reality would never return to her.

"I didn't mean to scare you or anything." One Eyed John said. "I am sorry, Miss. I've gotten to the point where saying and thinking are about the same for me. I've lost my sensor if you know what I mean."

Mary nodded. "It's nice to hear an honest thought every now and then."

* * *

A bulbous head filled the large television screen in Mary and Eliot's bedroom: "Have we all become pacifists? Liberals? Vegans? Grow some balls, New Hampshire, go out and hunt us some deer!"

"Can you turn that down, Eliot? It's irritating the baby."

Eliot put his hands on his wife's stomach to feel the child kicking beneath her skin.

"Maybe he's working on his sportsmanship—45 yards, and it's good. Baby Eliot wins the super bowl!"

"We're not naming it after you."

"I thought we were considering?"

"I've considered it and decided it's a strange thing to do, so egocentric. Can you turn it down!"

Eliot reached across to the end table to grab the remote, he turned the volume down two notches and continued listening to the news.

"It's interesting, isn't it? That accident I saw and now they're saying that overpopulation of deer has caused deer-related accidents to more than double in the past three months. I suppose hunting season isn't as popular as it used to be but still, it's strange. Don't you think? Maybe I'll go out and shoot us some deer."

"Don't be disgusting."

"What? I used to hunt with my dad when I was a kid."

"Eliot, you hate your father."

"How does that matter?"

"Turn it down lower, please. Or shut it off and light a candle."

"Gas again?"

"The candle is for romance. Not flatulence."

Mary rolled over onto her side and scooted her head forward on her pillow so that her mouth could almost meet her husbands over the bump of their child. Mary had always enjoyed kissing Eliot. It was something they were good at. And now, more than ever, she needed for him to need her, to want her. She needed to know that she was beautiful despite the child growing inside of her, or perhaps, because of it. She needed to know that she'd be loved still once the child had arrived and all the attention of the world which had once been hers had turned to it.

When they finished making love Eliot cradled Mary's head in his arms. Her knees were bent and arms compressed, he held her like a child. Her eyes filled with tears and she didn't want them. He kissed her forehead as if that would help. Mary used to like the feeling after sex, the mushy closeness of their bodies as if for a moment they weren't separate. But tonight she felt the world had stopped moving with her, stopped growing. It had stopped caring about her and there was nothing she could say to change its mind. This new town was silent and she could feel herself pulling away from what used to be her life.

"The faculty's friendly," Eliot said.

Mary pulled away from him and lay naked on top of the covers. She looked down to her belly. She liked the strange bulge of it. The tightness of skin. The dollop of her popped out belly-button. The way it hid her private parts—the lower by covering, and the upper by out-doing.

"I ran into a woman from the history department today. I told her about you and she wanted to know all about the baby. She said she'd love to meet you, if you're feeling up to stopping by one day," he continued.

"That's nice."

"I had a good first lecture, in case you were wondering. There were some interested eyes."

"And many more catatonic."

"You'll be excited to start teaching again, no?"

"What do I have to say that they all couldn't learn from a book if they cared to?"

"It feels good, you'll remember. 'Teaching early American history on the east coast will be revitalizing,' isn't that what you said before we moved? When I'm up there in front of them all it seems important."

"Don't you ever worry that you've gotten it all wrong?"

"No one expects that history could ever be totally accurate."

"I'm not talking about history, I'm talking about you."

"No then. I keep up to date. I went to that lecture just last month."

"I mean the principles, not the facts. Don't you ever think that the whole point of disease and contamination is to make us change the way we're living instead of coming up with ways to fix it? This curing of cancer we're on the verge of will be the worst thing that could happen to our society. It will make people give up trying to live in a better way. We'll all start smoking again and injecting our food with chemicals to make it shinier and brighter; goodbye organic."

"That's a strange way to look at it."

"It's the same with your water. If you can fix it, no need to improve. Keep on dumping in those chemicals, keep on building condo complexes up to the river. We'll take care of the consequences."

"What's gotten into you?"

"Let's kill the deer because they're getting in the way? *We're* getting in the way!"

"You didn't used to be like this."

"I've always been like this."

"No. You're negative. So full of, I don't know . . ."

There was a sound from the window to the side of their bed and they focused their attention to the darkness, to the face of a doe rapping its nose gently on the glass. Its eyes glowed like a cat's in the darkness and it stared right into their bed. Eliot sat up abruptly.

"What is it doing there? Why would a . . ."

A calmness came over Mary. She felt safe.

"I don't know what you're talking about."

"The deer, at the window. I've never seen an animal spy before. Is it dangerous?"

He stood up and pulled on some sweat pants.

"I don't see anything, Eliot. It's just some shadows, those trees, your imagination."

"Stop it. Stop lying to me."

"Eliot, there's nothing."

He looked at his wife exposed on the bed, allowing that deer to stare at her naked body. Eliot was overcome by a rancid jealousy, the kind that turns your breath and releases what you've been hiding.

Eliot grabbed the gun from his nightstand drawer. But the bullets were gone. He checked his tool box in the hall closet and then a small drawer in his desk.

"Where are the bullets?" he yelled to Mary.

"I threw them out."

"Why would you do that?"

"They were unsafe. You can't have bullets in a house with a baby."

Eliot grabbed his pocket knife and ran out the door.

The deer galloped down the road and then paused, waiting for him to catch up. She turned down the street, through the park, and stumbled down into the river. Eliot pumped his knife back and forth as he ran. His breath was heavy and he couldn't recognize anything around him. These streets he had walked in the daytime were now foreign and heavy like a dream that you know is a memory but can't quite place the when or why of.

* * *

The river was cool as it rose to Eliot's waist. The doe was still, standing in the middle of a river bend and waiting. Eliot held up his knife aggressively to scare her away but she did not move. He backed up and sank down to his stomach as he sat on a bolder at the side of the stream. The river was loud at night. Louder than the trees or the echoes from the highway. Louder than his breath or his beating heart.

"What do you want from me?"

The doe looked down to the water full of moonlight and licked at her own broken reflection. Eliot could hear the lapping of her tongue. She was beautiful, this creature. She was everything he meant to save when he'd begun his work in water treatment after graduate school.

Eliot look up and found that he was surrounded by deer. Does with their heads down and thick bucks with their antlers to the sky. They would trample him, he thought, it was a trap. He would die here in the Nashua River, inexplicably.

"I'm sorry," he called to them.

He approached her, the doe in the water with the flower on her cheek. He wrapped his arms around her warm smooth body as a killer holds his hostage for protection. He could feel what she was and was consumed by it. He slit her throat slowly and diligently. It was a hard thing to do with his dull knife but she waited patiently as the river filled with her blood, deep red streaks amidst the blackness. The forest watched as he hacked at her lovely flesh. The deer and the trees, the dirt, the rocks, the river—they made him do it. He was so ashamed.

III. September 2

It was a cool morning in Nashua. The birds were excited by the change in weather; they fluttered and clustered and flew from tree to tree. Eliot woke to find his wife absent from the house. He made himself a cup of coffee and waited for her return for an hour or so before he went out searching. On the streets he found that he was not the only one searching.

The women were gone. Vanished in the night. It had started in Nashua, spread up through Manchester to Lancaster and, within 12 hours of the doe's death, every woman within a twenty-mile radius of the Nashua River had walked straight out of her home and disappeared. Some women took their children with them, others left them behind, but none had left so much as a note.

There were men crying on the streets, screaming, swearing, thrashing as if possessed. Eliot walked slowly home watching his feet. He found his neighbor sitting outside in a rocking chair—the only piece of furniture placed in the middle of his grassy front yard. He rocked back and forth. Eliot stopped for a moment to glare at him.

"You're wondering why I'm so calm," he called out. "I've got no wife. They can't take nothing from me."

"Who can't? Who?" Eliot walked up to him, stared into his cavernous tired eye, overworked and lonely.

"I met Mary a few days back. A lovely girl."

Eliot wanted to muster hatred, this old man was taunting him, but instead he felt calm in his presence.

"You know what you've done," the old man said and nodded conclusively. "We do what we have to in this life. Me, I'd have done anything, but all I ever got to do was sit here waiting. All alone. Waiting until you came. Waiting to help them get where they were going. Waiting until they free me. "

Eliot broke down and cried, pleading at the old man's feet. "You know where they've gone. Help me. Please. Please!"

But the old man only rocked back and forth, back and forth.

* * *

It was early. The sun bubbled up from the trees and saturated the Boston Harbor with pink. The women floated with their arms out, their naked bodies warming in the light. The peninsula was empty. On this morning, they were free.

Mary wasn't sure of reality. Between the women there were only scattered memories of arriving. A pull. A jolt. A sudden escape into darkness. Mary felt stuck in one of her historic moments and she didn't ever want to return. This was the time she was meant for. A simple time where the soil was her bed and the harbor her sustenance. She had a sense of humor about it. Not sure how long it could last this way. Not sure if what she was doing was anything but rebellious. But she didn't care. Something had taken that from her—her caring—and she didn't want it back.

The women spoke seldom, their words untranslatable whispers from the back of the throat. No one expressed fear or asked for explanation. They seemed to trust that they would be led.

Mary knew where she was and what she had to do. She had known the moment she arrived on Deer Island. She could feel the story, the innocent people who had years ago been brought there to starve and die. She could hear their foreign songs, feel their desperation, the lonesome longing of a mother who knew she would not live to raise the child she had. A man who knew he could not protect the woman that he loved from the misery of the world. That had been King Phillips War, a Colonial war she had taught her students about many times. But she had never been able to make them feel what she felt now. The utterly unbearable pain of being promised amnesty only to be sentenced to death. The lie of the modern man. That was her failure.

As Mary climbed out of the water, she touched the hands of the woman next to her. A soft, gentle woman who she never would have known in her other life. As their hands met they shared a similar thought: the power plant. Mary whispered to this woman in words she herself couldn't understand. Mary held her belly with both hands. She could feel it would be soon.

As the day turned to darkness all of the women began singing. Deep melodic chants that carried across the water. There were thousands of them chanting, preparing the earth for its rescue, though it would take time.

IV. September 10–25

Eliot went in the mornings. He brought blankets, fruit and nuts, toothbrushes, children's toys, medicine, shoes. He placed them outside the perimeter of the deer. The women did not accept these offerings but sometimes when he returned the next day he would see that the apples had been eaten, or a bear taken into a child's care. Eliot called to her across the waters. "Keep our baby safe," he pleaded. "I love you."

The women wouldn't speak to their husbands, nor the news reporters or local police. No one could get near them. The deer circled the island like soldiers, marching, mesmerizing. For moments the viewers would forget to move, to speak, even to breathe. Once they remembered again and drew their guns, the women would run to the deer and throw themselves on top of the animals to protect them. A group of women ganged up and beat four policemen nearly to death for trying to sneak past the barrier and take a little boy away from the island and back to his father. And what could anyone do? They couldn't open fire and slaughter women and children in the middle of the Boston harbor with everybody watching. Some of the husbands had already hired lawyers to the scene, threatening that if their wives or children were so much as scratched they would sue.

The outside world seemed to hope it was a temporary hysteria that would pass if allowed to take its course. Eliot listened to the various explanations. *Something in the water. An airborne illness that only women are susceptible to. Maybe they've quarantined themselves here to save us all!* But Eliot saw the eyes of deer, cunning as the pair that had looked through the window of his house that night before his wife disappeared. He saw the Deer Island Waste Water Treatment Plant, the second largest plant in the United States, looming there on the island above them. He knew it was no virus or disease, no coincidence that the women ended up here on this particular island. They were pawns. All of them.

"For now the women are safe on the island. They are not harming themselves, their children or each other. They are surviving," announced the head of the police force. "We need to watch and wait."

V. September 26

The weapons had been gathered. Tree branches and bench boards. They crept into the plant in the night when none of the people patrolling their island would notice. They were acting in retribution of an old spirit, that of Monoco, leader of the Nashaway Indians, protector of the rivers and streams. He had been hung on this very day in 1676, after surrendering his way of life for the false promise of amnesty. They would not surrender. They would take something meaningful. It was not human life that was most precious now, so they would take instead the life of a machine, a spiritless construction.

At first there was a frenzy of wild hacking, banging, breaking of everything and anything that could be broken. They were summoning him with their fury. When their energy wore down they gathered around Mary, who told them what needed to be done in order to render the plant useless. This was a statement, she told them in their language, this was one of many events that would save them.

Mary pointed and passed. She made sure that things went as planned but she tired quickly. The plant came to a halt near dawn, it let out its long mechanical moans. The women took to their camp satisfied and began to get ready.

* * *

Mary sat in the corner of the hotel bathroom. It was the only place Eliot felt sure she couldn't escape. She was naked; she wouldn't keep clothes on her. Eliot sat and examined her scratched and scarred body.

Her feet were swollen and scarred. Her legs and arms seeped with blood from the scabs she was picking and picking. Her teeth had darkened, her breath had grown sticky and hot.

"Explain it to me again?" he asked her.

She took a deep sigh. "They are the reflections in the water of a different time, they are the illusion of everything. They care for everything, remember everything. And I'm on their side, which is the water's side and they won't betray me and they'll always save us. Like the time on the raft with our feet hanging off, you diverted us from the rapids, and you said that we'd be happy together. It was at the beginning, like a promise. That's their promise, this has happened before, whenever necessary. I can't even recall what raft, I've had a lapse of time. They say not to talk in this way, in this language, but you are part of me still and you can only understand this. I swear I'll save us, I made them let me come to you. There's always a chance I won't survive. You were my only request."

Eliot listened to her stammering and tried to make sense of it. "Colorado," he said. "The raft was in Colorado on our trip to the Rocky Mountains."

Mary didn't respond. She rocked back and forth. She stood and walked to a wall and began pounding her fists at it.

"Let me out, Eliot. Let me out. I'm trapped here. I'm not free. Let me out, Eliot. I came to you on my own and now you've trapped me."

He went to her and held her. She elbowed him in the face and kicked him in the groin. She pitied his poor shocked body as he stared up at her from the floor. She kept on pounding, her face growing red. There was water leaking down her legs out of her body. Eliot moved back in revulsion. She had become a savage. A crazy, incomprehensible beast, urinating on the floor. He was appalled, then suddenly, as if by magic, she stopped pounding on the wall. She straightened her hair behind her ears, put on the blouse and sweat pants that she had torn off of her body that morning when Eliot brought her into the bathroom.

"It's happening," she said with a smile. "Let's go!"

"What?"

"The baby. I'm having the baby. We have to get to the—hospital."

Eliot had no time to hesitate or decide. He opened the bathroom, threw some belongings into a bag and took his wife's hand gently as they headed to the door. Part of him believed it was all because of the baby. Pregnancy madness—was there such a thing? Surely, once they had the baby, things would go back to normal. He opened the front door and stepped out. They were surrounded.

Eliot screamed, a painful reverberating moan. The deer turned their heads at the abrasion of it. The deer surrounded the hotel, the cars. There were hundreds of them, standing in neat lines. He looked at his wife, her placid expression, her hand still firmly in his.

"What will they do to us, Mary? You can't have the baby here. It's a trap. Why are they trapping us?"

"We won't have the baby here," Mary said. "They need us to follow them."

Mary walked to the car and Eliot trailed behind her. She got into the passenger's seat and began breathing deeply with a contraction.

"We can do this," she said.

The deer began to march forward, down the road. He trailed them closely. He thought of running them down but it wouldn't have helped. He imagined the damage that all those deer could do to a car or a person.

The roads were clear, as if everyone knew they were coming. They headed through a ghost town, buildings, stop lights, but not a person around until they arrived at Deer Island.

The island was a cloud of smoke and the people were all gathered to watch it. The people were motionless and parted easily as the deer made way through the crowd. Eliot stopped his car on the bridge as was demanded of him and helped his wife out onto the island. The deer followed and closed in on them as they reached the camp, curious spectators as if at the zoo. The contractions were closer together now and Eliot understood that he would deliver his baby here, on this island, in the middle of a city where everyone had frozen. There was no one to save them.

The women held hands in a circle around Mary and the deer stood in their own ring behind the women. Eliot felt they might be trampled at any moment.

"I'm sorry I killed her," Eliot called out to them. "Is that what this is about?"

"They can't understand you," Mary said.

"Tell them then. Tell them I'm sorry about the deer. Ask them to let us go."

She shook her head. She screamed out and he lowered her to the ground, cradled her head and then let it rest on the ground. He realized he would need things. He took off his undershirt and wet it in a pot of water that had been placed before him. He washed his hands as best he could. He took off his wife's pants. Her underwear. He hated that the deer could see her exposed.

"They're not angry with you, Eliot," she said. "You helped them. She was their sacrifice."

The baby came out quickly and loudly. Covered in slime and mush. Eliot cut the umbilical cord with his knife, still stained with the doe's blood, and Mary held the baby boy in her arms. Even when he lay his eyes on his healthy child, Eliot knew that things would not be okay. He felt the wrench of helplessness.

"The baby will have two names," Mary said loudly, an announcement. "Eliot and Monoco. He will be ours and he will be theirs. He will save us all."

She held the child out and a buck came forward. He licked the child clean and took it in his mouth by the flesh of its back. He walked gently with it, away from Eliot and Mary. The other deer followed and so did the women until they were all gone.

Mary, striped with sweat and blood, took her aching husband Eliot in her arms. She rocked him until he was quiet. The smoke of the dying machine spread around them and saturated them with its wretched stench. Mary sang out an old, sad lullaby.

Catie Jarvis is an author of fiction and poetry. She received her BA in Writing from Ithaca College and her MFA in Creative Writing from California College of the Arts in San Francisco. Catie weaves her surroundings into her writing, from the subdued naturalism of the Finger Lakes to the lyrical, urban beat of the Bay Area. Having returned to the East Coast and currently residing in Nashua, New Hampshire, Catie continues to infuse both the history and the soul of places and people into her creative works.

Old Ruby Lane

Michael Alan

It's not your name on a deed that makes you part of a small New Hampshire town—it's becoming part of your neighbors' secrets.

A few years ago, at the peak of the autumnal display, my wife and I went for an idle Sunday drive through the Monadnock Mountain region. We made a wrong turn, found ourselves on Route 31, and got seduced by the Souhegan River as it wound its way through an ancient state forest. Leaping rivulets hurried to nowhere over smoothed stones. Stately evergreens watched their lunatic deciduous cousins burst into red and yellow and orange. If only for a moment, the timeless granite ledges eased the fleeting man-made calamities tugging at us. Nature had it all figured out.

We stopped for a late breakfast at a five-table café in the center of a little town called Greenville. The owner, a handsome woman in her early forties, sat at our table to take our order. "Haven't seen you before—new to the area?"

"This is my wife Bonnie and I'm Walter. We're just here admiring the scenery." I tried to remember the last time anyone noticed that I was new in town.

"Leaf peepers?" She squinted slightly to see if we would protest the label.

"Guilty as charged."

She nodded. "Coffee?"

The aroma of a freshly brewed pot hung deliciously in the air. "Absolutely. And how about a couple of short stacks to go with it?"

"Real maple syrup? Couple of dollars more—but trust me, it's worth it." She stared at my eyes as if trying to read something written on the inside of my skull.

"Sure. We're splurging today. It's our anniversary."

She smiled. "You'll love it. Everyone does. I get it from the sugar house just up the road."

She was right. The plate-sized pancakes were thick and fluffy. But it was the syrup that made the morning—a clear reddish nectar that went beyond sweet to a happy new place on our taste buds. Neither one of us had ever before had anything even close to it.

When we got our check I asked, "Where did you say that syrup came from?"

"Just up the road—Old Ruby Lane. On the left. Can't miss it. But sap doesn't flow 'round here till March. By now Jake's likely sold last year's run."

A few minutes later, our tongues still dreaming of maple, we were driving up Old Ruby Lane. Bonnie pointed. "I think that's it up ahead—the sugar house."

I saw a ramshackle barn of weathered cedar planks and rusted nails. The bowed roof looked like a swayed-back horse ready for a last trip to the vet. Patches of shingles were missing. A section of wall was charred black. The entire structure seemed to lean slightly to the right.

The building was set in a stand of brilliant red maples—as iridescent as any we had ever seen. A rustic sign, black with gold letters, declared Ruby Lane Sugar House, 1796. Bonnie said, "Let's go in." We parked and entered.

An old man, stooped and weathered as the barn, stood at a small counter. "Took you long enough, Mr. Walter. Last pint in the shop." He held up a tin for us to see.

"I assume you're Jake." I held out my hand to greet him.

He looked at my outstretched arm. "Nice hand. Ain't gonna shake it. Never know who's got what."

"How did you know my name?"

"Barb called from the diner. Good thing. Just about to split some wood. Would'a missed ya."

He read the handmade label on the pint. "Eight ounces. Genuine Maple Syrup. 100% Light Ruby."

"We'll take it. How much?"

"That would be $50."

"For one pint?"

"No tax. Nickel back if you return the can. That's the price—take it or leave it. You ain't gonna find nothin' like it. Worth every penny. Best Light Ruby anywhere—only Light Ruby anywhere."

I couldn't argue with that. But $50? I turned to leave but Bonnie held my arm. It really was that spectacular—and it was our anniversary. I paid him and we headed out.

Just past the sugar house was an overgrown graveyard with headstones dating from the 1700s. Markers varied from simple stone slabs to ten-foot-high monuments with carved cherubim and seraphim—but each wore the patina of a couple of hundred New Hampshire winters. All the graves stood in tall grass except for a couple of odd patches of freshly turned earth. There was no evidence that any living person had a connection to those buried there—no wreaths, no flowers, no ribbons.

I said to Bonnie, "Those markers sum up an entire life with two dates—started here, ended there. It's as if it didn't matter what they did between being born and dying. Talk about feeling small."

Just past the graveyard there was a small abandoned farm house. The building was falling apart and the yard was badly overgrown. Tires and beer cans, rusted tractor parts and large wooden utility spools lay everywhere. A small realtor's sign made me pull off to take a closer look.

Bonnie and I had been living in Nashua in a massive old mill building converted into apartments by some faceless corporation determined to squeeze every mean penny they could out of the tenants. Towing residents' cars on cleaning days, fines for violating trash disposal rules or forgetting a key, withheld security deposits for not cleaning bathtub grouting just so made us feel as if we were back in elementary school with hall monitors watching our every step. We had talked about finding a place in the country that would let us work with our hands and put some distance between us and the corporate pandemic. That old farmhouse looked as if it might have possibilities.

We found a back door flapping open in the breeze and entered. To our surprise the house still had much of its furniture. The kitchen table held dishes with dried remnants of a meal. I said, "Someone left here in a hurry."

The plaster walls and ceilings were badly cracked. Here and there holes exposed hand-hewn lathing through which outside air freely flowed. Upstairs the floors were random-width planks encrusted with layers of chipped black and blue enamel—the kind in old amusement park fun-houses.

The structure was easily over a hundred years old. Beams in the attic were bark-on raw timber. Every room had reminders that boards came from trees—not lumberyards. A two-seat outhouse set against a wall of the barn was made from recycled crates with shipping addresses still visible. Apparently when the house was built nothing useful was wasted.

Indoor plumbing and electric service were obviously afterthoughts added over the years by a succession of owners. What little wiring existed looked as if it was young Tommy Edison's first project. Exposed knife switches, thick bar fuses, and oxidized cloth-covered wires in a variety of sizes and colors came out of a half dozen rusted metal boxes. Doors, pieces of fans, knobs, and a headless Barbie doll with associated clothes were scattered here and there.

We walked down a rickety staircase into a dimly lit space. I felt a gentle tug on my cheeks. "Jesus! Get this off me." I turned to Bonnie to pull a mat of cobwebs from my face.

The basement was a five-foot-tall space formed from huge squared-off granite blocks each two to three feet across and a foot high. We had to walk hunched over to keep from hitting our heads. A single window illuminated a maze of spider webs with their makers frozen in place while waiting for prey. The spiders were huge and each one was covered with thick, white fuzz.

Bonnie said, "These guys froze to death last winter and that fuzz is mold digesting their bodies."

I rubbed my face again to check for cobwebs. "Obviously no one's been down here for awhile."

"Let's take a look out back."

We found a generous backyard filled with reminders of occupants past—a bicycle frame, rusted out wheelbarrow with a missing handle, a moldy stack of asbestos ceiling tiles half dissolved after years of exposure to rain and snow. I wondered who left the flagpole and bucket of screws to the rain and weeds? What task was interrupted, what news came that caused them to leave so suddenly?

The yard was framed by an old stone wall on three sides. I asked, "How did they move these stones into place? Some of them must weigh three-hundred pounds. No tractors, no front-end loaders—just muscle."

Bonnie said, "I'll bet the Kent family settled it and their son Clark put up the walls. Or maybe they just used horses and oxen."

I imagined trying to talk an ox into nudging a granite boulder into line and decided I had chosen the right era in which to be born.

At the far back wall there was a ten-foot break that led to a wooded area with a brilliant canopy of shockingly red maple leaves. Huge granite boulders the size of a car stood watch at the rim of a valley. The stone walls widened and ran down either side of a steep hillside. We could barely walk down the slope holding on to saplings as we went—but the stone walls continued uninterrupted until they were out of sight below.

"Look at the trees." Bonnie held a leaf. "Aren't they the same kind we saw at the sugar house?"

"I know what you're thinking, but before we get too excited we'd better find out how much they're asking for this place."

We went back to the car and called the number on the realtor's sign. I got the realtor's assistant. Apparently the house had been on the market for over a year, it was bank owned, and the broker couldn't be bothered to show it any longer.

I pressed the assistant for a price. She finally relented and named an amount.

Bonnie took the phone. "We'd like to make an offer."

The assistant said, "I told you we're really not able to show the property. I suggest you look at other listings in the area. There are plenty of other . . ."

Bonnie repeated her words more forcefully. "We'd like to make an offer."

"Okay, okay. I'll pass it on to Mr. Jackson. What is your offer?"

"How about we meet the bank's full asking price?"

A week went by and the broker wouldn't return our phone calls. We finally heard that our offer had been presented to the bank but apparently no one seemed able to approve anything. The broker seemed to be doing what he could to kill the deal. I began to think he wanted the property for himself, but after two months of wrangling with the comatose bank at last the property was ours.

It was December, leaves had fallen, and there was a crisp bite in the air. We were pioneers, settlers embarking on a great adventure. We moved a bed into the house and spent our first night in the new homestead. Bonnie improvised curtains for the windows and laid runners on the floors so we wouldn't pick up splinters in our stocking feet. I wrestled with leaky plumbing in the basement and blown fuses. We were home at last.

The first night in bed felt as if we had moved to a different planet. Compared to our Nashua apartment we now lay in pitch blackness and dead silence—no trucks grinding gears, no police sirens, no parking lots to act as perpetual nightlights. I lay still, trying to not wake Bonnie. An hour passed and then another.

"Are you awake?" Bonnie whispered.

"Spooky, isn't it?"

"Can you hear that?"

I listened carefully. "Sounds like tapping, something in the distance."

"I think it sounds like digging. Someone's using a shovel."

"I'll take a look tomorrow."

The next morning I took a stroll around the property but didn't see anything unusual. We spent the day scrubbing and hauling yard trash to a dumpster we had rented.

Late that night the tapping sound resumed. I grabbed a flashlight and headed out back. I saw nothing, but as soon as I shined the light in the direction of the graveyard the sound stopped. I wasn't about to wander off into the woods in the middle of the night, so I went back to bed.

For the next several days we hauled trash to the dumpster and at night listened to sounds too subtle at first for us city folks to pick up. We heard a flock of wild turkeys burbling deep in the woods, a solitary bark from a dog somewhere across the valley, the quiet scratching of a mouse preparing its winter nest in one of our walls. And every night there was the distant sound of someone digging, digging, digging.

On day six the ice came. And came and came. It was a freak storm that raged for an entire day and night with the temperature hovering around freezing the whole time.

Early in the evening we lost power and found ourselves in a dark, unfamiliar house without heat or light. Fearing that the plumbing would burst as the house cooled, I set up a propane heater in the middle of the dining room. It was clearly labeled For Outdoor Use Only! With the walls freely passing outside air into the room I decided that the risk of asphyxiation was far less than the risk of freezing to death. We watched as two-foot high yellow flames leapt out of the sides of the silver metal heater and pretended it was an indoor campfire.

Even with the heater on full I could see my breath when lightning flashed. Eerie shadows from the flames danced on the cracked plaster creating a surreal scene straight out of Dante's imagination. No television, no radio, no Internet. I tried to read but the flickering light was too dim and uneven. We were getting a taste of how original settlers passed their evenings. I was feeling primeval and wondered if the adrenalin kicked up by a night like this was what it took to muscle those three-hundred-pound boulders into a neat wall.

The old structure creaked and groaned as roof boards took on tons of ice. A vicious wind whistled through the openings in the walls. Suddenly there was a loud cracking sound. It was followed by another and another. In the flickering light I saw Bonnie's hand tremble. What was that noise? Would we be discovered under a pile of rubble? I tried calming myself by pretending it was all just a movie. Spielberg was messing with my mind trying to scare me senseless—and doing a pretty good job.

We snuggled closer in bed. A thunderous crack came—ten times as loud as the sounds we had been hearing. Bonnie buried her head in my chest. I pulled the covers higher to protect us as if we were kids hiding from monsters in the closet. A flash of lightning revealed that a huge tree had just fallen on our neighbor's house. I wanted the movie to end. It didn't.

Morning finally came and we ventured out to survey the damage. The sun shone brilliantly on a sparkling landscape. There was an inch and a half of clear ice coating on every branch, wire, and surface in sight. It was a Disney fantasy—a fairy godmother had touched Greenville with her magic wand. Except for the devastation.

Limbs had succumbed to the ice. Branches fell, trunks snapped with explosive force. Whole trees toppled under the force of the violent wind. The utility pole across the street had collapsed under the weight of ice on the power lines. It was leaning over the street at a forty-five degree angle being tethered by a single wire attached to our neighbor's house.

I chiseled my way into my ice-encased car and tried to make it to a store for batteries and more propane. The neighborhood looked like a bombed-out war zone frozen in time by a transparent force field. All roads were blocked by downed wires, fallen utility poles, and branches—huge branches everywhere. Large trees lay across taut power lines daring passersby to dart by lest they be flattened if wires gave way at just the right moment. We were completely cut off from the outside world. I returned home empty-handed.

Bonnie and I ventured out back to assess the damage. We cautiously made our way towards the woods, climbing over dozens of uprooted trees and fallen branches. Once through the break in the back wall, we decided to split up and examine the carnage separately. I walked west while Bonnie walked east. I had traveled a couple of hundred feet over a sturdy crust of ice when I heard it—a scream that sent my pulse racing. Bonnie was in trouble.

I scrambled as fast as I could toward the screaming. A couple of minutes later I saw her running toward me—pointing, gasping, incoherent.

"Catch your breath, honey. Tell me what's wrong. What happened?"

She couldn't speak.

"Show me. Take me back to where you were."

She shook her head. She wouldn't go back.

I persisted and she reluctantly guided me to the eastern end of the property nearest the old cemetery. As we approached Bonnie began shaking again. She pointed. "There! There!"

I saw an uprooted maple, fifteen-inches in diameter. Sinews of root stood six feet in the air as the base pulled out of the soil.

I looked at one of the exposed roots and tried to understand what my eyes were seeing. "Oh my God! My God!"

I turned my head to empty my stomach on the ground and noticed another fallen maple nearby—and another and another. Each uprooted tree held a nightmare that the most perverse fiction writer could not have invented.

I tried to keep Bonnie from seeing the other trees but I was too late. She began screaming again. I couldn't calm her.

I saw a figure in the distance approaching us. He must have heard Bonnie's screams and come to investigate. As he came closer I realized it was Jake, from the Sugar House. He held a pick-axe in one hand and a shovel in the other.

He shouted, "Mr. Walter. That you?" He continued coming closer.

I armed myself with a stout branch. "Yes. Moved in last week."

He stopped at the uprooted tree. "Guess you discovered our little secret. Not much I suppose to do about that."

"Secret? You mean the ice-encrusted corpses hanging from roots all over my property?"

"Come from the graveyard they do. First folks who planted the Ruby maples here knew a good thing when they tasted it. Some say it was just an accident in the beginning—tree sent a root into a grave. A few years later the sap came red as blood. But warn't nothin' touched the taste. By and by they got 'round to lendin' nature a hand until the whole cemetery was played out. Nothin' but empty boxes under them headstones."

"That's the secret?"

"Only a handful of us old timers know—and now you two. Tell, don't tell—don't make no nevermind to me. Ain't got but a few more years anyhow and the trees warn't gonna live forever. Good old Light Ruby—you'll never find nothin' like it. Never."

I could see Jake meant no harm. There seemed to be little point in having police tromp around all over our land for bodies that had been dead a couple of centuries. I helped Jake collect the bones and bury them in a granite pit on the south side of the property where it wasn't likely that anyone would disturb them.

Been a couple of years since that awful storm. Found a patch of land just up the road—another foreclosure. Happened to be next to a second abandoned town cemetery. Decided to run a crop—top shelf, all organic. Put up a little roadside farm stand—sign came today. Local carver did a great job—nice black background, raised gold letters: Sweet Ruby Corn—$10 an ear.

Michael Alan has spent a lifetime homesteading on the digital frontier, has several software patents for computers now only in museums, and founded several ventures that were almost wildly successful. He is fiercely anti-corporate, loves first-person tales of struggle, and is currently restoring a 1920 farmhouse on four acres of beautiful New Hampshire mountainside. He's written five novels (one of which, *The Lorelei Effect*, was named British Arts Council Book of the Year). He is blown away by Elisabet Sahtouris' *EarthDance*, thinks Sam Clemens got it about right and takes comfort that he's not going to live forever.

"The Exchange"

Seth Blake

From: timpb@gmail.com
To: fogeyfarm@hotmail.com
Cc:
Bcc:
Subject: URGENT! FROM YOUR SON! PLEASE RESPOND!

Mom, Dad, don't know if you know already, but something's gone horribly wrong—people roaming the streets, seem rabid, will attack and bite unprovoked. Nearly lost my hand to Effram from floor crew. Had to smack him with palette plank (Hope he's OK. Not a prank, not me, not isolated to NHBB. Kids are fine. School cancelled after phys. ed teacher found cannibalizing custodian in shower—nothing left but vertebrae and mop handle. Subdued by humanities dept. head and several members of lacrosse team. Horrible scene as impromptu bravery commendation ceremony turned bloodbath when tech. dir. Chet Conway sneezed loudly and was run through by overzealous Geometry I class wielding compass needles. Early dismissal traffic nightmare. Geo Prism crushed by Bus 36, later discovered to have been piloted by one of the "affected" after terrifying detour into the Contoocook River. Barely escaped unscathed from lot-turned-mudpit, forced to boon through football field and several young spruce—one stuck between axles, did not rupture oil-pan. Thank god I took the jeep. Community in total disarray. Gas stations and supermarkets mobbed, no one playing nice, and where there are people there "they" are, looking hungry. TV's still

smiling; no news online; sporadic, vague, unconfirmed reports coming into NHPR—still light in volume—never had cell service, anyway. Town meeting called for tonight. Don't know whether to go or get out. Please give status update immediately upon receipt of message. Getting supplies together for a trip up north. Be ready to leave at moment's notice.

From: fogeyfarm@hotmail.com
To: timpb@gmail.com
Cc: manray2012@yahoomail.com
Bcc: hottotrottoboston@comcast.net
Subject: Re: URGENT! FROM YOUR SON! PLEASE RESPOND!

Howdy!

Good to hear that you and the kiddos are doing fine. I wish we had been able to go to Holly's poetry recital back in December, but your Mom had that vein in her leg explode like I told you and it would have been a hell of a mess in the auditorium, let me tell you.

Something funny happened here yesterday—speaking of—and I wonder that it could be related and will tell Chief Menard about the possible connection when I get down to the Post Office to pick up the catalogs. Should be going later today as your Mom has been squawking about *Reminisce* the whole morning.

So the way our little episode started was, we're having our Cornflakes and all of sudden I hear this moaning and carrying on coming from the side yard.

Your mother, she says: "Rollie, you hear that noise?"

I say: "Of course I hear it, mother. You think my ears lost their gription?"

She goes: "That's the least of it."

So I take a little stroll around the premises with coffee cup in one hand, toad-stabber in the other and what should I find behind the woodshed but fella stumbling and acting bogus.

I ask him, real friendly, how's it going, but my inquiry elicits no response.

I ask him if he needs my help looking for something on my property, seeing as it's mine and I'm likely to know it better than he and furthermore I haven't ever seen him before and would he tell me, right off, on what account he's dickering around so I can decide whether to invite him to stay on, or give him the sign and tell him to go choge.

The guy looks up at me and starts saying something, but he's so mealy-mouthed I can hardly make it out, and my ears are sharp as Saskatoon scammels or I wouldn't have heard his galumphing for start-ers, despite what *she* said.

I tell him I'm an older gentleman and ask him to articulate himself and furthermore to halt his slow advance towards me, his arms out-stretched like so.

Anyway, he pays no mind and jiminy crickets does he ever start flashing me the Colgate smile. Summer here, summer there and there's crunchy critters crawling out of his mouth too. At that point I know what this pecker-head is out for and it's not tea and boo-boo cake.

I don't shoot first, but in that moment I can read with certainty the intentions spelled on his rabid face and the eagerness in his grop-ing hands.

I realize this ain't your average turd-burglar ranging over from Franklin and stepping to an old-timer for grins, but some real bonehead of the pleasant and fruit street sort, who'd maybe ruther not mind bru-talizing a boulevardier such as me if I happened to wind up tarrying too long between him and the object of his fancy, pop-tart or platinum ring.

It was about that time that I let the large, high-carbon stainless steel affair in my right hand leap to the dumb-cluck's most convenients.

The triple-rivet, full-tang slicer bit deep into the attacker's hide at the joint of his shoulder and collar, and before I blink he's minus an arm but determined as ever, mouth open like a fish out of water and hardly a drop of blood spilled.

Well, I take a step back and finish my coffee and try to keep my marbles from rolling away while this queer fella baby-steps his blasted self closer and closer. It's not to say that I wouldn'ta come to eventually and done what I musta, but I did appreciate the timely intervention of your mother with the old peppergun from the porch steps.

Before you start celebrating her as a heroine, you should know that I had to remind her about the break action. Also, she tagged the shed a bit and the meat wasn't even any good! (Pulling your leg).

So, I go inside and I call up Chief Menard right away and explain the situation to the answering machine. Haven't heard back yet, but I expect he'll be down sometime today with the coroner to have a peek.

Looks like we can still take care of ourselves up in this neck of the

woods, but we'd love for you to visit and to bring the kids if they're going
to have school off for a few days. Bring your fishing gear and I'll pick up
a couple gallons of freezey cream from Cumbies.

P.S. Copied Ray-ray and Gary in on the message, as maybe they've
heard something about the whole thing and could offer some explanation. Gary's a statie, as you know, and Ray-ray's usually got his finger on
the pulse one way or another—though I'm not sure if he knows how to
use the computer and has a slow Internet too (kidding if you read it Ray!).

* * *

Support for NHPR comes from you, our surviving members,
and from Subaru of Keene, now offering lifetime power-train
coverage and dedicated sales personnel who know how to stop
the bleeding and have working cars and short-wave radios.
Subaru of Keene: where there is free coffee and animal crackers in the heated, well-fortified lobby.

Reports continue to stream in from across the state of the
harassment of New Hampshire residents by the fetid, decaying
remains of former neighbors, colleagues, friends and family. No
word yet from Concord on whether the ill-intentioned-seeming
carrion are sentient beings bent on our annihilation, the spas-
modic flailings of inert flesh moved to haphazard violence by
neuro-electric stimulus of unknown origin, or some species of
hominid that has long stalked the hills and valleys of the Granite
State, heretofore unglimpsed save by those who—through drug
or dream—have met them in the most abhorrent recesses of
our collective unconscious.

Up next; "The Exchange" with Laura Knoy. With an extra
$140 million dollars needed to be cut from the budget, the House
and Senate have different ideas on how to close the gap. Rep.
Pamela Hubbard of Stafford has proposed requisitioning addi-
tional funds from Washington to ensure that embattled citizens
will have recourse to public shelters, while Rep. Clinton Bailey
of Rockingham maintains that it's an individual's responsibility
to fend for himself.

I'm Dan Colgan, please stay with us for continuing coverage on this story as it develops.

* * *

From: timpb@gmail.com
To: fogeyfarm@hotmail.com
Cc:
Bcc:
Subject: UPDATE! DO NOT LEAVE THE HOUSE!

Am astounded that you apparently killed someone and did not tell me immediately. Unfortunately, no time to get into the particulars now, but will certainly discuss in detail later. Seems phenomenon not isolated, situation more dire than guessed. Appears to have gone state-wide at least, reports streaming in from Bethlehem to Exeter of savage, random attacks against young and old of all creeds, backgrounds by individuals and groups matching description in last message—all unresponsive, non-communicative, often highly disheveled or disfigured to the point of the grotesque (open wounds, visibly gangrenous tissue, but oddly never bleeding) and undeterred in their pursuit of human flesh unless decapitated.

Did not believe it myself until abortive town meeting last night. Am still trying to scrape grey matter from timmies. Brought along Holly and Miles—too keyed up to leave them alone—and fear they have been traumatized by the experience. Not the way I would've hoped to induct them into our state's long and proud tradition of direct municipal democracy.

Had assumed uproar and shouting was simply reflection of passions stirred by terrifying circumstances of earlier in day, entered hall hoping to vent outrage in good company.

Instead found patriarch of the Bass family being disemboweled and summarily devoured at the lectern by several former members of the Recreation Committee. In desperate effort to save his young wife (a classmate of Holly's), Bob Walco from Valley Auto Parts had affixed what looked like leg of Fish and Game officer to spike of state flag, waving it totemically above heads of feral band of assessing clerks who had swarmed her.

Neighbors against neighbors, patrons against clientele. Citizens feasted merrily on the entrails of public servants.

Breathless elderly widow informed me that police, fire and rescue personnel had long since retreated to seek reinforcements. Before she collapsed into death, pressed a Beretta 92 into my hands, whispering that it would serve me well if well-oiled, always aimed a little above my assailant's mouth.

Seeing no hope of comity, fired shots into biggest clusterfuck of what I pray were bad guys, hightailed it out. Kids took it well, overall. Holly got more practice at wheel as I breathed into paper bag.

In light of situation, have decided that we have no choice but to come get you and travel as family to safety, wherever that may be. Please, do not venture out for any reason. You don't need to meet us halfway, don't need to go into town, don't need to draw attention to yourself. We are still not certain how/if these things have means of detecting human beings; however, keeping low profile as good a bet as any. Get cats in, shutter/shade windows, turn off lights in any but interior rooms, dead-bolt doors, reinforce weak points w/plywood, screws—+ chimney (= no fires). No Benny Spellman records, no Marty Stouffer videos, no tea-kettles, no canasta. Wear slippers, don't shower, don't clip coupons, slow breathing, don't cough, don't smoke, remove soft, non-perishable foods you may consume in next 24 hours from packaging now, if said pack-aging rustles, crinkles, clinks, thuds when dropped from chest height, and lay out neatly and carefully wherever most easily accessible. Do not use blender! Make sure plenty litter in box. Charge flashlights. Load guns. Kitchen utensils readily accessible, but! do not access under any save direst circumstances! Do not wear corduroy! Do not operate lever-adjustable footrest on recliner. Do not use rocking chair in den. Do not use hot water at pantry sink. Do not step on third step from top if going upstairs. Do not go upstairs! If Ray-ray invites out, decline and tell him our plans. If we've got room, we'll see if we can take him along. Do not have nightcap. Do not wear nightcap.

From: manray2012@yahoomail.com
To: fogeyfarm@hotmail.com
Cc: timpb@gmail.com
Bcc: hottotrottoboston@comcast.net
Subject: Funny Stuff

I resent that Rollie and I hope I can use the computer since you're the one as taught me!!! Your right about the Internet speed tho. I did

see this, http://www.zombiedance.com/ it's a cute site check it. Hope
this helps.

Ray-ray

From: fogeyfarm@hotmail.com
To: timpb@gmail.com
Cc: manray2012@yahoomail.com
Bcc:
Subject: Re: UPDATE! DO NOT LEAVE THE HOUSE!

Sounds like a real shit-twister up your way. Things are still pretty quiet
up here, except for earlier when I had to see to a bit of trouble out in
the out-of-doors.

I'm coaxing Kuskus from the sugar maple she tends to ascend in
times of distress with a handful of liverwurst I had bruised up specially
to get the smell going, when what do I hear except a distant drone like
cicadas. At first I pay it no mind and keep after the kitty, who is hissing
and spitting and generally acting the brazen tart. I use my best tricks
and even play hard to get like I'm done with her and would take the
liverwurst away for myself, when I realize that the buzzing, throbbing
sound hadn't yet reached a crescendo and in fact seemed to be getting
closer. I think that's funny enough and then I remember it's not even the
right season to be hearing the buzzing bastards. I start hollering for your
mother, but turns out she's in the house washing her hair with the radio
on, listening for signs of life and couldn't hear me over the roar.

At this point I turn around and what do I see down toward the end
of the driveway but a crowd of folks coming slowly my way, looking
like they need a hug and some hemorrhoid cream, and groaning up a
symphony. Must have been over a dozen and they're all murmuring the
same thing, but getting in each other's way, so to speak, so I can't make
out word one, and anyway, they're not speaking up. I hail 'em with my
best grump routine and try to make myself look bigger like they say to
do with the bears when they get uppity about the feeders. Of course,
that doesn't work and I start wondering how long I've got before they
close the distance between the house and me. Seeing as how I'm not
much faster than they, I realize it's going to be close, but I'd shit melons

before I left the little feline to their designs, even if she is a skank and I've seen her indiscriminate with the toms and the raccoons and the bull skunks, reminding me I've got to get her bits out.

I'm half steamed-half scarified by the circumstances, while Kuskus seems cool as a cucumber, and I can hardly think what I ought to do when the trajectory of my frantic machinations gives me an idea. I'll use the cat's most feared opponent to provoke her from the tree to the safety of the house, and maybe teach her a lesson in the mix.

Thinking nothing of my own safety, I hurry to the garage, getting pretty creative cursing Kuskus' name and praying that your mother isn't running the vacuum. There, in the soft light from the clouded-over midday sun is my lady in red all glowing like a what-starts- with "f"-and-ends-with "uck," polished up and ready to ride into the sunset. Ray-ray knows who I'm talking about when I say she's got a two-stage power max, two-foot berth, 45-foot lob distance and a 342 cubic centimeter heart of pure gold.

I sit and gaze at her for a few moments, recalling the purchase as if it was yesterday, allowing my mind to wander over the months of sweet, snow-free walks and drive we had worked tirelessly to maintain. Getting up early, going to bed late with never the slightest grumble or false start from her, and always at a reasonable pace due to her easily adjustable throttle. I don't think I exaggerate by saying I had forged something of a bond with Elaine.

Bending to prime her, I recall an instance shortly after the previous winter's first snowfall, when, alarmed at what then had first seemed like an abrupt stall, I noticed a pair of young lynx, wending their course through the wood aft of the bean plot. Together, we observed the tranquil scene until they vanished from our sight and then she thrummed back to life with no provocation whatever my side. From that moment forth I had been convinced we shared some portentous destiny.

In the garage she comes to consciousness purring sweet as you please, and as I rock her up onto the back wheels so as not to scrape the blades upon the concrete floor, I wonder if this cat is to be our Alamo. By the time we're outside, the crowd has filled out some and gained the better half of the front yard, fanning out wide with some seeming to make for the house, some for the garage and few more for the sugar maple, looking to me as intrigued as such folks are capable at the prospect of picking a certain, small, furry fruit that seemed to be growing there.

Well, I'm not about to let these asshats have it their way with any pussy of mine. I do a few light stretches like Dr. Oz is always showing your mother how to keep limber for me, and key Elaine up to cruising speed. She can really hit the high spots, and this first swatch we tear into those goons like Ray-ray at the rib-rodeo on fireman's muster. Arms and legs flying every which way in a fine dark mist of gore like some kind of Taranteeny movie and Elaine and I loving every bit of it. She neither clogs, cramps nor coughs the whole while, and I swung her around all loosey goosey for another pass. Despite the healthy roar of her engine, my closeness to the weird pricks allows me to better make out the strange kind of chant they've been reciting all the while, not even stopping to mourn the passing of their companions.

I'm no speech pathologist, as you plainly know, but I could've sworn they were moaning "more."

Running with it, I says:

"If it's more you want, it's right here and there's plenty left to go 'round," and that's that as they quickly succumb to the churning blades.

Yep, the cat's fine and Elaine has never been better—I made careful to check the tire pressure after the episode and to scrub her blades and body clean of bone meal and wound slur.

What bugs me about the whole thing is the fact that they kept on chanting the whole time. Sort of eerie, and what could it mean? Though I've cleaned the yard up and there's hardly any trace of the whole thing ever happening, the word, coming out of their cracked and peeling lips has stuck with me. I even had a nightmare last night. Something about Turkey Hill hoving off on rum raisin. Spooky!

Maybe you won't get this on account of being on the road, son and grandkids, and if not, I'll see you soon. Ray-ray, I hope you'll join us all for supper real soon.

From: manray2012@yahoomail.com
To: fogeyfarm@hotmail.com
Cc: timpb@gmail.com
Bcc:
Subject: Re: UPDATE! DO NOT LEAVE THE HOUSE!

Member that fishing trip we took down to Greg Lake this winter when we did some icefishing? Oooooh, we got a freezer full of fish burning a hole in the freezer here. Bass? You betcha? Trout? Ten-four. Pike—perty big, pissy looking ones? Oohoho. Perch? Please, my lord! We even got a few sunnies cooling off in dere! Went hornpouting the other night and got enough catfish to choke a zoo of kids and animals. Few of them Vandecamp sticks lying around somewhere. What do you say about a fish fry? Head down to nattyville and start cooking with gas, how bout it?

From: timpb@gmail.com
To: fogeyfarm@hotmail.com
Cc: manray2012@yahoomail.com
Bcc: hottotrottoboston@comcast.net
Subject: Tragedy at Noon

Grandmother, Grandfather
    Father cannot yet bring himself to write what must be told. Let my verse then, sing the tale.
    When your failing eyes did not
    Recognize
    That the syrup of ipecac was not dimetap
    And I was young and only
    Sniffling
    I learned that the road to hell is paved with good intentions
    Forgive us then, our youthful follies
    In the daylight of our lives
    And shortcuts do not illicit cries of
    "long odds!"
    Tragedy at noon; the zenith of our lusty decampment
    Transfig'r'd in an
    Instant
    to tenebrous Despair
    As Icarus, whose selfsame savior,
    Dearest Daedelus observes, is his shellacking
    Fates found our aged Jeep turned o'er
    Accompt slippery conditions and staggering no-necks, nigh blasted,
Blaisdell Lake
    Reports rang and Shield-Maidens sang upon our side, yet though
    My pathetic brother cried, victory found us as the gore-swell

Ebbed.
And One Hundred and Fourteen be the cursed concourse looming
Still forty miles hence, the homestead
Through the Barrows of Sutton
Their unquiet dead, pregnant for three centuries
With the desire to eat things
Delivered from that pale penumbra, unto ravish
The above
in feast.
A sordid sublimation rising.
We strive, unceasing for your door
And shall post notes at every store
We find
With Wifi.
Because we forgot the right cables at home
And even the sketchiest Mr. Mikes', perchance
Have password protection and IPs
Unknown.
As where
We huddle
Now.

While I briefly considered tetrameter, I concluded free verse to be the more practical and emotionally suggestive form. The poet can easily telegraph a rapid succession of information: images, thoughts, impressions, observations, feelings, witticisms, reflections, all as they occur and without regard to meter or other stylistic refinements. Raw? Definitely. Lyrical? I think so (and so did Goethe and Rimbaud, for that matter). Rather like the imbroglio in which we find ourselves enfolded. At once we are exhilarated by a freedom rarely known and cowed by its scope; one delimited only and truly for the first time by our own courage and imagination. Ironic that it should take the dead to ignite our passion for living (though hasn't it always been so?). I am as animate as I am appalled to have borne witness to these circumstances, and hope now only that I shall survive to see your sweet faces again, and that this horror was wrought by a quixotic and handsome vampire whose destiny bifurcates my own.

Holly

From: fogeyfarm@hotmail.com
To: timpb@gmail.com
Cc: manray2012@yahoomail.com
Bcc:
Subject: Jesus, Mary, and Joseph riding on a train!

Well, frost my pickle! Holly, you're growing into a fine young woman and your writ it sure does sound nice sliding down the old hearie-canals! What does your brother think of you? He still playing basketball?

So Ray-ray comes over last night (sorry for the redundancy Ray, or maybe you're hearing it for the first time!) and boy do we put a hurtin' on some fins (I ain't talking about going down to New Ipswich neither!). Beer-batter, artery sauce, John Holmes fries, ketchup and plenty of the good stuff to wash it down and dull the flavor of the more freezer-burnt specimens. We were hoping you'd join us, but it sounds like you're stopping in Sittinspin instead. You got some school friends there? Maybe this is the handsome fellow you alluded to? Well I wish you the best and hope to see you tonight.

Of course, Ray-ray was in rare form and all ready to give you each the old back-breaker. He got so carried away with the spirit he started singing Christmas carols and almost fell face first into the deep fryer! Wouldn't have eaten that, even it was extra-crispy. Towards the end of the evening he started acting so foolish we had to put him down for bed. Just muttering and listless and looking pale and peckish. Think maybe he had himself too much mayonnaise. Hasn't gotten up yet!

Anyway, we got plenty of leftovers and haven't been bothered by anybody since Elaine told those wingnuts where to get off.

* * *

Today on "The Writer's Almanac," we remember the death-day of that most morbid of minds, Mr. H.P. Lovecraft,

A writer largely unknown in his own time and whose body of work remains divisive today, inspiring delight from some and derision from others.

This is a man who once wrote: "Life is a hideous thing, and from the background behind what we know of it peer daemo-niacal hints of truth which make it sometimes a thousandfold more hideous. Science, already oppressive with its shocking revelations, will perhaps be the ultimate exterminator of our human species—if separate species we be—for its reserve of unguessed horrors could never be borne by mortal brains if loosed upon the world."

Born today, musician Sly Stone, who said: "Different strokes, for different folks."

* * *

From: timpb@gmail.com
To: fogeyfarm@hotmail.com
Cc:
Bcc:
Subject: YOU MUST BEHEAD RAY-RAY IMMEDIATELY!

Please, know this will be difficult for you, but must believe what I am about to tell you and do as I say. Ray-ray's symptoms, according to what we've been able to gather anecdotally and from media reports = totally in line with the final stages of transformation. Has likely been bitten by one of these creatures and condition will degenerate until he resembles them. Hate to tell you to do this and you should know it's no easier on me. Love that numbnuts, but I beg you do what subject line says b/ cause may have as little as 12 hours!

I know you've heard of zombies and maybe you don't believe in them—I know I didn't but mass of evidence too great to ignore. Believe it or not, they're upon us, among us and don't seem to be going any-where. In fact, they're flocking to New Hampshire in droves.

Why?

We've caught some wild fringe speculation from the few we've met on the road about everything from an apparent link to vast, subter-ranean radon vortices to psycho-motor compulsions from deep within the reptilian brain associated with the state motto. For some folks—and you know this, with the whole libertarian business—New Hampshire is a kind of symbolic promised land, the last vestige of what America ought to be. People hold it up in their minds like a kind of Jerusalem, as if we're an antidote to the depressing mantra about the only two sure things in life. A place where sure, we might die, but at least we don't have to pay (some) taxes! They do this up, not understanding (or not wanting to understand) that for the most part we're just as backward, just as miserable, just as clueless about how to approach the wrenchingly complex and constantly evolving struggle of attempting to ensure that the citizenry who aren't interned or on the lam, live the free and digni-fied lives they feel they so richly deserve without infringing on others' pursuit of the same. They do it because they have to, because to live under one of those little, custom-cut storm clouds might be worse than dying. And maybe that hope is stronger than death.

Give him the rest of the natty. Shit, give him whatever he wants and put him out. I can't stand the thought of losing three when it could be one. I don't know. Keep him drunk, I guess, and we'll hurry our butts up. We're in Hill now. "Best wieners in the state," this T-bird says, and I can barely touch one.

From: fogeyfarm@hotmail.com
To: timpb@gmail.com
Cc: ˎ
Bcc:
Subject: Re: YOU MUST BEHEAD RAY-RAY IMMEDIATELY!

You'll notice Ray's not copied into this one. I did that because I'm too ashamed to let him in on what you was discussing, even indirectly.

How's he doing you ask? (you didn't) Still sleeping it off, mild as a lamb on the living room sofa. Your face red yet? It's about to be.

This is not Kristallnacht, which incidentally I am old enough to remember as having been headline news. The systematic extermination of the "suspect" is something I'll never do despite whatever asshattery Pat Robertson is depositing on the heads of the swizzle sticks still tuning into the *700 Reasons I Barf*. What infuriates me most about the scrubs peddling apocalyptic eschatology is that they're fail-safe and can be eas-ily retrofitted to the heresy *du jour*, whether that's entertaining the notion of dinosaurs, farting in the presence of a child or cutting off the head of your neighbor. That said, I don't disbelieve in mystery.

There's an explanation for this, but our own brains—magnificent as they may often prove—have always been a limiting factor. One day, when this is all over somebody will start picking the fly shit out of the pepper. Until then I chalk it up to entropy and admit that I'm beat. What I've seen are municipal officials, public school teachers, children, sodomites, holy-rollers, pedophiles, little old ladies, immigrants, Yanks, short-bussers, turd-burglars, pecker-heads, jag offs, working men, working girls, good eggs, bad seed and every color of the goddamn rainbow, shuffling tits-up and sniffing around for the next bite. Maybe it's a good old fashioned Voo-doo curse, blowing its thanks up to CBN and the AM crowd on the trade winds. Maybe we had it coming.

Sure, I could cut Ray-ray's head off and be done with it easy as you please, but talk about storm clouds following you around. You think I could live beside myself knowing what I'd done? Thanks but no thanks. I'll put my cup on, open a bag of Sausalito's and see you when I see you. And suds ain't a bad idea either. Only sensible thing I made out in that grocery-list tirade. Son, call me stodgy but your old man misses articles; definite, indefinite, hell, even indeterminate would be enough to show you care.

* * *

I'm Brady Carlson, filling in for Dan Colgan, who could not be with us today for necrophagous reasons.

If you're listening, please pay close attention as we do not know how long we'll be able to maintain this signal at your particular frequency. We received a flood of e-mails and calls from across the state yesterday and this morning, reporting that alcohol, but especially beer, has had a mellowing effect on "zombies" who have been made to consume it and may even slow or nullify the transformation into "zombies" of those who have been bitten. Preliminary hypotheses point to the presence in hops specifically of 2-Methyl-2-butanol, also known as tert-amyl alcohol or amylene hydrate, which produces sedative and hypnotic effects in humans. While a thorough investigation of these allegations is currently being conducted by the remains of the state government at the Smuttynose Brewery in the Portsmouth Green Zone, early reports indicate a high level of optimism. Inventor and entrepreneur Dean Kamen has enthusiastically undertaken the ambitious personal project of delivering all the beer necessary to ensure peace in the Granite State via an intricate machine at once highly esoteric and idiotically simple, which he claims will revolutionize the way the world drinks and suppress those forces that would make it monstrous.

* * *

From: timpb@gmail.com
To: fogeyfarm@hotmail.com
Cc:
Bcc:
Subject: Sorry Dad

I've just been under a lot of stress lately, is all. Good news though—we've found some bicycles.

Spattered in a dozen shades of horrible, the kids are riding along with their chins up.

Miles laughed when he slid a severed, decaying hand from the grip shift.

"It's a deal," he said, pretending to shake it before placing it gently under a tree by the side of the road.

Big canopy, sawtoothed leaves. But there I go again, listing. Wish I had taken the time to learn its name. Then I could've been really terse and gruff.

When we get there, folks. Who am I going to write to?

Holly's peddling along. High shorts, tennis shoes, raincoat, wet, coffee-colored hair, big eyes going all over the compass and a funny secret sort of smile on her face like she's enjoying herself somehow. I can't help but list these things. How am I supposed to embellish a beauty I can't really comprehend? The whole situation is weird, obviously. Blood staining the rain, the rain washing the road, and us splashing through, and trees rising above us, and birds, chirping away just the same as always.

I feel like I should feel like I'm in hell but instead I'm taking a bike ride with my kids, and all I can think about is how I want to be their penpal or something so I can figure out what they're really thinking about up there that's so charming and mysterious.

Think they'd accept letters from down the hall? Would you?

We're going to have fun, Dad, Mom, if we ever get there.

From: hottotroinboston@comcast.net
To: manray2012@yahoomail.com
Cc: fogeyfarm@hotmail.com
Bcc: timpb@gmail.com
Subject: Re: Funny Stuff

Hey, what's up now? Bet you thought I ate the cake. Been in Hawaii for state highway patrolman's conference. Guess who learned how to uke?

Seth Blake was born and raised in Peterborough, New Hampshire. He attended St. Lawrence University in (way) upstate New York, graduating in 2009. His main preoccupations are fiction, film and music. He is currently enrolled at CalArts, earning his MFA in fiction. Wherever he lies, New Hampshire—weird and comely—features centrally in his dreams.

The Haze

Rebecca Rule

U p until the last minute, the hunter blames the hurt in his bones on his disease. Drugs helped some. For awhile. Lots of different ones—"Why don't we try this?" the docs said. "How about we change this up?" But there was no "we" about it. The cancer belonged to him. He'd been dying with it for four years, through four hunting seasons. At first the docs said he might last five, but that's not going to happen.

At radiation he overhead this story: The dying man hallucinated sharks swimming across the ceiling above his bed. He said to his wife, "When will this be over?" She said, "They say it's not over until the fat lady sings." He said, "Start singing."

This last November, he made a stab at one more hunting trip. His boy drove him to a likely field and helped him out of the truck. He sat on a camouflaged folding chair, thirty-thirty leaned against the stone wall because he couldn't stand the weight of it across his legs. If a buck appeared under that apple tree, he probably wouldn't have the strength to put the gun to his shoulder, let alone hold it steady. But for the sake of his boy—his gray-bearded boy off walking the woods—he play-acted that he might.

Mild for November, and the hunter had dressed in layers, but the boy wasn't gone ten minutes before the chill set in. His hands stiffened with it, even in insulated gloves. It got to his feet through felts and heavy socks. Christ, his feet had been cold in the truck with the heat blasting. What did he expect?

When the cold reached his core and he started shaking, he said,

To hell with it, abandoned the chair but took the rifle, and staggered to where the boy had parked the truck behind a screen of hemlocks, keys tucked in the visor.

He spent the next few hours turning the truck on for heat, then off to conserve gas. Slept some. Dreamed he was home in bed. Big bear outside concaving the wall with a shoulder. Gun at hand but he couldn't find the bullets. *Who stole my damn bullets?* Some under the pillow but the wrong calliber. Some in the drawer, but greasy; they slid through his fingers, clattered to the floor, and rolled away.

"How long you been sitting in the truck?" the boy asked.

"Ten minutes," he said. "See anything?"

"Tracks," the boy said. "But nothin' standin' in 'em. You?"

"Not a goddamned thing."

They'd driven three miles down the road before the hunter remembered the folding chair by the wall. The boy wheeled the truck around and they went back for it.

"I'll pick you up in the morning," the boy said. "We'll try a new spot."

"No," the hunter said. "I'm done. In more ways than one."

The boy laughed.

All his life, the hunter believed when your number's up, it's up. Death was not something to fear, it simply was. Animals knew it in their bones. The fear he saw in the eyes of the coyote caught in a leg trap was an instinctive fear of him—the human being—not fear of death. To shoot that coyote in the head was doing him a favor by ending his suffering. "Thank you very much," the coyote would have said, if he could talk. And if his blood wasn't pooling on the leaves, eyes dulled and glazed over. The haze, he called it. Before the rigor and the rot, came the haze. He'd seen it slide over the eyes of that coyote, still twitching. He'd seen it seep into the eyes of his beagle dog, run over, hit in the road right in front of him. Not a mark on that beagle, but she was gone in minutes as he cradled her in his arms, as his stupid sister said, "I'll go get Dad!" And ran off—as if there were anything he could do.

He'd seen the haze dozens of times in the deer he bagged. Before he stuck the knife into the warm belly, he looked into the eyes.

As a little kid, he asked his mother what happened after you die. She said you returned to where you were before you were born. Simple as that. When she died, he chose to believe she'd returned to that place—which, near as he could figure, was dark, silent, empty and pain-free. Sounded pretty good to him.

Walter, his brother-in-law, told this story. The old lady was dying. Her friend, holding her hand, asked, "Do you believe there's life after death?" The old lady said, "Lord, I hope not. I'm tired!"

When their father died, his stupid sister said, "He's gone to be with Mum and Andy." She said things like that. Just to say them. No one spoke of Andy, ever. And to bring up his name at their father's grave-side—*What the hell?* he felt like saying, *What the hell is wrong with you?*

When his ex-wife dropped dead from a bleed in the brain, his stupid sister said to the boy, "At least your Mum didn't suffer," and patted his shoulder. When that same sister skidded on black ice, rolled her van, crashed upside down and sideways into a pine tree, and survived, he said to the boy, "I guess her number wasn't up."

They visited her at the hospital. She was stove to hell—crushed leg, cracked pelvis, collapsed lung. They had to suck the blood out of her insides so she wouldn't drown in it. She had one of those pain buttons like he has now. You push it and the drugs go directly into your vein. She must have pushed it five times while he and the boy were in the room. "I'm so lucky," she said, "it wasn't my neck or back." Tears dripped from her blackened eyes. "I'm lucky to be alive. So lucky, Frankie." He had to step out of the room. *Lucky!* If she'd been lucky, she'd have missed that ice patch. Steered out of the skid. Or avoided the pine tree.

Now the tables are turned. He's the one in the hospital bed with the pain button. She sits at his bedside, holding his hand. *Never done that before.* Rubbing her thumb over his knuckles. *Never done that before.* The boy's in the room, too. Somewhere. When he opens his eyes, he sees the boy's jacket in a pile on a chair by the window. The shade is drawn, the room darkened, but it's daylight. He sees light through the shade.

"It's okay," his stupid sister says in his ear. "We're here, Frankie." Then something about Mum and Dad and Andy. Then the boy says something. The boy's hand presses the hunter's left shoulder. It hurts.

Someone raises the shade and he's in golden woods with Andy, his twin, and Uncle Frank, who he was named for. He and Andy are just boys. Father's working, so Uncle Frank takes them hunting. It's a sin to miss opening day. The boys carry identical four-tens. Big enough to kill a deer—though it might take two shots. Not big enough to dislocate a little boy's shoulder with a kick.

They separate. Uncle Frank whispers: *You stay here, Frankie. Lay in under this spruce. Rest your gun here. We'll drive one to you.*

He stays still a long time. The light shifts in the woods. He's flat out under the spruce. When he hears the hussssh of something moving through brush, he pulls off his right glove with his teeth, presses his shoulder into the rubber of the stock. He sees the head of a deer. The shape of it. The glint of an antler. He holds his breath and squeezes the trigger, like Uncle Frank and his father taught him.

"I know it hurts," his stupid sister is saying. "I'm sorry."
It's the cancer eating my bones, he thought. *Course it hurts.*

The hunter's eyes, when he looked in the mirror, were ordinary brown—like anybody else's: his father, Uncle Frank, his stupid sister, the boy. But Andy took after their mother. His eyes were pewter gray. No one ever mistook one twin for the other—not even when they were infants.

Uncle Frank pries the four-ten from his hands. *Stay put*, he says. But he doesn't. He crawls across the golden woods to where Frank bends over Andy. He puts his face close to Andy's and looks into gray eyes turned milky blue. The haze.

He tripped and his gun went off, Frank says. *Yours never fired. Smell the barrel.*
This is Andy's gun, he says.
It's not, Frank says. *It's yours and you never fired it. Andy fell.*
"Andy fell," the hunter says.
The boy says, "What, Dad?"

It's not the cancer hurts so deep in my bones, he thinks. *It's the lie.*

The boy bends close, breath to breath. The hunter looks into his boy's eyes. He sees the haze, milky blue. But this time, he's on the inside looking out.

Rebecca Rule gathers and tells funny New England stories. She's published three collections of short stories as well as a guide to New Hampshire, *Live Free and Eat Pie*. Her latest book is *Headin' for the Rhubarb: A New Hampshire Dictionary (kinda)*. She lives in Northwood and is currently working on a book about New Hampshire town meeting. "The Haze" is her first intentional work of horror.

Epitaph

Andy Richmond

"The girl's name Hannah is of Hebrew origin and its meaning is favored grace."

"I like it. You still think it's a girl?"

"I do. Hannah Anne Jarvis, to be exact."

"Oh, you've got a middle name picked out too?"

"I'm allowed to dream."

"Yes, you are, Love. I guess you are . . ."

She closed the baby name book and placed it on the makeshift night table beside the box spring and mattress as they lay back, wrapping into each other for warmth. Meg and Kevin Jarvis had been marking life's milestones at a rapid pace lately. Kevin's new job had brought them to New Hampshire just a month earlier. The farmhouse they now called home was their first. The bump in Meg's belly for which they nightly auditioned names was their first child. Four months pregnant, Meg had decided to take some time before getting back to her own work after the move. There was work enough, they both knew, in getting this new life started.

The latest addition to the to-do list was getting the furnace serviced. The fireplace had its charms, but Meg found herself feeling chilly all the time lately and September was mostly spent. Buying an ancient homestead in rural New Hampshire had seemed romantic last summer in Chicago, but reality had tarnished the dream a bit. Still, Meg was

coming to love the house and setting there in Harton. "Fourteen acres of river frontage, cornfields, rocky bluffs and woodland in rural New Hampshire," the real estate ad had said. "Nineteenth century charm abounds in this six-room farmhouse, outbuildings and barn."

Tonight though, the wind funneled down the river and rattled the windows as gusts from across the fields broke on the house. She'd been feeling good, just past her first trimester without much of the discomfort she'd read was possible. She'd prefer if Kevin didn't have to leave so soon after the move, but presenting at the symposium would really cement his position with the department head. Her days were plenty full, though: The pregnancy was going well, and the work of sorting out their new home matched her hormonal nesting instinct nicely. He'd only be gone for three days anyway. She settled in to sleep, comfortable with Kevin's warmth at her back and their cat Leo curled at her feet.

They woke early in anticipation of his departure. Early enough to allow for a proper goodbye, which sent the cat searching for his food bowl. Later, as the kitchen warmed to both stovetop and fireplace, they sorted the details of their coming days. Kevin powered up his laptop.

"Huh, the Internet connection's down. Must have been the wind."

"I'll see if they'll come out later today," Meg said, blowing across a steaming mug of tea.

"Thanks, Babe. I guess I'll just call from the road to confirm my reservations," Kevin said, unplugging his phone from the charger.

"Right, as soon as you get around the mountain . . ."

"At least your phone gets reception at the house. You going to be okay without the Internet?"

"They'll probably get to it today. Besides, I've been living in a time machine. Anyway, this will just make it more authentic."

"Oh yeah, the attic. Back to your classification project, Linnaeus?"

Since first exploring the attic, Meg had become consumed with the discovery; sorting, and arranging its contents.

"We'll be furnishing this house with what I find up there," she replied "and maybe paying off the mortgage. But yeah, the attic's almost done; I'll finish today."

"Well, wait on the barn 'til I'm back, okay? I don't want you to overdo it," Kevin said, holding her shoulders. "You know you could still drop me off and drive back so you'd have the car."

They'd driven to New Hampshire in their eight-year-old Nissan. It had spent most of its life in the city parked, and it was pretty good in the snow. But here they'd need a second car and on the advice of other faculty, they'd decided to get an all-wheel drive wagon. As of this morning, though, it still hadn't arrived at the dealership in Sargeant.

"Maybe the Subaru will come in and they'll deliver it," Meg said. "Either way, I'll be fine. It's three days, Kevin. I'm a big girl."

"And she's a really little girl," he said, rubbing Meg's belly. "You two be careful."

Their goodbye hug lingered until, finally, he had to go. She stood watching the car disappear down the drive, rounding a copse of trees. Turning away, she smelled the wood smoke rising from the chimney. Shafts of sunlight beamed through the mist that rose from the river and hung low in the field on these early fall mornings. The barn framed her view of the lower fields backed by the river, and the brilliant color of autumn trees on the far shore. The Shincracker, Harton's local mountain, loomed close from here, but it would take Kevin forty minutes to work his way around on back roads to the Interstate. Shrugging off a chill, she climbed the stairs to the farmer's porch that wrapped around two sides of the house, and went inside.

The attic was nice in the mornings. The window in the eastern eave spilled sunlight into the room. The angular space had taken on an ordered appeal as Meg worked through it. She'd used a sewing table she'd found as her triage area, deciding what stayed in the house, what went to the dump, what debuted on eBay. Her latest find was still spread out on the table. The surface was covered with bottles that had once held pills, elixirs and potions—now sorted by color, shape and size.

The eternal quest for a magic bullet, she thought, holding up a pill bottle to read the embossed surface.

"Not such a leap from Dr. King's New Life Pills to infomercial America, huh Leo?" she asked the cat who had climbed the steep attic stairs to join her.

This morning, she just needed to box the last of the bottles, clearing the sewing table so she could bring it down into her dining room work area and polish the wood. Nudging the bottles back as she slid an empty box onto the table, a small pill bottle fell over the edge. It dropped to the floor and rolled back against the wall. Hemmed in as the table was,

Meg realized she'd have to crawl under it to reach the bottle. Carefully, she maneuvered into the space.

"Easy, Baby," she said to her stomach, gaining just the reach she needed to touch the bottle. As she adjusted for a little more extension, she looked up and to her left. From this angle, she could see into a high corner she'd missed before. She'd overlooked two shelves built in to the space where the chimney rose against the attic's gable peak. The lower shelf was empty, but she could just see the ends of two tins on the upper one.

"Ooh, what have we here?" she asked Leo, who sat on the sunny top of a box, grooming. She'd have to clear a path to get to the coving. Fueled by the promise of new discovery, she carefully shifted things out of her way, moving thoughtfully and avoiding strain. It would still be a stretch up to the cobwebbed corner, but she thought she could just reach. She drew the edge of the left-hand tin off the shelf with the very tip of her finger. It wasn't heavy; in fact, it felt empty. As it levered off the shelf, dropping into her hands, something slid inside. She leaned back against a carton and worked to lift the tin's cover. It released suddenly and the shape inside hopped a little with the motion. Her heart raced, and the cat started at her inadvertent scream. Her hands tingled as she reassured herself with a laugh.

She'd been lucky up to now. All that time in the attic and she hadn't disturbed a bat or uncovered a big spider. In the tin though, was a dead mouse; mummified, really. Its movement when the lid popped, and seeing the fur, had scared her. She didn't really mind mice, though, and laughed at her own reaction now.

"Brave explorer, right Buddy?" The now sleeping cat rotated an ear in response.

"Poor thing" she said, resting the lid back over the tin, covering the small grey form along with the bits of yellowed newsprint and rust sifting inside.

"I'll take care of you later," she said, setting the first tin carefully aside and reaching for the second. This time, there was some weight inside. She coaxed it over the edge of the shelf, and it dropped, rattling, into her hands. With fresh caution, she held the tin at arm's length as she pried the lid off. It was half full of buttons.

Meg found herself reaching for handfuls of buttons and letting them run through her fingers like coins in a treasure chest, pattering back into the tin. The buttons, in so many shapes, sizes and materials were certainly not gold, but they were a treasure of sorts. Meg was transported through time, imagining the woman or girl who had collected the buttons in this same home, now hers. She cleared the table and sat down in the sunlight with the tin, digging into the find. By the time she decided to head down for lunch, Meg had found her two favorites. Their surfaces were marbled with a swirl of black and gold, their hexagonal shape unique.

Too early for Bakelite, Meg thought, flipping one of the buttons in her fingers. Maybe ceramic? She placed them both into the center of the overturned lid, swept the other buttons back into the tin and centered them on the table. Grabbing the first tin, she turned to the stairs.

"Want a snack, Leo? I hear mouse mummy is a feline delicacy."

* * *

Meg woke with a start to the sound of a crash.

"Leo?" She gathered herself in the dim room and looked at the clock. It was only 1:30 pm, but during her nap, the clear day had given way to a dark and drizzly afternoon. The wind had once again picked up, and at the sound of a second crash, she was able to pinpoint the source of her rude awakening. It was the shutter they'd noticed loosening on one of the front windows. The wind, now directly out of the north, had pulled it loose and was throwing it back against the casing.

Several times as she worked to nail the shutter fast, gusts of wind sent frozen pellets beating onto the window glass and the back of her parka and hood. At times the mix of rain turned entirely to white. With the shutter secured, she was happy to return to the shelter of the house, dropping the hammer in the mudroom with a sense of satisfaction. She lit the fire she'd laid before going out and called for the cat. Another slash of ice pellets on the window made her think of the cable company. No way they'd come out in this, but at least she could get her call into the queue. She opened her phone and was surprised to find a no service message on the screen. She'd always had phone service in the house. Maybe the weather was affecting it?

Meg moved around the house holding her phone out in front of her, seeking reception. Unsuccessful after circling the first floor, she climbed the stairs. She jumped back from the window at the landing, almost dropping her phone, as sleet again slammed into the glass. Deciding to head for the highest ground she could, she flipped the light switch and climbed the attic stairs. The phone's screen still read no service as she emerged into the small room.

"Phew," she said aloud, "I didn't notice Mr. Mouse had smelled so bad before." She unlocked the western window and slid it up a little to let the slightly putrid odor diffuse.

Well, I guess I'm not calling Comcast today, she thought, pocketing the phone and glancing at the table top. She smiled at the button collection. Her smile faded, though, as she looked more closely. The half-full tin and its overturned lid were just where she'd left them, but the two buttons she'd left on the lid were gone.

"Leo?" she called for the second time that afternoon. Come to think of it, she hadn't seen the cat since she'd been woken up. She looked more closely at the table. The lid was still positioned near the tin, exactly as it had been, but both buttons were gone. Could the cat have batted them out so precisely?

"Here we go again, Baby. Ready Hannah?" she let herself ask as she worked her body down to a position under the table once again, scanning the floor carefully. Neither of the two buttons was there. She shook the tin, quickly sifting through the other buttons. Had she dropped them back in without remembering? The two black hexagons were not with the others. She abruptly stood and closed the window.

"LEO?" She called as she came down the attic stairs, goose flesh prickling her neck, stomach unsettled from the smell up there. She quickly checked for the cat in the two upstairs bedrooms before descending to the first floor. She hit the power switch on the stereo and NHPR provided her some company. Feeling a little better, she circled the first floor again, this time looking for the cat. The cellar door off the dining room was closed, so she didn't bother with that. She looked under some of the furniture projects she'd spread out in her makeshift workroom. Finding nothing, she continued to the living room hearth.

I guess he could have taken a button in his mouth, but both of them?

she thought. She added wood to the fire, still working out the missing buttons. Weird cat behavior, she thought, but then, he's a weird cat.

"I would like to find the bugger, though," she said to herself, settling into a wing chair she'd reclaimed from the attic to enjoy the fire. On the radio, Talk of the Nation was taking calls on health care legislation. Another call I won't be making, she thought, sinking back into the chair.

A clatter on the porch caused her to lean forward, glancing out the window. She just caught sight of Leo's black tail as he scooted out of view away from an overturned planter.

"Outside!?" she said, thinking, I didn't let him out, did he get past me when I went to fix the shutter? She grabbed her mostly dry parka and ran out the front door. I must be losing it, she thought.

"Leo!" she called, hurrying now, off the porch and behind the house. While still overcast, the worst of the sleet had stopped. Gusty wind still blew sorties, but she ignored it, in hot pursuit. The cat ran through the waves of matted hay overgrown through a summer of neglect. Meg lost sight of him behind the barn. She rounded the big building, noticing for the first time a distinctly traveled path leading from the back of the barn toward the woods. Of course, Leo was bounding up it away from her.

The path stood out in white, graupel collected in the rut through the hay. She guessed maybe deer had walked this way often enough to mat down the deep grass and leave the track. She crossed over the stone wall and looked up toward the tree line. The path was vague through the ledge, but she could pick it up again where the white beads filled depressions in trampled moss between granite slabs. She couldn't see Leo; taller grass overhung the track further up, but she could sense his movement. He evaded her now, playful. They continued from slab into brush, crossing the tree line. The interstice was thin, allowing her to move easily into the woods, and really, the fresh air and exercise felt good. God damn the cat, he could stay out for the night, but now she was intrigued with the exploration.

She could see Leo's black and white rump ahead, moving upward on the matted path toward a ledge, really a big boulder set into the hillside. Her feet slipped from under her as she worked her way up the steep bank edging the right side of the giant rock. She felt a moment's worry, but she'd landed softly in thick moss and a layer of leaves blown into the corner. She lay there breathing in the earthy scents and listening to the cat pouncing in the duff, still playing.

"Okay in there, Baby?" she asked, confident her child was safely cushioned in a liquid home. From the corner of her eye, she noticed a dark shape to her left, where the ground leveled above her. Pressing up to stand, she saw it was a tombstone.

Where the boulder leveled at the top, the forest floor also flattened into the hillside, creating space for four graves. Dark slate slabs about an inch thick marked the small family plot. She brushed herself off, and came around to the foot of the first grave, keeping a respectful berth. Looking out through the foliage from the alcove set into the hillside, Meg had a view over the property. The eroded headstones stood in dark contrast against the dimmed autumn color below. Though worn by time and weather, she could clearly see the surname etched into the slate.

Wylde? What a name, she thought, already planning to research the house's history. The first stone was the largest, and apparently marked the patriarch's grave. She strained to make out the entire epitaph.

Sacred to the memory of Josephus Wylde
dead on the 18th of September 1839
in the 44th year of his life.

The stones told their tale of time as she moved along the plot.

Here Lyes Buried
the body of Mrs. Fidelia Wylde
Wife to Josephus Wylde
Who Departed this life
on the 12th of May 1850
Ae 51 years

Her breath caught as she read the tiny third stone.

Hannah Fortin
b Mar 4, d Jul 7, 1847
ae 4 mo.
Our Angel

Meg's blood ran cold. Hannah! She refused to think about the circumstances that might have led to the tragedy etched in the stone before her, and quickly turned away. She'd had enough of the cat and mouse game, and wanted to go home. Grabbing Leo, who had wandered close, she started working her way around the plot. She planned to skirt the last partially fallen tombstone and drop down the far side of the ledge, back to the track they'd followed in. Nearing the far edge, she now noticed the last grave had mostly slid away down the hillside. Its marker, barely standing, read:

Cora Wylde Fortin
Sorrowful Mother
b Nov 8, 1827, d Dec 12, 1859

The grave had dropped off the steep edge of the level alcove over time, the mossy surface scoured down to granite along the grave's outside edge. Meg pressed her eyes closed and backed around the way she'd come, heart pounding, arms wrapped around the wayward cat.

* * *

Listening to the empty house, Meg switched off the lamp. She lay back in the bed which tonight she shared only with Leo. She'd had no luck with the phone, and knew Kevin would be worried. She'd try from outside tomorrow. The weather had calmed, and the starry night promised a clear day to come. She skipped the baby names tonight, still trying to put the afternoon out of her mind.

Cradling her belly in her hands, she thought of her child.

"It's okay, little one," she said to the bulge. She forced herself to stop dwelling on the plights of the young mother and child whose graves she'd found. Her mind wandered through the day—back to the attic, the missing buttons and the crazy cat chase—ultimately back to the graves.

That poor family, she thought. As her mind finally settled and sleep approached, her memory touched on a detail that hadn't fully registered before. The trail she'd chased Leo on—deer had used it often enough to keep it visible, yet it didn't seem to really go anywhere. She couldn't remember seeing it continue beyond the ledge. It seemed to have ended at the Wylde family plot.

* * *

Frost steamed from the wide boards of the barn wall, warming as the sun topped the trees across the river. Meg left the porch, crunching through the long frosty grass, sienna tinted with crystal white, woven to a snarl through inattention. She cleared away the grass along the rail, and pulled the big door open on its rollers. Inside, sunlight beamed through gaps in the barn boards, striping the shadows with spokes of light. She breathed the comfortable smell of hay and long-ago livestock brought to life by the warmth.

She'd never really acknowledged Kevin's request the other morning to wait for him before starting on the barn. All she was going to do was take a look, anyway. She cast her eyes around the interior, standing in the entryway, open space all the way to the rafters. The rear part of the barn was a loft, sectioned underneath into stalls and small rooms. A narrow stairway climbed to the loft on the far side of the building. The trappings of the barn's working days hung here and there throughout. She wandered around the first level, enjoying the warmth and scent of the building.

She noticed a gap in the wall near the soapstone sink where the boards had loosened and bowed outward. It looked like something had been using this as a way into the building. A smudge of mud caked on the floor indicated the path of the raccoon(?) opossum(?), that had been getting into the building. Whatever it was had headed straight for the loft stairs.

Probably living up here, she thought, bracing herself for the next in the series of shocks she'd encountered lately as she began up the stairs. She noticed the smudged path was actually worn into the floorboards. The treads of the loft stairway were concave with the wear. She helped herself upward with her arms as she emerged through the loft floor from the stairs. The entire loft was filled with stored furniture, draped in dusty tarpaulins.

"Well, no rabid raccoons that meet the eye," Meg said to herself, eyeing the corners and crevices. She caught a slight scent of decay in the air, though.

Another carcass up here somewhere? she thought. Maybe whatever made this path crawled in here to die. She carefully pulled away tarpaulins, still following a trampled pathway. Cautious of another furry body, but eager to survey the extent of her find, she revealed the discovery section by section. There was a nice old grandfather clock, a set of ornate end tables; slowly she unearthed generations of furnishings, moving between groupings of odd shapes covered by tarpaulins. Rounding a tall corner that had blocked her view beyond, she entered an area where the other furniture had been pushed back. Centered in the small circular nook, uncovered, stood the find of the morning. Meg approached a delicate oak cradle and reached out to touch it.

Why would this one piece have been uncovered? It's not even dusty, Meg thought. Kevin must have been cleaning it up, that's why he didn't want me to start on the barn. He was going to surprise me!

The cradle was beautifully crafted, lightweight but sturdy. The rocker mechanism was a cleverly designed glider that worked effortlessly even now. The motion seemed as smooth as the day it was built.

* * *

Late that afternoon, she stood and looked proudly around her dining room workspace. Before the weather turned, she had brought the cradle, end tables and a small hope chest into the house. She'd uncovered and inventoried a good amount of the other stuff in the barn, and outlined a plan for keeping, dumping or selling most of what she'd seen. She'd worked carefully but steadily and felt a tired satisfaction with her accomplishments. Anticipating the excitement of sharing the secret cradle discovery with Kevin; mentally planning the nursery room, she put a pot of stew on the stove to warm. Meg grabbed her parka for a last trip to close up the barn since, once again, the fine day had deteriorated to a mix of rain and sleet with a steady wind off the river. Ducking her hooded head into the sleet, she made her way to the barn. Meg stepped through the big door and out of the weather. Moving to the ancient knob and tube switch panel, she flicked off the far set of lights. As her eyes adjusted, she noticed something at the base of the loft stairs. She walked toward the small bundle of fabric.

Did something fall out of one of the pieces I moved, she wondered.

Lifting the fabric form, she raised a simple doll to view. Crudely cut and irregularly stitched, it could have been made by a child. She turned the rustic but eloquent little figure over in her hands, and gasped, stunned. The face of the doll had been fashioned with buttons for eyes and a rough line of stitches as a mouth. The two hexagonal black and gold marbled buttons she'd found in the attic, the ones that had disappeared yesterday, were sewn unevenly to the doll's face as eyes.

* * *

Meg's vision blurred and refocused with the shock of her find. She dropped the doll to the barn floor, blood turning to ice. Someone had been in the house to take the buttons while she and her baby were sleeping! They must have been watching her movements all day and snuck into the barn when she'd left. She switched off the remaining lights, and threw the barn door closed on its runners, heart pounding. She ran back to the house, locking the door behind her. She found the hammer she'd left in the mudroom and hefted it, a powerful protective instinct she'd never known before emerging from deep inside her. She moved quickly through the house to the back door, and threw the lock. She tried to settle her breathing as she locked windows.

It could have been a coincidence, she thought as she finished—the house secure.

"No, those were the exact buttons, I'm sure of it," she said aloud. Meg ran upstairs and grabbed her cell phone from the charger beside her bed. She opened it to find no service available, but one message waiting. She must have had service long enough to receive a call. She keyed her code into the phone, hands shaking, and listened. Kevin—concerned, almost frantic in the message, asking her to please pick up, saying he hadn't heard from her, hadn't been able to get through until now. He'd rearranged his schedule and caught an early flight from the symposium. He was on the ground in Manchester and had left the airport half an hour ago, but it was still a two-hour trip in good weather.

"Thank God," she said to herself. He'd be here by eight. Leo mewed inquisitively as he joined her in the bedroom.

"Oh, Buddy, I'm glad to see you." She swept the cat into one arm and stroked his fur, beginning to relax. The smell of warm stew drew her down to the kitchen, flipping light switches as she went. Finally, with the house ablaze in light, a bowl of warm stew in her lap and a fire in the hearth, she settled down in her wingchair, letting the hammer she was still carrying slip to the floor.

Kevin will be home soon, she thought. As the stew warmed her from within, she fought the desire to close her eyes. Eventually, though, as Leo curled into a purring ball in her lap, emotional and physical exhaustion won out and her head fell to her chest in sleep.

* * *

Meg awoke to a door closing nearby. Immediate relief washed over her.

"Kevin!?"

There was no answer, save for a series of thuds beneath the floorboards.

The bulkhead! She hadn't locked it. She pictured the cellar stairs climbing to the door in the dining room. It must have been the cellar door's closing in the next room that had awakened her. She stood, scattering the empty bowl and dozing cat from her lap as she grabbed the hammer and ran for the dining room.

No one here. The door to the cellar was closed, but she held the hammer ready, scanning the room, enveloped by the sickly sweet scent of decay.

This time she fell to her knees with the shock of what she saw. The cradle she'd brought in earlier sat where she'd left it. Now, though, the hexagonal buttons of a rag doll's eyes stared back at her from inside. The doll she'd dropped in the barn had been carefully placed into the cradle on a quilt drawn from the hope chest nearby. A thick mat of wet moss was tucked tenderly around the doll as if to provide it with comfort.

In tears now, overwhelmed, she clung to the cradle. She wanted nothing more than to run and hide, to awaken from a dream. Still, she found herself pulling up on the cradle's edge to stand, gripping the hammer. She ran for the front door and onto the porch. Rounding the porch corner in the twilight, her eyes swept the yard. She could see the open bulkhead from here, and braced herself on the railing looking toward the barn. Movement beyond the building had caught her eye.

Meg watched in the dim light and blowing sleet as a pale figure moved up the hillside. With slow, lurching steps something vaguely human climbed toward the tree line. Meg realized she was witnessing the continuum that had formed the path she'd found—countless journeys from the small family plot to the cradle in the barn had worn down earth, stone and wood. The hammer slipped from her fingers, thudding to the porch floor. Profound sadness now replaced Meg's fear as she grasped the eternal tragedy unfolding before her.

"Cora?" she whispered through tears.

 **Andy Richmond** is a New Hampshire native with an undergraduate degree in fine arts (the visual kind) and a master's in library science. He's spent a lot of time reading—not so much writing. Two events last winter—happening onto a previously unknown (to him) family cemetery while snowshoeing, then finding out about *Live Free or Undead*—planted the seed of an idea that evolved into his first fully-realized short story. He says he is surprised and flattered to be included in the collection, and you can bet you'll find it on the shelves at Rye Public Library.

Lilies for Donald

Jeffrey R. DeRego

M y signature chicken soup bubbles happily on the wood stove as I
clean and reload the .38 revolver at the kitchen table. It's getting
dark later now and the wind's softening bite heralds a warm spring that
hides just over the horizon. I slip the pistol into the battered leather
shoulder holster and fix my apron. The house smells lovely now, thick
and rich. I stir the broth and pick out a handful of bones. I'll grind them
later for the chickens out back. Two bay leaves, a palm of salt, same
with black pepper, and some thyme, rosemary, and just a few diced red
peppers from the jar and it's perfect. I check the windows before sliding
the hardened oak shutters into their cast iron slats.

Donald made the window treatments by hand in his little work
shed when the electricity still worked. I lost him this autumn. His heart,
I think.

We don't have a doctor in town anymore.

Donald wasn't much for aesthetics but his sense of security has
proven a lifesaver in these strange times. I've managed to sit out
three, four, maybe half-a-dozen sieges since the world went to hell in
a handbasket.

Not bad for a gal of 71. Not bad at all.

I check the rest of the little house before settling in; living
room—shuttered; bathroom—shuttered; cellar—locked and bolted;
bedroom—shuttered. The oil lamp throws a dim circle on the still-fro-
zen ground as I walk the stockade fence around the backyard. Donald

built this too, back when all we had to worry about were wayward bears or lost hunters. Two years ago he buttressed each section with a six-by-six pressure-treated joist, two feet of which are sunk into the lawn.

We planted roses together along the fence, inside and out, and trained them up the buttresses and all along the inside surface of the stockade fence. Roses are so much prettier than barbed wire, but do just as well in keeping things out.

Chickens are counted and penned, 27, goats too, four.

Ivy, brittle and dead now from the long winter, creeps up over the south fence like slender fingers. I make a mental note to chop it down before the thaw.

In the darkness, over the occasional clucks and bleats of my animals, a soft moaning floats through the woods.

* * *

Phyllis Carlsen lies on the couch that Reverend Lyons and me dragged into the kitchen. Her fever isn't as bad today, but without aspirin or antibiotics there's no telling if she'll get well. She's just a little younger than me, 61.

"I heard them last night," she says softly.

I glance at the Reverend and see recognition on his face.

"Seems like the season is coming early this year. We had a couple of warm weeks in April, so I'm not surprised the ground softened enough to let them out."

Lyons gets the fire going. Phyllis only has a little stove, barely big enough to heat the kitchen, and it's hard to cook on. I ladle two servings of chicken soup into her pan and place it atop the stove. By now the kettle is hot enough for tea and I make it for the three of us.

The Reverend is nervous and doesn't sit. Rather he fingers the trigger guard on his antique Winchester rifle and repeatedly peers through the door slat. "We should move her," he says finally.

I drizzle honey (from my own apiary) into the teapot as the brew steeps. "Where?"

"You have room—"

I silence him with a sharp glance.

"I don't want to go," Phyllis' voice is hoarse but strong.

"And you shouldn't go." I stir the soup. The wood fire is starting to soften the quarter-inch layer of fat on top. "This would have been better if I didn't run out of rice last month. Is there any left in the storehouse?"

"About five hundred pounds—"

"Twenty should do nicely." I press against the door and look out. Thick snowflakes flutter down on the short walkway between Phyllis' home and the street. She lives closer to downtown; it's less safe but at least makes getting provisions easier. "We still have five hours of daylight, and it's only just below freezing."

"I'll send someone—"

"Just hurry back. I can hold the fort here until you return."

Reverend Lyons nods, but hesitates before opening the door. "You're loaded, right?"

I show him the revolver.

"Okay. I'll be back in an hour. Listen for the church bell. This close to spring means we need a headcount."

I bolt and barricade the door immediately after he leaves but it's more habit now than protection. The spring thaw will bring the zombies out, but we still have a few weeks of relative safety before that happens.

Phyllis eases up to sit on the couch. She smells like rotten fish but I can't tell if it's a festering wound or just poor hygiene. I hand her a teacup before checking the soup. The smell starts to fill her little house too. Phyllis isn't much of a housekeeper.

The back bedrooms are nailed or locked shut, windows encased in brick that's fitted then braced into the window frames. A few other windows are shuttered, like mine. Donald worked so hard helping to fortify the houses of we who stayed.

Dirty clothes lay heaped around dusty furniture and you can't see the carpet for a layer of grit and dirt. I start to tidy things, drag the clothes into a manageable pile and get a pot of water ready to boil so I can wash them, but on this little stove that could take all afternoon.

"Don't," she says.

"I'm just trying to save you some trouble, sweetie."

"I'll take care of it once I'm feeling better. I'm not an invalid."

"Of course not." I check her pantry. It's down to seven jars of jam, three of pickles, four green tomatoes, and a bunch of rubbery undersize carrots. "Almost time to start getting the gardens ready."

She sips tea and nods.

"Planting anything special this year?"

She pauses and stares at the boarded window over the kitchen sink for a minute. "Lilies."

"Lilies are nice. Donald used to love them. I'm going to try and get a better yield from my corn this year. The blight killed almost everything last season." I take the soup off the stove and pour a bowl for Phyllis then place the wash water in its place.

She begins to eat slowly, then, after only a couple of spoonfuls, breaks down into sobs.

"Oh sweetie, no." I sit beside her on the couch and rub her back. "Those tears aren't going to help anything now."

"Why did this happen? What did we do to make this happen?" She stares at me between sobs.

"The why's aren't important but perseverance is. We've done okay here, considering, and each spring it gets a little easier. In another five or ten years, who knows, maybe things will be just like they were."

"You don't believe that."

I shrug. "Everyone has to believe in something. Now eat your soup before it gets cold."

The church bell rings three times signaling the spring headcount in three days. We don't ring it often because it's not only the dead that pose a threat. Our little town is far enough off the highway that very few living people bother looking for us. I think most survivors of the comet strike, then the plague, are probably like us, insular, quiet, and unobtrusive.

Phyllis eats in silence.

We all lost friends, relatives when the end came. The cities took it worst of all. Within a month of the sky going permanent ashy gray, the densely populated areas fell into anarchy. The President declared martial law, but with a finite food supply it wasn't long before groups were at war over the contents of a supermarket, or tractor-trailer truck. Then the zombies came, millions of recent dead scrambling back from the grave in a never-ending quest for live food. Why can't the dead rest in peace? I don't know. Maybe there was something in the dust that choked the skies for months after the impact? Maybe the comet carried some germ or virus that we all breathed in and that lays dormant until we die?

We'll probably never know for sure.

"I'm feeling a little better," Phyllis says softly.

"That's a girl." I check the door and see Reverend Lyons crossing the street with a 20-pound bag of rice on his shoulder. "I'll leave the rest of the soup for later, and come back to check on you tomorrow? Maybe? Okay?"

She nods.

* * *

I pour all but a quarter cup of rice into a plastic bin just below the shelf of maple syrup and honey jars in my pantry. I limp into the kitchen. My hips aren't so good anymore and they ache worst at the change of seasons. I used to take aspirin but that ran out over a year ago.

The afternoon sun sneaks through the bare tree branches and casts long claw-like shadows on the tan, winter-dried grass. I crank two handfuls of rice and the chicken bones together through the grinder then scatter it out for the grateful chickens.

The crisp air revives me as I milk the goats and gather half-a-dozen fresh eggs. The ground is still too hard to turn over in my three rectangular gardens. Donald was going get a rototiller but, well—

I shake off missing him and herd the chickens back into their pen, then go inside to stoke the fire.

Headcount in three days.

We haven't done a headcount since autumn. How many more of the survivors starved or went crazy over the fierce winter? We lose an average of ten a year, and none of the young girls seem interested in making replacements. Not yet. I had five kids before I turned 30, and while we weren't dodging the undead back then, it was just as hard to keep food on the table and a house warm.

Don't think about the past. The past is gone.

I sit beside the stove. The soup bubbles nicely. I pull my Bible onto my lap and open it. I used to read Revelations. I used to wait for the end of the world to come, and Jesus with his arms open, to sweep us away to paradise. But Revelations wasn't right, there wasn't a serpent to devour us, and the chosen weren't taken to heaven.

I flip to a little note that acts as a permanent bookmark at Psalm 46. I read it aloud when I need strength, and today I need all the strength I can get.

I close my eyes and there—buried in the warmth of the stove, the smell of applewood and chicken soup—a hint of Donald. He hides in those smells like a ghost.

* * *

I hack at the brush with my machete until only slender stems of ivy poke out of the ground along the outside of the fence. No matter what we—I—do, the ivy comes back every year. Stronger I think, for all the abuse heaped upon it, chemicals, fire, and tearing it out by the roots, but nothing stems the growth for more than one season.

The sun beats down through the leafless trees with such intensity that I strip my wool jacket and work only in two layers of sweatshirts.

Reverend Lyons skids his bicycle to a halt at the end of the fence. I can tell he's been riding hard because his breath-cloud is thick enough to hide his face. Many people don't leave their property once the spring comes; even getting them together for headcount is hard, and right after that, the door-to-door checks for the families not present. Reverend Lyons hasn't become the de facto leader or anything, but he's made it part of his mission to keep communication open between the two hundred or so of us spread out in and around Pleasant Hollow.

"Linda," he yells, "Phyllis is worse. Come quickly."

I slide the machete into a canvas sheath and hang it over my back. The strap pulls uncomfortably against my breasts and my hip groans as I hobble along the stockade fence through the maple and oak saplings separating the yard from the deeper, darker woods.

"Honestly, Reverend, I can't stop taking care of my problems every time someone has a fever." I wait for his face to display even a hint of guilt—about four seconds—then start towards my gate. "I have some soup left. But I am not sure it's worth bringing. You've seen her place. She's given up—"

"But we can't give up."

"She's eaten through her stores, stopped washing her clothes, herself. There are other people who can make better use of what little extra some of us have."

"When we count heads I don't want to add another name to the dead for lack of caring."

"Caring!" I unlock the bicycle chain on the front gate and shove it open. "I have only a few chickens left. I killed one just to make the soup. Shall I kill another one today? Maybe I should slaughter a goat too, just in case. God knows we don't want to *look* like we don't care."

"That isn't fair."

I breathe deep and count to ten. Anger doesn't solve anything. "I heard gunfire this morning."

The Reverend closes the gate and slides the four-by-fours into the cast iron braces to seal the backyard. He fiddles with his beard that, while chest-long, is still neatly trimmed. "The Hendersons shot three. Slow moving. I haven't been over to see who it might have been. I checked on the Simmons over on North Farm." He shivers for a second. "They must've died around Christmas. When I forced the door open Jolene was on the kitchen floor with her cat's entrails dangling from her teeth. She couldn't have been mobile for long. The rest of the family was still mostly frozen, but they were all—"

"They were a young family and winter is hard." We'd send a gallon of fresh goat milk, or a dozen eggs over to the Simmons whenever we had a little extra. They had four children to feed; the oldest boy was only seven.

"How could all of them just die like that? We loaded them up with food before the first snow—"

"They gave up. Maybe one of the kids died and they couldn't bear to shoot it, maybe the weather did them in, we'll never know. We'll have to take back anything useful. Maybe move someone else into their place."

He leans the bicycle against the side of the house and follows me inside.

I slip the machete off and wriggle back into my wool coat. I double-check the revolver; it's loaded and ready. I dip my hands into the bucket of water beside the sink and rub it over my face. The fire crackles away comfortably in the stove and will stay that way for at least four hours.

Reverend Lyons sits at the kitchen table. "How do you do it, Linda?"

"What?" I'm blotting the cool water off my face with a hand towel as I answer.

"How do you keep on *this* well. I mean, look. Your house is clean and bright and happy. You have food, plenty of it, a more than useful garden, good fortifications, clean clothes. I thought most of us were doing okay, but compared to you we're like Neanderthals. How the hell do you do it?" Lyons' voice carries a touch of frustration.

I pause for a moment, just long enough to carefully word my answer. So many little groups of survivors wore out and turned against one another. We saw the results in some of the other little towns within walking and bicycling distance. Towns where dozens of survivors set up in supermarkets or shopping malls—it was worse in the suburbs of Concord or Manchester—but the food would run out, or they'd get on each others nerves, or someone would go insane and kill all the others.Some groups have flourished, the militia people, or the religious fanatics, the ones with bunkers and assault rifles and two years worth of fresh water and food and gasoline. They prowl the highways and back roads throughout the winter looking for places like Pleasant Hollow and sack them.

"I was poor, Reverend. I had to learn how to do all this survival stuff before things went apocalyptic. Buying strawberry jam costs money, making it costs effort. Buying a dead chicken costs money, raising chickens costs a fraction of a cent per pound. You have to find cheap ways to make things work when you're poor. And then, when you aren't poor any longer, you keep doing those things because they have become a satisfying habit. I can teach the others to do it, which is what I wanted to talk about. I can take two or three apprentices at a time and teach them how to garden, and find edible berries, and can, and milk goats, and tend to chickens and cook from what you grow. We're getting close to the point where whatever we can scavenge from the world *before* is all used up, or it's too dangerous to travel and forage. We'll discuss it at headcount. I have some other ideas too. Let's check on Phyllis first, then we'll come back here and talk. Leave your bicycle; I can't ride and we're safer traveling as a pair."

I gather the last of my soup and pour it into a plastic canister, then check the walkway before opening the door. "Clear."

Reverend Lyons leads me out to the street. Cracks in the asphalt stretch across the road to the gully that used to carry rainwater off. Three-years worth of leaves choke the culvert now and every spring rain will bring a mini-flood almost to my front gate. I can't bend over enough to clear it. We head north towards the center of town. The white and black steeple of the Pleasant Hollow Baptist Church pokes up over the trees.

My hip aches, and walking over the hard, uneven pavement grinds away at the last bits of cartilage. I nearly stop as the pain overwhelms. We're only a quarter-mile from Oak Grove cemetery, the smallest of the three we have in town. Donald is buried there, in a concrete and marble crypt his family erected almost 100 years ago.

I couldn't bear to shoot him after he died, but I would have if we didn't have the crypt. A few bicycle chains to hold the cast iron doors closed, and a dozen cinder blocks atop the casket means Donald can't go anywhere.

I plant a little square of lilies in my garden every year to honor his memory. Maybe this year I'll be able to leave a bundle of them at the cemetery gates.

"Almost there, Linda."

"Almost doesn't matter, Reverend. I wouldn't wish this hip on anyone." I grit my teeth and continue on, knowing I can sit at Phyllis' house until the pain ebbs. He offers an arm and for the last two hundred yards I have to lean heavily on him.

He knocks twice. "Phyllis?"

No answer.

"Phyllis? Open the door. I have Linda with me, and some soup."

A scratching sound escapes through the heavy oak, then a thud, and the door eases open. Phyllis is shivering beneath an afghan knitted from rainbow colored yarn. She shuffles to the couch and groans as she sits. Sweat beads on her forehead and mats down her gray curls.

I draw a thermometer from my satchel and slip it beneath her tongue; count to 120, then read the result. "It's not any worse than yesterday, Phyllis. Are you in any pain?"

Her eyes plead for a second, then she shakes her head. "I'm just cold and tired."

"Do you mind if Linda, um, checks you over—thoroughly, I mean?"

"Oh I don't think that's—"

"You've got an infection, somewhere. I can smell it. If we don't find it, I can't say if you're going to get better. Now I'll send the Reverend off for a bit so it's just you and me, that way you don't have to be embarrassed, and we'll see what we're dealing with."

"Oh no Linda, please. It's just a cold."

"Phyllis. Listen carefully. If you don't let me examine you I won't come back no matter how bad Reverend Lyons says you are feeling."

She stares at the Reverend for a few seconds. "I don't want to."

"There really is no other way. Come on, we'll leave Reverend Lyons here to warm up your soup. It will only take a minute. Come on." I have to almost yank her off the couch. "There's no need to be frightened. If you're hurt I might be able to help you—"

"It's not that." Phyllis' voice cracks and she resists my persistent tugging. "Reverend. Please! Don't let her—" She staggers against the door frame and releases a flurry of wracking coughs.

I try to steady her but she pushes me away.

Phyllis coughs thick globs of bloody phlegm that splatter against the wall and drizzle down her chin. "Oh God!" She drops to her knees and continues to retch.

"We can't do anything for her," I say while backing slowly into the living room.

"Linda, there must be—something?"

"She's dying."

Phyllis shudders and sways until her head drags along the wall. "I'm already dead," she says and begins to chuckle. "I always *hated* you, Linda. Always. You and your perfect Little-House-on-the-Prairie life. Never had to work. Always had Donald there to make things easy." She struggles to her feet. "You want to see my *infection*, Linda?" She laughs again until another coughing fit nearly pitches her to the floor. She recovers slowly then drops the afghan, and her sweat pants.

The overpowering stink of filth and rotten meat explodes from her.

"While he was fixing my windows, Linda. That's when I first seduced him. You remember that year? The Barlclay kids from down the road egged my house that Halloween. Donald was so nice to me. Getting him into bed was easy. I guess you just didn't have the appetites he did." She chokes up more blood. "All those weekday nights when he said he was going to lodge meetings, he came here and made love to me. I was easy, Linda, because I was barren."

"Get out, Linda," Reverend Lyons barks from the kitchen.

"No. I need to hear this."

"Endometriosis stole my chance for a family. Ruined my marriage. *Ruined it*! And where were you and your soup then, Linda? My insides were wrecked, but I was still a woman. I still had needs. And every time I saw you at the supermarket, with those kids following you like ducklings, at the post office, the hairdresser, church, especially when you were with him—I hated you more and more. Every time Donald left me to go back to you I cried myself to sleep. You did this to me Linda! You did this!" Maggots and thick yellow puss drips out of the gray dead skin of her thighs and pool at her bare feet. Part of her pelvis is visible through the slick black rot.

Reverend Lyons whirls around and vomits.

"And when he died I thought I'd lost everything. But I didn't, Linda! I didn't! If the dead can walk, then they can do other things too! I waited all winter until the graveyard was safe. I cut the chain on his family crypt. He was out of the casket, slumped over and frozen, just like he was sleeping. I dragged him all the way back without anyone knowing."

I slide the revolver out of its holster and thumb the hammer back. "Where is he?"

"All you need is a little duct tape, Linda. Just enough to keep them from biting and getting away—" She dissolves into sickly maniacal laughter. "A little duct tape." Phyllis slides down to the floor and groans. "I think he liked it." She shudders twice then falls silent. Her chest heaves for a moment, then ceases.

Reverend Lyons stumbles through The Lord's Prayer.

She'll start to move again in two days after rigor mortis begins to relax. "You can go," I say.

"I can't let you—"

"Go! Go, goddamn it!" I slam the revolver down and wait for him to leave. Phyllis' bedroom door is bolted from the outside. I contemplate shooting the lock off then stop and count to ten before searching her house for the key. This place is well-secured and there is probably a family in town that could use this house and the garden out back.

The key is in a little box beside a vase full of withered lilies.

I open the room slowly and a swarm of flies surges out into the living room; the stink immediately follows.

Donald struggles limply against Phyllis' cast iron bed frame. She's tied his wrists and ankles to the head and footboards with wire that has rubbed away the skin and muscle until it bites into scarred, ivory colored bone. He's naked, his flesh has rotted into the mattress top. Corrupted skin sloughs off his legs and the right side of his ribcage. His belly is black and gray and swollen. Two hand-shaped bruises sit on his chest.

Phyllis drenched the room, and Donald, with Aqua Velva, so the place smells like an abandoned meat locker and whorehouse. The urge to vomit wells up almost without warning but I manage to stifle it. "Oh Donald," I whisper.

His eyes soften at the sound of my voice. His quiet moans muffle behind a thick X of duct tape.

I reach down and stroke his leathery forehead. It's cold and wrinkled. The skin peels back around his eyebrows. "I knew, you son of a bitch, I knew all along, but I never said a word. I kept quiet and prayed and did all the things I thought were right, what you wanted, but that wasn't enough, was it?" I'm surprised at my anger, and for a second it's as if I am watching someone else speak, someone else place the revolver's muzzle under his chin.

Donald closes his eyes and I blow his head off.

I do the same for Phyllis on the way out.

* * *

Reverend Lyons' color is beginning to return as we walk back towards my house. We don't speak. A few curious faces, drawn by the gunfire, peer out through thick wooden slats, but no one comes out to see what's transpired. That's probably better anyway, because I don't know if I have the vocabulary to describe Phyllis' madness.

Louder moaning echoes out of the graveyard and surrounding woods. The zombies will be back in earnest soon but at least Donald won't be among them. I open the bicycle chains keeping my front door sealed. Reverend Lyons follows me in and helps put the heavy wooden bolts into place. I put the teakettle on and open the kitchen door leading to the garden. The chickens are happily scratching the cold ground, the goats bleat when they see me.

"Are you going to be alright?"

I step out into the waning sunlight and ease down onto a plastic chair. "I think so."

"I can stay a while. I can listen."

"The sun's going down Reverend. It's safer if you leave. Besides, I don't feel much like talking." I pause for a second and read the relief on his face. "Or praying. I'll see you at headcount tomorrow."

He stands at the foot of the steps and collects his bicycle. I follow him to the fence and seal the gate after he pedals away.

I kick at the ground and it's still too hard to turn over, but the top half-inch gives just a little beneath my feet. I put another log in the stove as my tea steeps on the table. I reflect on the day. Sure, things have gone haywire, but I'm still here, a little worse for the wear, sure, but I'm still here.

Not bad for a gal of 71. Not bad at all.

Jeffrey R. DeRego was born in New Bedford, Massachusetts. He is the author of the acclaimed Union Dues, and Pleasant Hollow series' of short stories. He also writes horror and cult film reviews for the website www.horrorview.com under the name Big McLargehuge. A graduate of New England College in Henniker, he lives in Derry, New Hampshire, with his wife, Cindy, and kids, Ian and Margaret.

The Spiral

J. Zachary Pike

Fletcher watched the mountains flow by, slow waves of maple and evergreen, cresting with bleached granite. The green forests and misty peaks reminded him of chopper rides over the jungle so many years ago, but there was nothing else to watch except the guardrail that occasionally wound alongside the road. He clicked his tongue irritably as the truck rattled on.

"Friggin' a, we're really up there," hissed Derek from the back seat of the truck.

"Yep," said Fletcher, as noncommittally as he could.

"We're like, what? A hundred friggin' miles north of home?"

"Something like that," said Paul with all the distraction he could muster. His considerable bulk rested easily in the driver's seat, and he drove with his wrists draped over the wheel, one hand dangling a Styrofoam coffee cup.

"Seriously," said Derek, his wiry frame bent forward in earnest. Their young apprentice reminded Fletcher of a coiled spring. "I mean, I knew the territory's big, but goddamn! We're gonna be in the friggin' White Mountains!"

Paul pulled a lazy swig of coffee. "We're already in the White Mountains," he said. "We're going fifty miles north of 'em."

"Holy shit!" roared Derek.

Fletcher shot the driver a dark look. "Don't encourage the kid," he said softly.

But the apprentice was already encouraged. "You know why PSNH calls it the Seacoast-Mountain division? Because all you hear is the Seacoast part. You think, 'Hey! Bars in Portsmouth! Rye beach! It's like a party compared to the Eastern Division!' So you sign up, and then they send you out to the boondocks! Can't they get a local crew to do it?"

"The local crews say they don't have the time or stuff to handle it."

"Pfft," huffed Derek. "Big surprise."

"Hey. A hawk," Fletcher said, trying to change the subject.

Paul leaned forward slightly, and Derek craned his neck to see out the passenger window. Above them, a dark shape spiraled on a warm updraft.

"Nope. Turkey vulture," Paul declared, settling back in his seat.

"Close enough, Mr. Discovery Channel."

Paul shrugged. A small smile sprouted beneath his dark mustache. "Is what it is, Fletch."

Fletcher smiled and clicked his tongue as he settled back and stared blankly at the rolling mountains. The mist among the trees was growing denser, and by the time they reached Franconia Notch, the fog had swallowed the linemen's truck altogether.

More than an hour later, they sat in a small diner tucked amid the mills of Groveton, reviewing the details of the job over an early lunch.

Paul intermittently shoved fries into his mouth as he went over the work order for the third time. "Headed to Northern Nash. Little village in the out-in-the-woods; got a small transmission station in it that's gone down. It's stressing the grid in the area and causing trouble in the park stations around the woods. So we're gonna check the fuses, check the transformers . . ."

"Hey, pay attention," Fletcher snapped at Derek. The review was largely for the scrawny apprentice's benefit, but he seemed unable to divert his attention from the plump waitress attending the diner's few customers.

"Any chance we'll be here overnight?" Derek asked, his watery eyes locked onto the supple siren as she refilled another patron's coffee.

"We don't want to be." Fletcher's salad was eaten and gone, and he rapped his knuckles on the table impatiently.

"Relax, Fletch," Paul murmured through his burger. "It'd suck to have a heart attack the day before you retire."

"It'd also suck to start my retirement out in the sticks. Hey, speakin' of blood pressure, you want another quarter pounder while you lecture me?"

Paul shrugged and smiled. "My doc's not after me. I've got great blood pressure. S'my good genes. And the yoga."

Fletcher couldn't help laughing.

"Anything else I can help you boys with?" asked the waitress, collecting a couple of empty dishes with one hand and refilling Fletcher's coffee with the other.

"Know a good place to crash around here?" Derek's ratty features were twisted into a juvenile attempt at seduction. "We might be spending the night in the area . . ."

Fletcher cut him off. "But not if we get the job done."

"Oh, yeah," said the waitress. "There's quite a few around. What's the job?"

"Some line work up in Northern Nash," said Paul. He offered her a half-empty coffee mug.

She obligingly topped him off. "Oh, then you'll want to stay around here. There's some real weirdos out there in the boonies."

"As opposed to the big city here," said Fletcher with a wink. She laughed and shook her head. "You seen some weird stuff out there?"

"Oh, I never been. Y'just hear things, y'know?" She noticed another customer in need. "I gotta get that table, boys. Try the Down Home Motel tonight. Right on Route 3—you probably passed it coming in. 'Scuse me."

"You guys are asses," whispered Derek harshly as she hurried away. "Why couldn't you just let me talk to her?"

Paul wiped his mouth, finally finished, and took another swig of coffee. "Because, my boy, we're here on business, not pleasure. Or whatever that would be."

"And besides," said Fletcher. "We ain't staying the night."

Nine hours later, Fletcher stormed into a musty hotel room, a wooden-paneled tomb filled with antiquities of a simpler era. Paul and Derek followed a couple paces back, too exhausted to muster anything close to the anger that Fletcher projected into his satellite phone.

"No, you listen, Steve! We circled those damn woods at least twice, and we asked for directions three times! We've been through every back road in the Nash Stream forest! We've been up and down Nash Stream Road, Northside Road, North Way Road, any friggin' road at all that sounds like the way to Northern Nash!"

Fletcher tossed his duffel onto one bed while the dispatcher ran through useless questions that protocol demanded. Paul claimed the other bed with a pointed glance at Derek, who scowled and dropped his bag next to the cot.

"Of course we used the friggin' GPS! It's what kept us circling the damn woods!"

On the other end of the line, Steve began to rally off some directions, but Fletcher would have none of it.

"You're not listening! We were there. We drove up and down that road at least six times. There's nothing there but a bunch of farms and covered bridges and an old church."

It only infuriated Fletcher further when the dispatch promised to ask local teams for help.

"You don't think we tried? None of the lazy bastards want to help! They're all feeding us bull about other jobs they need to be on. Look, I'm not spending two nights on a job I can't friggin' find. We'll try one more time tomorrow, and if we don't find it, we're comin' home!"

He hit the off button on the phone, cutting off any response.

"Relax, old timer," said Derek as he dragged an olive-green easy chair across the shag carpet.

Fletcher glowered at the apprentice.

"Look at the bright side. Every room comes with cable!" Derek laughed and switched on the television as he plopped into the chair, which creaked under even his slight frame. "Come on, sit back and enjoy the zombies!"

"Or the Discovery Channel," countered Paul, swooping from the bathroom to swipe the remote.

"Dude! That was *Splatter Shack Two*!" protested the young man as Paul flopped onto his bed and changed the channel.

Fletcher shook his head with a dismissive grunt.

"Seniority," said Paul. He flicked the remote to a nature documentary, wherein a coyote was carrying a dead prairie dog across the grasslands.

"Seriously, dude. It has a zombie moleman that burrows into this dude's chest!"

"If that's your cup of tea, you should watch more nature shows," said Paul. "Mother nature's a lot scarier than your average horror movie."

"Bull."

"It's true. Ask Fletch. He was out in the jungle back in 'Nam."

"Really?"

"Nature's a bitch," said Fletcher, who seldom spoke of his service at all.

"For example," Paul added, "there's a wasp that paralyzes spiders and lay eggs on 'em so the babies can eat the victim alive. And there's a parasitic fungus that takes over an ant's brain to make it infect others. There's man-eating crocs longer than boats. There's even a little parasitic fish that'll swim up your thingie when you piss."

Derek made a face. "That's wicked sick."

"Yep. And completely true."

The whole business sounded pretty sick to Fletcher as well. "I'm gonna go freshen up," he announced.

The bathroom was dimly lit by a flickering incandescent bulb. Fletcher scratched at his face. He had forgotten his razor, and his salt-and-pepper stubble was already filling in around the gray goatee he sported. His eyes were bloodshot, and his crows feet seemed deeper today. He felt old. Too old for this.

It probably would be good to relax, Fletcher decided as he headed back out into the room. Doctor Paulson had been advising him about stress levels since the divorce, anyway. He flopped onto the creaky springs of the bed and looked at the TV. The coyote had wandered too close to some wolves' territory, and was now frantically trying to outmaneuver the pack. The snarling wolves approached on either flank.

"This is wicked intense," said Derek.

Fletcher nodded. "Like I said. Nature's a bitch."

"Yeah," said Derek absently, watching the unfortunate coyote fail to evade its pursuers. A wolf grabbed it by its haunches and sent it tumbling across the prairie to the rest of the pack, who tore the yelping creature to shreds.

"Yes indeed," said Paul.

* * *

"Don't blink," said Paul. "You'll miss Stark."

A whitewashed covered bridge and the tiny Stark Unity Church materialized in the cold morning fog as the utility truck bounced along. Aside from a little farmhouse, there was little else in sight.

"Alright, that's the first church," Fletcher said. "The local crew said the road to Northern Nash is right after the second church.

"I didn't see two churches yesterday."

"Apparently we missed one."

"I guess," said Paul. "Did you know there was a World War II POW camp here in Stark?"

"No kiddin'."

"Yep. They say about 250 Germans came here for hard labor in the woods back in 1944." Paul's voice swelled with ominous tones for Derek's benefit. "And in '45, 220 went back."

"What happened to the others?" asked Derek, eyes wide.

"They really liked it here and settled nearby," smirked Paul.

Derek laughed. "Ass," he said.

"Hey!" Fletcher yelled, catching Paul's attention just in time. The truck swerved suddenly, barely avoiding the figure that suddenly appeared within the mist.

"Did we miss him?" asked Derek.

"Dammit!" swore a shaken Paul, pulling over. "Dammit, dammit!"

"Easy, bud," Fletcher said. "I'll take this." He hopped out into the soft gravel on the side of the road and trotted back behind the truck.

Their almost-victim was an old man with a hooked nose and a thick, white beard curled down over his chest. He wore a long leather coat over jeans and a plaid shirt, and a wide brimmed hat that concealed most of his weathered face. There was a pistol on his belt and a Bible in his hand.

"Hey," Fletcher shouted to him. "Hey, are you alright?"

"I'm fine, I'm fine, thanks be to God," murmured the old man. "Sorry to scare you. Just waiting for my groceries to come."

Fletcher huffed a sigh of relief. "He's OK!" he shouted back to the truck before apologizing. "Sorry. The fog . . ."

"I know, I know," said the old man. "I shouldn't stand around in it when it's thick as pea soup. The delivery boy always misses my house in the fog if I don't, y'see. Don't worry 'bout it." He extended a leathery hand. "Name's Quincy. Quincy Cote."

"David Fletcher. Call me Fletcher," he said, taking the hand and shaking it firmly. "We're with Public Service of New Hampshire. You must be local, then?"

"Oh, yes, yes. For some time now."

"Thank God. Listen, we're looking for the way to Northern Nash. Can you tell us how to get there?"

The words might as well have been a spell, for Quincy seemed to turn to stone as Fletcher said them. All the kindness drained from his eyes, replaced with cold, cutting iron. "You don't want to go there," he rasped.

"Well, no, I don't," Fletcher agreed, doing his best to stay upbeat. "But there's a relay substation that's gone down there, so somebody's got to go."

"What?"

"I'm afraid so, sir. If we don't go in, somebody else will have to get the station online."

Quincy looked around, uncomfortable. He glanced at his watch a couple of times, muttering to himself and to Jesus all the while. Fletcher almost felt like he was intruding upon a conversation, and the longer the dialogue continued, the more aware he was of the likely-loaded pistol at the murmuring man's hip.

"Where are you staying?" the old man suddenly snapped.

"At a motel down in Groveton."

"How long will it take to fix what you're fixin'?"

"I'm hoping a few hours?"

"Alright . . . alright," Quincy said reluctantly. "I'll show you the way. But hurry."

Fletcher hesitated. "But, your delivery—"

"Hurry!" rasped the old man, striding past Fletcher to scramble up into the truck.

"Uh, right." Already regretting this, Fletcher muttered an awkward thank you and followed the old pastor.

The utility truck bounced and jostled as Paul sped down the road, with Quincy riding shotgun. That left Fletcher crammed in the back with Derek. An uncomfortable silence had settled over the linemen, and to Fletcher's dismay it was the apprentice who eventually broke it.

"That your Bible?" Derek asked.

"Mmhmm," grunted Quincy. He clutched the book with whitened knuckles. "I pastor the First Church of Southern Nash."

"So you really believe that hoodoo bull . . . ?"

"Derek!" hissed Fletcher.

"It's alright," said Quincy. "I used to think like you, son. I did. But then I found the truth, and the truth keeps me free. Praise God, he keepeth me in perfect peace, because my mind is steadfast and I trust Him, Isaiah twenty-six three. He brought me to a haven, and I'm glad for the stillness, Psalm one-oh-seven thirty . . ."

As Quincy trailed off into a chant of muttered verses, the linemen fell silent once more. While the pastor mumbled, his fingers repeatedly tracing a twisting spiral pattern across the pebbled leather cover of his old Bible. Looking closer, Fletcher could see the pattern etched in smooth grooves across the book's cover, worn in by ages of nervous tracing by old, calloused fingers.

Paul didn't seem too perturbed by the old man's ramblings, but Derek nodded at the old pastor and twirled a finger near his temple. He hated admitting it, but Fletcher found himself agreeing with the apprentice.

The utility crew recognized the small, white building that Quincy directed them to. They had passed it several times on the previous day without realizing its significance, but this was understandable, as there was little to distinguish the First Church of Southern Nash from any of the other small homes and farms scattered alongside the road.

"Damn," whispered Derek as they pulled up next to the small, brown house, with crooked gray shutters and sagging roof. "First church I ever seen with its own farm." He pointed, and out in the mists Fletcher could see a herd of sheep grazing in a field beyond the house, dwarfed by a few scattered cows moving among them.

"He must take tending the flock pretty literally," Fletcher whispered back.

The only distinguishing feature of the church, and indeed, the entire village of Southern Nash, was an old wooden sign that had been overgrown with thistles and thorny trees. Even with Quincy pointing it out, the linemen could barely make out the letters among the dark weeds.

Fletcher felt uneasy as soon as he was out of the truck, and he noticed that a few locals were watching him with dark eyes from the farmhouse across the street.

"Ho, brother Thomas!" Quincy yelled to an old Latino who emerged from the church with a hunting rifle. "It's alright, it's alright! These gents need to go to the northern village."

Brother Thomas clearly had his doubts, but he nodded and settled into an old rocker on the church's porch. Once seated, he took a log of firewood and a long hunting knife from a crate next to him and set about carving something into the birch bark. Even as he whittled, his eyes never left the Fletcher as the old preacher guided him around the truck.

"There's the road," said Quincy, gesturing to his field.

"Well, I'll be damn-darned," Fletcher fumbled as he noticed the scattered trail of pulverized asphalt, barely visible beneath a sea of weeds and overgrowth. The nearly-invisible road wound back through the church's field and into a narrow parting in the Nash Stream Forest.

"Now listen to me, David Fletcher," hissed Quincy, grabbing Fletcher's arm. "Northern Nash ain't like other towns out here. It is forsaken by God! His wrath is revealed from Heaven upon them for suppressing His truth in unrighteousness, Romans one eighteen!"

Fletcher gently tried to dislodge Quincy's grip, "Sir, we're just here to do our job. . . ."

The old man's iron talons only squeezed harder, his eyes wide and wild. Flecks of spittle flew from his mouth as he rasped a rapid litany of orders. "Don't talk to them godless folk, for the wicked strut about while vileness is exalted, Psalm twelve eight! Get your work done and then be gone from them, may God keep you! And for the Lord's sake, don't stay after dark! Don't stay in that valley of the shadow of death!"

"Sir, we won't! We're just going in and out," Fletcher assured him.

The old preacher finally loosened his hold on Fletcher's arm and backed away. "God be with you and watch over you and bring you back to this land, Genesis twenty-eight fifteen."

"Uh, thank you. And thanks for the directions," Fletcher called as he quickly rounded the truck and climbed back in the door.

"Well that was a strange one," remarked Paul as Fletcher climbed into the truck. "You okay, Fletch?"

"Fine," said Fletcher. "We've seen stranger. That gravel path's actually the road. The town's up in the woods."

"Seriously?"

"Yeah, I know," said Fletcher. He could see the reflection of the old preacher in the rear view mirror, still muttering verses and nervously pawing the same twisting pattern on his Bible. "Let's just go and get this done."

"Hell yeah," grunted Derek as the truck turned down the bumpy trail and headed across the field. "These freaks are creepin' me out."

"You have no idea," said Fletcher softly, watching the back of the church recede in the mirror. Behind the small building, hidden from view of the road, were several stacks of firewood, every log carved with innumerable spirals.

Fletcher was the first to spot the dead sheep, a headless mass draped across a massive hunk of granite next to the road.

"Shit," Derek said.

Most of it was missing, but the bones and wool that remained behind were at the epicenter of a ring of carnage. Dried blood and bits of decaying meat were sprayed over the stone, the road, the thick ferns. Paul even pointed out a gibbet of flesh and wool dangling from a branch high above the road.

"Bear?" asked Fletcher.

"Probably," said Paul. The truck started forward over the bumpy gravel road.

"Shit," Derek said again.

Northern Nash wasn't an interruption of the ancient woods, but rather an extension of them. Amid the dark pines and fog loomed a couple of buildings in various states of decay, their peeling paint revealing wood ravaged by ants and termites and the woodpeckers that coveted them. Few of their shattered windows showed signs of any attempt to fix them. Skeletal cars and trucks lay marooned amid the trees, floundering in the spongy earth or wrecked on cinderblock shoals. Some vehicles showed more signs of habitation than the houses around them, like the rusted school bus that brooded at the center of a web of archaic clotheslines.

"You ever wish they'd let you bring a gun on the job?" asked Derek. He hadn't really said much since the headless sheep twenty miles back.

"In and out, gentlemen," Paul reassured them. "In and out."

Fletcher just nodded and stared out the window as the truck slowly picked its way along a narrow road winding down into a small valley

The buildings were sparse here, old capes that must have once looked clean and white and official. One bore half a sign that read "Office." Down the slope, through the trees, he could just make out the rotting rooftops of more buildings in the mist

"There's the juice," said Paul.

Fletcher looked up just as they passed underneath some lines crossing the street. The power ran through a clear-cut area bisecting the town, a thin electric scar on the woods. Looking down the slope through the clearing, he could clearly make out the buildings below. There were a dozen or so long, low houses spread out along the winding road. They looked like carcasses rotting in the misty woods, the mold and maggots already overtaking them.

The road wound around the valley twice more before the utility truck reached the main village, which was really just two houses placed within a few hundred yards of Northern Nash's center of commerce: a general store and motel crammed into a gray Colonial house.

It was here that the crew saw the first signs of habitation. A teenage shop-hand stood on the store's small porch, methodically sweeping the top step. A little girl in pink corduroy overalls ran and danced in circles on a patch of grass up ahead. Several residents were emerging from the houses, including a young man with blonde hair, a shaggy beard, and friendly blue eyes who stepped up to the truck as Paul rolled down the window. "Morning, folks," he grinned. "Name's Jude. Welcome to Northern Nash."

"Well, we're glad to see a friendly face," said Paul. "It took us forever to find this place."

"Oh, did Pastor Cote give you trouble?" asked a lovely young woman, joining Jude.

"Not too much," said Paul. "We wouldn't have found the place without him."

Jude shared a smile with the young woman. "Well, maybe old Quincy's coming around," he said hopefully.

"Paster Cote and his church usually don't care much for our community," the woman explained to the crew, pushing back her long, dark hair. "He think's we're a bit too close to nature, if you get my drift. I'm Belle, by the way."

"Nice to meet you. I'm Paul, and this here's Fletcher. Fella in the back's Derek."

"We're here to check out a substation that's gone off the grid," Fletcher cut in. "Went down about three days ago."

"Oh? We hadn't noticed," said Jude.

"Really? You folks have power?"

"Oh, we usually don't use much electricity," said Belle. "We prefer natural light."

"But hey, don't mind us hippies. We prefer natural grown foods, fresh mountain air, baths in pristine springs, that sort of thing," laughed Jude.

"Doesn't sound all bad," said Paul. "But we do need to get that substation up."

"Sure, sure," said Jude. "It's actually right across the valley from us—maybe a mile and a half straight through those woods. If you want your truck there, you'll have to follow the road for another half-loop around the valley, though."

"Well, these things do come in handy," Paul quipped, banging the truck's door. "I think we'll do that. Thanks for the help."

"Not at all," said Jude. "Good luck."

"We'll see you around," said Belle.

Paul was much more at ease as the truck pulled out. "Well, that sums up why nobody likes Northern Nash," he chuckled. "Nobody wants a tree-hugging commune in the backyard. They're probably a bunch of drugged-up nudists."

"Frig, I hope so! That chick was hot!" exclaimed Derek, still looking back to catch a glimpse of Belle.

Paul followed standard procedure and ignored him. "You OK, Fletch?" Paul asked.

"Hm? I'm fine," Fletcher said.

He didn't feel fine, though. Something about this place set him sideways. The people waving from the side of the road and the couple that the crew had spoken with seemed nice enough, surely nicer than many of the folk in Southern Nash, but something kept gnawing deep in the back of his mind.

He found himself second-guessing vague shapes in darkened windows that caught his eye. It seemed to him that the shop-boy on the store's porch hadn't moved an inch, and was still vacantly sweeping the same step. And the child in pink overalls was still spinning without so much as a hint of dizziness. As the truck passed, Fletcher stared at the deep spiral groove beneath her, worn into the ground over uncounted hours of the little girl's dancing.

The substation sat where the road faded to nothingness, the dirt and gravel path gradually fading into the scrub brush and leaf litter. It was a small facility, little more than a pair of steel towers supporting several lines, atop an ancient concrete slab. Most of the visible equipment was from the early sixties and somewhat weathered, but in remarkably good condition for its age. In keeping with Northern Nash's theme, a rusting PSNH truck sat nearby, likely dating back to the early nineties

"Jeez," said Derek, trotting towards the old vehicle. "Wonder why'd they'd leave a truck here?"

"Quit screwing around," snapped Fletcher, still unloading the truck. "Let's get this done!"

As they approached the substation's gate, Fletcher pointed out the spiral designs scratched onto the wooden PSNH sign, and painted in deep red onto its cement base. "Someone's a little obsessed," he said.

"'S just graffiti," Paul said dismissively. "Happens everywhere we go."

"Graffiti's usually dirty poems or notes about who puts out. What's with all the spirals around here?"

"It's probably some Indian new age mystic mumbo jumbo," said Paul. "Gate's grounded. Open her up, kid."

"Just seems weird," said Fletcher, looking closer at the spirals covering the sign.

"Well, quit screwing around and let's get this done then." Derek wore a snarky grin as he opened the gate.

Fletcher grunted irritably, but followed them in.

Once in the substation, the crew fanned out to find the problem. "It might be in the basement," Paul said, noting the heavy trap door on the concrete floor.

"I'll check it. Derek, make sure everything's grounded," said Fletcher.

He set about opening the trap door while Paul and Derek continued their inspection. It was heavy, much more so than he expected. It took a lot of effort to pull it up, and he nearly dropped it as soon as he did. Beneath the heavy door, a rickety set of wooden steps descended into darkness. Every one of them was carved with hundreds of spirals.

"What the hell?" breathed Fletcher.

"Fletch!"

Fletcher startled and dropped the heavy trap door lid with a heavy thud. Paul waved to him from by the transformers.

"No point going down there," said Paul. "We figured out the problem."

Somewhat relieved, Fletcher followed to where Derek stood looking at the transformer's box.

"Check it out, Fletcher," said Derek, holding up a dead fuse. "These friggin' things are from, like, 1926 or something.

"Seventies, by my guess," said Paul. "They don"t last forever."

"Shit," said Fletcher. "We'll have to replace the whole board."

"Yeah," Derek agreed. "We're going to be here a while."

There are few tasks for an electrician as miserable as integrating old equipment with new technology, but the thought of returning to Northern Nash later wasn't an option for Fletcher. He assured his dispatch that they had everything they needed to do the job right, tossed the phone back in the truck, and then immediately set about scavenging odds and ends to jury-rig the box.

"You sure this will work?" Paul asked, sorting through the random electronic gear in the back of the truck.

"We'll make it work," said Fletcher.

The crew didn't get a start until nearly twelve, and it was almost two by the time that they figured out a solution. Before they could get started, some of the locals arrived with a late lunch to share.

"We don't have time for this," grumbled Fletcher as he and Paul made their way to the blanket that Belle was spreading out.

"We'll be quick," Paul assured him. Fletcher took it for the lie that it was; Paul never rushed anything that he enjoyed, and he enjoyed nothing so much as a meal.

The food and company were good. Belle and Jude shared canned fruits, pickled onions, and cold roast venison, and politely refused the peanut butter crackers and cheese curls that Derek offered in return.

The locals shared some of their history as well. Northern Nash had once been one of several labor outposts for the POW camp of Germans held in Stark. Every day the prisoners were sent out to a few of the surrounding camps, worked in the woods, and then returned to the bunk houses. The Nash Stream Outpost was originally slated to be a foresting site, but signs of tourmaline had set the workers digging in the middle of the valley.

The war ended before anything could be found, but many of the Nash Stream workers and even a few of their guards remained hopeful. They pooled their resources, purchased a grant, and founded the Nash Mining Company.

By 1962, the Nash Mining Company had closed. Even after carving down nearly a quarter of a mile, the dig had produced little of value except some carvings and tools made by a small tribe of Pennacook that died out long before the white man arrived.

Even after their venture failed, the quarry workers felt that they couldn't leave their home of some two decades. The village of Nash was established, and for a time enjoyed a small but bustling economy. It was an especially popular destination for those interested in New Age culture, intrigued by the remote setting and the Native American mysticism of the quarry. The differences between these mystics and Nash's established German Lutherans, Jude surmised, were likely responsible for the rift that resulted in the founding of Southern Nash by 1968.

"Thanks to the church's gossip and religious intolerance," Belle concluded, "Northern Nash got a bad reputation. And now we're a dwindling village."

"I don't know about dwindling. You all seem so young," Paul remarked, watching a couple of children running in circles around the crew's truck.

"Oh, all of the old timers have passed on now," said Belle. "A couple people here are their grandkids, but most residents are people who came to Nash and loved it enough to stay. Jude and I found the place on a hiking trip, and we settled down almost immediately."

Jude smiled and nodded. "What can we say? There's just something in the air here that makes you want to never leave."

Fletcher couldn't disagree more. As friendly as the townsfolk were, there was something unsettling about them that he couldn't put his finger on. Their mannerisms lagged behind or jumped ahead of their speech, almost like a video with the audio out of sync. The more they talked and friendlier they acted, the more he wanted to get the hell out of Northern Nash for good.

He changed the subject. "Hey, what's with all the spirals everywhere?"

"Oh, the spiral was sacred to the Majigemidup tribe," said Jude. "Most of the carvings and artifacts unearthed in the Nash quarry were their religious icons of spirals."

"The spiral is in so much of nature," Belle added, her voice heavy with adoration. "We see it in the snail shell and the fern shoot, and also in time. See that fallen tree?" She indicated a fallen stump grown thick with lichens and a black, creeping fungus. "For decades that tree has been winding down, spiraling towards its death." She drew a spiral in the loose gravel and sand next to the blanket, stopping at the tree's death at the center. "And now," she continued, tracing the same spiral back from the center, "it feeds a whole generation of plants and fungi. From one death, many lives spring forth."

"We see the spiral in hierarchies as well," said Jude. "Look at these ants come to join us for lunch. They're the outer ring, the foragers, But the closer you go to the center of the colony, the more important the ants become, like nurses for the young or big soldiers. And the farther in you go, the more dense the rings and the ants are, until you reach the whole point, the queen, at the center. The whole colony's a spiral."

"It's a very sacred symbol," said Belle.

"Ah," said Fletcher. He checked his watch; it was almost three. "Well, we should probably get back to it. We've got a lot to do."

"Sure, sure," said Jude. "Don't let us keep you."

"Hey," said Belle. "If you folks are around tonight, you're more than welcome to join us for dinner."

"Or stay at the motel. Best accommodations in Nash," joked Jude.

Fletcher forced a smile and nodded. "That'd be nice. Maybe we'll do that."

As soon as the locals had headed home and the linemen were back to work at the station, however, Fletcher dropped the facade. "We ain't staying," he said.

"Seriously, dude, I'm thinking about it," said Derek. "That chick was making eyes at me."

"Give it a rest, Casanova," grunted Fletcher. "We're gonna finish fast and get the hell out of Dodge. Remember what that old pastor said?"

"I sure do," said Derek. "Remember that he was friggin' crazy?"

"I'm tellin' you, this place gives me the heebie jeebies!" Fletcher snarled.

Paul stepped in. "Relax, guys. Look, we don't have much left to do. We'll be home soon enough."

For all of their initial concern, the rest of the work went fast, and by four the crew was ready to switch on the power. Derek, having completed his first big job, was allowed the honors of closing the box back up and turning on the juice. "Here goes nothing," he said, and threw down the switch.

Sparks showered from the transformer above, but the linemen were completely focused on what was below them. From the cement basement came the sounds of an electric blast and thud, followed by an unholy shriek and a frantic scrabbling.

"Turn it off! Turn it off!" screamed Fletcher and Paul in unison. Derek scrambled to hit the power again, and the readings on the meters plummeted. The howling continued, a warped wailing seemed to scrape over the brain, followed by a loud bang, the screech of metal twisting, and a great clatter.

Fletcher and Paul were already running, but by the time they rounded the transistor array the trap door was just a twisted piece of scrap laying next to the gaping maw of the basement. In the distance, they could still hear some large creature fleeing through the woods, shrieking as it ran.

It took all of Fletcher's courage to will himself into the basement, but once there he and Paul found little more alarming than the ubiquitous graffiti. Spirals were carved into every wooden surface, scratched into any paint, and drawn in various pigments all over the floor. Little patches of the same black, creeping mold that was ravaging the log outside grew along some of the pigments, curling into vile fractals of decay.

Beneath the spirals on the walls were older graffiti, some spray-painted on, some splashed on by brush. There was garbled gibberish—it looked German to Fletcher—and new-age sounding messages about the center of life. One in particular caught Fletcher's attention, a hurriedly scrawled line reading:

Run away, run away
When you see a dead man pray.

He stared at it for a long time, trying to discern its meaning. It could have been a line from some hippie song—although Fletcher himself had been quite wild and free when he first got back from the war, and he couldn't remember any such lyrics. Still, a folk variation was possible, perhaps one with a message about the spiritual or mental deadness of the Lutherans, or even a threat against them. For folk music, however, it was undeniably eerie.

Paul dug through a pile of old supplies heaped unceremoniously by the stairs. "Old blankets. Rusty fuses. Broken lamp. Couple cans of kerosene. Nothin' special," he declared, standing. "I think we're all set here, Fletch."

"What do you make-ah-that," said Fletcher, pointing to the verse.

"I dunno," shrugged Paul. "Some teens on a dare? Kids are stupid."

"Something ain't right here," muttered Fletcher.

"Know what's really wrong? The way you're starting to sound a little like that crazy old preacher."

Fletcher just grunted and shook his head.

"What do you think happened?" Derek asked as Fletcher and Paul climbed the stairs to join Derek.

"I think," said Paul, "that some animal, a bear or maybe even a cougar, was down there near one of the the secondary lines, and when we threw the switch it got a shock."

"Shit," said Derek, looking out into the woods.

"I almost went down in there with it." Fletcher shook his head. "I almost went into the basement."

"Yeah, well, that wouldn't have been good, but I think you probably would have been okay. It was hiding down there after all. Hell, it was probably terrified of us."

"I suppose. How'd it get in, though?"

"Oh, who knows? A panicked animal can do a lot," said Paul. "And I imagine it was pretty panicked."

"I can't believe it survived that much juice!" exclaimed Derek.

"Yeah," said Paul. "Probably won't make it much longer. Probably already dead."

"Let's hope so, Paulie," said Fletcher. His eyes were drawn to the heavy trap door that had been so quickly mangled and discarded, and he couldn't help but wonder what kind of creature could do that much damage after getting tagged with a thousand volts. "Let's hope so."

Fortunately, the animal hadn't damaged anything vital. After a hasty replacement of the trap door with some old boards and a couple of rocks, Derek re-activated the power without incident. By a quarter to five the crew was already picking up, and Fletcher's mood had lifted considerably by the time they loaded the last of the gear into the truck.

"This isn't going to last more than a couple of years," said Paul, wading through electrical flotsam and jetsam in the back of the truck.

"Not my problem," grinned Fletcher. He was nearly giddy as he and Paul joined Derek in the truck.

"Alright, alright," said Paul. "Let's head on . . ." His voice trailed away as he turned the key and the truck's engine failed to turn over.

"You gotta be friggin' kidding me," said Derek.

Paul wasn't. The engine would do little outside of choking, even after multiple attempts to jump it with the battery backup.

"Alright, damn it," said Fletcher. "Call the dispatch and let them know there's a problem."

This alerted the crew to a second problem—the satellite phone was missing. There was a lot of yelling, finger pointing, and general exclamations of amazement that a foot-long piece of neon yellow electronics could go missing, but in the end, there was little else to do but make for town.

"Man, Fletch," said Derek, dropping a can of bug spray into his pack. "Maybe you were right. This is freaked out."

"I hope not," said Fletcher. "Sometimes, I really hate bein' right."

"Yes, indeed," said Paul. He hefted his own pack, and the three started down the dirt road back to Northern Nash. "Yes, indeed."

The crew arrived in the village around half past six, where Jude and Belle greeted them. They expressed concern over the car not starting. "We've more than our fair share of cars that won't run," Jude quipped, but unfortunately, the nearest mechanic was in Groveton, and he didn't do service calls this far out.

The townsfolk were even more concerned when they heard about the missing satellite phone. "I'll go ask some of the kids if they took it," Belle offered. "Maybe they thought they were being funny."

"We have our cells, but there's no service since before Groveton," Paul continued. "You folks have a phone we could use?"

"Not a one." Jude shook his head. "We've never had much interest.

If you folks want my advice, you'll stay at the inn tonight and hike out to Southern Nash in the morning. Someone there might be able to give you a lift into Stark or Groveton. They'll have phones there."

"We could just make the hike now," said Fletcher.

"You could," said Jude. "But I really don't recommend it. It's a ten-mile hike to Southern Nash, and sundown's in an hour. It's not really safe to wander alone at night—the road isn't too easy to follow in the dark, and there's been animals taken by some big predator lately. Probably a bear."

Derek got a little excited over that. "Dude, yeah, remember the friggin' sheep? And that thing at the substation?"

"Thing?" Jude asked.

"We saw something in the woods. Probably a bear, right?" Fletcher interrupted. "We'll talk it over," he told Jude.

"Sure, sure. Take your time." Jude smiled and pointed back to the inn and corner store. "I'll be in there if you need me."

"I say we get the hell out of here as fast as possible," said Fletcher as soon as Jude was out of earshot. "Walk it if we have to."

"Are you friggin' crazy?" asked Derek.

"No, I ain't," said Fletcher. "There may be bears out there, or worse. And the road may be hard to follow. But these people are definitely up to something, and I'll take the evil I know any day."

Paul shook his head. "Fletch, all due respect, but we're not sure they're up to anything."

"You ain't. I am. There's too much goin' wrong here to be coincidence. First someone warns us not to stay here, then they ask us to stay in their rink-a-dink hotel, and then suddenly everything breaks or goes missing in a way that makes us stay? Ain't it a bit too much? Don't you know when you're bein' set up?"

"Maybe," said Paul. "But that's speculation. And big animals in the woods are a certainty."

Fletcher nearly shook with frustration—if he wasn't getting anywhere with Paul, then the kid was a lost cause. "Fine," he said, turning and starting . "Just don't put it on me."

"Put what on you?" asked Derek.

"I don't know yet." Fletcher scowled as he turned back to the decrepit inn. "But it's gonna be bad."

The check-in for the Northern Nash Inn was also the cashier's desk at the Northern Nash General Store. The store's creaking floors were lined by oak shelves of ancient preserves, canned goods, and dried jerky. The whole store and inn were mostly free of the spiraling graffiti that plagued most of Northern Nash, though Fletcher noticed sevaral tiny curls idly scratched into the desktop behind the register.

"Sorry things aren't going your way," said Jude, filling out some old paperwork. He slid an old, leather ledger across the desk to the crew.

"Not your fault, I'm sure," said Fletcher, taking the pen and book.

Jude nodded uneasily and turned to Paul. "We'll waive the room fee, naturally, given the circumstances."

"Mighty kind of you," said Paul.

As Paul and Jude spoke, Fletcher signed the crew into the ledger. There were only a handful of names each year, and the page he was on dated nearly back to the mid-eighties. As he looked, he noticed one Josh Froning, who had stayed on a late August night in nineteen ninety. In the "Reason for Visit" column, Mr. Froning has written that he was a lineman working for PSNH. The truck by the substation must have been his, Fletcher surmised.

The reminder of the company sparked another thought, which ignited the first smoldering ideas of a plan. " 'Scuse me," he interrupted. "What time you got?"

"Oh, uh, 6:50," Jude said.

"Thanks," said Fletcher, noting it in the ledger.

Belle arrived just then, regretfully announcing that her search for the phone had come up empty. "I even searched a couple of the kids' rooms," she added. "I really don't think anyone around here has seen it."

"Well, I'm sure you tried your best," Fletcher managed, already moving towards the back. "Anyways, we'd best be getting up to our room."

"Maybe you folks would like to join us for dinner?" Belle asked.

"That's mighty kind of you," said Paul.

"Sure, sure," said Fletcher. "But let's get settled into the room first."

That seemed fine to Belle, who started looking along the shelves for something to go with dinner. Jude, in turn, grabbed a couple of bags and started to lead the crew up to the Inn's room.

"You got somewhere to be, Fletch?" Derek asked as they ascended the old stairs.

Fletcher just nodded. "We'll see soon enough," he said.

Compared with the Down Home Motel, the room was actually quite spacious, if a bit musty. Fletcher thanked Jude for his hospitality, and set his bag on the bed as if he planned to settle in. Once Jude was gone, however, he picked his luggage back up, flopped down in a floral easy-chair by the window, and pulled his old knife from the bag.

Paul settled down on the bed and started unpacking. "You Ok, Fletch?"

Fletcher grunted in assent as he strapped the knife to his leg.

Derek eyed the blade warily. "Are you having, like, flashbacks or what?"

"What time you got, kid?"

"Almost seven."

"Good." Fletcher straightened and started rifling through the bag. "Tell you what. If you still want to go to dinner with them folk at five after, I'll go down with you, right as rain. If not, you start listening to old Fletch. Deal?"

Derek looked at his watch again, checking it for some trickery. "Deal," he said eventually.

"Deal," said Paul.

"Good," said Fletcher, smiling. He slipped a couple of flashlights and a headlamp into his pockets. "Hey Paulie, you remember that night we got stuck out in South Cemetery?"

"Oh, God yes," Paul laughed. "That was the worst."

"What happened?" asked Derek.

"You tell it, Paulie."

"Oh, we was running late one night, 'bout ten years back, when a transformer blew out in Portsmouth. We wound up working right next to a candlelight vigil for some kid who'd died. And we was trying to get done fast and quiet, so nobody called dispatch to check in."

"Big mistake," laughed Fletcher.

"Well, we all forgot dispatch would check on us after end of day if we didn't check in," Paul continued. "And Fletcher always keeps the phone going so loud, when they called it interrupted the whole ceremony. And of course, he's the only one of us who ever really uses it."

"But I was up in the cherry picker," Fletcher added.

"Right. So I had to turn it off, right? And the whole dang crowd is watching me wrestle with this damn phone!" Paul was grinning as he pantomimed combatting the satellite. "But I tell you, these heavy duty satellites, if you never used one before, it's damn hard to shut one of them ... things ..." Paul trailed off, his mirth evaporating.

From below them, the tinny tune of the dispatch calling was faint, but still clearly audible. So were the scrabbling of feet on the oak floor, and the smacking of hands on plastic as someone made hurried attempts to surreptitiously silence the device.

"Damned hard to shut 'em off quietly, yeah," said Fletcher. He hated being right.

"Shit," said Derek, eyes wide.

"What the hell do they think they're getting at?" Paul demanded.

"I dunno, but there's a lot more of 'em than there are of us," whispered Fletcher. "Keep your voice down, and act natural. Don't look out the window!" he snapped

Derek startled. "Why?"

"'Cause they're looking in," said Fletcher. From the corner of his eye, he could already make out well over a dozen townsfolk walking towards the inn in the fading sun, making poor attempts to look inconspicuous as they glanced into the inn's room.

Paul feigned interest in his pack again. "What do you think we should do?" he asked.

"I already told you," said Fletcher. "We should get the hell out of here."

It was only a couple of minutes later that Jude knocked on the door with some old mints for the pillows. His smile was friendly, but his sharp eyes darted about, searching for signs of suspicion in the linemen. Fortunately, Fletcher had foreseen such a visit. He and Paul maintained an amicable and nonchalant facade, while a panicking Derek hid in the bathroom and ran the shower.

"You sure you have everything you need?" asked Jude.

"Oh, yep. We'll come on down once we're all cleaned up," Paul assured him.

"Great," smiled Jude. "The whole village is coming to dinner."

"Who'd want to miss that?" said Fletcher.

Once Jude had gone, however, the crew sprung into action. Curtains were drawn, bags were hastily repacked, and headlamps were donned. At Fletcher's direction, Paul and Derek quietly set a dresser in front of the door, on which he carefully arranged all of the decorative plates and silver platters he could find. When he was satisfied with the arrangement, the three men set about their escape.

Twilight was setting in when they slid open a rear window, gaining access to a rooftop that sloped down to the tree line behind the house. They moved as quietly as possible, their footsteps softened by the mosses that carpeted the roof and masked by the running shower. An old pine sat near the inn, it's broken branches forming a manageable ladder. One by one they stepped across the gap and climbed down, taking care to avoid being visible from the road and whispering prayers to any god listening that nobody would look out the back window.

It wasn't until they had slipped into the forest and began pushing through its concealing web of scrub brush that the linemen looked back. When they did so, Paul had to slap a hand over Derek's mouth to suppress a shocked expletive.

More of Northern Nash's residents were streaming towards the inn, emerging from the shadowy houses and descending along the road. Unlike the youthful, energetic townsfolk that had been the norm so far, these were shambling degenerates, grunting and groaning as they limped and stamped towards the inn. Their arms were uniformly curled up to their chests, and in the deepening twilight their faces had dark shadows and odd highlights, as though bulging with grotesque deformities. Their hair, wild and unkempt, seemed to ripple and rustle independent of any wind, so that they resembled bloated Medusas congregating just outside the doors of the inn.

"Come on," whispered Fletcher. He wasn't certain what exactly he was seeing, but he was sure that in this case ignorance was bliss.

Crossing the street was out of the question, forcing them to sneak deeper into the forest. "We'll head through the quarry to the power station," Fletcher whispered when they were out of earshot. "Then we can head straight up the path of the power lines up the valley, and hit the road into Southern Nash near the top."

Quietly and carefully, they picked their way through the woods by the light of a gibbous moon. The whole forest was a maze of silvery blue moonlight scattered among deep pools of black, reaching shadows.

Thin tendrils of mist were beginning to snake through the trees in the cool evening air.

By Fletcher's reckoning, they made it over half a mile before they heard the distant crash of platters and plates. The din was almost immediately followed by a chorus of shouts, punctuated by warped, piping howls.

"There's our cue to run!" he exclaimed, already breaking into a sprint.

They ran blindly through the trees, spurred by the twisted screeching that pierced the night air. Thorns and branches whipped by Fletcher, scratching his face, but he barely registered the pain in the wake of the weird howling that raked across his brain and and vibrated in his spine.

He had almost lost track of everything else when he tripped over something like a wet football, sending him pitching forward into the spongey earth. He skidded in the muck until crashing up against a rock and something that clanged like a bell.

"Fletch!" Paul yelled, skidding to a stop. "You okay?" He flicked on his flashlight. The whole ground was thick with the creeping black fungus from the substation basement, covered with yellow spots that opened in the moonlight. The dank mold spiraled among uneven chunks of granite, covering several ancient digging tools like the old shovel Fletcher had slid into. Sputtering expletives, Fletcher stood and snapped on his headlamp. In its yellow glow, he saw what he had tripped over—a sheep's head. It was covered with the black creep that wound around everything else here, growing in foul black spirals from its eyes and ears.

"What the hell?" Fletcher muttered, standing. "My god . . ."

Dismembered chunks of animals in every state of decay were scattered amongst the tools of the old dig site. Their lights revealed skulls of deer and sheep, a cow's rotting haunches, a decaying cat, and even a femur that looked human protruded from the moist earth and swirling black mold. Even as he rocked back on his heels, Fletcher thought he could hear the faint clicking of bones just below the squelching surface of the soft earth beneath him.

Paul wheezed a little as his flashlight locked onto a human skull, black spirals spilling from its eyes and mouth. "What the hell, Fletch? I mean, what the hell?"

A sudden squeal of foul language and burbled tears reminded them of Derek. Sprinting towards the sound, they found him staring and shining his flashlight at a massive granite dais, twice as wide as Fletcher was tall, carved with thousands of spirals. Wood, stones, bones, and other trinkets were laid at its base, all inscribed with the same hypnotic design. Atop the dais, the black fungus was thicker and more vibrant than elsewhere, mounded into a great, twisting black mass that boasted speckled, yellow, fruiting bodies the size of a man's hand.

But it was what was before the dais that had Derek trembling as he pointed. "That's . . . ! That's . . . !"

Fletcher looked. It was a man, or at least the corpse of one, curled up on his knees as ancient people did when worshipping great idols; face down, with bloody and cracked hands extended out in front of his prostrate body. The skin that Fletcher could see was burned and bruised, and wrapped in the tattered remnants of jeans and a flannel shirt. The misshapen body beneath the clothes looked to be infected with giant tumors that seemed to shift and squirm in the dim light. It was his hair, however, that was the most noteworthy, for it wasn't hair at all, but thick black tendrils of Northern Nash's ubiquitous mold.

"Calm down, kid," Fletcher told Derek, trying to do the same himself. He wondered if this poor soul was the creature that had been electrocuted by their work that afternoon—certainly the burns and bruises looked like electrocution.

Something caught his eye, and from the fungus and leaf litter he extracted a laminated card dangling from the corpse by a singed lanyard. The ID tag was burned and surrounded by melting laminate, but he could still make out a faded portrait of a smiling blonde man, and text identifying him as a PSNH worker named Josh Froning. Fletcher stepped back, his head swimming.

Paul softly called out to him. "Fletch."

"Yeah, Paulie, what?" Fletcher looked to where Paul pointed. What he saw took his breath away.

Their flashlights swept across a clearing, carpeted with the black fungus and filled with dozens, if not hundreds, of skeletons and rotting corpses, curled into the same pose of adulation and pointed inward at the dais. Each skull had a large hole bored through its top, and several had something like long, gray hoses protruding from them. They looked like fossilized Hare Krishna, complete with petrified topknots.

"This is really bad," said Paul.

"Run away, run away," Fletcher breathed. "When you see a dead man pray."

"What the friggin' hell?"

The two turned to Derek, who was slowly backing away from the corpse of Josh Froning. The carcass was beginning to twitch, stirring in its shoulders. With a sickening cracking sound, the back of his head split, and from it a long, snaking tuber quickly sprouted. Its tip glowed a faint yellow in the deep blue night, so that it seemed a rising point of flame. Dripping chunks of bone and gore, the growth rose until it was at least a yard in the air.

"Run!" Fletcher shouted, but before he had taken his first steps, the protuberance suddenly gave a small, shrill whistle. Fletcher felt a small rush of air breeze by him, and his nose was assaulted by the stench of sulfur and decay. Something stinking and powdery cloyed and clung to the inside of his nose, the back of his throat, the rims of his eyes. All three of the men rubbed their faces and spat to no avail as they choked on this noxious powder.

They weren't the only ones to hear the the whistle of the glowing tuber, however. The weird, warped howls resumed with renewed intensity. Something nearby was crashing through the woods. Fletcher turned in horror to see what emerged from the dark shadows.

It was the young girl in pink overalls, shielding her eyes from the glare of flashlights and headlamps suddenly focused on her.

Paul let out a sigh of relief. "Hey, kiddo," he began. "Are you . . ."

Brandishing a rusty knife, the child let out the most hideous shriek any of the men had ever heard. Her eyes were wide and bloodshot, and something black and viscous whipped around in her mouth where a tongue should have been. She launched herself blindly at Paul, who nearly fell over in the face of her reckless onslaught.

Fletcher was already in motion. He grabbed the girl by her knees and hauled her off of the struggling Paul. That was harder than it should have been, because black tentacles protruding from her mouth had wrapped themselves around the workman's arm. Her rusty knife stabbed at his arm wildly, drawing a couple of long gashes in his ample flesh.

Paul screamed. Wrestling the girl's weapon away from her, he hacked at the black protrusions wrapped around his forearm, and they loosed themselves with a wail. With all the strength in his wiry arms,

Fletcher lifted the girl above his head and slammed her down onto the dais. A sickening crack ripped through the air, and the child collapsed in a heap and lay still.

"Oh my god, oh my god," Paul sobbed. His arm was lacerated and bleeding where the tentacles had clutched him, and he had a shallow stab wound in his chest.

Derek stared at the twitching child, already curling into the prostrate pose of the other corpses. "Shit, dude! You just killed that little girl!"

"No, I just killed that little demon zombie girl," Fletcher snarled, helping Paul to his feet. "It's the friggin' Viet Cong all over again—you never trust a local, no matter what! Now let's go!"

Their flight was wild, over stinging scrub, under reaching branches, around lurking rocks, pushing towards the flashing red beacon of the tower. Fletcher lost track of time as he sprinted through a nightmare, his lungs burning. They could hear their pursuers crashing through the woods, howling and screeching. Above the hellish din they also heard the high whine of an all terrain vehicle in the distance behind them.

"Bastards are trying to head us off," Fletcher grunted.

"Where do we go?" Paul wheezed.

"The substation! We can at least get the lights on there, and its fenced in."

"We shouldn't have come here," said Derek.

"Now you get it."

Dark forms were closing in behind them, and he could hear low snarls in the forest. The substation was just ahead, its warning light pulsing red in the distance. "Go!" he hollered. "Go for the station! Don't stop for anything!"

They had almost reached the station when the ATV pulled up in front of it. Jude and Belle extended hands from the ATV, their faces terrified, and called out to the sprinting crew.

"Come on!" Jude shouted. "We can . . ."

Fletcher's fist caught Jude full in the face. The crunch of bone was clearly audible, as well as a piping yelp, as Jude was thrown backwards off the ATV. "Go go go!" Fletcher screamed, grabbing Derek and running harder to where Paul was struggling with the gate.

"But they . . ." Derek protested.

"Shut it and move it, kid!" As Paul finally opened the gate, Fletcher threw Derek ahead of him. He turned and slammed the gate shut just in time for Belle and Jude to leap against it.

"Let us in!" Belle cried. "Those things are out there!"

"So get on that ATV you never told us about," Fletcher snarled, padding the lock.

"Please," said Jude. "Please, they'll . . ."

Fletcher bent down and grabbed a twisted piece of rebar left over from the mangled trap door. "Back off this fence, or I'll kill ya."

"Goddamn, Fletch!" protested Derek.

"Fletcher, come on, it's us," said Jude. "Let us in! Those things will . . ."

"Those things ain't howlin' now, are they? And I don't hear 'em running out either."

They all paused, listening. The forest was silent now, and eerily so. Belle frowned and took a step back.

Fletcher grinned with grating teeth. He really, really hated being right. "Nah, unless I miss my guess, those things are waiting to see if we let you in. But I won't. I'll kill you. Last warning."

Jude shook his head. "Fletcher, I don't . . ."

With a shrug, Fletcher tossed the rebar to his left, where it jammed between a tower support and the fence. Sparks flew as twenty thousand volts surged through the fence and into Jude.

"Careful boys," said Fletcher. "Live wire."

Jude twisted and shrieked as arcs of blue light danced across his frame, and with another blast he was flung screaming from the fence. He crumpled into a small pile near the edge of the forest, almost out of the substation's light.

He hadn't hit the ground before the woods erupted in utter chaos. Dark shapes ran through the shadow. The forest echoed with a burst of howls and inhuman shrieks that shook the leaves from the trees.

"What the hell, man?" Derek protested. "Stop friggin' killing people!"

"They ain't people," said Fletcher. "And I didn't kill it. Look."

Jude was, impossibly, still moving. With grunts of effort, he pushed himself to his hands and knees, his whole body jerking like a marionette. His breath came in short, irregular gasps, as though his lungs were being manually operated. Dark tendrils wound out of his mouth and writhed around his face.

The howling fell silent as Jude looked up into the blackness of the woods; the hint of a shadow fell over him. There was a low breathing from above him, a predatory growl, as something loomed above the man, considering.

Ignoring the linesmen, Belle ran to the fallen man's side. "No!" she shrieked. "No! He'll heal! He'll be . . ."

A warped scream from within the woods cut her off. Something dark grabbed Jude by the legs, and with an inhuman wail he was yanked back into the woods.

"My god," whispered Paul.

The trees shook again, and the air split with Jude's screams and a chorus of monstrous snarls. Mixed in the din were the sickening sounds of meat and grist being torn from crunching bones.

"No!" shrieked Belle again, falling to her knees.

After a couple of minutes, the din subsided, and several creatures could be heard striding back into the woods, towards the old dig site. The rest, however, still prowled around the edge of the light, growling and murmuring just out of sight. Some of the more normal of Northern Nash's residents were emerging from the shadows, their faces twisted masks of hatred.

Belle approached the fence again, tear-stained eyes burning like embers. "You!" she snarled at Fletcher. "You think you beat him? He's going to be with the spiral now, and from him new life shall spiral forth forever!"

"Didn't seem like he wanted to go," Fletcher taunted her. "Probably didn't like the idea of getting hacked up and fertilizin' mold."

"Shut up!" she screamed. "You laugh now, but you'll serve in the same way! You'll join the same cycle of life and death as he did, as we all must somehow! The spiral has you! You can never leave! It's life and death! It's nature itself!"

"She's right!" Derek screamed. Paul and Fletcher looked at him in alarm, but the young man took no notice of them. He stared straight ahead, his eyes wide with hysteria. "All paths lead into into the spiral's center! It's all around us! The spiral will . . ."

Fletcher slapped him, hard and fast. A bit of blood flew out the side of the apprentice's mouth as his head snapped to the right.

"Don't you snap on me, kid," the old man snarled, his finger an inch from Derek's face. "If you can't take it, you shut up and let me think."

"But the spiral . . ." Derek's whine cut off when Fletcher raised his hand again, and he slunk off behind the power shed to cry.

"What do we do now, Fletch?" Paul said despondently.

Fletcher looked past the fence, where Belle and the more human locals circled the substation with dark eyes. Beyond them, faint shapes of more grotesque creatures creeped through the darkness. "I suppose we wait," he said.

Fletcher had Paul drag the ancient supplies up from the basement. The rusty lamp was far too dilapidated to make any use of the kerosene, and so the old, musty blankets were all that they had to keep warm.

The hours were long under the gaze of the lurking things. Fletcher and Paul sat back to back, watching the dark woods in the pulsing red light. Time seemed to stretch out and wrap back on itself, tying itself into a massive headache. Fletcher struggled to keep his wits and will about him. Paul had a harder time doing so, often growing listless and despondent. The kid was a wreck, crouched in a corner and alternately sobbing and singing softly to himself.

"Are they demons?" asked Fletcher at one point, watching the townsfolk creep around the fence. He rubbed his arm nervously.

Some of the more deformed of them were occasionally caught in a pulse of light, their twisted bodies writhing like a brood of snakes creeping beneath thin, pale skin. Their eyes, whenever visible beneath their dark mass of fungal hair, were like fish eyes, bulging and unblinking. Black tentacles hung from their mouths, whipping around in a frenzy whenever the creatures sounded their warped voices.

"I dunno," said Paul. "Maybe. Maybe they're mutants, like toxic waste, y'know? Maybe it's that damn mold, that fungus. What's it matter, though? Either way, this place is hell."

Fletcher nodded. It *was* hell. He talked to Paul periodically, trying to keep their spirits up as the night wore on in a haze of red light and dark shadows and shrill howling. It was a losing battle, though—his own head was splitting, and there was no denying the hopelessness that had descended on them. The pain and the despair wound together with time itself, until Fletcher couldn't tell any of them apart.

It wasn't until Derek stepped in front of him that Fletcher realized the townsfolk had fallen silent. Thick mist had rolled into the woods, but even so it was lighter than it had been before—just over an hour before dawn.

"I . . . I think they're gone," said Derek. His mouth was still bloody where Fletcher had struck him.

Paul and Fletcher immediately scrambled to their feet. The woods beyond them were silent, and no townsfolk were visible.

"Why would they go?" Fletcher wondered aloud.

"It's the light," Paul whispered with mounting excitement. "Those monsters hate the light, and the sun's coming up soon! It's already getting lighter. Maybe they're going back to their dens."

"Yeah. Yeah, that makes sense," said Derek.

"You sure?" Fletcher asked.

"Of course I'm not friggin' sure!" Paul snorted. "But if it's true, now may be the time to run."

"Hell, they could all be going to get guns," said Derek, "and just save themselves the trouble."

Paul nodded. "When else are we gonna have a chance like this?" He licked his lips, curling a lock of his hair around his finger. "I say we go for it."

Fletcher was skeptical, but he had to admit that it seemed an opportune moment. They checked and re-checked, walking the perimeter quickly as they eyed the forest, but they could see no sign of the creatures nor the townsfolk in the shadowy woods.

"Okay," said Fletcher, when they re-convened. "I'll cut the power, real quiet like. Derek, you're fastest; you run out first. You see or hear anything, you run back as fast as you can, you hear? I'll turn the juice back on once you're in."

"Yeah," said Derek.

"You don't hear anything, follow the lines up the valley. If you make it to the first posts without having to run back, Paulie and I will be right behind you. You just run as hard as you can until you're back in an actual city. Got it?"

"Got it," Derek nodded.

"Good. Once we're out there, we run no matter what. And if we don't all make it—it's been a pleasure workin' with you, boys."

They exchanged similar sentiments, and then moved swiftly. Fletcher counted down in a whisper before flipping the switch that cut the whole station off, its red light dimming and flickering out. Quickly,

Paul opened the gate and Derek was off, sprinting up the hillside as fast as his scrawny legs would carry him.

"Go, kid, go," Fletcher whispered, his knuckles white as he gripped the switch. He and Paul watched the apprentice's flight intently, but there were no signs of pursuit, no dark howls from the woods. Derek quickly reached the first set of poles, where he turned and waved to them, barely visible in the mist.

The two senior linemen looked to each other and nodded in affirmation. Quickly, Paul slipped out the gate and headed for where the apprentice was waving. Fletcher started to follow, but something caught his eye.

Derek's pack and jacket were left in the corner where the kid had spent the night crying, but the jacket was more than just discarded. It almost looked arranged. His stomach turning, Fletcher paused and picked up the coat.

Hundreds of red spirals, hours worth, were scrawled onto the cement in Derek's blood.

"Paulie, no!" Fletcher cried, slamming against the chain link fence. "Come back!"

He could already see that he was too late, though. Dark shadows broke from the forest and swiftly glided through the mists, brushing past Derek. By the time Paul realized the deception, the creatures were almost on top of him, snarling and baying. He tried to evade, dodging and turning back, but his pursuers were larger and faster, and the shadows quickly closed in.

"Paulie!" Fletcher couldn't even hear himself over Paul's screaming. The pack fell upon the journeyman, and all Fletcher could see was churning darkness in the fog. With a final scream Paul's limp form was tossed into the air, breaching the mists for a moment before plunging back into silver obscurity. The hill fell silent, except for the grisly sounds of rending flesh.

In his grief and terror, Fletcher barely had the presence of mind to notice that the gate to the substation was still open. Cursing, he sprinted across the station. Already he could see howling creatures pouring from the woods and running towards the open fence. With all his strength, he lunged for the gate and slammed it shut, clicking the lock into place just as the largest of the creatures slammed into the fence.

Fletcher fell back at the sight of the monster. Its head was a human skull, bare except for black tendrils that flailed from its orifices and the wide eyeballs staring from the bone sockets. The terrifying visage perched atop a mane of black, rubbery tentacles that ran over its shoulders and down its back. The rest of the creature was a mass of pale, sickly skin with similar tentacles spiraling beneath its surface, occasionally bristling though in patches of writhing hair. Its arms were almost human from the elbow up, but a mass of black, curling appendages from the elbow down. These tentacles extended far beyond the length of a man's hands, and the abomination ran on all fours, like a great ape.

Now it clutched at the gate, its rubbery appendages slithering through the chain link fence and reaching for Fletcher, wrapping around his ankles and cutting into him with serrated barbs. It let loose one of the shrill, warping howls, a black mass of tentacles pouring from its mouth as it did so.

Screaming, Fletcher clawed back along the pavement, stabbing at the reaching protrusions with his knife as he did so. Severing a couple, he freed himself and staggered to the power box with a curse and a whimper. In a daze, he hit the switch.

Blue and yellow sparks erupted all around him as the howling monster and several similar creatures were blasted from the fence. The dark things hadn't even rolled to a stop when an even larger monster stepped from the shadows. It stepped over the limp form of the shocked howler by the gate and looked Fletcher directly in the eye before piping a garbled, hollow whistle. At the sound, a pack of similar abominations emerged behind it, staring with bare eyes and hissing their hatred at Fletcher.

Fletcher glared back with his own hate and defiance as more and more figures materialized from within the mist, joining the howlers. Belle smiled cruelly as she appeared, regarding Fletcher within his electrified cage. "Well, well," she purred. "One left."

A moment later, Derek stepped from the fog as well. "Hey Fletch," the kid said, as though he hadn't just betrayed Paul to his death. As though nothing had happened at all.

"You son of a bitch," Fletcher snarled. "You killed Paulie."

"Derek here was just serving the spiral," said Belle, fondly stroking Derek's chin. She nodded to him, and he ran off to the abandoned utility truck. "We all serve it somehow. It is life and death."

"I don't!" Fletcher countered.

"You will. We all do, in so many ways." Belle rested a hand on the tentacled monster next to her. "The eldest of us hunt food for it, and kill those who would harm it."

More townsfolk were walking through the mists, bug-eyed, deformed creatures shambling towards the dig site with chunks of human flesh in their twisted arms. Some set about dismantling the electrocuted howlers, callously ripping the weakly protesting creatures apart and bearing the pieces back into the woods.

Belle pointed to the macabre parade. "Those of us well along the path of the spiral bring it food and tend its needs."

Fletcher winced and turned away as one of the grotesque troglodytes passed the substation carrying Paul's severed head, the dead man's face twisted in a silent scream. Belle smiled. "Some, like you and your friend here, will never find the path, and are destined to join the great spiral of life as sustenance. But those of us who have only just found it," she added, "guide wanderers to the spiral, and make sure they find their place within it."

"You're bait," grunted Fletcher. "You're the pretty face on this hellhole until that black shit takes you over and shows you for the monster you are."

Belle frowned. "That's just ignorant," she said. "You don't know the glory of the spiral, of all nature, of all that is wonderful here. But Derek does," she added, turning as the ratty kid returned from the truck. "And he'll help you find your place."

Derek smiled and walked up to the great howler. He was wearing lineman's gloves, and he held a long pair of clippers. He pointed to the wires, and the great beast extended its tentacled arms for him.

"Y'know, Fletch," said Derek, stepping on to the writhing mass that served as the monster's hands. "It's too bad you don't see it. The spiral, I mean. It's amazing, once you do."

"Stop it, Derek," Fletcher said, walking over to Derek's discarded pack and bag. "You don't want to do this."

"Oh, I do," said Derek. The beast was lifting him up, high over its head, bringing him within reach of the wires entering the substation. "I mean, I get rid of your cranky old ass, I prove myself to my new friends, and I serve the spiral. Win, win, win, man."

"That's not you," said Fletcher. He was emptying Derek's bag, removing almost everything from it. He tossed in the broken lamp, and the can of kerosene. "That black crap's got in you somehow."

"It's in all of us, in everything! We've seen it, and heard it, and breathed it! It's life, man." Derek reached up and cut one of the four main wires to the station. It flopped to the ground, sputtering blue energy. "Careful boys," he grinned, looking right at Fletcher. "Live wire."

Fletcher walked back to near the fence, hefting the bag. "Look at that thing you're on. You really want to be that? Fight it, kid. Try to fight it."

"Oh, come on, old man," said Derek. "I'm one with nature now. I've found my place. Do you really think that's gonna work?"

"Nope," said Fletcher. He tossed the bag over the fence. It tumbled end over end as it sailed through the air, spilling the aerosol cans, the broken lamp, and the kerosene within. One canister landing directly on the live wire on the ground.

It lit up in a man-sized fireball, igniting the can next to it, and then another. The howler carrying Derek screeched at the flash of heat and light, dropping the youth as he did so. With a squeal, Derek fell straight into the flames.

Propelled by spouts of fire and gas, cans spun into the scrub brush where they ignited plants, trees, and even a couple of residents who shambled away too slowly. Derek shrieked in agony, rolling about to put out the flames. The large howler stepped back from the flames, directly onto the live wire. With another howl, it was blown into the igniting woods.

Fletcher didn't miss a beat. Before Derek had hit the ground, the senior lineman was already in motion. He killed the power to the station as he ran by the switch to open the gate. Knife in hand, he sprinted through fog and chaos to where the ATV sat.

"Oh, there is a God," he breathed when he saw the key sitting in the ignition. He kicked the vehicle into gear with a quick twist of his wrists, and the vehicle roared forward. As he passed the substation, he could see several howling creatures descending on the burned and feebly struggling form of Derek.

"You never listened, kid." Fletcher muttered under his breath. "Nature's a bitch."

He didn't have long to ponder the apprentice's demise. Some of the howlers and townsfolk had clearly noticed him. Already, they were in pursuit, their voices shrill with rage and hate. Even with the ATV roaring at full throttle, Fletcher was barely gaining ground as he sped along under the power lines, dodging dark shapes in the twilight fog.

Fletcher had just crested the road at the top of the valley, and his lead wasn't half what he would have liked it to have been, when the ATV began to sputter and wheeze. "Dammit!" he cursed as the machine chugged to a halt, but there was no time to waste. He leapt from the vehicle and sprinted for the road, running as fast as his exhausted frame would carry him.

It didn't take long for him to hear the sounds of his hunters. The townsfolk had fallen back, but it sounded like three or four of the big howlers were still on his trail. He could hear their otherworldly baying as they closed in, could hear them scattering leaves and stones as they pounded through the forest.

The road seemed to go on forever, and a part of him was sick of running. Sick of fighting. Sick of trying to leave what was inevitable. His heart was pounding in his chest. His legs felt like lumps of mud. He heard odd, low moans in the distance.

Unable to go on, Fletcher fell to his knees. "Dammit," he sputtered, turning. Three howlers ran up the road behind him, thundering along with their skeletal mouths open and their black nests of slavering tongues. Fletcher couldn't even find the will to raise his old knife in defense. The foremost beast leapt for the kill. Just as it reached the zenith of its final pounce, its head exploded in a spray of bone and black ichor.

Foul goo sprayed over Fletcher. A sound like a thunderclap hung in the air. The howler's body flopped down, its wriggling tentacles drawing misshapen spirals in the dirt as it twitched and jerked. The other two howlers skidded to a halt and hissed at several figures emerging from the fog behind the prone lineman.

"Back! Back, you foul things!" hollered Quincy, raising his Bible into the air. Brother Thomas followed after him, hefting a smoking hunting rifle. Behind him, several of Southern Nash's residents wore determined faces and carried high-caliber weapons.

Quincy waved the holy book like it was more potent than any gun. "You brood of vipers! Back to your pit! You've wandered too long from your black mother anyway, that whore of Babylon! Can you stand to be so far from her?"

The creatures hissed and howled, pawing the ground in agitation. The townsfolk needed little excuse to fire another volley of bullets, and a second howler disappeared in a mist of lead and gore. The third fled, limping away and howling in fury.

"You . . ." began Fletcher. "You've gotta—we need to . . ."

"I know, my son, I know." Quincy's voice was kind as he knelt next to Fletcher. "Did your friends . . . ?"

Fletcher fought tears as he shook his head.

"Ah," said Quincy sadly. "Hell has opened her mouth without measure, and the multitude descends into it, Isaiah five fourteen."

"It isn't demons!" Fletcher hissed, gripping the old man's arm. "It's like a—like a . . ." He paused, puzzled. The words wouldn't come out. "It gets in your brain! We have to—we have to . . ."

"I know it ain't fire and brimstone, my boy, but you tell me what else it'd look like for God to turn His back on a place."

Quincy shook his head as he helped Fletcher to his feet. "We all been through that hellhole," he said, nodding to the villagers as they dumped a can of gasoline on one of the howler's convulsing carcass. "Every one of us."

Fletcher watched as Brother Thomas dropped a lit match on the body. "You've seen—you've seen the . . . ?"

"'Course I have. I was there when it was just a mining camp. I was in the first crew to find that vile blackness, like Satan's blood! I watched it turn the young folk against us old timers, and I heard 'em kill my friends as the years went by. I seen what those kids have turned into. I hate it, I hate it with all my soul. But I can't leave here. I just—we can't never leave. And neither can you, God bless you. You've breathed it in. It'll be all you can do not to go back."

Fletcher shook his head. The headache was coming back. "No, that's not true."

The old pastor's face was not unkind. "Ain't it? Look what you're doing, my son."

Fletcher felt a lump in his throat as realization struck him. He knew without looking that he was rubbing his arm again. Already, the skin just above his elbow was raw and painful from where he had traced and retraced the same, sinister spiral.

"You can't speak of it, can you?" whispered Quincy.

"No," said Fletcher. "No, I- I- nnng." Fletcher's words cut off in a spate of choking groans, a pathetic hacking that was all he could muster when he tried to speak of the fungus, or the howlers, or even of Paulie and that bastard Derek.

"It can never touch us the way it takes the young ones," Quincy said slowly. "Maybe we're too old, too set in our ways for its evil to take root. But it's still in you, and in me, and in all of us, that foul thing. It won't let you reveal its secrets. It'll fight you if you try to threaten it. You cannot bring yourself to leave it. There's probably even a part of you that wants to lie down and let it have you, let its blackhearted brood shred you and feed the pieces to it. It'll be all you can do to haunt the edge of Hell."

It was that thought that finally broke Fletcher. Spluttering and choking, he couldn't stop the tears as he crumpled onto Quincy's shoulder.

"There, there, my son," Quincy comforted. "I know. We're here."

Wiping his face with one hand, Fletcher took a step back. The other villagers were praying over a burning mass that had once been a monster that had once been a man.

Quincy smiled at Fletcher, and patted his old Bible. "Come," he said, setting off into the fog. "The godless destroys his neighbor, but through knowledge the righteous will be delivered, Proverbs eleven nine. We will teach you. We will show you the way. Yes, the way, and the truth . . ." Still muttering verses, the old man disappeared into the fog.

With nowhere else to go, Fletcher had no choice but to follow.

 **J. Zachary Pike** is an active writer, director, and animator in the New Hampshire film community. His ever-expanding portfolio includes several award-winning shorts and trade animations, and more film and writing are currently in the works. Most notably, he wrote and directed the animated short *The Toll,* which has won a dozen awards in more than sixty festivals worldwide. He has no prior experience working in horror, is easily frightened by any scary book or movie made after 1965, and will probably be too terrified to finish reading this book.

The Waiting Room

James Patrick Kelly

"How sick are you?" said the man, as he dropped *Entertainment Weekly* onto the end table. The magazine was two months old: Mitch Gellman, the drummer who had hung himself, had the cover. He was grinning like the devil on crack.

Sherry blinked at the magazine and then at the man. "What?" She'd slumped on the sofa, wrapped so tight in dread that the waiting room seemed nothing but a blur of blonde wood and dark cushions.

The man nodded at the door behind the receptionist's desk. "Waiting for the doc?"

Sherry didn't have time for prying strangers. "None of your business." She didn't have any time at all.

The man sat next to her. "Right." He picked up a copy of *New Hampshire Magazine*—the "Top Doctors" issue—and fanned himself with it. He was as bland as the furniture: forty-something going gray, middling build, midnight blue suit, red check tie. "It's just that I've seen you here before."

"I've never seen you."

He winked and tugged at the knot of his tie. "Maybe you haven't been looking hard enough."

Sherry got up then. She found a new seat next to the front desk. Dawn, the receptionist, was on the phone. She glanced up briefly to see if Sherry needed anything then went back to what sounded like

a difficult call. "I'm not collecting anything, sir," said Dawn. "I'm just calling to remind you that Louis Desmarais has an appointment at two-fifteen tomorrow."

Sherry wanted to grab the phone out of Dawn's hands and scream into it. *Don't come in. Don't come anywhere near this place.*

"It's the pancreatic, isn't it?" The man settled onto the chair beside her. "Doc has seen a lot of that recently." His voice purred with sympathy.

Sherry felt as if hands were pressing against the sides of her head. She fumbled a Kleenex from the box on the end table and touched the corners of her dry eyes. In advanced Stage III, her oncologist said, it moves from the pancreas to the large blood vessels and lymph nodes. She'd been dying for a long time as it turned out—years maybe, and hadn't known it. Palliative care, her oncologist advised, ease the symptoms. Maybe take part in a clinical study. Leave a legacy.

"It's not so bad," said the man. "Could be worse."

Anger boiled out of her. "Worse?" She grabbed the man by the lapel of his blue suit. The material was odd—not wool, or silk or synthetic. It felt thin as a spider's web. "He's giving me *months*." She couldn't believe what she was doing; this wasn't the kind of woman she was. But then Sherry wasn't anyone she knew anymore.

"That's hard." The man frowned. "But believe me, it could be worse."

"That's right, Mrs. Nute," Dawn said. "Tomorrow at three. No, I don't know what's in the lab report. The doctor will talk to you tomorrow. No, I'm just the receptionist, ma'am. I understand you're concerned. I'm sorry, I have no access to charts."

With an effort, Sherry released her grip on the man's lapel and then smoothed it with her thumb. "So," she said, "how sick are *you*?" Since he seemed to know all about her, she felt she had the right to ask. She knew it was monstrous of her, but she was hoping that cancer was eating this nosy son of a bitch too. That it would put him in a grave.

"Oh, I'm not sick." He settled his hand on hers. His touch was smooth as glass and as light as air. "I'm dead."

"Mr. Goff," murmured Dawn.

"What?" He started.

The receptionist curled a finger.

"Me?" His eyes were suddenly wild. "Already?"

"Yes, Mr. Goff," She was grinning at them like the devil on crack. "The doctor will see you now."

James Patrick Kelly has had an eclectic writing career. He has written novels, short stories, essays, reviews, poetry, plays and planetarium shows. His most recent book, a collection of stories, was *The Wreck of the Godspeed*. His short novel *Burn* won the Science Fiction Writers of America's Nebula Award in 2007. He has won the World Science Fiction Society's Hugo Award twice: in 1996, for his novelette *Think Like a Dinosaur* and in 2000, for his novelette *Ten to the Sixteenth to One*. His fiction has been translated into 18 languages.

Uneasy Lies the Head

Brendan DuBois

On a cluttered street in Lawrence, Massachusetts—a mill town that had last seen better days about a century ago—Roland Miller sat in his Ford Escape SUV, waiting. With him were two other men, Jasper Duncan and Lucas Wilton. It was early evening and Roland was tired. They had driven four hours to meet a man in the nearby three-story tenement with peeling paint and a Chevy pickup truck on blocks parked outside.

Roland looked around the narrow street. He couldn't imagine living in a place like this, with so much concrete, asphalt and buildings crammed in together. The window was rolled down some and there was no scent of trees, of grass, of holy soil. Just the smell of burnt oil and wet garbage. Next to him Jasper said, "The quicker we get this done and out of here, the happier I'll be."

Behind them, Lucas piped up. "That makes the two of us."

Roland said, "It's not like we're on the moon, fellas. It's just Massachusetts, that's all."

A car came crawling down the street, with low wheels and lots of bright neon paint on the side. Music pounded from speakers set in the rear window, actually making the Ford tremble as it went by. The car was packed with young men, who shouted at them in a foreign language.

"Well, that now makes the three of us," Roland said. "Let's get this thing done. We've got a long ride back when we're through."

Next to him Jasper said, "What? Can't we stay at a motel?"

"Only if you pay your own way," Roland said. "You know the town can't afford it."

And with that, the town fathers of the small village of Arkham, New Hampshire got out and walked into the tenement building.

Roland wrinkled his nose at the smell of burnt food, urine and other strong odors in the open lobby. It was filled with overflowing green trash bags, a bicycle with no wheels, and a child's tricycle on its side. Jasper looked at the mailboxes to the right, running a thin finger across the names. "Here," he said. "Harold Monroe. Apartment 2-A."

Roland said, "Let's go then."

Behind them, the heavier Lucas said, "Thank God he's not at the top of the building."

"No matter where he is, you know we need him," Roland said.

"I know, I know," Jasper said. "And like before, what our town really needs is . . ."

Roland interrupted, "Oh, God, please don't say that. Such an old cliché." And the other two men laughed.

Up on the second floor, they stopped before a dirty yellow door that had a stick-on letter and number that announced 2-A. Roland said, "Are we ready?"

Both of the men nodded. Roland said, "All right. You know there's no going back."

Jasper said, "Oh yeah, we know that."

And Lucas added, "You're the chairman, Roland. Go ahead and take the lead. We won't mind."

Roland knocked on the door. Waited. Knocked again, harder; he could hear somebody shuffling around on the other side. He looked to his two companions, shrugged, and knocked again.

A sound of a lock being unsnapped, and then the door opened up a bit, a chain lock holding it back. There was a rumpled-looking man peering through the narrow slit.

"Yeah?" he asked, in a low, surly voice. From behind him, Roland heard one of his fellow travelers sighing, and he knew what Lucas or Jasper was thinking: *This? This is the man who's going to save us?*

He tried not to sigh himself. He said, "Mister Monroe? Mister Harold Monroe?"

"Who's asking?" came the voice.

"We are," Roland said.

"And who the hell are you guys? Cops? Immigration?"

"Nope," Roland said. "We . . . we represent the town of Arkham, New Hampshire. And we need your help."

There was a pause, and Harold said, "The hell you say."

"No, it's true," Roland said. "May we come in?"

Another pause, and then Roland reached into his coat pocket, removed a crisp fifty-dollar bill. He slipped it through the opening and Harold plucked it away.

Roland said, "That's just for talking with us, Mister Monroe. And you can keep it, no matter what you decide. Doesn't that sound fair?"

Harold, rubbing the fifty-dollar bill in his hand, suddenly shut the door. Jasper whispered, "Well, that went okay," and there was a clattering noise as the chain was undone. Then the door opened and Harold beckoned them in. "Okay. Come on in, but I don't got much time."

Roland entered the apartment, followed by Jasper and Lucas. He tried to keep his expression friendly, though he was disgusted by what he saw. A tiny room with a sagging couch, a chair covered with a flowered sheet, and a coffee table covered with men's magazines and paper plates and cardboard pizza boxes. More pizza boxes were on the dirty orange carpet, along with newspapers and crumpled fast-food bags.

And Harold wasn't much better. He had on dirty gray sweatpants and a stained New England Patriots T-shirt. He was in his early thirties with a paunch, fleshy face and a two-day-old stubble of beard, and he was barefoot. A television set on mute squatted in the far corner. His brown eyes were set in, beady, and flickered around the three of them.

"Well?"

Roland took a breath. "Mister Monroe, my name is Roland Miller. These two gentlemen are Jasper Duncan and Lucas Wilton. We are the selectmen for the town of Arkham, New Hampshire. Sort of like city councilors. We're elected to run the town and that's why we're here. We need your help."

"Me? What kind of help?"

Roland smiled. "This is going to sound unusual, but do bear with me. We have a position in Arkham that needs to be filled, and we've done some research, some genealogical research, and we've determined you might be able to fill this position."

Harold rubbed at the bristles on his chin. "A job? You're offering me a job?"

Roland said, "In a manner of speaking, yes, we're offering you a job. A job that pays quite well, and which isn't particularly . . . burdensome."

Harold looked at Roland, and the other two selectmen. "What kind of job?"

Another breath. "Mayor."

"Mayor? Hunh? Did you just say mayor?"

"Yes, I did."

The eyes got a bit more beadier. "Is this some sort of joke?"

Our savior, he thought, *our savior*. "I assure you, Mister Monroe, it's not a joke."

"Of course it is. I mean . . . hell, how can I be your mayor? I don't got the experience."

Roland said, "Experience doesn't count, Mister Monroe. Your last name is what counts."

"My last name? Man, this is too weird. For fifty bucks, it really ain't worth it."

Roland held up a hand. "Please. Let me talk, just for a few minutes. And you can ask any questions, and then we'll leave. And you'll still be fifty dollars richer."

Harold folded his arms. "Go on, then."

He looked to his fellow selectmen. "Our little town is in a remote area of New Hampshire, and we're one of the oldest in the state. For all these hundreds of years, we've governed ourselves through the selectmen, the oldest form of governance in New England . . . but Arkham being Arkham, we also have a mayor. The mayor is a ceremonial position for the most part, but . . . we've had a tradition that the mayor always comes from the same family, the Monroes. An odd tradition, but our townspeople have found that keeping such a tradition alive leads to . . . harmony, as strange as that may sound."

"So my last name is Monroe. So what."

"Yes, but according to our research, your great-great-great uncle was once a resident of Arkham, so you have a direct family link back to our town . . . and, alas, there are no longer any Monroes still living in Arkham. So when the time comes, we try find a direct descendant of the Monroe family in Arkham who resides somewhere in New England, and offer him the job."

Harold eyed each of them. "Why are you the only one talking?"

He shrugged. "I'm the chairman of the board. It's my role, to take the lead in a matter such as this."

"And it's a paying job?"

"Yes."

"How much?"

Roland named a number, was pleased to see the look on Harold's face. "And what exactly would I do?"

"Attend selectmen meetings. Sign official documents. Represent Arkham at civic functions. Anything else that might come up during the course of events."

"But I have to live in town."

"Yes, you do. And you get a nice home, rent free, to call your own."

Harold rubbed his chin again. "Sounds too good to be true."

"No matter how it sounds, it's legitimate. Are you interested?"

"Maybe, maybe not," Harold said.

Roland shook his head. "I'm sorry, Mister Monroe, but we don't have time for negotiations, or extended discussion. We need an answer right now. You say yes, and we'll make arrangements to move you to Arkham. You say no, then you can stay here in Lawrence and enjoy these lovely accommodations, and your part-time job at the Wal-Mart warehouse. What's it going to be, Mister Monroe?"

Roland was definitely not a prayerful man—only during the right occasions—but he was hopeful, as whatever passed for a mind there in that pudgy man worked through its thoughts.

And then Harold smiled and said, "Guys, you just hired yourself a mayor."

A week later, Harold Monroe got off a Greyhound bus in the northeastern part of New Hampshire, stretched his cramped legs. The bus station was just a Greyhound sign nailed to the side of a gas station and cafe at a lonely crossroads, and Harold had never seen so many trees in his life. He had a zippered duffel bag at his feet, and it was a cool June day. He looked around. So damn quiet. *So,* he thought, *what the hell am I getting into?*

A dark blue Ford Escape came down the road, and pulled to a halt. The head of that selectmen crew, Roland something-or-another, got out. He was dressed pretty nice in clean jeans and a green L.L. Bean jacket.

Funny thing, even though they were in New Hampshire, the guy had dark skin . . . not as dark as his neighbors in Lawrence, but dark enough.

Roland came over, held out an envelope. "Welcome, Mister Monroe, and I'm pleased to present you with your first payment."

What doubts he had went away when he opened the envelope and saw the collection of 20 and 50 dollar bills inside. *All right*, he thought, *let's do it*. "Okay," he said. "I'm ready."

He tossed his duffel bag into the rear of the Ford and got in the front seat. Roland got back on the road and in a few minutes, the road started climbing and climbing, going up a steep series of switchbacks, as they went up into the mountains. At one point his ears popped, and then they started descending once they crossed over on the other side. The slopes of the mountains and hills seemed to close in on the road.

Harold looked out at the passing granite boulders, the scraggly trees and said, "How in hell do you get out of here in the winter?"

Roland seemed happier, descending into the narrow valley. "Sometimes we don't, if the snows really fly and the state plows get hung up. Been a few times when we were cut off for a few days."

"Sounds awful."

"You get used to it."

There was an overlook, and he saw Arkham, down there below them. It was a small collection of buildings, with a river going through the middle, surrounded on all sides by high peaks. And in a few more minutes, they were in town. Roland pulled the Ford into one of a number of empty parking spots. He got out and looked around, smiling, as Harold joined him.

"Welcome to your new home, Mister Monroe."

"Please," he said. "Makes me sound like an old man. Call me Harold."

He looked at the collection of homes, small brick buildings and shops. Seemed so quiet, so different. Roland said, "Pretty small, isn't it. But sure is peaceful. In fact, nobody locks their doors at night. Nobody. Bet you can't say that in Lawrence, can you."

Harold smiled. "No, you can't," he said, thinking of that envelope full of money in his pocket.

At the selectmen's meeting that night at the Arkham Town Hall, the meeting room was packed with residents of Arkham. After the conclusion of the regular business, Roland stood up behind a long polished table and said, "And for our special event tonight, I want to introduce our next mayor, Harold Monroe, late of Lawrence, Massachusetts, and now, of Arkham, New Hampshire!"

The townspeople—sitting on folding wooden chairs—stood up and cheered and applauded, and Harold, blushing, stood up and looked around, like he wasn't sure how he ended up here. Roland joined the applause, and smiling, joining him, were Jasper and Lucas, his fellow selectmen.

Later there was spiked punch and cookies and more celebrating, and handshaking, and when Harold got a bit loopy from the punch, Roland took him aside and said, "Mister Mayor, just a few official papers to sign." And Roland took him to a corner of the room, where the partying hadn't reached yet, and took out a folder from a desk drawer. He gently placed a pen into Harold's right hand, and smiling at all the attention and good wishes, Harold scrawled his signature at the bottom of the papers.

And when Roland took the papers away, he felt someone touch his elbow. He turned and bowed his head. Before him was the oldest resident of Arkham, Molly Wilton, known to everyone as Auntie Molly. She was short, wizened and wrinkled, wearing an old black dress, sensible shoes, and large round glasses. She was smiling widely and went up to Harold, pinched his cheek. "So glad you've joined us, young man. So glad you're our new mayor!"

Harold blushed and Roland thought, *It's all right, it's going to be all right.*

Later that night, Roland stood outside the town hall, breathing in the cool air. Their new and drunk mayor was safe in his own home. There were footsteps and he was joined by the other two selectmen, Jasper and Lucas. They flanked him and he held out his hands, and first one, and then the other, took a hand. He squeezed them and they squeezed back.

"We did it," Jasper said.

"We did it," Lucas said.

Roland nodded. "We did it."

Up in the distant and cold mountains, a fire erupted, a fire celebrating the start of a new era in Arkham.

Two weeks later, Harold Monroe walked down Arkham's Main Street, shaking his head. Something very weird was going on here. Oh, the townspeople treated him like the new big guy or something, and his bank account with the First Arkham Savings & Loan was nice and fat—fatter than it had ever been in Lawrence!—and his job, such as it was, was no heavy lifting. Damn, that was for sure. Just attend some meetings and lead the Pledge of Allegiance a couple of times, and that was that.

But . . . it was still too weird. For example, even though it was pretty damn quiet, he found it hard getting to sleep at night. There was always the sense that he could barely hear voices, out there in the woods. Whispering, chanting, singing, such that he'd sometimes sit up, quivering a bit. And during the day, even though the people were friendly, he always had the feeling they were talking about him when he wasn't around.

He went into a small brick building that held the office of Roland Miller.

Roland stood up when Harold, wearing jeans and a green turtle-neck shirt that had stains in the front, walked in. *But he's our savior,* he thought, *our savior,* so he offered him a smile and a handshake.

"Welcome, Mister Mayor, welcome," Roland said, sitting back down behind his desk. Harold took a chair and looked around and said, "What kind of work do you do here?"

Roland said, "I'm a lawyer."

"Are you good?"

"Best one in town," Roland said. "Of course, I'm the only one in town, which helps."

Harold shifted his seat and said, "You know, I'm having a hard time settling in . . . adjusting."

Uh-oh, he thought, and he said, "What seems to be the problem?"

Harold shrugged. "This town is too damn small. No good restau-rants, only one bar, no cell phones because there's no cell-phone towers. And you don't have Internet access, except for dial-up, and that's usually out of service. Hell, what's worse is you don't have cable television. How can you live without cable TV? I'm getting bored out of my skull. And I don't like it."

Careful, he thought, *careful.* Roland said, "So. What can we do to help?"

Harold snorted. "Christ, I don't know. What do you think you can do?"

Roland picked up an old-fashioned fountain pen, grabbed a legal pad. "How does a satellite dish for you sound?"

Harold's beady eyes widened some. "Are you serious?"

"Of course I'm serious," Roland said. "We'll make it happen. We want you to be happy in your job . . . and we'll probably never ever get cable television to this valley. Too remote."

"Remote . . . you sure ain't lying," Harold said. "How do you guys make a living out here?"

Roland scribbled some on the legal pad. "Started off as a farming community, of course, self-sufficient in the beginning. There's a set of falls up yonder on the Piqwaq River, so we did some leatherwork and spinning work. And light industry and dairy. Even today, we do hang on, though it gets challenging, especially since most of our goods have to come over the single mountain pass down here. But we stick together."

Harold grunted. "Maybe so, but I'm thinking . . . well, maybe I made a mistake coming here. You know? No offense."

Roland tightened his grip on his fountain pen. "Sure, I know what you mean. Look, give it a bit more time, will you? Can you promise us that?"

The mayor got out of the chair. "Sure. But not that long. See you around."

When the door closed, Roland waited just a minute, and then picked up the phone and made three phone calls. And to each resident, he said, "We have a problem. Meet me at the town hall at seven tonight."

The Arkham Town Hall housed a couple of small offices for the town clerk, the assessor and the public works director, and also had an office in the rear for the selectmen's daily business. The room was cozy, with shelves holding copies of the town's annual report going back to the mid-1800s. There were framed certificates and awards on the paneled walls, including one back from 1976 naming Arkham an official Bicentennial community. A heavy iron safe, containing precious documents and artifacts from the town's history, squatted in one corner.

Roland sat at the head of the table, looked at Jasper and Lucas, and at the other end of the table, Auntie Molly.

"Let the record show," Roland said, talking to Lucas, who was acting as recording secretary, "that the board of selectmen has gone into executive session to discuss a personnel matter."

Lucas moved his pen across a legal pad—donated to the town from Roland's firm—and said, "So recorded."

"Good," Roland said, folding his hands. "We have a problem with the mayor. He's already getting antsy, regretting his decision."

"Holy crap," Jasper said. "It hasn't even been two weeks yet."

Roland said, "His environment, I guess. He's complaining about Internet access, about cable television. I told him we'd get a satellite dish installed at his house as soon as possible and consider other things, but I'm concerned. He might not want to serve out his term of office. He finds the town . . . boring."

Lucas said sharply, "He's obligated. He has to stay. That's it."

Auntie Molly spoke up. "Don't be so quick, Lucas, or any of you. The poor boy feels isolated, alone, friendless, out of place. The electronics and gadgets that he craves, those can be supplanted, if we offer him something else. Something real."

At that, the back of Roland's hands felt cool, and he was glad he and his wife had only produced two young boys. But Jasper and Lucas . . . they exchanged looks and Auntie Molly said, "You know how we've survived here, in isolation, for centuries. By pulling together, by sacrificing. And to maintain tranquility, we have always followed those old ways. Lucas and Jasper, you know I'm right."

Meekly, Lucas nodded and whispered, "Yes, Auntie Molly." And after a second, Jasper said the same. "Yes, Auntie Molly."

She smiled at them, like an old schoolteacher pleased with their grades. "Boys, I know this is a tough decision, so I'll have to make it for you. I know your families. Jasper, your girl, Elayne. How old is she now?"

"Nineteen, Auntie," Jasper whispered, staring down at the old wooden table.

"Then it's settled," she said. "Roland, is there any other business set before the board?"

"No, Auntie," he said, feeling relief that this burden had passed him by.

"Very well," she said, and Jasper looked up and said, his voice strained, "Auntie, before we adjourn, would you mind leading us in prayer?"

She smiled again. "Absolutely not. Roland?"

"At once, Auntie," he said. He got up and knelt down at the old iron safe, and after deftly spinning the combination dial, opened it up. He reached in and took out old sheets of vellum, and stones, and worked iron, and brought them out. Gingerly and with great reverence, he placed them before Auntie Molly.

Then the board of selectmen for the town of Arkham, New Hampshire, and its oldest resident, Auntie Molly, held hands around the table as the old woman spoke in a language that had not been heard in public for centuries.

Two days after meeting with the old guy, Roland, the mayor of Arkham sipped on a Budweiser and admired his new satellite television system. It was pretty cool and it was nice to see something without looking through the fuzz of static, but still, what the hell had he signed up for? For one thing, the town was so small. He could walk up and down the main street in less than twenty minutes, and see most of the buildings. There was no bus or taxi service, so unless he hitched a ride with someone, he was stuck here. And there was one other odd thing—not that he minded much, but he thought all these small New England towns were real religious—there wasn't a single church in Arkham. Once he had asked Roland about that and Roland said, "Oh, the folks here make their own arrangements, that's all." And then Roland had changed the subject by asking if the landscaping for his home was okay.

The nearest other town was clear on the other side of the mountains and, besides the people and the buildings, the only thing Arkham had was farmland, mountains and a river that cut through it.

Yeah. One warm day, he was walking by the river, and an old guy was there, fishing, and he had said, "Anybody tell ya the history of this river?"

"Ah, no, they haven't," Harold had said. And the old guy waited a bit, and then said, "Well . . . long, long time ago, 'fore there were landslides and such, this river flowed wide all the way through Maine, and then to the ocean. It's cuz of this river that Arkham is Arkham."

And bored, he had said, "That's nice," and walked away.

Sure, he thought, raising his beer up, there were some good things. Like a nice bulging bank account. And a work routine that was pretty simple. And yeah, you could sleep at night with the door unlocked.

But he never did. He always kept his door locked, like he was back in Lawrence. There were things at night that creeped him out, like those distant whispers, the chanting, the singing. And sometimes, just bored, he would go out in the rear yard and look out at the dark mountains. On a couple of nights, he had seen fires on some of the mountain peaks. Harold knew he wasn't too bright—he had barely gotten through high school—but he figured that if he could see fires flickering up on the distant mountain peaks, they had to be pretty friggin' big fires.

Once he had mentioned that to Roland, who had said, "Our young'uns like to fool around, that's all. If they don't hurt anybody's property, we leave 'em alone."

Yeah, right. Harold knew the hell-raising he had done when he was younger, and he knew his buds would have dumped beers on him if he had suggested climbing a mountain to set off a bonfire—meaning you either had to spend the night up there, freezing your butt off, or try to climb down a dark mountain trail and break a leg.

Didn't make sense. Lots of things didn't make sense. Like being treated so friendly and loving, like . . . royalty, yeah, that's it, for doing such simple stuff.

He finished his beer. Not a bad gig, but man. When the snows started coming, it'd be worse, and he couldn't help himself, he shivered, and he knew when the first threat of snow came, he would . . .

There was a knock at his door. He looked up. He wasn't expecting visitors. Harold got up and opened the door, then stepped back.

A cute—hell, a real good-looking girl was standing there on his white porch, a wide and friendly smile on her face, holding a paper bag. Like most everyone else in the town, she had light olive skin and black hair. She had on jeans and a tight white turtleneck sweater, showing prominently that it must be cold outside, and she said, "Hey, Mister Mayor, how are you doing?"

Harold grinned. "Please, that sounds like I'm fifty or sixty years old. Call me Harold."

And it was like she curtsied, and said, "Hi, Harold. I'm Elayne Duncan."

"Nice to meet you, Elayne."

She laughed. "Harold, this is sweet and all, but are you going to invite me in?"

"Oh, hell, yes," he said, and she came in, and set the paper bag on the kitchen counter—cluttered with dirty dishes and crumpled up napkins—and she opened the bag and peered inside. "Here," she said. "My family's famous lasagna. Mom thought you'd like a home-cooked meal. What do you say we have some dinner?"

He struggled with what to say, and then, giving up with a smile, he said, "Sure."

The lasagna tasted fine, a bottle of wine she had brought tasted even finer, and the best part was when she had cleaned up and smiled and said, "What would you like for dessert?"

He blurted out, "What I'm looking at, I guess."

He instantly regretted saying that, knowing this fine-looking woman before him was nothing like the hard-drinking and hard-worn women he knew back in Lawrence, but her smile grew wider and she said, "Funny, that's what I was thinking, too."

So that was the first time that Elayne Duncan, daughter of select-man Justin Duncan, spent the night with the mayor of Arkham.

Early the next morning, the phone rang in Roland Miller's bed-room. He reached out and picked up the receiver, and a cheerful young lady said, "Done."

"Very good," he said, putting the phone down. His wife Tammy grog-gily reached over and rubbed his shoulder. "What was that, sweetie?"

He rolled over. "Town business."

His wife yawned. "Why am I not surprised."

Harold liked to play street hockey and a hard rubber ball once struck him right in the forehead, making shiny lights dance around in his eyes, making his head seem like it was spinning. After a couple of weeks with Elayne, it was like his head was always spinning. He did his mayor duties and Elayne would show up every few days. After seeing a DVD or going for a walk, they'd go back to his house and well . . . it was wonderful. But it was different. It was a bit disturbing. Like eating a sweet cake that had the slightest off taste, like something nasty had been added to it when it was baked.

One night, waking up with Elayne slumbering next to him, he had that flash that it was all a fake somehow. He rolled over and looked out the window. Out there in the darkness it looked like another flame was flickering on top of a distant peak.

A fake. How could it be anything else? Doing stuff in Arkham that anybody could do, getting paid lots of money, getting his house cared for, the satellite dish installed and now a girl who came and went whenever Harold wanted her. No whining, no hanging around. When she sensed he was bored, she left. When she sensed he needed some company, she showed up. And let's face it, he thought, she was gorgeous. No bad complexion, bad teeth, saggy belly or tattoos on the arms or wrists like the girls he had known back home. Nope, she was pretty hot. So why was she spending even a minute with a guy like him?

He looked at the gleaming flame out there. He didn't know. But he sure as hell was going to find out.

One late afternoon the board of selectmen of Arkham, New Hampshire were by the banks of the Piqwaq River, walking through the fields of one of the town's largest farms. Every now and then, they knelt down, and ran their fingers through the grass and soil.

"Looks good for spring," Roland said.

"Sure does," Lucas said.

"Best I've seen in a while," Jasper said.

Roland got up, brushed his hands and looked out at the fields and farms and the distant buildings of the town he loved and protected.

"Gentlemen," he said, "I do believe our new mayor is working out."

A week later, Elayne came over for dinner and she brought another fine meal and a bottle of wine. Like before, Harold saw that Elayne would only have one glass, as if she was afraid to get drunk. But Harold had other thoughts. As the evening moved along, he kept refilling her lemonade glass. The girl just loved lemonade. This night, Harold was adding vodka to it.

They were watching the latest Spiderman movie and Harold asked, "Don't you ever want to leave Arkham?"

She was cuddled up against him on the couch. "Why?"

"To get out in the world, make friends, get a living."

"Mmm," she said. "I can get a living by working for my Uncle Roland, as a paralegal, when the time comes. And I got all the friends and family I need here."

"But don't you want more?"

"More what?" she asked. "More crime? Pollution? Drugs? Here . . . here we're safe . . . have been safe for hundreds of years. And you know what's special? I can walk down the street and know everyone, and they know me. And we're all related . . . all of us . . ."

"Including Auntie Molly?" he asked.

"Auntie Molly?" she repeated. "Oh, she's so sweet . . . so strong . . . she's our eldest, you know, she's our town's . . . well, she's our eldest . . . everyone loves her and trusts her."

Something, he thought. Elayne was about to say something more about that old broad but she had caught herself. Time to keep this conversation going.

In the kitchen he refilled her glass with lemonade and more vodka and went back to the living room. "You said something about being related to everyone else. Is that why your skin is dark?"

"Mmm?" she asked, smiling up at him. He sat down and passed over the spiked lemonade to her. "Your skin color, you're darker than most people in these parts. Why's that?"

She sipped delicately at her lemonade. "Old stories are . . . that the first settlers, when they came into this valley . . . there was a Micmac tribe living here. There was a terrible, terrible winter. The Micmacs said to survive . . . the first settlers . . . they needed to join the tribe . . . to marry . . . to live. So that's what they did. I mean . . . you'll do anything to survive, won't you?"

"Sure," he thought. "Anything."

Elayne took another big swallow and then yawned. "God. I think I'm going to fall asleep, right here on your couch. . . ."

Something came to him, something he had wanted to ask but had never gotten around to it. Now was the time.

"Elayne?"

"Mmm?" she said, yawning again.

"The mayors."

"What about them?"

"They've all been Monroes, haven't they?"

She firmly nodded, and then belched, and giggled. "Yes. Tradition . . . the king . . . I mean, the mayor, must always be a Monroe. Always."

"How come there are none living in town?"

She burped again, and then put a finger to her sweet lips and said, "I don't know the whole story . . . secret, it is . . . but centuries ago . . . there was a feud . . . a fight . . . and the Monroes . . . they fought their way out. I mean, they moved out . . . and left. A terrible time . . . famine, no fish in the river, disease. But we got it back . . . once a Monroe came back to Arkham . . . to bring us peace and security."

Her words were slurred, but something about each one of them made his skin tingle. "So I'm your king. Or your mayor."

Elayne gave him a wet kiss on his neck. "Yes . . . our king . . . our savior. And be strong, Harold. Remember what Shakespeare said . . . 'Uneasy lies the head that wears a crown.' That's you, sweetie . . ."

She then drifted off, snoring. Harold sat still, thinking things over, and then nudged her once, and twice. She yawned. "Harold. Please. I wanna sleep . . ."

"The mayor before me. What happened to him?"

"Oh, he . . . he died in office. . . ."

"And the one before him?"

"Died in office, too. . . ."

"And before?"

She fell back asleep, stretched out on the couch. Harold got up and went to his bedroom to pack. In a manner of minutes, hands shaking, he threw some clothes and stuff in his duffel bag, made sure he tossed in his bankbook, too. Lots of money there but damn it, he wasn't going to stick around to see what dying in office meant. He could get it closed out later, when he got the hell out of this town.

He left through the rear door, not bothering to lock it behind him.

Another late night phone call from a woman, but this time, the voice wasn't cheerful at all. Roland had said crisply, "I see," and hung up.

He got dressed in the darkness and his wife said, "What's up?"

"Town business."

"At this hour?"

"It's trouble," he said, and in the downstairs kitchen, he made a number of phone calls, each one a bit more frantic than the previous.

Harold was shivering. Maybe he should have gotten a heavier coat but no, it was time to get out. And he wished he had picked up a bit more in the hell-raising stuff when he was younger, 'cause it would have been great to hot-wire a car and get the hell out of Arkham, but he didn't know how to do that. He did know it was time to leave. He took the main road out of town, heading up into the mountains, knowing it would get colder the higher he got. If he kept moving, he thought, he'd be just fine.

Out of town there were no longer any streetlights, just an occasional light from a home on a side road or a long driveway. His footsteps sounded loud on the asphalt. He shivered again. It was damn spooky, out here in the darkness, but he just kept on walking, one foot after another. There were other lights out there as well—car headlights in the distance on one of the parallel roads; and the stars; and again, up there in the mountains, someone burning something. Whatever. He was getting the hell out of Arkham, and if the selectmen or anybody else cared, they could look him up in Lawrence. Or someplace else. A place with noise, buzz, parties, fun, and girls. Well ... maybe girls not as good looking as Elayne, but at least they wouldn't talk about kings and dead mayors and ...

A noise.

He stopped. Chest thumping. Breathing hard. Looked around. Almost whimpered, that's how scared he was. Why oh why had he left that Wal-mart job, his place in Lawrence, to come here on such a crazy offer.

Because he wasn't bright. He was greedy.

Harold took a breath, looked up. It seemed like the road was starting to rise up into the mountains. Keep moving, he thought, one foot after another. Keep moving and everything would be fine.

He took one more step, and as the world exploded about him, Harold knew things were definitely not fine.

Roland Miller stepped out of the shadows, as the lights illuminated the poor pathetic figure of Harold Monroe, looking around wide-eyed, a duffel bag on his shoulder. There were vehicles parked on a turnoff and their headlights had nailed the mayor as he started up the first rise of land.

"Mister Mayor," Roland said gently. "Let's go back to your home. One of us will give you a ride, and then we can talk."

Harold looked around at the townspeople now emerging from other cars and trucks, some carrying flashlights. "No," he said. "You can't stop me. I want to leave. I want to go home."

Roland held out his hands. "Harold, you signed legal documents, the first night you were here. You can't leave. And this is your home now. You can have anything you want in Arkham, anything at all, so long as you stay here."

Harold shook his head. "What? To be a crazy king for you? Until I'm dead? Is that it?"

"No, nothing like that," Roland said, as the townspeople circled around their mayor.

Harold said sharply, "Who are you people? Some long lost tribe of Indians? Is that it? Some crazy lost tribe?"

"No," Roland said, keeping his voice low and soothing. "Not lost, but a tribe of sorts with a mix of blood . . . of Englishmen from the 1700s, from a remote tribe of Micmac Indians before that, and before that, centuries earlier, blood from another tribe, from across the sea, fleeing their island home from invaders from Rome and Gaul. They found refuge here, up a river and into the mountains. Our old ways have allowed us to thrive."

Harold looked around again, interrupted. "I don't care if you came from Mars. I don't care what papers I signed. I quit. I'm not your mayor anymore, or your king, or your damn emperor."

Roland closed his eyes as he heard his fellow townspeople take in a quick breath. "Very well," Roland said, opening his eyes. "That's your choice."

When Harold said those magic words, that he quit, he thought, *Well, let's get a move on.* He walked two more steps before he was grabbed from behind, had his hands bound, a bag placed over his head, and was tossed into the rear of a pickup truck. The drive was bumpy and long, and there were other men keeping him company until they stopped, high up on one of the mountain peaks. Harold was dragged out of the truck, placed against what felt like a wooden pole, and then the bag was pulled from his head.

He blinked from the lights of the flames and the hand-held torches and looked about him. There was one large bonfire set in a circle of tall stones, like pillars. The townspeople from Arkham were there—including Elayne—and their faces were serious and set, like they were at some high holy Mass or something. Then he saw something that almost made him turn around in shock and terror.

The old woman known as Auntie Molly was coming to him. She was naked and all of her wrinkled skin—save her face, neck, hands and feet—was covered with blue, elaborate tattoos.

The last thing Harold saw was the long knife in her hand, and the last thing he felt was the strength of the old woman, driving the sharp blade into his stomach.

Some while later, the board of selectmen for the town of Arkham, New Hampshire knelt in a circle on the dirt around the bloodied corpse of their king, as their priestess looked at the blood spatter and the entrails, murmuring the old language to herself.

She looked up, her face solemn. "This time . . . this time you will go west. And the one you choose to be king, he will be with us for a while. A very long while. And all will be well."

And so the three men stood up, and Roland said, "All right, west it is. Once we get the genealogy straightened out, the three of us will leave."

Lucas said, "I hope it's Vermont. I don't like New York."

Jasper smiled. "Wherever we go, we'll do what needs to be done. For you know what I've always said, what this town needs is . . ."

"New blood," Roland chimed in, followed by Lucas. "New blood."

And with that, the three men grinned widely, their teeth white and sharp by the flickering flames of the torches and the bonfire set among the stone pillars.

Brendan DuBois of New Hampshire is the award-winning author of twelve novels and more than 100 short stories. His short fiction has appeared in *Playboy*, *Ellery Queen's Mystery Magazine*, *Alfred Hitchcock's Mystery Magazine*, *The Magazine of Fantasy & Science Fiction*, and numerous other magazines and anthologies including *The Best American Mystery Stories of the Century*, published in 2000 by Houghton-Mifflin. His short stories have twice won him the Shamus Award from the Private Eye Writers of America, and have also earned him three Edgar Allan Poe Award nominations from the Mystery Writers of America. Visit his website at www.BrendanDuBois.com.

Love in the Time of Zombies

Jason Allard

Vigilance watched Prudence's slender hands as she held the rod, her index finger caressing the line. Every time they fished he was amazed how she could tell the tremors caused by the gentle waves from those of a fish nibbling at her worm. Her hand twitched and she started reeling in the line.

"Seven," she said with a laugh. "How many have you caught?"

"Two."

"And one crayfish who let go. Pity, he would've made great bait."

Vigilance nodded. His hair fell into his eyes again. He still hadn't decided if he was going to grow it out long enough to braid or if he should take the shears to it. He pulled in his line as Prudence's rod bent nearly double. His worm was gone. Again. She hauled a rainbow trout the length of his forearm into the boat. It stopped flopping the second time she clubbed it.

"We should probably head back," Prudence said, tucking an errant strand of long black hair behind her ear. "Father won't be happy if we're out after dark again."

"Mine wasn't too happy about it, either," he said.

As she stowed the gear, he set to with the oars, falling into an easy rhythm after a few strokes. The blue waters of Lake Winnipesaukee were calm, but it was miles from their fishing spot near Moose Island to the dock at the southwestern tip of Rattlesnake Island.

Vigilance stopped rowing.

"What's wrong?"

He held up a finger and cocked his head. For a moment, there was nothing more than the creak of the oarlocks and the slap of water against the aluminum hull. The breeze picked up and he heard it again—a faint, strange drone, like the distant buzzing of a hundred cicadas. Prudence twisted around, a hand shading her eyes. She pointed with her other hand.

Something flew high above the trees. It seemed to be following Route 11, between the western edge of Alton Bay and the eastern edge of the ridge. Squinting against the setting sun, Vigilance could make it out. A small airplane. It coughed, like tearing fabric, and smoke poured from its nose. It banked and wobbled before it dove into the trees below Mount Major's bald summit.

"Was that what I think it was?" Prudence asked. Her green eyes were wide and the blood had drained from her cheeks.

Vigilance nodded. "An airplane. I saw some on the ground while foraging with Dad in Laconia. Dad said his grandfather told him they used to build them big enough to carry a few hundred people at a time." A thread of smoke rose from the trees where the plane had vanished. "I never thought I'd see one flying."

"There would've been someone in it, right? Shouldn't we go up and see if they're still alive? They might be hurt."

"No. We'd never make it up there before nightfall. Besides, we don't have any guns. I'm not going to risk meeting a rotter in the dark with just a fish club." He hauled on the oars, the muscles in his back and arms straining. "We'll tell the others. Dad and I and Mr. Standish can go up."

Vigilance kept an eye on the thin column of smoke. It had been a dry summer. The wind would bring a fire right down to the shoreline. They would be safe on the island, no sparks could cross so much water, but their corn and wheat and other crops between the shore and the old highway would be destroyed, and harvest was only days away. Prudence trailed her fingers in the water and stared back as well.

By the time they reached the dock, he was sore. Up on the mountain, the smoke was gone, leaving only the faintest hint of haze. The sun had sunk behind the ridge, but it wasn't quite dark. Vigilance scrambled to secure the boat. He took the heavy bucket of fish, then helped

Prudence out. He held her hand as they hurried through the village to find her father.

Most of the villagers lived in ancient cottages along the shoreline, or homes made from salvaged materials. Some land had been cleared a little ways inland for a communal meeting hall, a bare patch of ground as a town square, and a ways from everything else, a locked concrete and brick armory. That was where the older, machine-made firearms and ammunition was kept and new black powder was made.

"An airplane, you say?" Prudence's father said, smoothing his salt and pepper beard. They'd found him in the meeting hall, looking over some of the bales of wool the trading party had brought back from Moultonborough the day before.

"Yes, sir," Vigilance said. "Don't you think it would be a good idea to investigate?"

"You know harvest time means *they* will be migrating south again for the winter. Like as not, some are already on the move. I would not send men to look for a crashed relic when rotters are likely to be out there. Especially not at night."

"But, Papa, if it was an airplane, then there had to have been a pilot."

The old man pinched the bridge of his nose. "Enough, you two. If it crashed, the pilot is dead, or will be before we could reach him. I have enough to worry about in taking care of the people here. I don't need to add anyone or anything else. Now, get going. I need to finish this before I'm late for dinner."

Outside, Prudence slipped her hand into his again. "Can you come have supper with Dad and me?" Vigilance asked as their fingers twined.

"I'll have to ask," she said. "Mother will say 'yes.' I think she'd rather take care of feeding little Charity by herself than worry about you burning down your house."

"I still don't think your Dad likes me too much."

"Father likes you. He wouldn't let you take me out to fish if he didn't."

Vigilance shook his head. "But he's always watching me."

"Of course he is." Prudence bumped her hip against his thigh. "You won't be old enough for us to get married until next spring. He's worried you'll drag me off into the bushes and have your way with me while nobody's looking. He was 15 once, too, you know."

"I would never," he stammered.

"I know," she said. "But what would you do if I decided to have my way with you in the boat sometime?"

Vigilance felt heat as his blood rose. His jaw opened and closed, but nothing came out of his mouth. Prudence snickered, then kissed his cheek.

Although Vigilance was as large as most of the adult men, and half a head taller than his father, his father was nearly twice as broad in the shoulders. He could've been carved from granite. He excelled when it came to working in the heat of his forge but when it came to cooking a meal, he was lost. Vigilance wasn't any better. As the two of them made dinner under Prudence's direction, he told his father about the plane. He tried not to be disappointed when his father sided with Mayor Eaton's decision not to put anyone at risk.

"Have you spoken with Mr. Kerr about learning some carpentry?" his father asked, forking a bite of trout into his mouth.

"Yes," Vigilance said. He pushed a piece of fish around his plate, swimming it between islands of carrot and potato. He glanced across the table. Prudence winked at him.

"And?"

"He's going to start me on some small projects before the snow comes. The sort of things that will get me used to the tools I'd be using to make gun stocks."

"Good. What about you, Pru? Any plans for the winter?"

"My mother wants me to start teaching Charity to read. And, I was hoping I might get started on a new dress."

Vigilance coughed, choking on his trout. Father looked to see both of them trying to hide grins as he snatched up his cup, an ancient ceramic mug with a faded drawing of a fat black and orange cat. He gulped down water.

Someone pounded on the door. His father dropped his napkin beside his plate and went to answer it. Vigilance couldn't hear any of the short conversation, distracted by Prudence's foot on his ankle. She speared the last bite of the fish on her plate and popped it in her mouth. She smiled as she chewed.

"Your father's here to take you home, Prudence."

She scooted back her chair and stood. "I hadn't realized it was getting so late. See you tomorrow," she said, and then headed for the door.

Vigilance's father sat back down. "Seems the pilot survived the crash. Somebody fired a flare from the top of Mount Major a few minutes ago. Mayor Eaton has reconsidered his decision. He wants me and James Standish to take a look first thing in the morning."

"I want to go with you."

"No."

"Why not? If he needs to be carried, I'm almost as strong as you. I can shoot almost as well as Mr. Standish. I'm faster and quieter in the woods than either of you. I can track. I'm the best hunter here."

"I know, Lance. It's not a matter of not being up to it. It's a matter of risk. It's not feasible to risk both of us on this. God forbid, what if something happens? If we don't come back, you know enough to run the forge by yourself. Nobody else here does. If you came along, where does that leave the village?" He leaned over the table. "Where would that leave Pru?"

"But, Dad . . ."

"No 'buts.' I need you get the dishes and the kitchen cleaned up."

Vigilance leaned back in his chair. He crossed his arms and stared at his plate, muttering under his breath.

"And don't whine about it. Men don't whine. I don't have time to argue with you, Lance. I have to get my things together and get to bed. We're heading out at first light." His father stood and headed for his bedroom. Vigilance pouted for several minutes, listening to his father gathering his gear. The musket, powder and shot, some bandages, a water skin, and other items. When he thought he heard his father returning, he gathered the plates and carried them to the sink. As he scrubbed them in the cold water from the cistern, he looked out the window and saw a faint glow on top of the mountain. He couldn't be sure if he imagined it or not.

When Vigilance woke, his father was gone. He rolled out of bed and dressed. He scrounged for something to eat, settling on a piece of bread and chunk of hard cheese as he headed out the door. He tried not to think about the mountain or the plane or the possibility of the pilot being alive as he worked with Mr. Kerr. They built and repaired several hot boxes, wooden crates with old windows for tops, where small plants could grow during the winter, kept warm enough by the sun.

Shortly after noon, he headed down to the shore. They'd made enough boxes for each household to have two, and Mr. Kerr had decided to call it a day.

Vigilance sat on an old stump and watched the water. The ducks had started flying south for the winter already, leaving only the jays and other small birds. He took a deep breath. He could smell the clean scent of the lake, the greenness of the pine trees, and someone was baking bread. His stomach rumbled. He stood, thinking of lunch, when he spotted Mr. Standish's boat sailing up from Alton Bay. He ran for Prudence's house, to tell her father they were returning.

By the time they docked, everyone not on the mainland tending the crops or looking after livestock was waiting for them. There was a third man in the boat. He was young and handsome with swarthy skin, mustache and goatee. Many of the women whispered about him. Even Prudence leaned forward to peer more closely at the stranger.

The boat secure, the three of them retrieved their gear and marched up the dock, the stranger in the middle. The dock thudded and creaked with each step. The stranger carried an unfamiliar gun and his clothing, colored with a random smattering of green, black, and brown splotches, was made of an unfamiliar fabric. He walked with a limp and a clenched jaw.

They pushed through the crowd without a word. Vigilance's father and Mr. Standish kept their eyes forward but the stranger's head swiveled back and forth. He tried to pass off his grimace as a smile. Vigilance noticed he paid most attention to the younger women. One or two people asked questions, but Mayor Eaton held up his hand.

"There will be a meeting later, after we've had a chance to talk with our new guest," he said. He tugged Reverend White's sleeve. "Would you join us, Moses?"

The crowd lingered for a few moments after they had gone, then fragmented as couples and families went off to finish chores and speculate amongst themselves.

"I wonder where he's from," Prudence said. "Maybe he's from Durham. Or Boston. Or New York City." Her eyes went wide and she grabbed Vigilance's hand. "Maybe he's from Washington D.C.! The government is reforming and he's been sent by the president to make contact with whoever he can find."

Vigilance shrugged. "Durham might have electricity and other old technology, but they don't have an airport. Dad's been there. He'd have said something about it. He's got to be from somewhere, though," he said. "Guess we'll find out tonight." He'd spent hours looking through atlases and reading volumes of the encyclopedia in the meeting hall. He knew those names and where they were on the maps. Washington, D.C.? It was possible, but he doubted it.

Shortly before sunset, the meeting bell rang. Vigilance found a seat in the front row, sitting on a bench with Prudence and her mother. Once everyone was settled and quiet, Mr. Standish related their trip up the mountain and then turned it over to the stranger. He hobbled to Reverend White's lectern and leaned against it. He smiled, revealing his teeth, bright white against his dark skin.

"Bonan nokton," he said. *"Mia nomo estas Esteban Aguilar."* He paused, sketching a bow. "Good evening. My name is Esteban Aguilar." His English was accented, with odd vowels and vibrating r's. "I am from the Azores Free Zone." He picked up Mayor Eaton's old globe and pointed to a tiny cluster of islands in the middle of the Atlantic Ocean.

"Many years ago, the islands were cleared of the *nemortaj*. There hasn't been an instance of the dead walking in over 15 years. We have plenty of land to grow many crops, raise much livestock, and plenty of room for people to live safe and sound. We have all the modern conveniences, hot and cold running water, electricity, schools, and computers, even a television and several radio stations."

Most of them knew the words, and many had seen the devices, ruined relics, but only the handful who had traveled as far as Durham had seen any of them functioning. Prudence leaned forward, hanging on Esteban's every word.

"We're beginning to take back the world from the *nemortaj*. We have many bases in Europe, and a few in Africa. Now, we are looking to help free America. We have allies in the Caribbean, who are moving from island to island, making room for people to live there in safety."

A woman at the back of the hall stood. "How did you get here?"

"Our ship, the *Pizarro*. We stopped at the islands off the coast. There are a few people living there. They call themselves 'Pelicans.' They did not want to leave their homes, but told us many things about where we might find safety and other people on shore. We landed at the ruins of a shipyard, and made our base there. We cleared a road along a pier to make a narrow runway, just big enough for my plane to take off and land." Esteban shook his head. "The only thing scarier than landing there was crashing into your mountain.

"Some of us have visited the settlements the Pelicans told us about."

"Did you visit Durham?" an older man asked.

"Yes. Most amazing. They have a generator which runs on gas piped in from an ancient trash dump, and it still works. I think the library there is bigger, and has more books than any library still standing, anywhere in the world."

Vigilance felt a pang of jealousy shoot through him. One of these days, we would make the long trek southward, and just spend days and days reading.

"And Dover?" Mrs. White asked. Her sister had gone there with a trading party and decided to stay.

Esteban knuckled his chin. "Yes, Dover. They're in fortified brick buildings between the falls and a bend in the river."

"What do you want from us?" someone else asked.

Esteban smiled. "We would like your aid. You know the area better than we do. You know how the *nemortaj* travel and where they gather. Our only other interests are trade and offering to take anyone who wants to go back with us. We come to free, not conquer."

Vigilance snorted. He'd read several books about the world before the rotters took over. He'd lost track of how many times a liberation force had become an occupation force.

"Wouldn't it be wonderful to live where we don't have to worry about running into rotters?" Prudence whispered to him. She grabbed his hand. "Let's go. We could live in a big house with electric lights and a bathtub you don't have to heat with a fire."

"Doesn't sound like they've learned anything. None of that stuff stopped the outbreak, and for all we know, it might have been responsible somehow," Vigilance said. "I'd rather stay here." Prudence dropped his hand and turned back to Esteban, who was explaining his mission to find settlements from the air, mark them on his map, and drop cans with written greetings from his commander.

"So, now what are you going to do?" one of the younger women asked.

"I must stay for a few days. I hurt my foot when I crashed. My radio was broken, so I will have to walk back. We only brought one airplane," Esteban said. "Anyone who would like to come with me is welcome."

"Idiot," Vigilance muttered. Prudence elbowed him in the ribs.

"You should wait, Mr. Aguilar," Mayor Eaton said. "The coast is a good 50 miles or so, as the crow flies. This time of year is bad, with the rotters migrating south for the winter. It would be better if you waited until the lake freezes over and the snow piles up. Go on skis."

"We didn't bring enough supplies for a long stay. The ship will be returning to the Free Zone in three weeks. I could be stuck here."

As the meeting wore on, many people asked more questions about the Azores and other places Esteban had been. After a chorus of offers for a place to stay, Mayor Eaton announced the stranger would be staying in his guest room. Vigilance bristled. When the questions started to be of a more personal nature, he walked out.

Outside, Vigilance took a deep breath and slowly exhaled. A ghostly mist hung in the moonlight for several seconds. He walked home, where he pulled a faded book, *Goode's World Atlas*, from the bookshelf. He set it on the kitchen table and studied the map of the Azores as the tallow candle burned low.

Over the next few days, Vigilance saw little of either Prudence or Esteban. Most of his time was spent helping his father prepare tools for the harvest. There were several blades to be sharpened or straightened, and handles to be replaced. When not working in the forge, he was helping Mr. Kerr build storage bins.

When the harvest began, Vigilance took a post on one of the short wooden towers, where he could watch for rotters and shoot them before they could threaten the men and women working in the fields. Late in the morning of the third day, he felt the tower tremble as someone climbed up the ladder. Esteban stepped onto the platform, wearing more normal clothes, but carrying his weapon.

"*Saluton,*" he said. "*Sinjor,* ah, Mr. Standish told me I could watch here with you today. I don't know how to farm, but I can do this to help."

Vigilance shrugged. "Suit yourself." He scanned the slope up to the old paved road. Maybe the rotters had taken a different route this year.

"Do you farm?"

"No."

Esteban scratched his head. "Mr. Eaton made it sound like everyone here did."

"Tried as a kid. I'm no good at it. No green thumb."

"What is a 'green thumb'?"

Vigilance rolled his eyes. "If someone is good at farming or garden-ing, they're said to have a green thumb. I don't know why." He ignored Esteban, who looked over the lake as often as anywhere else. Several long minutes passed.

Esteban started to speak, but Vigilance hissed at him and pressed a finger to his lips. He pointed. A pair of rotters, a man and a woman, shambled towards them. They stopped at the edge of the slope, looking down at the people in the fields. Both of them were in rough shape. Most of their clothing had decomposed, leaving little more than scraps and rags hanging off them. Here and there old wounds gaped. Vigilance could see some of the woman's ribs and the blackened tangle of her intestines. He raised his musket.

"Would you like to try mine?" Esteban asked. The gun he held out was all metal and plastic, with a collapsible stock. "It's an MP5 9 mil-limeter submachine gun." He pointed to a switch on the side. "You set it here for semi-auto, or flip it all the way to rock and roll."

Vigilance shrugged and they exchanged firearms. He pulled the stock out, flipped the switch to the red "E" and shouldered the weapon. The sights were different than he was used to, but they lined up easily. He centered the post on the woman's head and squeezed the trigger. The gun made a small pop. There was little recoil and no smoke. He could hear the small brass casing tinkling and skittering on the floor. The rags, once a shirt, fluttered over the dead woman's breasts. She reached up and touched the new hole at the base of her throat. He aimed a hand's breadth over her matted brown hair and fired again. Her head snapped back and she dropped.

"You like?"

Vigilance shrugged. "It's quiet and light, but not practical for hunt-ing. The bullet's too small for deer."

"May I try yours?"

"Be my guest."

Esteban looked down at the gun for a second, then pulled back the hammer. When Vigilance nodded, he raised it to his shoulder. He aimed for several seconds, then pulled the trigger. There was a flash and puff of smoke as the hammer snapped down, then an instant later, the gun roared, belching smoke and flame. A clean miss.

Esteban rattled of several strange words and rubbed his shoulder. "Ow," he said. "What happened? What went wrong?"

Vigilance waved at the harvesters, who looked up at them. He waved and shook his head. "You missed. You need to keep the stock tight against your body or it will kick. Now, I'll show you how to reload—you can try again." He walked Esteban through the process, from measuring the powder and seating the ball to priming the pan. By the time they were done, he could have done it twice on his own. The rotter had reached the bottom of the slope. He was only a few yards from the low stone wall marking the edge of the field.

Esteban aimed again. This time he didn't miss. The rotter's head cracked in half. Pieces of skull and brain sprayed out behind. The body took one more step then fell on its side.

Esteban shook his head. "Why do you use such guns?"

Vigilance traded with him again. "You have machines to make those, right?"

"*Ja,* yes."

"We don't. I made it. The steel was salvaged, melted down, and reforged. I hand carved the stock." He picked up one of the spent shell casings. He held it up and tapped the end. "Do you have the means to produce smokeless powder and more primers?"

"Yes."

"We don't, but we can make black powder." Vigilance dropped the brass shell. "We have factory guns and ammunition, but we save them for emergencies."

As the sun oozed towards the top of the mountains, the harvesters set aside their tools and piled into the waiting boats. No more rotters appeared, but more would come. Prudence was waiting at the dock.

"I missed you," she said, taking Vigilance's hand.

"I missed you, too. Sorry I haven't come to see you. Between Dad and Mr. Kerr, I've been hopping." Vigilance glanced at Esteban, who ignored them as he stalked away. "Besides, I thought you might be mad at me."

"I wasn't mad at you," she said. "A little annoyed, maybe, but not mad." She twined her fingers with his. "I was thinking we might take a walk."

Vigilance dropped off his gun and shooting bag at home, then they followed the old dirt road away from the village. They walked without a word. Although the threat of winter loomed, the evening was still warm.

A slight breeze off the water rustled the leaves that were turning more red and gold by the day. Vigilance could smell a hint of the dried flowers Prudence had put in her bath water, but he couldn't think of anything to say. He was content.

They followed the road, now mostly reclaimed and narrowed to a path by trees, around the large cove to a smaller one halfway to the island's southeastern tip, a favorite haunt. They sat by the shore on a large rock heated by the afternoon sun, where they could watch the lake and the mainland. Summer cottages once stood nearby, but they had long ago been torn apart; their materials either put to use in new buildings and furniture or burnt for firewood.

Prudence pressed close to his side and Vigilance slipped his arm around her. She rested her head on his shoulder.

"I'm sorry I made you think I was mad," she said. "I've been pretty busy as well. Mama and I have been discussing dress patterns."

Vigilance kissed the top of her head. "I guess I should ask your father. I don't think he'll say 'yes' until after my birthday."

"I know. Mama and I have been keeping it a secret." She pulled away and smiled at him, mischief in her green eyes. "Want to go for a swim?"

"Now? Water's pretty cold."

She stood up and began unbuttoning her shirt. "Yeah, but it'll be fun warming up."

Vigilance's heart pounded. His ears burned. They'd been skinny-dipping several times, years ago, when they were little. He shook his head. "No," he said, hating himself for it. "It wouldn't be right. We should wait until we're married. I'll talk to your father, maybe he'll agree to let us do it early. Maybe make it part of the midwinter celebration."

"Damn it, Lance. I wish you'd stop being so worried about what's right or proper." She crossed her arms. "It's not like either one of us would get into trouble or anything. I'm an adult. Besides, it's not like anybody is going to know." She leaned towards him. "Can you give me a good reason why not?"

"I can't. I don't know why. It just doesn't feel right, doing it out here. Sneaking around like this." He wished he'd shut up.

"Fine." Prudence started back towards the path, buttoning her shirt as she went.

"Pru, wait." Vigilance jumped to his feet and followed her.

"Leave me alone."

Once on the path, she ran. He might've been able to sprint faster, but once Prudence found her stride, there was no way he could keep up. He swore loudly at himself and started the long walk back. Once home, he ignored his father and the dinner kept warm on the stove, and collapsed on his bed.

Vigilance woke at dawn. Prudence would be going out to fish before the sun climbed too high. If he could catch her at the dock, he might smooth things over. He changed his shirt before slipping out into the cool morning.

People were already swarming over the dock, getting into the boats to continue the harvest. Tribulation Howland, a year younger and his frequent hunting partner, waved.

"She's gone already," he said.

"What?"

"She and Mr. Aguilar rowed out about twenty minutes ago." He pointed to the small boat sitting between the southern tip of Sleepers Island and a small cluster of tree-covered rocks. "They were chatting like they've known each other for ages."

Vigilance swore under his breath and stomped back up the dirt road. He plowed into the brush and undergrowth, heading towards the rocky ledges at the island's highest point. He stopped every few dozen paces to pitch stones at random trees. Before he reached the summit, he decided it was a waste of time. He turned around and went to find Mr. Kerr. Perhaps driving some nails would help him work it off. The carpenter didn't need anything pounded, but he had firewood that needed to be chopped.

As he finished piling the split logs, they returned. Esteban tied up the boat with a sloppy knot, as Prudence stepped up onto the dock. She didn't have any fish.

Vigilance went home for lunch and had almost finished eating when his father spoke. "Something wrong? You haven't been yourself today."

"Pru and I had a fight." He shrugged. "I think she's starting to be interested in Esteban."

"Have you tried talking to her?"

"No, not really."

"You should. I'll take care of washing up."

Vigilance considered it for a few moments, then pushed his chair back and stood. He put his plate by the sink and headed out. He had no more idea what to say when he reached the Eaton home than he had when he stepped outside. Heart in his throat, he knocked.

Mrs. Eaton opened the door. He frowned.

"May I speak with Prudence, please?"

"Wait here. I'll see if she wants to talk to you." She closed the door. A moment later, it reopened. Prudence leaned against the doorframe.

"I'm sorry," he said.

"For what? It's not like you did anything wrong."

Vigilance ran his fingers through his hair. "Yeah, well, I wish I had."

Prudence snorted, then spoke in hushed tones. "I'm going with Esteban when he leaves. Why should I stay when I could have a life like everyone here only reads about? I want to be able to store food in a refrigerator instead of hoping we have enough ice to keep an icebox cold all summer. I want to listen to music on a radio. Music we don't have the instruments to play. I want to watch television and movies. I want to walk outside at night and not worry about rotters or bears or coydogs. I want more than I can have on this little island."

Vigilance absorbed her speech, silently.

"What about you? What do you want, Lance?"

He met her gaze and held it. "Everything I want is right here."

She shook her head. "I'm sorry, but I have to go." She slammed the door. A curtain moved in an upstairs window. Vigilance glimpsed Esteban smirking down at him. Prudence's bedroom window.

"Come on, Pru," he shouted. "Come out and talk to me."

The door opened and Mrs. Eaton leaned out. "Run along now. My daughter has said all she has to say to you for the moment."

Seething, Vigilance ran to the farthest, northernmost point of the island. He wore himself out heaving rocks into the water. Blame for all of this could be laid at the stranger's feet. She'd been happy enough before he showed up.

"Fine, go with him," he said, skipping a stone across the waves. "See if I care."

For the next few days, he threw himself into his work. He helped haul baskets of grain and potatoes and pumpkins from the fields to the boats. He took his turns in the watch tower, hoping for more than a trickle of rotters to wander into his sights.

Esteban pitched in as well. He carried his fair share of loads, but if he took his gun into one of the towers, Vigilance never saw it. On the island, he often saw the stranger with Prudence, who still refused to speak with him. They'd started holding hands.

Two weeks after Esteban's arrival, the last of the harvest had been collected and the livestock transferred from the mainland barn to winter quarters on Sleepers Island. The rotters would soon be coming in a steady stream. It would be unsafe to leave the islands again until the snow started falling.

Vigilance woke to voices in the kitchen. It was still dark. He could hear his father and Mayor Eaton, but he couldn't make out what they were saying. He slipped out of bed and snuck down the hall.

"She's gone, Hiram," Mayor Eaton said. "That boy left, taking her, Tribulation Howland, and Felicity Turner with him. They broke into the armory before they left; took some boxes of ammunition and maybe a few guns. They've taken one of the smaller boats and I have no idea where they've gone."

Vigilance sucked in a breath and froze. His father glanced over Mayor Eaton's shoulder, into the hallway's gloom. "What do you want to do, Jonathan? I can get James and a couple others and go after them. We can bring our kids home."

Mayor Eaton shook his head. "No." His shoulders slumped. "Let them go. They know the risks. I can't, in good conscience, send anyone after them. Not now."

"Alright," Hiram said. "You go home and look after Mrs. Eaton."

"Will you tell your son I'm sorry?"

"I will," Hiram said, showing Mayor Eaton to the door. Once the older man was gone, he turned to the hallway. "You heard everything, I take it."

"Yes," Vigilance said, stepping in the kitchen. He leaned against a chair.

"It would be best to let them go."

"I know."

"It wouldn't have stopped me from going after your mother."

"I know."

"I'll have some food packed for you by the time you're dressed."

Vigilance hugged his father. "Thank you."

Ten minutes later, Vigilance ran towards the dock. The eastern sky was already brightening. People would be up and moving soon. He wore warm layers of wool and leather, and toted a backpack filled with extra clothing, blankets, dried fish, smoked venison, a pair of small apples and a few other supplies, as well as his musket and a hatchet. Mayor Eaton was waiting for him, holding a rifle.

"I'm going to get Prudence," Vigilance said. "Please don't try to stop me."

"Give me your gun, Mr. Brewster."

"I can't let her go like this. Please."

James Standish stepped out from behind a tree. "Powder and shot, too, Lance."

Vigilance hung his head and held out the musket. Mr. Standish took it. He shrugged the powder horn from his shoulder as well as the bag with his shooting kit and handed them over.

"This should serve you better," Mayor Eaton said. He pushed the rifle into Vigilance's hands. It was old and heavy. Made of sturdy wood and steel, with a box magazine and bolt action. It had been built for fighting in the First World War, a hundred years before the first rotters. "I trust you know how to use it. It's loaded. Ten rounds." He held out a spare magazine.

Vigilance looked at the bullets. Smooth, gleaming brass cases. Shiny copper jackets. He had no idea what to say.

"Factory rounds, not hand-loads," Mayor Eaton said.

"I thought you were going to stop me," Vigilance said.

"We should, but she's my daughter." Mayor Eaton held out yet another gift: a large, thin book with a faded red cover. It was one of his favorites to flip through with Prudence—a New Hampshire atlas. "I hope this will help."

"My guess is they're taking the most direct route," Mr. Standish said, ushering Vigilance down the dock. "They took a sailboat. They're probably just going to the end of Alton Bay and walking from there, following Route 11."

"Be careful," Mayor Eaton said.

They helped him into another small sailboat and gave him a shove. The wind was out of the north, bringing with it the promise of snow. Another boat sat at the tip of the bay, beached near a handful of sun-bleached pilings jutting up from the water like fingers.

Vigilance landed his craft. He guessed they had a few hours head start. Esteban was in for a surprise. He might know how to fly an airplane and shoot a fancy gun, but the islanders had been working hard all their lives. He'd probably be the one dragging by the end of the day.

He slipped through Alton's remains. Carefully dodging from building to collapsed building, he avoided the shambling population of transient rotters. He skirted the edge of the town square, keeping a careful eye on the handful of dead men loitering in front of the old brick clock tower. The minute hand had fallen off long ago, but the hour hand still pointed to the top of the three. Vigilance hurried on. He cut through the overgrown cemetery. At least the dead here were at rest. Near a worn marble headstone, he spotted the print of a hard-soled boot.

Every time he spotted a rotter, Vigilance would pause to study them. Most had some scraps of clothing, but it wasn't unusual to see one naked—pale, bluish skin streaked with dirt and dried gore. If they wore anything, it seemed to be shoes. It made sense. A hundred years of shambling from one place to another was sure to wear out soles, be they rubber or flesh.

They weren't intelligent, but had instinct and cunning. They understood they couldn't heal. They avoided rough terrain and other hazards which might do harm or hasten decomposition, such as freezing and thawing, or becoming waterlogged. He'd seen some seek shelter from the rain.

As darkness fell, Vigilance found himself outside of Farmington, across the road from a collapsed drug store. He was still seeing signs of Esteban's passage and hints of other feet clad in less distinctive footwear. He was gaining on them, he was sure.

He found two sturdy trees in which to camp for the night. He hung his pack with the food he wasn't having for dinner in one tree. The food might not interest a rotter, but a bear, preparing for hibernation, would come a long way for dried fish and smoked venison. With a piece of rope, he secured himself in the comfortable crotch of another tree, high enough from the ground to be safe from a bear or worse.

Vigilance woke at sunrise. He retrieved his bag and consulted the atlas. He tried to guess the route Esteban would lead them along. There were back roads he could follow, smaller lanes not as likely to be traveled by rotters. He might be able to catch them near the south side of Rochester. With his pack cinched tight to his back and rifle in hand, Vigilance loped through the trees and down overgrown roads.

Shadowing the highway, he came to a shallow river. There were footprints in the mud. The tracks had been made since sun-up—boots with heavy tread and three pairs of smaller, plainer soles.

Though the river meandered like a blind rotter, it flowed more or less parallel to the main road. Several times, the trail left the edge of the water to cut across narrow spits between bends. It forded where another river joined in, bringing deeper water downstream. Vigilance followed. At times, he could imagine hearing Prudence and Felicity.

After the river passed under a crumbling concrete bridge, Vigilance began to see more signs of former civilization, toppled ruins of homes and businesses. After several more bridges, he was surrounded by the carcass of a city. Skeletal buildings loomed on either side of the river. Ahead, he could see a collapsed bridge and, beyond it, a massive brick building spanning the river. Between the two roared an unseen water-fall. Dover.

A line of laundry swayed in the breeze, hung between two poles on the roof. Small trees stood in large pots nearby. Vigilance followed scuffed footprints, abandoning the riverside, and ventured into the unnatural remains of city streets.

He stopped when he noticed a small, filthy, bloodied child. A boy or a girl, he couldn't tell. It reeked of sickness and sweat and had soiled itself. Seeing him, it opened its mouth and toddled toward him at top speed.

The child lunged at him, its jaw snapping. He kicked it in the chest, knocking it away. It sprang to its feet and came at him again. Long hair shifted, revealing the ragged, oozing wound where the child's ear had been ripped away. Vigilance knocked it down again, pining it to the ground with his foot. He brought up his rifle and slammed the butt down against its skull. There was a wet crunch and the child's head lay misshapen. Dark blood pooled, trickling along the cracks in the pavement. Vigilance sagged against the rusted hulk of a large truck and vomited.

Wiping his bitter mouth, he slunk towards the corner where the street ran into a nexus of other streets. Brick and stone buildings towered over him. High windows looked down like empty eye sockets while lower ones yawned like mouths with jagged, crystalline teeth. A clock face, stopped at 4:30, peered down from a building like a pale moon. Across the square was a weed-choked amphitheater. To one side was a once-blue sculpture of a crab. It was ringed with pots of dead flowers and burnt out candles. Offerings to a scuttling god.

A scream echoed through the concrete canyons. Vigilance looked around. It was hard to tell where it came from. He saw Prudence sprint from between two brick buildings, heading towards the crab, Esteban hot on her heels. Panting, Felicity lagged behind. Bloodied men and women ran after her, hands reaching, fingers hooked into claws. Tribulation, half his face missing, led the pack.

Vigilance's breath caught in his throat. Runners. Live people who'd been bitten by a rotter, but escaped. They were like rabid animals, vicious until they were dealt a mortal wound or succumbed to starvation, only to rise within hours as a fresh rotter.

"Run!" Esteban screamed. He slowed and raised his weapon, taking quick aim.

Vigilance didn't hear the shot and no smoke belched from the barrel. He saw the spurt of blood and heard a shriek as the bullet punched through Felicity's thigh. The snarling runners were on her before she hit the ground. Tribulation bit into her arm as the others tried to tear her apart. The sound rising from Felicity's throat was inhuman.

Shaking, Vigilance shouldered his rifle. He hovered the front sight's post on her head and jerked the trigger. The factory round was louder than his gun had ever been, and the recoil jolted his shoulder. The bullet, copper jacketed and sleek, punched through Felicity's chest. Blood sprayed. The screaming stopped. Her body, whatever was left of it, might rise again, but her pain was ended. Vigilance fumbled the bolt, loading a fresh round. His second shot tore away the top of Tribulation's head.

He dashed around the amphitheater. He spotted Prudence and Esteban along the edge of the river in what had been a park. Across the water was another section of fortifications. A hundred yards in front of them a rowboat sat on the bank.

Vigilance shouted, "Prudence!" She stumbled and fell to one knee when she looked back. Esteban nearly ran her over. He skidded to a stop, swinging his weapon around.

"He shot Felicity!"

Esteban fired. The bullet whizzed past and struck the wall. Hearing footsteps, Vigilance glanced back to see runners bearing down on him. The closest was only a few steps away. He stopped, planting his foot, and thrust the rifle butt backward. It caved in the runner's face and it fell, dead. He fired. A runner dropped. He worked the bolt and did it again. And again. And again. The last one tumbled at his feet.

"Get to the boat, Pru," Esteban said. "The noise will bring more." He pointed his weapon at Vigilance's chest. "You shouldn't have followed us."

"What are you doing?" Prudence shouted as he squeezed the trigger. Nothing happened.

Vigilance raised his rifle and pulled the trigger. There was a sharp click. He snapped open the bolt. Empty. He dropped the gun and fumbled at his belt as Esteban rushed towards him, a knife in his hand.

He managed to catch the blade with the rifle. The knife whispered across the back of his hand. The gun fell from pain-splayed fingers as he scrambled to his feet. As Esteban came at him again, Vigilance yanked the hatchet from his belt.

He swung, hoping to plant the blade in the stranger's head. Esteban caught his wrist with one hand, and drove the knife into his belly with the other. They fell one on top of the other. Vigilance had no breath to scream. Lightning and fire shot through his guts.

"She might have come back, eventually," Esteban whispered, twisting the knife. He jerked the knife free and held up the blade, blood dripping from its point.

There were three loud pops and a line of little white holes appeared in Esteban's forehead. A heartbeat later, blood poured forth in streams, coursing down his face and spattering on Vigilance's chest. It sounded like rain. He pushed the dead man away and looked up to see Prudence holding a small, silver revolver.

"They're coming, Lance," she said. "I can't carry you."

Vigilance found his feet and half ran with Prudence, his arm over her shoulders and hers around his waist. They reached the boat and he pitched forward, collapsing into it. She emptied her gun at the runners, then shoved the boat into the water. It stopped with a jerk. She screamed in frustration, wordless, primal.

"It's tied," she said. Vigilance dug out his pocketknife and handed it to her. The sharp blade made short work of the old rope. She dropped it in the bottom of the boat and pushed them into the sluggish current. He could hear the snarls and splashes of pursuit as Prudence put out the oars and pulled with all her strength. They passed under a sagging covered bridge, scraping on the bottom, then reached deeper, swifter waters.

"Stay with me, Lance," Prudence said. "Portsmouth is just downstream a little ways. The Azores ship's there. They've got a doctor. You'll be all right. Just don't leave me."

Vigilance smiled. He stared up, past the trees with their leaves beginning to turn red and gold. The sky was bright blue with soft, puffy, white clouds. "I'm not going anywhere without you, Pru," he said. He closed his eyes and let the rowing and the waves rock him. "I love you."

Although **Jason Allard** grew up as a semi-nomadic Army brat, his familial ties to New England extend as far back as the Mayflower and the early days of Gosport, on the Isles of Shoals. He graduated from the University of New Hampshire in 2000, and from the Odyssey Writers' Workshop in 2001. He now lives in the Seacoast region of New Hampshire with his wife, Rebecca, and a mischief of rats.